THE
SORCERER'S
APPRENTICE

DOCTOR WHO – THE MISSING ADVENTURES

Also available:

THE SORCERER'S APPRENTICE

Christopher Bulis

DOCTOR WHO

THE MISSING ADVENTURES

First published in Great Britain in 1995 by
Doctor Who Books
an imprint of Virgin Publishing Ltd
332 Ladbroke Grove
London W10 5AH

ISBN 0 426 20447 6

Cover illustration by Paul Campbell

Typeset by Galleon Typesetting, Ipswich
Printed and bound in Great Britain by
Cox & Wyman Ltd, Reading, Berks

Prologue

The system took care of everything.

Once it had been different, but now that fact was all that mattered.

There *had* been a few restless spirits who never fitted in, some dimly recalled. But they had departed long ago, leaving the contented behind. That must have been, oh . . . when was it? Never mind. The knowledge was there *somewhere*, of course, but as nothing, fundamentally, changed anymore, why trouble to count?

And so it was, and so it continued.

Then, one night, Klist (an otherwise quite ordinary person) looked up at the stars, and decided he was getting bored with them. They altered their relative positions, of course, but only very slowly. Why couldn't they be more interestingly arranged to start with, he wondered, or at least more colourful.

So he chose a new pattern for them, including plenty of interesting colours. Nothing happened.

It was unbelievable. It was frustrating, and Klist could not remember when he had last felt that. Baffled and annoyed (there was another novel sensation), he actually had to consciously ask why they wouldn't change as he wanted. He was told that it was a third order adjustment, and to even attempt it required a Nodal. That meant the tedium of obtaining group consent. Oh, well, he might as well finish what he had started.

Klist gathered together some of his friends, once they could be prised away from their own indulgences, and talked them round to his idea. They transferred to the nearest Locus, where Klist used the Nodal interface to command the stars to move into the aesthetically tasteful

1

pattern they had all, more or less, decided upon.

And was told he was asking for the impossible.

Klist was embarrassed and amazed. How could *any-thing* be impossible? Hastily, to cover his confusion, he demanded *some* sort of change; at least put more colour into the stars, he said. That was possible, he was informed, but it would take a little time and a lot of power. Was it a priority?

Yes, said Klist, it was to him. Do it!

Yes, said the others, already getting bored. Do it!

Promptly, every light in the sky went out and black silence covered all the world.

Punctuated only by the screaming, of course.

Time passed. The blackness lifted. But things were not the same as before.

More time passed. Klist's colour *did* appear amongst the stars. But by then nobody seemed to appreciate it much.

Much more time passed. Others came. But as they weren't *real* people, it took a while for them to register . . .

1

Apprentice

The first cold wind of morning whispered across the moor.

It stirred the tussock grasses, the clumps of heather and straggling dwarf furze. It blew over the humped granite mass of the tor, whistling about dark caves in the rock, bringing forth a cacophony of grunts and strange, chattering voices from their depths. It keened about the sheer walls of the tower, which rose like a single black fang from the rocks. On the tower's broad, turreted roof, inhuman sentries kept watch far out across the rolling heathland.

In one high window a light glowed.

Marton Dhal smoothed down his raven black robes with their silver thread tracery and reclined in his carved, high-backed chair in satisfied reflection; watching the candles throw dancing shadows about his chamber. At last, that interfering old woman was out of the way! However, he must perpetrate just a little more random mischief to ensure the correct . . . he pondered over the appropriate word . . . yes: *atmosphere*.

On the table before him, mounted on a tripod, was a globe about a foot across. It was perfectly smooth and milky white, perhaps made of polished stone or glass. He reached forward and touched the sphere, and his cold, dark eyes closed. The globe began to shine with a soft, pearly radiance. He stiffened, reaching out for what he sought, searching . . . He drew in his breath sharply as he made contact. His mouth twitching in a half smile, he once more insinuated his will into the other. They had done good work together yesterday. What might today bring? His eyes opened again – but now they were red as fire.

3

2

Forest of Death

Ian Chesterton had just stepped out into the corridor when he heard the first low, pulsing, tones of the materialization effect. Frowning, he turned quickly on his heel and re-entered the TARDIS's control room.

'What's happening, Doctor?' he enquired. 'Surely we can't be landing again so soon?'

The Doctor, busily fussing over the complex controls set about the hexagonal console and muttering under his breath, ignored his question. Ian sighed, thinking that such equipment should, ideally, have been attended by technicians and scientists in white lab coats. In practice, it was operated by an eccentric old man in his sixties, perhaps, with collar-length silver hair and wearing a black frock-coat. This strange dichotomy also pervaded the rest of the chamber, where complex machinery jostled with a scattering of antiques and curios from many different periods. A room of anachronisms, Ian thought; even I fit in at the moment. He was wearing a striking black silk tunic, patterned and decorated in the Chinese style. It was absolutely authentic thirteenth-century workmanship, being an impromptu souvenir of the last place they had visited: the court of Kublai Khan himself.

The rise and fall of the materialization pulses grew louder. Ian coughed loudly and repeated his earlier enquiry.

The Doctor briefly lifted his gaze from the console to transfix him with sharp blue eyes. It was the sort of look normally exchanged between stern schoolmasters and particularly dull pupils.

'Really, Chesterton!' he snapped impatiently. 'For a supposedly intelligent man, you sometimes ask the most obtuse questions. Self-evidently we *are* materializing.'

Ian tried to overlook the slur on his intellect. 'But we only left China two minutes ago. Does this mean we're landing back on Earth again?'

'Possibly, possibly,' replied the Doctor, circling the console once more. 'Of course, the duration of travel time experienced within the TARDIS has little to do with our eventual point of arrival, you know. Millions of miles, or years, may have passed outside.'

'And I suppose you're no nearer getting the ship under control again and actually taking us back to our proper place and time?' replied Ian contentiously, reacting to the Doctor's patronizing manner. The Doctor turned upon him, eyes dangerously hard and sharp, and thrust out a belligerent chin as though preparing for another argument. Fortunately, at that moment the other two members of the TARDIS's crew entered the room.

Barbara came to Ian's side. Susan, still pulling on a sleeveless dark green top over her loose shirt, ran quickly to the console to examine the readings for herself.

'Oh, we're landing again so soon, Grandfather,' she exclaimed to the Doctor. 'Do you know what kind of place it is?'

'Just a moment, my dear,' replied the Doctor tolerantly, 'the readings are not clear yet.'

Like Barbara, Susan had managed to find time for a quick clean-up and change after their departure from China, and her fresh face gleamed with excitement. She looked like any girl in her mid teens, with her close, urchin-cut hair and her half-shy, half-challenging manner. But Ian had seen depths in her eyes that suggested experiences far beyond those of most teenagers. Of all of us, he thought, she is still the most eager and enthusiastic traveller. She hasn't developed the Doctor's intense, but rather clinical curiosity yet, nor is her appreciation clouded by our desire to get home again.

Beside him, Barbara looked on as the TARDIS began to materialize; hope and apprehension mingled on her

5

concerned, intelligent, strong-featured face, crowned by her bouffant of dark hair. She was wearing a simple loose jumper and slacks, with sensible flat shoes, having already learned the value of practical dress when travelling with the Doctor.

'Might it be Earth again?' she whispered, unwilling to disturb the Doctor's activity about the console.

'I don't know. The Doctor won't promise anything.'

She managed a rueful grin. 'That's nothing new, is it?'

The thrumming beat of materialization had grown deeper. Suddenly it reached a crescendo with a solid thump. Then all was quiet.

The scanner screen, mounted high on a section of wall close to the console, lit up. The grey of the interdimensional void had resolved into a stretch of rough grass, scattered with flowers and backed by a wall of trees. It seemed so normal, so like a section of traditional English woodland, that Ian felt his pulse quicken. He stepped closer to the screen.

'They look like oaks, don't they? And I think those are buttercups in the grass.' The Doctor set the scanner rotating. More of the same type of scenery rolled across the screen. The TARDIS had evidently landed in a small open glade.

'And looks can be deceiving,' the Doctor warned. 'However, the instruments do show the composition of the air and temperature are both satisfactory. Susan, dear, what is the radiation count?'

'It reads normal, Grandfather.'

'Are you sure?' Ian asked quickly. 'We don't want a repeat of what happened on Skaro.'

Susan grinned back. 'I'm quite certain the meter's working properly this time.' There was an assured certainty in her reply at odds with her apparent youth. Sometimes Ian found it disconcerting.

'Then we can go outside,' said Barbara quickly. Her eyes were bright. 'Ian, it *must* be Earth. It might even be England.'

He didn't want to dampen her hopes, but he felt he had to be cautious. 'Yes, but *when* is it? What's the date? If we've simply moved in space and not time, then it's still the Middle Ages out there.'

'And there could be a tarmac road on the other side of those trees carrying nice normal people in cars having a summer's day out. This could be the New Forest, for all we know. Wouldn't that be lovely? Petrol fumes and picnic lunches . . . Ian, we *have* to find out.'

'Of course,' he acknowledged gently, 'but don't build your hopes up too high just yet.' She smiled back in understanding. 'Of course,' Ian continued, turning to the Doctor, 'it would be useful if all this equipment could simply tell us where and when we've landed first, wouldn't it, Doctor?'

The Doctor sniffed haughtily. 'And as I keep reminding you, Chesterton, until I am allowed a little peace and quiet to complete some minor repairs, and have a chance to properly calibrate the instruments, I simply cannot provide that sort of precise information.'

'We'll simply have to go outside and find out for ourselves, won't we, Grandfather?' Susan said quickly, adding cheerfully: 'Besides, it's more interesting that way!'

Ian felt the usual brief moment of disorientation as he passed through the main doors of the TARDIS and stepped out into the warm sunshine. He looked back. The ship had not changed since they left China. The time-space craft, a miracle of science and technology far beyond his understanding, still stubbornly (and much to the annoyance of its owner) preserved the outward appearance of a British police call box of the mid-twentieth century.

While the Doctor and Susan wandered over to the nearest tree, Barbara knelt down close by, examining the grass around the TARDIS with mounting excitement.

'You were right, Ian. Buttercups! And daisies and

clover too. And look,' she held up a pink, wriggling form, 'a worm. Isn't it lovely?'

'Hardly the word I would have chosen, but it certainly looks like one,' he agreed.

Barbara carefully put the creature down and wiped her hands, looking around at the tranquil scene. 'Smell the air. It's so fresh and warm, just like an early summer's day. And listen to the birds. We *must* be on Earth.'

'Yes,' agreed Ian, half to himself, 'but *when* on Earth are we?'

Together they crossed the glade to where the Doctor was examining the bark and leaves of a sizeable, and familiar, tree.

'Mmm . . .' the Doctor was deliberating. '*Quercus robur*, I believe.'

'It's an oak, Doctor,' said Barbara.

'Precisely what I just said: the common oak. And note that the acorns are not yet developed, indicating it is still early in the season.'

Susan, who had wandered on a short way, suddenly called out, 'There's a sort of path over here!'

'Just a moment, my dear,' the Doctor called back, 'don't get yourself lost.' He brandished his silver-handled walking stick and set off briskly after her, with Ian and Barbara following close behind.

The path curved away to the left and right under the green canopy, weaving between the trees and thickets. The compressed mud and old leaf litter that formed its surface bore fading parallel ruts, suggesting it was used occasionally by some type of wheeled vehicle. In one soft spot there was also an imprint resembling that of a horse's hoof.

The Doctor was looking up and down the track with interest. 'Well now, Chesterton. The answer to your question should lie at one end or the other, eh? We should soon come to some settlement or more substantial thoroughfare and be able to establish our location.' He beamed genially. 'Yes, a fine day for a walk, and no danger of getting lost as long as we take the elementary precaution of remembering where we joined the route.'

He fished about in his pocket and withdrew a small compass, and noted the bearing. Then, with Susan at his side, started off up the path. After a few paces he turned and waved his stick commandingly at them. 'Come along then, no dawdling!'

Smiling, Ian and Barbara followed.

They must have gone a little over a mile, Ian estimated, when they made their first discovery.

It seemed as though there had been a large bonfire beside the path which had scorched the lower branches of the surrounding trees, then burnt down to the earth leaving only a fire-blackened, twisted mound of clinker in the centre. Flies buzzed around it. Curiously, lying on the edge of the circle, was a large wooden bow.

Then the nauseating smell of burnt flesh assailed them.

Susan went rigid, staring at the shape in the middle of the blackened circle with widening eyes. 'It's a body,' she whispered hoarsely, then clapped her hand to her mouth.

Barbara turned her head aside in disgust, put her arm about Susan's shoulders and led her off a few paces.

Ian gulped, fighting to control his stomach. The Doctor looked pale, and mopped his brow with a large white handkerchief. 'Dear me. This is most distressing,' he managed to say dully.

Ian forced himself to be detached. Carefully, he pressed his hand to the burnt earth. 'Cold. This must have happened yesterday. No later than last night, anyway.'

'Quite so. What about the bow?'

Gingerly, they circled the blackened grass. Ian put his handkerchief over his nose and mouth and tried not to look at the ghastly remains. Not that there was any detail visible. Such had been the heat of the fire that flesh and clothing had fused together into one cracked and charred shell. He could not even tell if the body was male or

9

female. Cautiously they examined the weapon.

'It's a kind of longbow,' said Ian. 'Yew, I think, with a leather strap grip, and a gut string. Scorched a bit by the fire.' He looked at the old man's taut features. 'Well, Doctor, what do you make of it? An accident . . . or some kind of ceremonial cremation, perhaps?

'If it were a deliberate ceremony, I would expect it to be in some more suitable site, instead of half-under the trees like this. And is it not usual for weapons, presumably belonging to the corpse, to be deliberately burnt with their owner, instead of carelessly left to one side? Besides, where is the ash from the funeral pyre? There should be a fair quantity of wood to have generated that much heat, yet I see hardly any ash.'

'Perhaps it was accidental . . . a lightning strike, maybe?'

'Perhaps so,' the Doctor mused, brow furrowed in thought. 'It does, however, suggest this path is unfrequented, or someone would have dealt with the body by now.'

'But it can't have been here that long, or else scavengers would have been feeding off it, and there are no signs of that yet.'

'Assuming there are any. Have you noticed any larger animals so far?'

'No, only birds. But I wouldn't be surprised if there are foxes about. If this is Earth's past, there might even be wolves.'

'Unless something has frightened them off, of course.'

'Have you finished, Grandfather?' Susan's voice came plaintively from a little way along the path, where she and Barbara were waiting.

'Just coming, my child,' the Doctor assured her. 'There's nothing more to learn here.'

Ian recounted what they had found to Barbara, as they continued down the path in a subdued manner.

'And it seemed such a lovely day for a walk,' she said bitterly, then sighed. 'I suppose this isn't our own time, then.'

'From the looks of the bow, I think it's unlikely.'

Barbara walked along silently for several minutes. Ian touched her arm lightly in sympathy, and she forced a brave smile. 'You did warn me not to get too hopeful,' she admitted.

'Never mind. Next time, maybe.'

'Maybe . . .'

It was Susan who alerted them to their next find. The path had just joined a wider track, with deeper rut marks in, when she paled and wrinkled her nose.

'I can smell it again,' she said in a small voice. 'Smoke – and burnt things . . .'

They followed the track as it curved around a densely thicketed copse, and found themselves at the gateway of a stockade.

It was ringed by a shallow circular ditch, with the inner bank of the excavation topped by a man-high wall of roughly trimmed stakes. Over the top of the fence they could see a cluster of low roofs. Or rather, the blackened poles that had once supported roofs.

The air was heavy with the tang of stale smoke and the odour of death. It was very quiet. Even the birdsong in the surrounding trees seemed muted. The gates of the stockade hung open, sagging half off their hinges.

Cautiously, they entered.

A crudely fortified hamlet was the best description Ian could think of. There had been a dozen or so simple, single-storey dwellings with their small adjacent stock pens, clustered round a tiny central square containing a traditional crank-and-bucket stone-walled well. Now a shattered handcart lay beside the well and the buildings were a collection of jagged, charred timbers projecting through mounds of ash. To one side, a few scrawny chickens, apparently oblivious to the change in their surroundings, were scratching in the dirt for food. They pecked around the edges of several scorched circles with blackened, contorted forms in their centres. Flies buzzed

11

industriously. The travellers did not need to go any nearer to know what they were.

'More burnt circles surrounding human remains,' observed the Doctor. 'That suggests a similar cause.'

Ian pointed to the far wall of the compound. The fence poles had been smashed inwards and the earth churned and scraped. 'Somebody, or something, came in there. But who, or what?'

Susan suddenly stepped forward and picked something up off the ground. It was a broken arrow, nearly a yard long, fletched with feathers and tipped with a viciously sharp, bright metal head. The Doctor examined it closely. 'Most intriguing. This very probably belongs with that bow we found in the woods. Certainly it could only be fired from a weapon of similar size.'

Ian looked grim. 'Do you realize what you're implying, Doctor? Whoever, or whatever, did this followed the archer after he fought it here. And whatever it was, heavy longbow arrows didn't stop it!'

They looked uncomfortably around the devastated settlement and at the looming forest beyond. Though the sun still shone brightly, it suddenly seemed to be getting colder.

'Look,' Ian said bluntly, 'I think we'd better just go back to the TARDIS. It's obvious that something very dangerous is on the loose and may still be around. There's nothing else to see here and, frankly, I don't fancy being out after dark.'

For a moment it seemed that the Doctor's single-minded curiosity would overcome Ian's commonsense suggestion, but then he relented.

'You may be right, Chesterton. Let us be going.' At his side, Susan gave a relieved smile.

They were turning to go when Barbara stopped short and pointed to an impression in the soft earth close to the well. 'Does that remind you of anything?' she asked faintly.

It was like the print of a bird's foot, but with three long

12

toes projecting forward, and a shorter one behind. The tips of each toe print were deeply indented, as though by a curving talon. From end to end it was at least four feet long.

'It's like one of those fossilized dinosaur footprints they sometimes find in old river beds,' Ian exclaimed.

'Except,' added the Doctor, kneeling down beside the monstrous spoor, 'this cannot be more than a day old! Most remarkable. Are there more of them?'

Recognizing the signs, Ian caught him under the arm and almost hauled him upright. 'No Doctor,' he said, defying the old man's indignant expression, and holding him firmly as he tried to pull away. 'We agreed to leaving *now*, remember? We're not going out of our way to find trouble!'

'Have you no sense of curiosity, young man?' the Doctor demanded angrily.

'Yes, but I also have a sense of self-preservation!' Ian retorted.

'Ian's right, Doctor,' said Barbara supportively.

'Please, Grandfather,' added Susan.

The Doctor glared back at them, but they held their ground. 'Oh, very well,' he conceded, almost petulantly, and stomped off through the gateway and down the track.

The others followed gratefully, with many a backward glance at the shattered hamlet and at the great wall of the forest that rose, impassive and mysterious, over their heads.

An itch started up along Ian's spine and centred itself between his shoulder blades.

They had reached the stretch of pathway that passed the first burnt circle when the Doctor halted to consult his compass.

'I believe we can save ourselves some time if we cut through here.' He gestured at an angle through the trees. 'The path curves that way further down, if you recall, so

13

there's no danger of us missing it.' He glowered at Ian. 'If that meets with your approval of course, Chesterton?'

Ian ignored the barb. Anything that got them back to the TARDIS earlier was worth considering, and keeping off a well-marked, and exposed, pathway for a while might not be a bad idea. Just in case. He looked enquiringly at Susan and Barbara. They nodded.

'All right, Doctor. Lead the way.'

The Doctor bowed slightly, with mock courtesy, and started off through the wood.

Within five minutes, Ian was regretting their decision.

The undergrowth grew thicker under the trees, and they had to pick their way around numerous tangled clumps of brier and bramble, or push through shaggy curtains of ancient ivy that hung from trunks and branches in graceful catenaries. Fallen boughs, rotting and furred with moss, turned their progress into something resembling an obstacle course. The Doctor, unwilling to admit his short cut would probably take longer in the end, pressed ahead briskly. Barbara and Susan exchanged ironic, knowing glances, but made no comment. Ian, bringing up the rear, decided that they might as well press on now. At least the denser wood gave plenty of cover, and they would not get lost while they had a compass.

Then he saw the Doctor stop abruptly, and kick at something half buried in the grass. There was a dull metallic clang.

They crowded round him as he tugged a buckled section of metal plate free, and brushed away the debris clinging to its surface. In places it still gleamed brightly. Edge on they saw the plate was formed of two curving metal sheets sandwiching several layers of honeycomb insulation. A length of bracing rib was welded to the inner side.

The Doctor gazed at his find in delight. 'You know what this is?' he demanded. 'A section of spacecraft hull panel! A product of advanced engineering technology. What is it doing adjacent to the remains of a settlement

14

more appropriate to your Middle Ages, hmm?'

'But where's the rest of it?' Barbara asked practically.

They all turned to look about them. There was a hollow in the trees to one side, filled with tangled undergrowth and slender saplings, and half covering what Ian first took to be a cluster of large boulders. The Doctor pushed his way up to the nearest one and thrust his stick through the tangle of grass and ivy that smothered it. There was a hollow metallic resonance.

Gradually, Ian made out the shape of the vessel the forest was steadily burying. It was perhaps sixty feet long, and had originally comprised two spherical compartments linked by a short section of cylindrical hull. Four outrigger landing legs, now twisted and broken, had once projected from the sides of the spheres. The regular lines of the craft had clearly been distorted by the terrific impact of a crash landing. Cracks showed in several places, and some hull panels were missing. As they circled the wreck, they found themselves looking into the shattered viewports of the control module, crumpled around the remains of a thick tree stump.

'I doubt if anyone in the cabin survived such an impact,' the Doctor said solemnly.

They continued on round the wreck.

'Look, the side hatch is open,' exclaimed Susan.

A door set in the middle hull section hung twisted and gaping, as though the shock of the crash had sprung its catches. As they got closer they saw a faint pathway had been trodden into the grass leading from the hatch.

'Maybe there *are* still survivors, former passengers perhaps, sheltering inside,' said Barbara, half-whispering.

'After all the years this has clearly lain here?' pondered the Doctor. He pointed with his stick at some gaps in the panelling along the side of the hull. 'Far more likely some of the locals have been using the wreck as a source of ready refined metals, I should think. The head of that arrow we found probably came from here. But why not strip the entire craft, I wonder? Perhaps some thought it taboo? Still, we'll just have to see . . .' He started for the open hatch.

'Doctor,' Ian said firmly, 'we're on our way back to the TARDIS, remember?'

The Doctor looked dismayed. 'We must at least make a cursory examination, Chesterton. This is a first-class mystery. Don't you want to know what happened here?'

Ian sighed. The trouble was he was just as curious as the Doctor, but he couldn't forget the unknown danger the woods might contain. Still, everything had been quiet so far.

'All right,' he relented, and tapped his watch. 'Five minutes *only*, understand?'

The Doctor beamed with almost boyish triumph and stepped up to the hatchway.

The interior of the ship would have been pitch black except for light filtering through the rents in the hull. Vines and probing tree roots had also penetrated, spreading their tendrils over bulkheads and deck plates alike. They were clearly in the ship's small hold and utility space, which was perhaps twenty feet long and ten wide. Apart from conduits snaking along the inside of the hull connected to flat, fuse-box-like terminals, it was empty, and gave no indication of recent occupancy. A heavy door at one end suggested access to the engine compartment, while a short corridor in the other direction led to the crew section. Its further end, however, was crumpled and choked with impacted wreckage.

'Well,' said Ian, after peering about for a few moments, 'there's not much to see here, Doctor, unless you want to inspect the engines.'

'Not a bad suggestion, Chesterton. They might give us a clue as to why the ship crashed.'

'What's this?' said Barbara. She had noticed a small plate set on the bulkhead opposite the entrance hatch, gleaming dully under a growth of intruding ivy. She and Susan tugged the strands away to reveal a brass plaque:

Armstrong Transolar Aerospace
—Inc—
'*Mercury Starhopper .C.*'
Model No: 1427
Year of Manufacture: 2976
Empire City, Tycho, Luna.

' "Twenty-nine seventy-six"?' said Barbara.

'Clearly this is the late thirtieth century,' the Doctor concluded.

'But the village belongs to the tenth century rather than the thirtieth. Yet, if this is the future, surely we should have heard aircraft flying over by now, or something – unless . . .' Barbara's expression darkened. 'Unless civilization has fallen somehow, and the survivors have been reduced to a primitive level of existence.'

'That's a depressing thought,' Ian said.

'But a possibility,' conceded the Doctor. 'Now, if we could find out why this craft crashed, if it was accidental or if it was shot down, for instance, then we would have more information to work with.'

'Grandfather, look at this!' Susan sounded excited. She had opened the front of one of the wall-mounted units to reveal the components within, and had pulled out a thin transparent wafer with intricate patterns traced upon it. 'It's an old-fashioned beam etched micro circuit card, but look . . .' She squeezed the card gently in her fingers and it snapped and crumbled to dust.

'Most unusual,' agreed the Doctor, pulling a card free himself and crumbling it between his fingers. 'Now what could have caused this?'

'Corrosion?' suggested Ian. 'It's been lying out here for years, after all.'

'No, no. This type of component, though rather primitive, is extremely robust and durable. It really shouldn't have –'

His words were cut short by the long-drawn-out bass tone of an animal roar rumbling through the woods.

17

For a moment all four of them froze. Then Ian leapt to the hatch and peered out. He could see nothing but the encircling forest wall. Then it came again; a sustained and resonating throaty bellow. It seemed slightly louder.

'It's between us and the village,' Ian hissed. 'Come on, back to the TARDIS before we're trapped here! Try not to make too much noise.'

They scrambled out of the wrecked ship and back on to the Doctor's original short-cut trail.

The Doctor himself set a good pace, consulting his compass as he went, with Barbara and Susan beside him. Ian was a few steps to the rear, constantly turning to watch behind. At this speed he reckoned they were ten minutes from the TARDIS. But did they have ten minutes? How fast could whatever it was travel if it followed them? A distant rasping sibilation, like escaping steam, whispered through the woods. He cursed himself silently for letting them stop at the wreck.

Five minutes later they regained the original pathway, and turned along it towards the glade where the TARDIS lay. They were all breathing hard, but maintaining their pace now they were on smoother ground. The Doctor was exhibiting once again an unusual vitality for his years. They heard the bellow again from behind them, but it seemed no closer.

Another two minutes and we'll be safe, Ian thought

Then came a snuffling hiss, loud and urgent, as though something was scenting their trail. There was a rushing crack and swish of branches. Ian twisted round in time to glimpse some huge, bulky form moving between the trees. Iridescence sparkled off rippling flanks, then the curve of the path hid it.

'Faster!' he yelled at the others.

They were on the last stretch now. The gap into the glade was only a hundred yards ahead.

From down the path came the growing thud, thud, thud of heavy feet, devouring the distance between them in monstrous strides.

The opening was only yards away, the Doctor was scanning the trees intently lest they overshoot. There was a terrible roar from behind them, louder than any before. The pounding tread made the earth tremble. Automatically Susan looked back, saw what was pursuing them and let out a cry of fear and amazement:

'It's . . . a *dragon*!

Ian turned, knowing it was madness to waste even a second, but unable to ignore Susan's incredible words.

It *was* a dragon.

From twenty feet above the path, baleful red eyes glowed out of a great horned and bearded reptilian head. A forked tongue flickered between cruelly fanged jaws. A weaving snake neck ridged with spines descended to a massive body, coated in scales, shimmering with blue and green iridescence over its back, with a vivid yellow underbelly. Claw-tipped bat wings were folded against its sides, while its great taloned feet ripped the turf as it surged towards them, trailing a long, sinuous barbed tail in its wake.

With an effort, Ian forced himself to overcome the dreadful fascination of the fantastic beast. 'Run!' he yelled at the petrified Susan, and saw Barbara grab her hand and drag her on through the trees. Then he realized the Doctor had also paused in his flight; helplessly enthralled by their pursuer.

'Impossible!' the old scientist declared; standing in its path as though his disbelief would somehow shield him from its lethal intent.

Ian heard air rush in to fill the creature's huge lungs. He threw himself forward at the Doctor, knocking him to the ground. With a furnace thunder a torrent of fire erupted from the dragon's maw and billowed just above their prone bodies, scorching their exposed flesh, singeing their hair and setting the branches of an oak ablaze.

Before the dragon could draw in another breath, Ian hauled the Doctor to his feet and together they ran through the screen of trees.

19

The glade opened before them with the TARDIS in its centre. Ian thought he had never seen such a welcome sight. Susan and Barbara had almost reached it. He saw Susan holding her key ready to plunge into the lock. Good girl!

Behind them branches snapped as the dragon tried to force its bulk between the close set trees. Just ten seconds more and we're safe, Ian thought.

Then he realized Susan was twisting the key frantically, but the door wouldn't open!

The Doctor at his side, they stumbled, panting, up to the TARDIS. Susan turned a pale, distraught face.

'It won't unlock, Grandfather!'

The Doctor tore out her key and thrust his own in the lock, twisting it urgently left and right even as the dragon burst through the trees into the glade. Suddenly, blue sparks crackled and licked across the TARDIS's skin, causing the Doctor to jerk his hands away.

'The defence circuits are activated,' he gasped. 'The TARDIS has shut us out. We're trapped!'

3

For the Empire

The firm knock on his door came precisely on the hour, as Nyborg had suspected it would.

'Open,' he commanded from behind his desk. The door slid back to admit Captain Shannon.

He entered, saluted crisply, deliberately watched the door close behind him, and took the seat indicated. Nyborg surveyed Shannon's immaculate space marines uniform. It fitted him a little too perfectly for regulation issue. But then, that was not surprising in the circumstances.

'I must confirm the room is shielded, Admiral,' Shannon said.

Nyborg swivelled the comm unit on the desk around to show the *CONFERENCE* and *SCRAMBLE* lights were on.

'Communications silence has been established?'

'As of two minutes ago. Look, "Captain", I know how to follow orders. Even the S.S.D. should realize that!'

'The Special Services Directorate is fully aware of your record, Admiral, and has no doubt that you *will* follow orders.' He withdrew a memory wafer still in its security seal from an inside pocket. 'And these are your orders from this moment on, including details of our objective. And my own authority. Please check that first before we proceed further.'

He watched impassively as Nyborg inserted the wafer into the comm unit reader and entered his personal decode sequence. Nyborg flicked his eyes over the text for a few moments, then turned back to Shannon with a trace of grudging respect and renewed interest.

'You're operating under instructions direct from the Empress's private office.'

'I am.'

'I didn't realize. This mission actually has her personal backing?'

For the first time, emotion seemed to animate Shannon. A faint flush showed on his lean, hard cheeks, and he leant slightly towards Nyborg.

'Admiral. Our success may mean the difference between life and death for the Empire itself!'

4

A Knight's Duty

The dragon's terrible bellow of triumph as it closed on them blotted out all other sounds, leaving their ears ringing as they stumbled around the side of the TARDIS. There was the rush of indrawn breath filling huge lungs, then a hissing roar as a gout of flame poured over the ship; licking around its edges as they huddled in its lee, setting an arc of grass around its base alight and sucking the air from their lungs in its scalding wake.

The TARDIS remained undamaged; buying them a moment's grace even as it denied them sanctuary. But Barbara knew the creature had only to circle it or crane its neck over the machine and they were lost. Again the dragonfire spewed out, setting them coughing and gasping for air. Then there was an agonizing pause, as though the beast was puzzled by the strange structure, neither rock nor tree, that defied its power, and had temporarily forgotten about them. Barbara wanted to scream: If you're going to kill us do it quickly!

With a rasp of scales it moved closer. Then came a snuffling and the TARDIS swayed as the dragon nuzzled it curiously. They could smell its foul breath. The TARDIS rocked again more forcefully. Electric sparks licked across its surface in response, causing the travellers to flinch away. The dragon shrieked in rage: the trumpeting scream of annoyance cutting the air so sharply that they clasped their hands over their ears in pain. There was a ripping sound as huge talons clawed the turf and the beast turned. Its tail whipped and thrashed in the air, then cracked against the side of the TARDIS, rocking it

23

dangerously. The very tip of the tail curled about the farther side of the craft and caught Barbara sharply across one shin, the horned scales tearing open a gash in the material of her slacks. She cried out, feeling blood flowing hot from her wound, and, sick with shock, started to collapse. Suddenly Ian was supporting her, his eyes full of desperate concern. The dragon's tail beat against the TARDIS again. The machine heeled over, crackling with sparks, and began to topple. Barbara felt Ian sweep her up into his arms and start to run.

'Make for the trees!' he shouted.

The Doctor and Susan just got clear before the TARDIS crashed on to its side. The dragon turned, saw their frantic dash for cover, and pounded after them.

The nearest trees were twenty yards away, and Barbara knew the dragon would overtake them first. With ghastly fascination she saw the great sea-horse head rise up, eyes glowing like coals, forked tongue flickering. Jaws gaped and saliva flowed about its jowls and dripped to earth. Every detail seemed to be imprinting itself upon her mind, as though she was packing her last moments of life with as much sensation as possible to delay the inevitable end.

Then came the swelling beat of hooves.

An improbably magnificent white charger, tail flying, burst into the lower end of the glade. Astride it, as though torn from the pages of a history book, was a knight in a red-plumed helmet bearing a shield and lance. Sunlight glittered off chain mail. The horse reared with a shrill neigh, heavy front hooves pawing the air defiantly, nostrils flared and steaming. The knight held his lance aloft dramatically.

'Turn and face me, foul beast!' he cried.

The dragon's head twisted round and it roared as though accepting the challenge, tail whipping to and fro in renewed fury. Suddenly forgotten, the TARDIS crew stumbled into the shelter of the trees and collapsed into the long grass. Even if they could have run further, it was impossible to turn their backs on the impending confrontation. Susan pulled out a handkerchief and began tying it about Barbara's injured leg, but even through her pain, Barbara's eyes, like the others, were riveted on dragon and knight.

With a malevolent hiss the dragon made a splay-legged, waddling advance on its foe. The knight's visor snapped down, his lance lowered. His mount's powerful hindquarters bunched and extended and they surged forward in a spray of torn earth and grass. Barbara gasped at the suicidal headlong charge. Surely no armour could protect horse or rider from the dragon's fire?

She heard the terrible rasp of indrawing breath and saw the serpent neck lift the head then snap it forward. A blossom of flame billowed across the grass, just as the charger, with remarkable agility for such a bulky animal, swerved to one side. The knight threw up his shield. Incredibly, the fireball seemed to flatten and spread, as though it had struck an invisible wall extending beyond the shield itself, warding the flame clear of both man and mount.

Then they were through the flame, past the dragon's head and circling round behind it, evading its thrashing tail. The creature twisted about to follow them but they were too swift. Before it could strike again, the knight tilted his lance and charged the dragon's exposed flank. Horse and rider staggered with the force of the impact as the lance plunged home between the beast's ribs.

In his chamber, Marton Dhal gasped and clutched his side. For a moment, the red glow in his eyes flickered.

The dragon roared in pain and rage and its sinuous body bucked and writhed. Three feet of lance tip broke off, lodged deep in the wound. Hooves tearing at the turf, the charger tried to back clear of the convulsing beast, but a coil of tail snapped round and caught its side sending it sprawling to the ground and tossing the rider from his saddle. The horse struggled to its feet and skittered away, panicked and confused.

With a dreadful trumpeting moan, the dragon staggered, clawing futilely at its side, then reared over its fallen foe. A torrent of fire beat down on to the earth. But, dazed though he was, the knight had retained his shield. Again the flames were deflected clear of his body. The dragon raised one heavy clawed foreleg over him. What it could not burn, it could still tear and crush.

At that moment Ian sprinted forward into the heart of the fray.

'No!' Barbara cried in horror.

Ian snatched up the knight's broken lance, still twelve feet long, and charged on, shouting at the top of his voice. The great head twisted around towards him. Taking advantage of the distraction, the knight rolled clear of the descending talons as they thudded on to the ground. The beast's strength was going and the head hung lower. As it tried to focus on him, Ian seized his chance and thrust the lance into one red eye. With a terrible shriek of pain and rage the creature clawed at its bloody eye-socket. Ian and the knight fell flat as it writhed and thrashed and churned great gouges in the grass.

Then Barbara heard distant cries ringing through the woods and the sound of many running feet. Suddenly, soldiers clad in chain mail and steel caps, armed with crossbows, pikes and spears, were pouring into the glade out of the trees.

'Fire at your will!' came a shouted order.

The twang and snap of bows filled the air. Spears were hurled. Many bounced off the dragon's hide, but some penetrated. Ten yards away a party of three soldiers appeared, dragging a large, wheel-mounted siege bow behind them. They turned it about, fired a heavy metal dart into the beast's side, and feverishly started cranking the bow back for a second shot.

Under the new onslaught the creature's convulsions subsided, its moans muted and the pulse of its lungs faltered. As its head sank to earth, the knight ran forward, clasped his longsword in both hands, and drove it clean through the eye socket and into the brain. There was a last spasmodic shudder, a final death rattle, and the thing was still.

For a moment the glade was silent, then the soldiers began to cheer and slap each other's backs.

Light-headed with both shock and relief, Barbara got to her feet, supported by Susan and the Doctor, and limped over to Ian, who was standing beside the huge body, staring at it in wonder. She didn't know whether to hug or scold him, but the others spoke first.

'That was very brave,' said Susan, in slightly awed tones, 'wasn't it, Grandfather?'

'Mmm? Oh yes – most courageous,' commented the Doctor, absentmindedly shaking his head at the remains of the creature that still clearly offended his rational senses. 'It shouldn't exist!' he muttered.

'Did you have to take such a risk?' Barbara managed to say at last.

Ian managed a dazed grin. 'Well, I couldn't leave our rescuer in the lurch like that, could I? Anyway, no harm done.'

The knight, after calming his frightened horse and checking it was uninjured, now approached them. Emblazoned on his surcoat, as on his shield, was the image of a dragon in red and gold, set on a black field, overarched with a bow of seven stars. He removed his helmet, and Barbara was surprised to see proud, brown-skinned features, capped with dark curled hair, suggesting African ancestry. But if his appearance was unexpected, his manner was undeniably chivalrous. He drew off a gauntlet, bowed slightly and clasped Ian's hand.

'I am in your debt, sir; that was stoutly done.'

He spoke with dignity and self-assurance, with a slightly archaic inflection to his words.

'It was only fair,' Ian replied sincerely. 'If you hadn't turned up when you did, we'd all be a dragon's breakfast by now.' Ian nodded at the company of soldiers now milling around the dragon. 'It's a good thing you were ready for it, Sir . . .?'

The man straightened. 'I am Bron of Westhold, and have the honour to be in the service of Sir Stephan Palbury, Baron of Fluxford and Steward of the South Share of Elbyon. We had news yesterday that such a beast had despoiled several small settlements in the forest, and I was commanded to seek it out. We have been hunting it since dawn.'

'We found some ruins a couple of miles down the track. We didn't realize how it had happened.'

Sir Bron looked at them curiously. 'You must live in a much favoured land not to know dragon's work when you see it.'

'Yes, this was our first dragon,' Ian remarked dryly. 'We are from . . . abroad.'

'Forgive me, but it is then my duty to ask you to give an account of yourselves and your intentions here.'

Barbara could see Ian was uncertain how to explain their presence. Fortunately, at that moment, Sir Bron realized she was injured and chivalry smoothed the way. He called for the wagon, which had carried the bolt guns and their crews, to be brought to the glade to provide her with a proper seat so her leg could be tended. Meanwhile, he insisted she should rest a little way clear from the dragon's grisly corpse. This seemed to make introducing she and Susan much easier, and he bowed politely to them in due course. The Doctor's introduction as a 'learned man and explorer', together with his distinguished appearance, seemed to impress Sir Bron. He also accepted Ian's, slightly circumspect, explanation that they were travellers from a 'distant land' called 'United Kingdom'. But the TARDIS was harder to pass off.

'It's a sort of . . . travelling device,' said Ian, glancing meaningfully at the Doctor, 'but it doesn't always work properly. We were just trying to find out where it had landed us, when we met the dragon.'

The Doctor interjected impatiently.

'It is simply a mechanical contrivance which has temporarily malfunctioned,' he explained, glaring back at Ian.

'Ah, a *magical* device,' said Sir Bron. 'I did not realize you had wizardly skills, good Doctor.'

The Doctor smiled tolerantly. 'Mechanical, not magical, sir; neither am I a wizard.' He clasped his lapels and thrust out his chin. 'I am a scientist.'

'Forgive me, but I do not know of this word.' Bron stepped over to the fallen TARDIS where it lay in a circle of burnt grass and examined it curiously. 'But surely,' he continued, 'your box must be of magical origin. What else could have withstood dragonfire unscathed?'

He reached out to touch the TARDIS and Ian said quickly: 'Careful. You'll get a shock doing that.'

'Only if it is roughly handled, Chesterton, or the lock is interfered with,' the Doctor amplified.

Sir Bron looked puzzled. Ian turned to one of the pikemen who was standing a respectful few paces back. 'May I borrow that for a moment, thank you.' Ian held the pike by its wooden shaft and struck the TARDIS sharply. On the second blow, blue sparks crackled across its surface, causing the soldiers to step back, muttering in surprise.

'Clearly this is a device of strange power beyond my understanding,' stated Sir Bron. He appeared to reach a decision. 'This must be taken to Fluxford for examination by Gramling, our wizard, to determine its nature,' he stated. The Doctor looked dismayed, but the knight held up a placating hand. 'We will carry your travelling box with great care, Doctor, you may be sure. If it is judged to be safe it will be returned to you.'

The Doctor looked intent on arguing further, so Barbara said quickly: 'Thank you, Sir Bron. We realize you are only doing your duty.'

The knight bowed. 'And you and your companions will of course come too, Mistress Barbara. Your injury

must be properly tended.' He paused reflectively. 'I fea
this an inconvenient time for your arrival here. There i
both joy and unease abroad in the land . . .'

Dhal sipped a goblet of wine to take away the taste o
death. His side and one eye still troubled him with a
memory of relayed pain. Curse the meddling stranger! He
had stayed with the beast too long in trying to finish
Bron, and now he had lost a useful tool. Still, it had
served its purpose, and he had others like it, in one form
or another. But who were these strangers with their
strange fire-proof box? Where had they come from? And
why come now of all times?

Half an hour later, together with a small escort, they were
bumping along the dappled forest road towards Fluxford
The TARDIS was now securely lashed upright in the
wagon, while the four travellers sat on rough benches
behind it. Sir Bron rode a few yards off on his own
mount, which they heard him call 'Ambler'. Every so
often, Barbara felt him giving them curious glances. Still,
she had to admit his treatment of them had been nothing
but correct, and she was certainly glad to leave the
glade and the monstrous corpse of the dragon. As they
departed, a detail of soldiers was already preparing for the
grisly task of dismembering and burning it, except for
those parts which had special medicinal or thaumaturgical
properties, Bron had explained. The head he wanted for
his own trophy, but magnanimously he offered Ian a
talon as a memento.

Barbara noted that, while Susan was looking around
her with bright interest, the Doctor was sitting tight-
lipped, frowning, deep in thought.

'Well, Doctor,' Ian asked at length, 'what do you make
of all this?'

'And what's happened to the TARDIS?' Barbara
added. 'Why won't it let us in?'

The Doctor appeared not to hear, but Susan turned

to fix them with her serious, dark eyes. 'The defence mechanism comes on if there's a danger of something harmful getting inside,' she said simply.

'Harmful!' exclaimed Ian sharply. 'You mean dangerous to us, like a gas or an infection, or just something which might damage the ship itself, like the dragon?'

'It could be any of those, if it's working properly,' Susan admitted. 'Though if it was the dragon that triggered it, it should have turned itself off again by now.'

'As it hasn't,' said Ian tersely, 'that leaves us with some unpleasant possibilities. If there is something harmful out here, will it affect us, and if so, how?'

'But there's obviously plenty of life here, including people like ourselves,' Barbara pointed out, 'and they seem all right.'

'Perhaps they've become acclimatized to whatever it is,' Ian suggested, darkly, then brightened. 'Or perhaps the TARDIS is simply malfunctioning again, Doctor?' He gave him a nudge.

'Mmm . . . what?' The Doctor came out of his reverie. 'Really, Chesterton, do you have to interrupt my train of thought like that?'

'It depends whether you were thinking of anything useful.'

'I was trying to piece together what we have learned so far into some kind of order. Once we understand the nature of this place, we will know what has happened to the TARDIS.'

'And have you managed to fit crashed spacecraft and dragons into their proper places yet?' asked Ian, a touch sarcastically.

'The dragon, superficially at least, is an absurdity,' the Doctor replied firmly.

'But it exists,' Barbara reminded him, 'even if it does seem to have come from a fairy tale. It nearly killed us! Isn't that real enough for you?'

'Of course I'm not denying its existence,' the Doctor replied sharply. 'But I am questioning whether it is what it seems to be. I wish I had had the chance to examine it more closely.' He frowned. 'I have seen many strange creatures in my travels, but a giant, winged, fire-breathing dragon is, as you say, a creation of pure fantasy; belonging to the myths and legends of your world's past, along with harpies, pixies, elves –'

'Dwarves?' suggested Barbara, in slightly strained tones. 'Like those over there?'

Their little column had slowed and Sir Bron rode forward to where a group of stocky, bearded figures, none over four feet tall, waited by the roadside. Barbara saw him speak to them, apparently imparting good news, for they began to look more cheerful. After a few minutes they bid farewell. The file of dwarves marched on as the wagon started off again, and they glimpsed compact, ruddy features between beards and caps, and saw they were all carrying picks and shovels slung with their packs. The dwarves gazed curiously at the TARDIS as they passed, then turned off the road and disappeared into the greenwood.

Barbara couldn't help smiling at the Doctor's expression. She called to Sir Bron, who rode up beside them.

'Who were they?' she asked.

'A party of miners who have excavations in the forest, Mistress Barbara. They were asking if it was safe to proceed, having heard tell of the dragon. I was able to reassure them, and they were pleased to be able to return to their workings, for dwarvish folk have a great passion for burrowing into the ground.'

'I suppose,' said Ian, straightfaced, not looking at the Doctor, 'that there are quite a few pixies and elves around here as well?'

'Not so many elves in these parts,' Sir Bron replied matter-of-factly. 'There are more in the Silverwood, which is close to my own home of Westhold. Here we have too many mischievous goblins and slinking cephlies for comfort. But then, they are ever to be found close to great cities such as Fluxford.'

'And dragons, of course,' Susan reminded him.

Sir Bron chuckled grimly. 'More than there used to be, Mistress Susan. In the past it was just the odd guivre in a fen, or a lindworm out on the heath. You wouldn't hear of a full-grown fire-herald, like the one you encountered, more than once a year at most. But since Beltane Eve, I've raised my shield three times to such beasts.'

'Yes, I noticed your shield was rather . . . er, special,' Ian commented mildly. 'The dragon's fire just seemed to spread without touching it.'

'A prize of my family,' Sir Bron said, proudly. 'Handed down from my father and his father before him. A runic enchantment of great power is inscribed on the rim to turn back fire from its bearer.'

Barbara heard the Doctor mutter under his breath: 'Enchantments!' in exasperated tones. But then he appeared to think of something and asked aloud: 'May I ask, Sir Bron, what today's date is? We . . . ah, have lost count during our recent travels.'

'Today is the fifteenth of June.'

'And the year?'

The knight looked surprised. 'You must have travelled far and long indeed to have lost count of the year, Doctor.'

'Indeed. Just how far we will know when you tell us what it is.'

'Then it is the fourteenth year of the reign of Magnus the Third, eight hundred and forty six AL.'

'Ah,' the Doctor appeared pleased with himself. 'But what would it be by . . .' his lips pursed speculatively, 'the old calendar?' he hazarded.

Sir Bron's puzzlement was clearly deepening. 'Why, none use the old counting anymore.'

'But if they did,' persisted the Doctor, 'would it not be the end of the thirtieth century now?'

'I suppose so. But why trouble about it?'

'And just what does "AL" signify?' continued the Doctor, regardless.

33

Sir Bron now looked increasingly suspicious. 'How can you not know that?' he demanded. 'All lands count from then.' His eyes narrowed. 'Just where is this United Kingdom of yours?'

The tense silence that followed was broken by quick, chittering voices and a patter of feet from the track behind them. Barbara saw a party of three stooping creatures, with mottled pelts, large heads elongated at the back, and spindly bodies, scamper across the road. One flashed them an apprehensive, hang-dog glance, then they were gone.

Sir Bron must have seen the expression on her face, because he asked levelly: 'Do you not recognize common cephlies, Mistress Barbara? Do any of you?' Reluctantly they shook their heads. 'And you have never encountered a dragon before. That is unbelievable. Again I ask: where do you come from?'

'Sir Bron,' said the Doctor, sincerely. 'We didn't say more earlier because we were not sure how you would treat our somewhat unusual origins. You see, our . . . travelling box, has carried us much further than you imagine. I shall try to explain, but I genuinely believe it would help if I knew what AL means.'

'It means "After Landfall", naturally.'

'But landfall where?'

'Here on Avalon, where else? The landfall of Merlin's skyboat *Prydwen*, when it bore the body of Arthur through the Veil from the last great battle, to his rest amongst the stars.'

5

Mission Specialists

Doctor Jen Komati shifted uncomfortably in her seat. The uniform still pinched her. She'd have to go back to the auto-tailor again. Of course, she conceded, it might simply be that she was not a natural soldier. She'd only been in the forces for three weeks. Just time enough for the briefest period of intensive training, of a very particular kind, and learning who to salute. The fact that she was already wearing the double stars of a lieutenant had little to do with her martial prowess. It was intended, she realized, to put her unquestionably within a command structure and under military discipline, where orders would be obeyed. She glanced across at professor Ivanov, similarly uniformed, and suspected he felt equally uncomfortable.

The door of the small briefing room slid back and Shannon and flight lieutenant Monadno entered. Komati and Ivanov stood in as military a fashion as they could manage.

The first time she'd seen them together, Komati thought they were related. Later she realized they had simply come out of the same training mould. Physically lean, narrow waisted and broad shouldered. Clear, steady eyes that tended to bore through you. Hair trimmed down so close its colour hardly showed. Necks bunched with thick tendons leading up to resolute jaws. Not square jaws, particularly, just absolutely, singlemindedly, determinedly set. Undeniably capable men. Capable of anything.

'Be seated,' said Shannon, briskly. He did everything briskly, Komati realized.

'We are now approximately thirty hours from our objective. This briefing is to acquaint you with the details of that objective and the wider purpose of our mission. All mission details are classified ultra secret, and are to be discussed with no one outside our team. That includes the rest of the marine contingent aboard. You are to report solely to me. Any questions?'

Komati and Ivanov exchanged glances, and Ivanov coughed slightly and spoke up.

'Well, Captain, only the obvious one: why us? We've still not been given a proper explanation. Doctor Komati and myself were both involved in reserved research work when we were, as the old expression has it, "drafted". My work will suffer, as I'm sure will the doctor's. It had important defence implications, you know.'

'I am aware of your previous work, Lieutenant, but this mission has absolute priority. You were serving the Empire in your laboratories, and now you will do your duty in the field.'

'But surely there are other military scientists and technicians amongst the marine corps on board who could —'

'You are to hold yourself apart from them as I have already indicated,' Shannon cut in. 'They will provide our backup as necessary after we have made the initial sortie.' He surveyed them coldly. 'Frankly, I would also have preferred regular military scientists. But that was not possible in the circumstances, as you will learn. Now, if there is nothing further . . .'

And very shortly Jen Komati discovered their purpose.

And began to be afraid.

36

6

Wizard

It was fortunate that Ambler knew the road to Fluxford well, for during the rest of the journey, Bron paid it little attention.

Voyagers from beyond the Veil.

People from the oldworlds travelling inside that tiny box!

An incredible story, but he found himself believing it.

Apart from the box itself, with its half-tamed lightning, there was Ian Chesterton's word, which he judged to be good. It also explained their incredibly foolish behaviour in walking through the forest unarmed with the signs of dragons all about them. Bron had seen the look of concern on Ian's face as Barbara's injury had been tended, and he knew he would never lead her into such danger had he known better. Yet the man was evidently no fool. So he must truly not have known better, which set him apart from all other Avalonians with any sense.

And yet they looked so ordinary. Bar their strange dress, he might have passed them without note. Well, perhaps not the Doctor. There was a quality about him, which was as wizardly as he had ever felt, never mind what he chose to call himself. There was more than a touch of it in his grandchild too, unsurprisingly. What would Sir Stephan make of the arrival of such people today of all days, he wondered? For that matter, what would old Gramling make of the Doctor and his travelling box?

The sphere glowed into life once more at Dhal's touch. He hunched over it intently, straining to achieve the link

37

with the least possible disruption. This was not like riding an animal mind, this had to be delicate. There, he had it! He spoke aloud to reinforce his commands.

'Listen to me. There are strangers coming to Fluxford. I wish to learn more about them.'

Susan watched the forest thin and fall behind them, and they emerged on to a better road that wound between fields and scattered farmhouses. They crested a slight rise, and a river valley opened before them. Behind high, curving walls jostled the huddled roofs of Fluxford; spreading over both banks of the river and linked by a single wide bridge. Dominating the valley from a hilltop on the further bank was a great castle. Tall towers rose from within encircling rings of turreted outer walls. Early afternoon sun sparkled from its windows, and pendants flew from every mast and pinnacle.

'Oh, that looks wonderful,' she said.

'The finest castle in the southlands,' Bron agreed. 'Only the King's own fastness at Glazebry is grander.'

They followed the winding road down into the valley and up to the city walls, where they passed through heavy studded double gates and into a long cobbled street. Half timbered three and four storey buildings ran along each side, throwing out overhanging eves and gables. The thoroughfare bustled with carts, horses and people, who were dressed in variations of the medieval kirtle, or tunic and hose, with occasional puffed sleeves and hooded caps. Moving amongst the ordinary folk were stocky dwarves, and a few tall, graceful figures with golden hair and pointed ears. Are they elves? Susan wondered. The TARDIS and the four travellers received many curious stares, but their escort cleared the way, and they rumbled steadily on towards the river. They caught a glimpse of a busy quayside as they passed through the arch of the gatehouse and on to the bridge that linked the two halves of the city.

The bridge was a shallow bow that leapt the broad

river in a single span. It was apparently made solely of *glass*.

Susan grasped the side of the wagon a little tighter and looked over its side. The road surface itself was finely dimpled and frosted, presumably for traction. She could see, slightly blurred, the flowing waters thirty feet below. The bridge structure was only a few inches thick.

'Sir Bron, who made this?' asked the Doctor.

'Why, 'tis said to be the work of Merlin, when men first came to Avalon. But the secrets of such craft have long since been lost. Surely you have such things on your world?'

'We tend to make them . . . ah, a little more substantial,' Ian replied mildly, exchanging helpless glances with the others. Barbara shook her head in bemusement. The Doctor's thoughtful scowl deepened.

They crossed over into the other half of the city and began to ascend towards the castle. The winding street twisted between even older and more closely packed houses than those on the other bank. The castle walls loomed over them and they began to appreciate its vast bulk. Topping the hill they found a wide dry moat separated the last of the houses from its outer walls.

Here they had to pause as a company of twenty mounted men, bearing pennants on their lances and riding immaculately groomed and harnessed horses, trotted out over the drawbridge past them. They were led by a sturdy, fresh faced youth, hardly out of his teens, who drew up briefly beside Bron, surveying the TARDIS and the four travellers curiously.

'I thought you were hunting dragon, Sir Bron,' he said cheerfully. 'But what have you here?'

'The hunt was successful, Master Edmund. But I found these people and their box along the way. And a strange story they have to tell.'

'I look forward to hearing it. But I must not tarry now. Well done!' And he spurred his mount on after the others.

Boards rattled under the wagon's wheels as they crossed the drawbridge and entered the shadowy portals of the turreted gatehouse, passing under two portcullises and between massive double gates.

They emerged into what, Susan remembered, was called the outer bailey. It was a broad stretch of open grass entirely surrounding the inner walls and the castle keep, which rose majestically from a great mound at its centre. To her surprise, the space was dotted with brightly coloured tents with conical roofs, each having a distinctive banner flying from its central pole, and lances and shields displayed before them. The figures of squires and pages in tabards bearing many different heraldic designs, flitted about the forest of tents and across to the inside of the wall, where horses were tethered under lean-to shelters.

'Do you usually have so many visitors?' she exclaimed.

Sir Bron laughed lightly, white teeth flashing against his dark skin. 'I forget you do not know what all Elbyon has been talking about for weeks. Tomorrow, Princess Mellisa, the King's youngest daughter, will be wed to Sir Stephan's youngest son Edmund; he who just passed us on his way to escort the royal party over the last miles. It will be the grandest celebration in years, with tournaments and entertainments every day for a week up to the midsummer fair. There are parties here from all over the land and a few beyond.' He smiled. 'Though you must surely now count as our most travelled guests.'

Their little column crossed a second moat, this time water filled, and through a gatehouse no less substantial than the first, then up a paved ramp flanked by high walls and roofed by an iron grating. Susan noticed many slotted openings in the stonework and realized what their deadly purpose would be, should any invading force reach this far. The castle might look romantic, but it was clearly built to serve a very practical function. They passed through another solid gate and into the inner bailey. Built up against its walls were buildings that must have been the main stables, a smithy and store houses. Sections of the grounds within the enclosure were walled off, presumably forming private gardens. In the middle was the castle keep: a cluster of round towers built of pale stone, with only slotted loopholes on their lower levels, capped by turrets or conical pointed roofs, and bridged between by battlements and crenellated walkways. The wagon clattered up to an archway, passed under yet another portcullis, and emerged within the central courtyard. This was overlooked by the large, colourful traceried windows of staterooms and many hanging balconies. The wagon swung round and drew up beside a flight of steps ascending to a large doorway. An attendant ran up to take charge of Ambler, and Sir Bron dismounted.

'Please descend,' he requested. 'Your box will be taken where it may be examined later. Can you walk a little ways, Mistress Barbara?' he asked solicitously, as Ian helped her down from the wagon.

'Thank you, Sir Bron,' she replied with a wry smile, rubbing her seat delicately, 'but after that ride, a walk will be welcome!'

Bron smiled understandingly. 'I will try to contrive a meeting for you with Sir Stephan, though you appreciate he is much engaged with arrangements. The royal party will be arriving in but a few hours.'

Sir Bron spoke briefly to the guards on the door, and they passed through into a long, stone flagged corridor, busy with pages and maids in flying skirts, dashing to and fro. The homely smell of food suddenly impinged on Susan's senses, and she gazed hungrily at the laden trays and platters, clearly destined for a feast, being carried past them. They were led along the corridor, sometimes having to stand aside to let more food and cases of tableware by, and then up a broad flight of stairs to the entrance of a grand hall.

It was a spacious chamber, with heavy beams supporting its high vaulted roof. A minstrels' gallery bridged across one end. On opposite walls, two huge fireplaces gaped under massive chimney breasts, flanked by tall arched windows. Presently, the hall was a hive of activity as servants prepared tables. At the far end of the room they could see a compact, dapper man, wearing fine robes, who was directing some details of the operation. He was flanked by a slightly harassed looking scribe carrying a small wooden desk top, supported horizontally by a strap around his neck and a belt, before him. This held his paper, quill and inkpot, and allowed him to walk whilst taking notes.

They waited by the door while Sir Bron approached Sir Stephan and spoke intently to him for several moments. They saw the Baron cast several curious glances in their direction. He gave some instructions to a pageboy, who hurried out of the room, then the travellers were beckoned over. Sir Bron introduced them, and the Doctor made a small, dignified bow.

'Please excuse our arrival at such an inconvenient time, Sir Stephan. It was, I assure you, quite unplanned.'

'So Bron has explained, good Doctor.' The Baron peered at them intently with bright, intelligent eyes, that contrasted with his iron-grey hair. 'But if you are indeed travellers from the oldworlds come safely to us at last, as Bron is inclined to believe you are, then your arrival is surely propitious. And this travelling box he describes, that is so different to the skyboats we know of, that intrigues me.' He looked thoughtful. 'Even though time is short, I am minded to inspect such a remarkable thing.' He nodded to his scribe. 'I believe Master Harding can manage quite well without my aid for a while. Show me this strange vessel of yours.'

The TARDIS had been placed in a small walled yard adjacent to the castle gardens. The Baron inspected it closely and had the Doctor explain its functions. With another borrowed pike, the defence shield was again demonstrated.

'And yet you say it is a device constructed purely of mundane elements, without any magical principles at all?' he queried at length.

'That is so,' the Doctor replied firmly. 'I know nothing about what you call "magic".'

'Well, I have sent for one who is more expert than I in such matters. Ah, here he comes now.'

An old man with a flowing white beard was approaching. He wore a wine-red cloak which swept the ground, over a long tunic belted with a wide gold sash, decorated with runic inscriptions. On his head was a tall pointed hat patterned with silver stars. He walked with the aid of a staff of dark, twisted wood, nearly as tall as he was. He bowed stiffly as he came up to Sir Stephan.

'You sent for me, my lord, and I have come.' His gaze passed over the travellers and the TARDIS. 'And these are the strangers and their . . . device.'

'Indeed. A mechanical travelling box of the Doctor's, here. And it appears to have shut them out against their will. What do you make of it, Master Gramling?'

The old wizard circled the TARDIS, tapping it with his staff, sniffing suspiciously. 'It has a strange quality, certainly.'

'We really would be grateful if you could open it,' Barbara said politely, ignoring the Doctor's withering glance.

Gramling swelled slightly. 'Open it, lady? Yes, I'm sure I can do that, if your companion has lost the means. A simple unlocking spell should suffice.'

The wizard made a complicated pass with his free hand, chanting under his breath, and gestured with his staff. To the amazement of the travellers, they saw a flare of bright green light surge from its tip and strike the TARDIS door, tracing the outline of its edges for a moment and sparkling around its lock, then fading away. Gramling tapped the door expectantly. Nothing happened. His face fell. He struck it harder.

'I would advise against that,' the Doctor warned,

quickly concealing his surprise at the show of magical pyrotechnics.

Sparks crackled over the TARDIS and licked out towards Gramling, who leapt back with a start. 'Aha,' he said, recovering himself. 'It is protected by an elemental, I see.'

'Nonsense,' exclaimed the Doctor. 'It is protected by a high voltage surface electrical discharge!'

'Allow me,' said Gramling icily, taking a step towards the Doctor in emphasis, 'to make my own observations in a field of knowledge in which I have made something of a study, having identified forty-three distinct types of elemental beings!'

'And allow me,' said the Doctor, taking a step towards Gramling in turn, 'to point out that the TARDIS is evidently quite outside any such field of knowledge.'

'I think I recognize the actions of elementals when I see them!' Gramling replied haughtily, edging still closer to his detractor.

'Your pardon, sir, but you do not!' retorted the Doctor, stepping closer again.

The two were practically nose to nose now, and Susan realized that, except for Gramling's flowing beard, they were very much alike, with the same defiantly thrusting chins and domineering manners.

'Now just a minute,' said Ian moderately, trying to get between them. 'Perhaps you're both just disagreeing over semantics here –' He trailed off as two pairs of aged diamond-hard eyes stared him into silence.

'My lord,' said Gramling suddenly, turning to Sir Stephan. 'I believe my competence has been questioned by this man. May I make a more substantial demonstration of my powers?'

Sir Stephan was looking amused by the confrontation. 'Very well, Master Gramling. But nothing dangerous, mind.'

The wizard stepped back from the Doctor, eyes blazing. Under his breath he spoke an incantation, stirring the air with his staff. A thread of vapour appeared from nowhere, swirling like a streamer, and grew more solid. In moments it had taken on the form of a vividly coloured snake, coiled about the staff. Growing larger, it slithered to the ground. Susan gasped and shrank away instinctively. Barbara clasped Ian's arm, but he stood firm, fists clenched. The snake was twenty feet long, and it still seemed to be uncoiling and growing. Hissing menacingly, its fanged head reared over the Doctor, forked tongue flickering.

Then the Doctor suddenly smiled in understanding.

'It's an illusion,' he said triumphantly, and stepped forward and slashed his stick through the snake's neck.

It met no resistance. The others blinked. And there was only a thin streamer of vapour in the air that slowly drifted away. The idea that it had ever been a snake suddenly seemed ridiculous.

Sir Stephan laughed. 'I believe you have met a worthy opponent, Gramling.'

The wizard coloured and frowned angrily at the Doctor. 'How did you recognize the illusion so quickly? It was perfect.' He became suspicious. 'Only one trained in the magical arts could have done that.'

'Not so,' countered the Doctor sharply. 'I am a scientist, an observer. And your illusion, excellent though it was,' he allowed magnanimously, 'lacked one important detail: it cast no shadow on the ground!' Gramling seemed taken aback, and the Doctor pressed home his advantage, a mischievous smile now playing about his lips. 'Yes, I sometimes see things others do not.' He pointed dramatically. 'That egg in your beard, for example!'

'What!'

'Right there, sir, under your very chin!' And before anybody could move, the Doctor stepped quickly forward, thrust his hand into the flowing mass of hair, and appeared to withdraw from it a brown hen's egg, which he held up for all to see.

There was a momentary surprised silence, then general

45

laughter filled the yard.

The Doctor beamed and bowed genially to his impromptu audience. 'And all done without magical intervention,' he added, turning back to Gramling. 'Now, sir, let us forget our little difference and agree not to trespass on the other's territory, hmm?'

There was a moment's hesitation, then Gramling bowed slightly. 'Perhaps that would be wisest, Doctor.'

'Well said,' applauded Sir Stephan. 'Two such learned men should not set against each other, especially on such a happy occasion as this. Now, Master Gramling, do you believe there is any evil in the Doctor's vessel?'

Gramling recovered some of his poise. 'It is a strange contrivance, but no, I sense no evil.'

'Just so. And I in turn judge these people to be good folk, and offer them the hospitality of my house, in return only for some tales of their travels and news of the oldworlds, when time allows.'

The Doctor, now at his courteous best after his little triumph, bowed. 'Thank you, Sir Stephan. We accept your most gracious offer.'

'Well,' observed Ian, half an hour later, 'I think we could say we've been rather lucky, all things considered.'

They had been found a couple of rooms on an upper floor of the crowded castle, which, if not the best, were comfortable enough. Ian was sharing with the Doctor, and Barbara with Susan. A tray of food and a flagon of wine had been provided to tide them over to the banquet that evening. At the moment they were all in the women's room, where Barbara rested her injured leg on the bed. Boiled water in a glazed bowl had been supplied, together with clean bandages and a small bottle of raw alcohol for a disinfectant. Susan was cleaning and re-bandaging the wound. Barbara would probably be limping for the next few days.

'I could have done with slightly more luck, thank you,' Barbara said, wincing as Susan cleaned her wound, 'but I suppose it could have been worse.' She glanced at the Doctor, who was sitting with his hands clasped over the handle of his cane, apparently lost in thought again. 'So, Doctor, what have you to say about magic, now that you've actually seen some practised?'

'Talking of which,' Ian added quickly, 'how did you do that trick with the egg?'

The Doctor seemed annoyed. 'Now why is it that you assume what we saw demonstrated was "magic", while my own little contribution was merely a "trick", eh? Can you tell me how I did it?'

'Some sort of sleight of hand, I suppose,' said Ian.

'Precisely. But where did I get the egg from in the first place? Did I "magic" it out of thin air? No. I picked it up unobtrusively when we passed all those food trays in the long corridor, because I noticed my Susan was looking hungry, and I thought a boiled egg would be better than nothing.'

Susan smiled. 'Thank you, Grandfather.'

'Of course, I had no idea that I might be able to produce it to such good effect. You realize, I trust, that my somewhat dramatic words and gestures served as a distraction, while I palmed the egg and then appeared to retrieve it from Gramling's beard.' He grinned almost boyishly. 'A little trick I picked up while I was in the United States once. Fellow named Harry . . . something . . . showed me.'

'Houdini, Grandfather,' Susan reminded him gently, as she finished tying Barbara's bandage.

'Yes, that was him. Better known for his escapology, but a talented illusionist as well. Anyway, that is an example of what I know of as "magic". Now, how do you explain what you saw Gramling do?'

'Well, I can't,' admitted Ian. 'The light that came out of his staff, the giant snake – and in the open in broad daylight. Even if that was an illusion without substance, it was a clever one.'

'I see. So you immediately jump to the conclusion that

47

it must be a product of mystical forces and paranormal phenomena, just because you can't see any other obvious explanation.'

'But it does rather fit the pattern,' put in Barbara. 'We've actually seen a dragon, dwarves and elves, and Bron's flame-proof shield. They're no illusions. And King Arthur and Merlin seem to be part of their history. This world is called Avalon, which in the Arthurian Legends was meant to be his last resting place. He was carried there on Merlin's boat called the *Prydwen*. I don't pretend to understand it, but it does make a sort of sense.' She frowned. 'Couldn't we have gone somewhere beyond our ordinary universe, where magic actually does work, and where myth and fantasy become reality?'

'There are dimensions, in the darker recesses of time and space, where the laws of nature as you know them are distorted,' the Doctor admitted solemnly. 'But there was no indication we made such a leap to get here. In any case, what of the spacecraft we found, and why do they talk about "skyboats" so freely, if this is such a place? What need or understanding would they have of them? No, I am convinced this is the end of the Thirtieth Century, by your calendar, and that these people, perhaps originally an Earth colony, have, over time, somehow confused real and mythical history so they believe they are descended from the followers of Arthur and Merlin.'

'Hold on, Doctor,' said Ian. 'I can see how a pseudo-medieval society might grow up if a colonizing attempt failed for some reason. But all the confusion in the world is not going to make "magic" work or dragons actually appear. There is something unusual there, whatever you care to call it.'

The Doctor beamed benignly. 'At last, my boy, you're starting to consider the problem objectively, and not leaping to conclusions. I have never denied that the dragon was a reality, Bron's shield has special properties, or that the wizard has access to powers I do not, as yet, understand. But I will never call on the supernatural to explain it away before exploring every other possibility first. To do that we must learn more facts about this world and its history.'

'But will that help us with the TARDIS?' wondered Barbara.

'But of course,' exclaimed the Doctor. 'It is too much of a coincidence for the unusual conditions here not to be linked to the misbehaviour of the TARDIS. Once we know the facts behind those, the problem will be explained.' He hooked his thumbs under his lapels in his deliberate way. 'Believe me, I'm certain of it.'

7

The Cat

The tiny cottage stood dark and silent amid the tall
trees of the deep wood. Its shingled roof sagged and
its single chimney stack twisted like a corkscrew, not
quite reaching up to the outflung lower branches of the
nearest trees, which overhung the dwelling and sheltered
it from all but the highest noonday sun. A faint, little
used path meandered up to the front door, which was
blackened and ridge-grained with age. The tiny lead-
latticed windows with the rippled glass panes were dark
and cold, and reflected no cheery sparkle. It was almost as
though the cottage was dead.

A cat, yellow eyed and black as night, flitted silently
through the trees. Reaching the front door, it scratched
to be let in, then sat on the time-worn step with its tail
flicking impatiently.

There was no movement from inside.

The cat scratched again, more determinedly.

Still nothing.

It yowled stridently, its piercing tone normally a
guarantee of immediate attention.

All remained silent.

Irritated, it began a tour of inspection around the
cottage, looking for a window ajar. There was none.

The cat paced in frustration to and fro before the front
door for a minute, then trotted over to the lean-to
woodshed. There was a scrabbling and it appeared on the
woodshed roof. A springing leap, and it was on the main
roof. It padded over to the crazy chimney stack, reared up
to hook its claws between the bricks and began to climb.
Reaching the top, it peered cautiously down the smoke-

blackened flue, but no fire burnt in the grate below. It curled itself over the lip and disappeared.

No sound came from the cottage for several minutes.

Then there was a rapid scrabbling up the chimney and the cat appeared again. It leaped from the top of the stack on to the shingles, then from shingles to ground in practically one movement. It landed bonelessly and silently and sprinted off through the trees without a backward glance.

Its eyes still flashed yellow. But now, deep within them, burned a purpose that had not been there before.

8

An Unwelcome Guest

'Now tell me, Doctor,' Ian heard Kilvenny Odoyle enquire, 'how is it with the oldworld? I would dearly like to hear tales of the Emerald Isle after all these long years.'

Odoyle sat on the other side of Susan and the Doctor from Ian. He wore a bottle green tail-coat, breeches with buttoned gaiters and silver buckled shoes. He had his own specially raised chair, necessitated by the fact that he was slightly under two feet tall. Which was probably quite a good height for a leprechaun. They had all, including the Doctor, accepted him with hardly a second glance. After what they had experienced so far that day, Ian thought, being introduced to a leprechaun as your table companion required little additional mental adjustment.

In the space between the tables, a jester, apparently engaged in a dispute with his own stick-and-bladder, executed a pratfall, to the delight of the diners. In the minstrels' gallery, a small company of musicians plucked and blew at harps, horns and pipes; producing a reedy but merry accompaniment to the festivities.

'Ireland,' replied the Doctor carefully, raising his voice above the noise, 'was still the same charming, whimsical place as always when I last visited it. Of course, that was a while ago . . .'

Ian lost the rest of his noncommittal response as a fresh wave of laughter washed through the Great Hall of Fluxford Castle.

Three hundred guests sat at an extended 'U' of adjoining tables, which stretched the length of the hall and across its further end. From his own place, well down one side, Ian could see the high table where the royal party and their host sat. This was the closest they had yet been to the royal couple, there having been no chance to include them in the official introductions earlier. As far as he could judge, King Magnus and Queen Leonora made an impressive spectacle in their fine robes and crowns; balancing regal reserve and dignity nicely with an easy conviviality. Beside them was Palbury, who they had learned was a widower, together with his elder son Giles and his wife, and Edmund. Next to Edmund was a pretty girl, with golden hair worn in one long waist-length plait, who could hardly have been more than seventeen. This was Princess Mellisa, his bride to be. The two kept exchanging long, silent, slightly embarrassed smiles amid the noise and clamour of the feast.

Barbara, seated beside Ian, had also noticed the pair's behaviour, and now leaned closer. 'Where have we seen expressions like that before?' she asked.

Like Susan, she was now wearing a loose-sleeved, floor length dress suitable for the occasion, chosen from a selection which Sir Stephan considerately had sent to their room earlier, together with night clothing for all of them. Ian suspected that, apart from the need to replace Barbara's torn and bloody clothing, the sight of women in slacks was not thought quite proper. His own costume and that of the Doctor had, presumably, been judged unusual but acceptable, considering their peculiar origins.

Ian grinned back. 'I know, on the faces of any number of lovesick sixth formers.'

Barbara frowned, pursing her lips experimentally, 'Lovesixth sic formers – oh – I don't think I could say that quickly. It's all this wine . . . it's gone to my head.' She shifted in her chair and winced, as though her leg still pained her.

Ian noticed her discomfort. 'Do you want to go to your room and rest?'

53

'I'll be all right for a little while longer. I just wish there was some plain water to drink.'

'Maybe a spot of wine's the best thing for you at the moment. Besides, I'm not sure I'd trust the water.' A troop of jugglers and tumblers had taken the place of the jester in the space between the tables. 'At least there's a free floor show, and we're certainly not going to starve.'

'Oh, there's plenty of food, if you like meat. I just wish it wasn't all so richly flavoured!'

The tables groaned under platters piled high with haunches, ribs and slices of every type of meat. Venison, suckling pig, mutton, pheasant and woodcock, jostled together with breaded salmon and some dried sea fish they could not identify. There were few vegetables present except roast potatoes, beans and peas, and nothing as simple as plain gravy, but instead a variety of heavily seasoned sauces, pungent with onion, pepper, cloves, cinnamon and ginger. Apart from the fat golden rolls of bread that were torn up to mop the plates, and some fruit, mainly last year's carefully preserved apples, the blandest item on the menu was a side dish of almond flavoured rice. Custard flans and sugared wafers provided a sweet diversion.

The feast seemed to be without fixed courses, and all were apparently expected to eat their fill as they chose. The only interruptions were when the servants brought forth fresh pitchers to replenish their cups. There was white wine, red wine, wine sweetened with honey or spiced with nutmeg. Ale and beer was being consumed freely on the lower tables. With each serving, a new toast was proposed, and goblets of silver and gold were raised to the King and Queen, to the Steward of the South Share and to the future of the two betrothed. As the banquet progressed and the toasts became more slurred and merrier, Ian wondered who would be fit for tomorrow's ceremonies.

As he observed the banqueters, he realized how racially diverse they were. Fairy tale beings aside, he saw many black, brown and oriental faces amid the revellers, giving an additional exotic quality to this pseudo-medieval feast. Presumably the original colonists had come from all parts of the Earth. But that still didn't explain where the elves or leprechauns came from, of course.

While he mused, Barbara was engaged in conversation by Sir Peridor, who sat on her other side. He was a blond giant of a man, resembling a reincarnated Viking, in the service of the King. The Doctor was still conversing with Kilvenny Odoyle, and Susan was chatting brightly with one of the ladies sitting opposite, sipping quickly from her goblet as she did so. This action inspired a sudden feeling of schoolmasterly responsibility in Ian, possibly reinforced by the knowledge that he was feeling a little light-headed himself.

Taking advantage of a break in their conversation, he leaned closer and murmured: 'I wouldn't have too much wine, if I were you, Susan. You might regret it in the morning.'

She blinked in incomprehension for a moment, and Ian had the feeling she was translating an unfamiliar concept. Then she replied simply: 'Oh, it doesn't matter what I drink. We don't get inebriated. Unless we want to, of course.'

And Ian had a brief glimpse, once again, of the gulf that separated him from this seemingly normal girl and her grandfather.

As the evening light slanting through the hall's tall windows mellowed, candles were lit in scrolled wall brackets, or in great wheels suspended from the ceiling; filling the room with dancing shadows and the heavy scent of wax. And as the mood of the banqueters mellowed in sympathy, the minstrels took their rest, and a troubadour was presented to the royal table, to sing a lay specially composed for the occasion. Feeling well fed and relaxed, Ian leaned back in his chair and closed his eyes and let the gentle, liquid, mellifluous words drift softly over him.

From outside he seemed to hear a breeze wash over the traceried window panes.

Then there was a louder buffet of wind. Somewhere a shutter banged suddenly.

The singer faltered for a moment as a cry of surprise rang out from within the castle. There was a boiling, rushing noise that grew sharply in pitch. The guards at the hall's big double doors turned, dropping their pikes to the ready. The sound rose to a wailing scream.

The doors burst open, knocking the guards aside. A cold hurricane blast tore through them, snuffing out the candles in an instant and plunging the hall into grey half-light. A window pane blew out, tableware toppled and spilled on to the floor, banners and hangings billowed and snapped. A woman screamed and men's voices rose in surprise and anger.

Slowly the gale subsided and the last gusts faded and were gone. People started to gather their wits, groping about almost blindly in the gloom. The King's voice could be heard over the confusion calling for light.

And out of the murk in the middle of the hall came a cool, sardonic reply: 'Light, your Majesty? Certainly you shall have light.'

A shadow moved with a rustle of cloth. There was a faint multiple popping sound, and it seemed as though fireflies had exploded about a candle bracket at one end of the hall, and a flame suddenly danced over every smoking wick. Then the next bracket came to life, and the next. A wave of illumination rolled around them, finally causing the great hanging candle wheels to blaze afresh.

A tall figure, wearing flowing dark robes and a wizard's hat, stood in the open space between the tables. Ian saw dark eyes gleaming out of the handsome, sardonic face of a man no older than himself. Power and arrogant self-assurance burned in the gaze that passed across the assembly before coming to rest on the occupants of the high table. Sir Bron and Gramling sprang to their feet as

56

the man strode up to the King, but the intruder only bowed low before him, with a mocking exaggerated flourish.

'Pardon my late arrival, your Majesty, but my invitation to this happy gathering seems to have gone astray.' There came the sound of feet pounding up the corridor outside. The man in black waved his hand negligently at the big double doors and with a rush of wind they slammed shut.

The King had recovered himself by now and stood to face the man across the table.

'There was no invitation, Dhal, as well you know. I would not have the good humour of this day tainted by bloodshed, but I swear if you do not leave this instant, I will have you removed from here by whatever means necessary!'

Dhal's voice lowered menacingly for a moment, ignoring the thumping fists pounding on the outside of the doors. 'Dare you risk the consequences of such foolhardiness? I think not.' Then he brightened again, as though dismissing the threat from his mind, and became full of transparent charm once more. 'But there is no cause to bear me ill will, when I seek only to convey to your – beautiful – daughter, and her husband-to-be, my best wishes for their future life together.'

And he bowed elegantly towards Princess Mellisa, but then let his eyes linger so suggestively on her that Edmund sprang to his feet, his face flushed with outrage, and lunged forward. His older brother managed to restrain him, saying quickly: 'Don't, Edmund! He's just trying to bait you!'

'Ah, the voice of maturity,' purred Dhal. He crooked an eyebrow at the furious Edmund, then regarded the Princess again. 'A trifle headstrong, isn't he, Princess?' he observed. 'Perhaps you might be better advised to find a more mature mate after all.'

Sir Stephan clenched his fists at the new insult to his son. Ian could feel the tension in the hall steadily rising and heard angry shufflings and mutterings. He saw Sir Bron appear ready to fly at Dhal even though he was weaponless. Gramling, eyes blazing, held his staff and hand poised as though about to cast a spell. Kilvenny Odoyle was standing on his chair holding a tiny silver hammer before him, and Ian sensed an aura of power about the little leprechaun. All eyes were on the King and Dhal. But while Dhal restricted himself only to words, Magnus held himself in check.

'You have said your piece, Dhal. Now begone!'

'There was just one other matter,' Dhal drawled casually, as though the King had not spoken. 'When is my appointment as Wizard Supreme, Sorcerer of Sorcerers and Magician to the Royal Court to be confirmed?' The assembly gasped as though he had excelled his previous insults. Out of the corner of his eye, Ian saw two castle guards, armed with crossbows, appear at the rail of the minstrels' gallery.

With a visible effort, the King maintained his composure. 'Not another word! Go now! Or else —'

'Or else what?' sneered Dhal.

There came the snap and zip of crossbow bolts discharged from the gallery.

They struck Dhal square in the chest, only to pass clean through his body to shatter against the flagstones.

Dhal laughed and gestured upwards. There was a tearing rush of wind in the gallery, and the two guards were blasted out over the rail and plunged to the floor of the hall. Screams and cries of horror rang out. Gramling's staff spat a fireball towards Dhal at the same moment as a searing blue-white lightning bolt crackled from Odoyle's hammer. Dhal flung out his hands towards the two magic users, and fireball and thunderbolt flared and burst a foot from his palms.

For a moment the tableau held. Dhal, arms outstretched to ward off further attacks, Gramling and Odoyle weaving their hands about as though probing his defences for some weak point. The rest of the banqueters frozen in various

58

cowering postures, realizing that material weapons were useless against the intruder.

'You know what I desire,' Dhal said, his voice carrying clearly to all corners of the chamber. 'You will deliver it to me or else!'

And with that final ultimatum hanging in the air, another rush of wind swirled about the hall. A second window blew out and darkness filled the chamber again. By the time a handful of candles could be re-lit, there was no sign of Dhal.

'Just who was he anyway,' asked Ian, 'and what was he after?'

The banquet had ended with Dhal's dramatic departure. Both Palbury and the King had extolled their guests to remain calm and not let the intrusion spoil the next day's ceremonies. Ian thought this was a forlorn hope; one of the guards Dhal had blasted from the gallery had broken his neck, which was hardly the ideal prelude to a wedding day. Now the travellers were gathered in Ian and the Doctor's dimly lamplit room before turning in. Kilvenny Odoyle had accompanied them. After the events of the evening, the castle still felt too restless to think of sleep.

Odoyle, perched on the side of a bed, considered Ian's question while he filled a long stemmed, silver banded pipe from his pouch and snapped his fingers to light it. The leprechaun's puckish face creased in thought and his long upper lip twitched as he puffed away.

'Well to be sure, it would be a long tale to tell in full of all the doings that led Marton Dhal to where he is today, and I'd not want to keep the ladies from their rest.'

'We'd really like to know,' said Susan brightly, 'and we couldn't sleep anyway after what's happened.'

'As you will then, lass. I'll try to tell the story in brief.' He puffed on his pipe. 'Twenty years ago, it would be, when Gramling took on young Dhal as his apprentice. The boy was keen and a quick learner and all thought he would make a fine addition to the chapter of magical practitioners, someday following Gramling as Wizard Imprimis to the House of the Stewards of the South Share. But there was an ambitious and calculating streak in the boy that none had guessed at, and which now Gramling, I know, bitterly regrets not spying earlier. As young Dhal became more experienced in the craft he started practising its darker side. In secret, as it would later be known, he experimented on the transmutation and metamorphosis of living things, a task normally only undertaken by the most skilled in the field, for fear of the consequences of such work. He also began to challenge his master more often in magical matters to test their respective strengths and abilities. Soon he had proved, to his own satisfaction anyway, that he was the stronger. But he was no longer content to supplant Gramling alone. Dhal now wanted to be the first in all Elbyon, and so he petitioned to become apprentice to the King's own court magician, Tregandor of Arndell, who had lost his own apprentice in an accident not long before. And Tregandor was considering taking him on, when Gramling discovered strong evidence that Dhal had caused the death of his apprentice. So Tregandor challenged Dhal to a wizard's duel, so that justice might be served.' Odoyle paused to puff at his pipe which was in danger of going out.

'And did they fight?' asked Barbara.

'Indeed they did, lady,' Odoyle confirmed, 'and a terrible and wonderful battle it was, and all who witnessed it will never forget it to their dying day.'

'But what was the outcome?' the Doctor demanded impatiently.

'Well it as near as killed both of them. Tregandor never recovered properly and died later, while Dhal retreated to his fastness on the moor to lick his wounds. His ambition remained unchanged, however. So he waited on Tregandor's passing, then put himself forward for the vacant post, which he could do, because the evidence against him was not proof positive.'

'But surely the King can choose someone else if he's so unsuitable?' said Ian.

'Indeed he can,' agreed Odoyle, 'but only if they put themselves forward. And none have, knowing their first task would be to face a new challenge from Dhal. To have fought Tregandor to death's door like that made it clear he is terribly strong. I wouldn't take him on, and that's a fact.'

'But can't several wizards band together to defeat him?' asked Barbara practically.

Odoyle chuckled ruefully. 'That would be plain common sense, would it not, lady. But common sense does not rule in this case. It's hard enough for magic users to combine their powers on the most abstract matters. 'Tis our nature, you see. Fearful as we are of the strength of one, the dangers of a cadre might be even worse. Yet it might come to that in the end, if Dhal is perceived by enough of us as the more immediate peril. But so far he has confined his activities to the south of Elbyon alone, and not antagonized more than he must, while at the same time not allowing the King to forget that he must appoint someone soon. By way of doing this, and testing his own strength, he is, I fear, behind the strange happenings and unexplained manifestations that have plagued the Share of late.'

'Including the dragons?' Barbara asked, with an involuntary shudder.

'Ah, your own lively encounter in the forest. Yes, very likely so. And now we witness his boldest move yet, though I do not see how it has promoted his cause to have insulted both Ruler and Steward so publicly. They are stout men and not to be cowed by threats.'

'Perhaps he hopes to force the appointment of a wizard in a hurry, who he can then beat easily and take his place,' suggested Susan.

'That maybe so, young lady,' conceded Odoyle.

The Doctor snorted. 'All this for a title and position!'

'That's not the half of it,' Odoyle replied. 'You being

61

strangers to these parts don't know what is entailed with the job. The holder has access to a fine and rare collection of magical writings, formulae and other devices of great power, Merlin's own staff amongst them. What use one of Dhal's make would put them to is not a pleasant thought, but they'll need someone capable to watch over them soon, for the position can't be left untended long.'

'But if Dhal's so strong, what's to stop him simply taking them?' queried Ian.

'Ah, now, surely he would if he could, but he can't. There's a binding laid upon them.'

'A what?' exclaimed Barbara.

'A binding. A spell of compulsion set up in olden times that has become part of the very fabric of the things and which none can break. They can only safely be kept by the strongest magician in the land, to prevent them being misused. But counterwise, such a magician can only be rightfully appointed by the freely given word of the King, at a gathering of his peers and other persons of rank, who must also add their consent to his choice.'

'But if these items are so powerful,' the Doctor pointed out, 'couldn't any suitable magician be properly appointed, and then use them to overcome Dhal?'

'These things, Doctor,' Odoyle replied darkly, 'are not intended for everyday use, but only in the direst need. If one of lesser quality should use them to win position against another, then the threat would only have changed its name, for such power is temptation for all but the strongest, and even they should beware.'

While they thought on this, the leprechaun stowed away his pipe and slipped lightly off the bedside to the floor. 'Well now, the ladies must have their rest, and I'll be away myself. But I'll be wanting you to show me this remarkable travelling box of yours, tomorrow, Doctor, if you will.'

'Just one thing,' the Doctor said. 'Am I right in believing that was not actually Marton Dhal himself we saw in the hall earlier, but merely an illusion?'

Odoyle smiled. 'Ah, you have a seeing eye, Doctor. I thought none but Gramling and myself would have realized that. No, 'twas a third level mirror simulacrum of the rogue, I'd hazard. Dhal was probably safe in his tower all the time. But he perhaps wanted us to think that he could transfer himself bodily hither and yon, for that is power indeed.'

'And the wind that accompanied his, rather theatrical, arrival and departure?'

'No doubt an air elemental under his control, hopefully of no more use to him after the work he put it through. But now I see your granddaughter is yawning while we chat on.' His eyes twinkled:

'So I'll be gone and out the door,
until the morrow when we'll talk more.
From bed and rest no more will I keep,
so I bid you all a sound night's sleep.'

And the little man tipped his hat, clicked his heels, and was gone.

63

9

The Veil of Guinevere

'Have you learnt anything more about "magic" yet, Doctor?' Ian asked, with the trace of a smile. Susan and Barbara had gone to their room, while the Doctor and Ian prepared to take to their own beds. Ian had just finished splashing his face in the washbowl and was drying himself with a rather rough towel.

The Doctor was sitting up in his bed still looking remarkably alert and thoughtful. 'There has hardly been time to reach any firm conclusions yet, Chesterton. But I admit I have noted certain interesting details concerning the phenomena. So would you if you would only apply yourself a little harder. Constant observation, that's the ticket.'

'Well that can wait for tomorrow, like our leprechaun friend said,' he paused and shook his head in wonder. 'I can hardly believe I just said that! Leprechauns, dragons, wizards! I am going to try and sleep,' he stated firmly. 'I don't suppose I shall manage it, but I'm going to try anyway. I've had quite enough surprises for one day.'

'Grandfather, Ian – look at this outside!' It was Susan's voice, sounding excited, and apparently coming from their window.

'I spoke too soon,' Ian sighed.

Their room, like that next door, opened out on to a tiny balcony. Ian pulled aside the heavy drapes and they stepped out into the night. A few feet to his left, Ian could make out the pale, nightclothed forms of Susan and Barbara, standing on their own balcony. Around and below him were the flickering yellow torches of the castle grounds. Beyond those was the faint constellation of lights that marked Fluxford itself. The air was clear and mild. As his eyes adjusted to the dark, he looked up into the night sky.

His jaw dropped.

Just lifting clear of the eastern horizon, turning with the stars, was a glorious nebula of misty light that stretched almost to the zenith. It resembled a huge and ghostly blossoming flower hanging in the sky, with each unfolding petal sculpted in translucent streamers of purple and violet about the edges, with tints of cerulean, emerald and viridian towards its core. It was probably the single most breathtaking thing he had ever seen.

'Isn't it beautiful!' came Barbara's exclamation from out of the darkness.

Even the Doctor seemed moved by the simple splendour of the spectacle. 'Most arresting. Merely the remnant of a stellar explosion, of course, or perhaps a condensing cloud of dust and gas out of which new stars will be born. But undeniably a majestic sight.'

A spray of three shooting stars flashed silently across the darker portion of the sky as though in tribute to the scene.

'Guinevere's Veil!' Barbara said suddenly. 'Somebody said it at the banquet, but I didn't realize what they meant. Bron talked about travelling beyond a veil when we were on the road here. This must be it.'

'There's a moon,' said Susan, 'just on the horizon.'

Ian could see a grey disc, a little smaller than Earth's moon, as it rose over a distant line of hills. Another shooting star trailed across the sky. His eyes automatically followed its track and saw that a circular notch seemed to be cut out of one of the outer streamers of the nebula. 'Hallo. There's another one a bit over halfway to the zenith. Looks about the same size as the first.'

'It's rather dark, isn't it,' commented Susan. 'I can't see any markings.'

The Doctor had been leaning over the balcony rail scanning the western sky. Now he pointed upwards in

65

turn. 'Look there. A faint crescent on the edge of the sunset afterglow.'

'So there is,' agreed Ian. 'Three moons. And look at the one that's just risen. It's already well clear of the horizon.'

'Then they must be both smaller and nearer to this world than your own is,' the Doctor stated. 'Mmm . . . would you say they were equidistantly spaced and travelling along the same plane?'

'Yes, I think so.'

'And is their separation about one third that of the whole arc of the sky?'

'About that. What of it?'

'It means that, if we waited long enough, we should see another moon rise as the one furthest west sets. There are not three moons orbiting this world, but six.'

'Why should there be six?'

'Because they would form a more stable arrangement, gravitationally, whereas three moons, spaced as they appear to be, would not.'

'But can such an arrangement occur naturally?'

'Most unlikely, especially in view of their uniform size and appearance.'

'You mean,' cut in Barbara, 'that they've been placed there somehow?'

'I suspect so.'

'But that's fantastic!' exclaimed Ian. 'Moving entire worlds. Who did it . . . and why?'

'That is a very good question,' conceded the Doctor, 'but one which must wait until tomorrow for further investigation. Even I must admit, we have now had sufficient problems presented to us for one day.' Then he chuckled lightly. 'However, you will agree that whatever other shortcomings the TARDIS may, occasionally, exhibit, it never fails to take us somewhere interesting.'

'No, Doctor,' said Barbara dryly from the darkness, 'we'd never say that! Goodnight.'

They withdrew to their rooms.

Ian took one last look at the nebula before pulling the drapes again. 'Well, you'd never get tired of looking at the sky if you lived here, I'll say that.'

'Oh I don't know, Chesterton,' replied the Doctor, mischievously. 'The people here probably take it entirely for granted!'

Barbara had also gone to bed with the feeling that sleep was sure to elude her. Her confused mind, stimulated by the incredible experiences of the day, together with the ache of her injured leg, would, she thought, prevent any chance of proper rest. Neither did her bed's rather coarsely woven sheets, its straw mattress, or the rope webbing in lieu of springs greatly help matters, she decided resignedly. What she wouldn't give for the comfort of her own bed back home in London, a thousand years and heaven knew how many million miles away. She could almost picture herself in it now; curled up warm and content after a night-time mug of cocoa and ten minutes read of a treasured book. A Jane Austen, perhaps, or maybe a Wodehouse . . .

Catching her quite unawares, nature took its course and she fell into a deep, exhausted, sleep.

Susan listened to her friend's breathing slow and deepen and smiled to herself. Barbara needed the rest. She really shouldn't have gone to the banquet at all, but she had a stubborn streak and wouldn't admit that her leg was troubling her. It was very human. That was one of the reasons why Susan liked her. Susan yawned again. And now she needed her rest too. Not as much as humans did, of course, but still some. In a few years time, when she had passed into her first maturation and had mastered the physiological intricacies of her body fully, an hour or two a night would be quite sufficient. Meanwhile, she mentally put aside those thoughts and speculations that would interfere with relaxation and concentrated on slowing her body functions in the age-old manner of her kind.

Within ten seconds, she too was asleep.

Bron of Westhold slept in the manner of a warrior; which was to say lightly, as though he were on a battlefield, with his consciousness on a hair trigger, ready to spring into full alertness at a moment's warning. He would rather have gone without sleep that night, but he also knew he needed it. He had checked the castle security with the captain of the nightwatch before retiring, and knew that all reasonable measures had been taken. There was no cause to suppose Dhal would make another move that night, and indeed, in conference with the King and Palbury before his rounds, they had agreed that some sort of disruption to the wedding itself was more likely. All the more reason to be fresh for what the new day would bring.

And so he lay in his spartan chamber with a candle burning, still wearing shirt and breeches, with his longsword *Invictus* by his side, and let sleep take him . . .

And in a while he dreamed.

He was hunting a dragon – no, *the* dragon of that morning, as it pursued the strangers in the forest. He saw it loom over him, saw its red glowing eyes, felt its fire. He struck out but the beast was receding. He smote again but it was slipping away from him. Was it running? No, it was flying. He could hear its wings beating, so many wings –

Then he was awake, *Invictus* in his hand.

Fire flashed red at his window. There were cries of alarm, the clash of steel and, swelling into one continuous throbbing pulse, the beating of many wings.

Bron tore open his door, dashed out into the corridor and sprinted for the stairs that led up to the nearest battlements. The beat of wings grew louder, and with it the rise and fall of inhuman, jabbering, whooping voices. He pounded up the spiralling stairs three at a time. The heavy door at their head was open, and he could smell burning and hear somebody screaming terribly. Then he was out on to the wall-walk and into a mêlée of struggling figures and pools of burning fire. Billowing acrid smoke swirled about him, catching in his throat and stinging his eyes. In his blindness he stumbled over the body of a guard and felt the slick of blood underfoot.

There was a snap and rush of wings from above. Instinctively he twisted and swung upwards, feeling *Invictus* bite into sinew and bone, even as a leathery membrane slapped across his face. The thing crashed to the ground, writhing and squealing, its entrails spilling out. In the flickering light he saw a creature with the hairy, long-armed body of an ape, perhaps five feet tall, with a curling prehensile tail, but sporting the naked black wings of a bat on its back. It wore a simple harness from which hung throwing stars and round flasks, with wicks trailing from their stoppers. Still clutching a light scimitar in its clawed hand, the beast snarled at him in pain and defiance, bearing its fangs. Bron thrust cleanly through its heart and it was still.

Ten feet away, another winged ape tore at the throat of a fallen guard. Bron leaped upon it, *Invictus* sang through the air and parted the creature's head from its shoulders. A throwing star rebounded from the flags beside him. He snatched up the fallen guard's crossbow and loosed a bolt at something swooping above the walls. There was a yelp of pain and the thing tumbled out of the sky in a flurry of wings.

Further along the battlements, a knot of guards were being set upon by a dozen of the flying apes. The men were defending themselves with their swords but had no chance to reach cover or re-cock their crossbows. Bron ran to a rack of spears beside an embrasure, snatched one up and hurled it into the swirling mass of beating wings, skewering one beast. He threw a second and third. The apes scattered in confusion for a moment.

'Make for the turret!' he shouted. Together he and the guards dashed for shelter, piling through the door of the turret room and slamming it behind them. Bron looked into frightened and confused faces and did not allow them time to think.

69

'Re-arm!' Use bows, spears or throwing darts,' he commanded. 'Pick the beasts off from shelter and don't try to engage them on the open walls. Pass the word along.'

From the narrow barred windows of the turret, he saw several small fires already blazing about the castle, with smoke billowing from windows and pools of burning oil. The targets seemed mainly the inner walls and keep, though some of the tents in the outer bailey were burning, and Bron could hear the terrible shrill neighing of frightened horses. At least Ambler was in a proper stable! He saw the creatures circling overhead like wasps invading a beehive, diving out of the darkness and smoke to hurl firebombs or glittering throwing stars. Some dropped low over the heads of the defenders in sudden swooping dives, slashing down at them with swords or simply clawing and biting with talon and tooth.

The dreadful realization struck him that any window would allow these agile creatures access to the castle's interior.

'Hold fast here!' he cried, 'the King is at risk!' and he raced down the stairs towards the lower levels. A squad of guards were pounding up to the turret top as he descended, and he shouted instructions as he tore past them.

Down the stairs, along a corridor dimly lit by night candles burning in their niches, through a heavy door and into the floors of guest rooms. He burst through the last door and straight into a struggling mass of apes and men that filled a broad hallway. Here at close quarters a sword would tell better than a bow, and he launched himself upon the nearest ape-thing. *Invictus* sang through the air once more, weaving a net of flashing steel about him, and he cut a path through to the side of Sir Peridor, who held the mouth of the passage to the King's apartments with a handful of guards.

'Is the King safe?' Bron cried, between blows.

'Yes. In an inner room!'

'Thanks be! Now let us finish these things!'

Together they pressed forward into the hall, driving

back the apes in a jabbering, whooping line before them, cutting steadily into their ranks, slipping and skidding on a floor slick with the blood of friend and foe alike. With a spark and crackle of lightning, the doors at the other end of the hall burst open and an ape fell through them, a hole burned in its chest. Gramling appeared, clad in a nightshirt and hatless, but clutching his staff, which he levelled at another ape. Fire streamed from its tip and the creature was blasted off its feet to crash lifeless against the wall.

Then came a cry: 'They're retreating!' Sure enough, the apes were suddenly turning and running on all fours, knuckles to the ground. Towards windows or balconies they fled, with the castle defenders at their heels, vengefully cutting down the stragglers. The clamour of battle diminished as the last of the apes fell or were lost in the night.

Gradually the sound of beating wings faded and was gone.

For a moment or two, Bron and Peridor rested on their swords, panting from their exertions, silently contemplating the carnage about them; knowing they had done their duty well, but rueing the cost. The King emerged from his chambers, still grasping his sword, with the Queen, pale-faced, by his side.

'Is it over?' he asked simply.

'Yes, your Majesty, they are all dead or fled. You are safe.'

'For the moment,' said the Queen despairingly. Then she appeared to gather her composure. 'I must assure Mellisa all is well,' she said firmly, 'then we and our ladies shall help with the wounded as we may.' Bron and Peridor bowed as she departed.

Sir Stephan, Edmund and Giles appeared at the run, bearing bloody swords. Their relief was almost palpable when they saw the King safe.

'Your Majesty . . .' Sir Stephan faltered, 'that this should happen under my roof. I have failed –'

71

'Nonsense, Palbury,' said the King dismissively. 'Glaze-bry itself could not have withstood an attack from such creatures any better. Now, what about the fires these creatures started?'

'None too serious, Sire. They are being contained —'

'Bron . . . Sir Bron!' It was Ian Chesterton's voice. He burst into the hall, dressed in a nightshirt, but carrying a bloody ape-man scimitar. His face was ashen. 'They've taken Susan!' he gasped.

But even as Bron started forward, a woman's cry of despair from the royal chambers froze him in his tracks. The King blanched and ran for his daughter's room, the others following after him with dreadful foreboding in their hearts.

The Princess's bedchamber presented a tragic scene.

The body of a lady-in-waiting lay crumpled and bloody in a corner. Windows were wide open to the mild night air. Bedding was strewn across the floor and the big canopied bed itself was empty. Queen Leonora was kneeling at its foot, clutching a sheet of parchment to her chest, and staring sightlessly out into the night. Without a word, the King rested his hand on her shoulder and gently drew the document from her grasp. He glanced over it for a moment, then handed it to Sir Stephan. Standing by his side, Bron read it too.

For the attention of Magnus III, King of Elbyon.

Majesty,
You know of my desires, now learn of my power. Have what I require brought to Fluxford and prepare a suitable Convocation for the assigning of rights. You have until Midsummer's Day, after which the welfare of my new guests cannot be guaranteed. Any move to recover them by force, or any intrusion whatsoever into my private domain would be most unwise.

Marton Dhal.

10

Merlin's Helm

Komati and Ivanov sat in the most secluded corner of the *Prince Randolph*'s officers' mess; though they could have sat in the very centre of the room for all the attention they received. The clatter of plates and the buzz of conversation seemed to pass them by, as they were studiously ignored by the other diners.

'This is ridiculous,' said Jen, with quiet vehemence. 'They're behaving as though we don't exist.'

'No doubt they've had their orders, regarding us,' Ivanov replied moderately. 'They know we are part of the special mission team and understand the need for security.'

'How can they? They don't know what we're after yet.'

'The general principle is part of military discipline.'

'Well I'm sick of military discipline and secrets! There are too many of them. Maybe it's a sign of the times. You can't pretend to rate them highly either.'

'Certainly not. This should be an open, purely scientific expedition. Still, in view of the potential of what we might find, I suppose it is inevitable, in the circumstances.' His tone betrayed suppressed anticipation.

Jen looked at him closely. 'But aren't you afraid at all?'

'Well . . . yes, I admit I am. I'm trying not to think about it. I know the landing might be dangerous, but afterward –'

'No. I mean about what we might find down there!'

He blinked. 'My dear Doctor Komati, it is what we might find afterwards that makes this tedious charade worthwhile. Surely you've speculated about its potential?'

73

'Yes. And I don't like where it takes me. You know how it could be misused!'

'All the more reason why it should be in the hands of the Empire, then. We have a unique chance to render signal service both to science and our Empress, surely you see that.'

'I'm not sure I want to. Actually, I can't think of anybody I'd trust with it. Certainly not the Empire!'

'Please, Doctor! He looked about him in alarm, then leaned closer. 'I assumed you would recognize where your obligation and duty lay.'

'Obligation and duty are not necessarily the same thing, you know. I've had quite enough talk of "duty" from Shannon.' She hung her head. 'And, if I had the courage, I'd tell him so!'

'The universe is not perfect and never will be,' Ivanov said, not unsympathetically. 'Our options are sometimes limited and equally short of the ideal. But we must all decide eventually where our loyalty lies.'

Jen forced a weak smile. 'Yes. But by the time we decide, will it be too late?'

The Steward's Chamber of Fluxford castle became grey and sombre as the pre-dawn light shrank the lamps to feeble yellow flickers. Of course, Ian thought, as he scanned the faces of those seated about the chamber's large round table, its occupants hardly enliven the scene, myself included.

Beside him the Doctor sat stone faced and intent; not allowing his anxiety for Susan to show, except for a few brief distracted moments. Across the table, Ian saw much the same conflict between emotion and iron self-control visible in the face of the King. On either side of him sat Palbury and his sons, Edmund looking rather pale. Beside them were knights and captains, lords of the dwarves and elves who owed allegiance to Magnus, then Gramling, Odoyle and scribe Harding, who would record their plans. All were members of what was now a war council.

Ian wished Barbara was with them. But she had taken a nasty blow to the head the previous night, and the Doctor had told her firmly to rest.

Thinking of the assault made Ian shiver again. The memory of being jerked awake by Barbara's scream for help, the wingbeats and inhuman voices of the flying apes outside their window, dashing madly out of his door, only to collide with one of the brutes in the corridor, as much to its surprise as his, and catching it with a purely reflex right-cross to the jaw that had laid it out (Ian unconsciously rubbed his bruised knuckles). Bursting into the women's room just in time to see the apes lift Susan's limp form off the balcony, Barbara sprawled on the floor, blood on her forehead, for one terrible instant thinking she was dead, turning to see the Doctor staring aghast at Susan's empty bed . . .

Ian jerked himself back to the present with an effort. This would not help get Susan back.

Captain Morgane, commander of the castle guard, had just finished giving a report of their casualties, the enemy dead, the damage sustained and the repairs underway. At the end, he formally offered his resignation from his post. Sir Stephan refused.

'You have not been derelict in your duty, Captain, unless failing to anticipate the true depth of cunning and artifice of Marton Dhal is dereliction, in which case I am just as culpable. I will bear the responsibility of letting guests under my roof come to harm, and that is all.'

'The fault is mine,' the King stated gravely. The eyes of the table turned to him in surprise. 'I should never have let the matter of the wizardly succession go unresolved for so long. Alas, I am now being sorely punished for my indecision.'

'Excuse me, your Majesty,' the Doctor interrupted sharply, 'but I understood we are here to discuss action, not guilt. These admissions are very fine and noble, but are quite irrelevant to the situation we now find ourselves in. The only question that must concern us now is how to get those we have lost back safely!'

There were annoyed mutters at the Doctor's blunt manner, but the King silenced them with a wave of his hand. 'No. He speaks fairly. Continue, Doctor. If you have a plan, I will hear it.'

The Doctor bowed slightly. 'Thank you. First, however, I must confirm one point. There is not, I take it, any question of acceding to Dhal's demands?'

Heads shook all round the table. 'Even for my own daughter,' said the King, in deadly earnest, 'I could not do this. Dhal has miscalculated if he thinks he can force me to grant him what he wishes, even if I truly believed such action would guarantee her safe return, which I doubt. The consequences for the country would be too terrible to risk. Dhal simply cannot be trusted. I am sorry if that gives you little hope for your own child, but that is how it must be.'

The Doctor nodded solemnly and resignedly. 'I suspected as much.'

'Had there been even the slightest hope that Dhal would have proved worthy of such power and position, Doctor, that was lost last night,' said Gramling. 'He must now be opposed with all the strength we can muster.' There were nods of agreement.

'But what of Mellisa?' Edmund Palbury said fearfully. 'If we move against Dhal, what will he do to her?'

'Steady, lad,' his father murmured.

'She will understand,' the King said simply. 'She knows that there are some sacrifices that must be made −'

'Wait a minute,' interjected Ian hotly. 'We're all talking here as though there's no chance of getting them back. But there must be something we can do. Is this place they're being held really totally impregnable?'

'Quite so,' agreed the Doctor. 'What of this tower of Dhal's? Just where is it situated in relation to Flux-ford, and how is it protected? Let us study the problem methodically. Remember, we do have one advantage. The consequences of inaction are as grave as action, so

76

we may dare anything to destroy Dhal and free the hostages.'

'As you say, we must try,' agreed Sir Stephan. 'Master Harding, be so good as to bring out the maps.'

The scribe shortly unrolled a large, hand-drawn map of the South Share, which he hung on the wall, together with a more detailed map of the moor itself. For the first time, Ian began to get an idea of the land they were in. Elbyon seemed to be situated rather like France was in Continental Europe, with an ocean to the north-west, and a long curving coastline of sea, where the Mediterranean would have been, to the south and east. Glazebry, the capital, was almost exactly in the centre of the land, where the boundaries between four local regions, or 'Shares', met. The South Share extended along part of that curving sea coast, then ran westwards. On its western boundaries, putting Ian in mind of Dartmoor or Bodmin Moor, was an oval of high country with few roads or settlements marked on it. On the more detailed map, Harding indicated a spot almost in its centre. 'Here is Raven's Tor, whereon Dhal's tower is set.'

After a moment's study, Ian asked: 'How long would it take to reach the tower from here?'

'By wing, as of those creatures of last night, perhaps two or three hours,' Harding said. 'On horse, with clear roads, two or three days,' he ventured, looking at Sir Bron, who nodded. 'By foot, a week at least.'

'And we have barely eight days,' said the Doctor. 'Hardly time for a substantial force to reach the tower.'

'But just time enough for me to have the artefacts sent down from Glazebry, and arrange the convocation,' the King observed. 'This was planned well.'

'But what about the tower itself?' Ian asked.

'It is situated on a great mass of rock,' replied Sir Bron. 'This provides a natural defence from ground assault. Caves are also said to lie within it. A sufficient force could certainly take the tower, but not quickly, or with any chance of surprise. With the natural disadvantages of the terrain, which is heath and bog, and any mischief Dhal cares to throw at us, it would be a costly enterprise.'

'These flying apes that he has bred are a worrying factor,' Peridor added. 'I have not met their like before. They must also be taken into the calculations for the success of any assault. In open country like the moor they would be a deadly foe, quite apart from their use as scouts. How many more such beasts does he have hidden away?'

'Well, what about magic?' said Ian, turning to the magicians. 'Even if you can't use it to defeat Dhal out-right, couldn't it at least help? Maybe you can whip up a flying carpet or something?'

Gramling and Odoyle regarded him tolerantly. 'Flying spells take the most effort to perform and maintain,' Gramling explained, 'and in any case, Dhal is sure to have set protective wards about his own domain, as I am now protecting this castle against such intrusions of his so he may not spy upon us. Or there may be negation spells. Would you care to encounter one of those whilst flying? I'm afraid you have little understanding of magic lore and method.'

'No,' agreed the Doctor quickly, 'magic is, er, a lost art on Earth. Men use complex machines to perform such tasks now.' Ian alone heard him add thoughtfully under his breath, 'which do not seem to work here.'

'For a start, a small force will be sent to watch Raven's Tor,' the King said decisively, 'without making any move that might imperil the hostages. With carrier pigeons they can keep us informed should Dhal venture from his stronghold. And I will have reinforcements sent here from Glazebry, as it seems Fluxford is the focus of Dhal's actions at present.'

Gramling appeared to have been wrestling with some internal conflict while the King spoke. Now he seemed decided. 'There is one other possibility,' he said quietly. 'A means to defeat Dhal for ever, and most probably rescue the hostages. But there is a risk – and a price.'

Everybody was staring at him, sensing the gravity of his tone. 'Speak out, man!' implored Sir Stephan fervently. 'If there is any chance let us hear it.'

'There is one relic of supreme power not among those kept in Glazebry. Indeed, its exact location has been lost for centuries. But with its aid, anything would be possible!'

'Gramling, my friend,' said Odoyle softly. 'You surely don't mean –'

'Yes. Merlin's Helm!'

Gasps of surprise and incredulity echoed round the table.

'Pardon our ignorance,' said the Doctor, 'but what is Merlin's Helm?'

'None other than the cap worn by the great wizard himself,' Kilvenny Odoyle explained, almost reverently. 'It is an amplifier and concentrator of thaumaturgic power, you see. With its help he constructed the great skyboat *Prydwen* that carried our ancestors across the sea of stars to Avalon. The Glass Bridge that spans the Flux is but a small sample of its powers.'

'But the Helm was lost with the *Prydwen* and the remains of Arthur and Merlin in ancient times,' exclaimed Bron, turning to Gramling. 'How is it you now know where they might be found?'

The old wizard looked weary. 'It was no one thing I discovered, but the summation of years of research into ancient texts and relics of the founding days. A mention here, a clue there. Gradually I pieced together enough to learn the likely resting place of the *Prydwen*.'

'You have proof of this, Gramling?' asked the King, a flicker of hope dawning in his eyes.

'To my satisfaction, I do, your Majesty. I learned that the resting place of the skyboat would be protected, apart from diverse physical means, by a field of negation in which no magical activity could occur. It was this, and not the relic itself, that I searched for; sending the power of my divination out to its furthest limits. And I found it.

A discontinuity in the thaumatic flux. Almost unnoticeable, but it is there!'

'Why not speak of it sooner?' asked Odoyle.

Gramling bowed slightly in tired acknowledgement. 'I made my discovery a year or two past, but have been unsure of whether good or ill would come of it, even in the face of the threat from my treacherous assistant. But now I am decided that there is no other choice. The Helm must be used.'

'But where is it hidden?' asked Sir Stephan urgently. 'Can it be found in time?'

'Please bring forth a map of the Circle Sea, Master Harding,' Gramling requested. The scribe quickly unrolled and displayed the chart. Ian now saw that the curving south-east coastline of Elbyon was only part of the coast of an almost perfectly circular sea, some five hundred miles across by the map scale, which was landlocked on all sides except for a short section of its most eastern edge, where it opened into a larger ocean.

'A most extraordinary formation,' the Doctor murmured.

Gramling pointed at the chart and a spot of light glowed amongst a cluster of dots and symbols in the very centre of the sea. 'There lies the *Prydwen* and the Helm.'

'The Shadow Isles!' breathed Sir Peridor. 'Those are treacherous waters. Plagued by fogs and whirlpools and all manner of strange creatures, I have heard.'

'True, sir knight,' agreed Gramling. 'But where better to hide such a treasure?'

Sir Stephan had also been studying the chart intensely. Now he turned to the King. 'It could be done in time, Sire. The swiftest boat from Fluxmouth port could just make such a journey and return before midsummer's day, assuming it could recover the Helm without delay.'

'I can provide aid for such a trip,' Gramling assured him. 'At least to assist in reaching the isle of the Helm safely.'

'Just a minute,' Ian said. 'I'm a little confused here. If

this Helm is as powerful as you say, why aren't there the same objections to using it as there are to the other magical items? If Merlin's staff is too risky to use, why isn't his Helm?'

The rest of the table went quiet, as though Ian had touched on an unpleasant point. Gramling sighed, suddenly looking old and tired. 'Three ways is the Helm protected. First by its location. No magic may be used on the Isle, and there are subtle guardian devices. It is written that only those seeking selflessly for a just cause may take the Helm from its resting place. Second, it also carries a binding upon it, which may only be unlocked by the freely expressed will of a gathering of rulers and seniors of the land.'

'Well, Dhal wants you to assemble a convocation anyway, so you can arrange that.'

'True. Thirdly, however, using the Helm, even briefly, carries a price. This is to protect it from misuse in all but the most desperate times. Quite simply, to use the Helm means death. Its power is too great to endure for long; perhaps just for minutes. But it is only after the death of its wearer that the Helm may be removed again.' There was a moment of absolute silence. Gramling added calmly: 'Naturally, this duty shall fall to me.'

Barbara lay on her bed, with a cold compress pressed to the large bruise on her forehead. The Doctor and Ian sat beside her on the edge of what had been Susan's bed.

She squinted at them through her throbbing headache. 'I just wish you weren't both going so soon. And I wish I was fit enough to come with you.' She shifted her injured leg uncomfortably. 'But I know I'd only be a burden like this. Don't worry, I'm not going to make a fuss.'

Ian felt equally unhappy about the arrangement, but knew he had to be resolute. He smiled sympathetically at her, trying to win her understanding. 'It's only going to be a small party, and we're going to slip out discreetly in case Dhal's watching somehow. We have to leave soon so we can reach the port before nightfall.'

'But are you really sure it's worth it? I mean, a journey like this one seems so ridiculous, it's –' she searched for an analogy – 'It's like a fairy tale quest that Sinbad or Jason would have undertaken.'

'But that is precisely the point, my dear,' said the Doctor soothingly. 'On Avalon it is not ridiculous to embark on such a quest to solve our problems.'

'Doctor,' replied Barbara firmly, 'I know we've kidded you about the magic, or whatever it is, but this isn't a fantasy world we're on.'

'No. But it is a world shaped by fantasies and legends, in some way. And if there is an answer to be found, then reason suggests it should be on the craft that brought these people here. There are bound to be clues to the early history of Avalon there. Such knowledge may explain how this "magic" functions. And then I will know what action to take against the man who is holding Susan!'

For a moment, his passion showed, and Ian and Barbara looked at each other uncomfortably. Then the Doctor was his usual collected self again.

'But you will not be idle yourself, either,' he told Barbara briskly. 'There are certain tasks I need you to perform while we are away.' He held out a key on a length of black ribbon. 'This is Susan's TARDIS key. Every day you must test that the defence system is still active. Then try the key to see if it works. I'll explain the correct turning sequence within the lock in a moment. If you can open the doors, then at least you will have a safe retreat should the castle be threatened again.'

'I understand,' said Barbara confidently. 'What else?'

'Continue to try to find out all you can about "magic", the Helm and the history of Avalon. You may ask Gramling, but I suggest you attempt your own researches first. A fresh approach with an unbiased mind may be more productive. A castle this size must have a library. See if you can gain access to it.'

'All right. Anything more?'

82

'Well, if you take care to be discreet, and do not put yourself at risk, then you might watch out for the spy in the castle.'

'What!' Ian and Barbara exclaimed simultaneously.

The Doctor seemed surprised at their response. 'It is highly probable that one exists,' he stated simply. 'Dhal might have used his powers to determine all he needed for his plans remotely, but such a link would surely be very tenuous and subject to interception, therefore an additional physical agency is likely. Think how quickly he modified his plans to include one of us in his kidnapping plot. We had only been in the castle a few hours, but his creatures knew exactly what room to enter, which could hardly have been chance. His note to the King spoke of "guests", indicating he was anticipating taking more than one hostage. Yet, if he wanted another person of position to gain a hold over the King, why not the Queen? No. This was the only other room the ape-hybrids entered with the intent to kidnap its occupant. Either Susan or you, my dear, were their targets.' Barbara shivered as the Doctor's expression darkened, his lips tightening. 'We are strangers here, and have roused Dhal's curiosity. I only hope my Susan does not pay the price for it!'

11

The Hostages

It was the smells that Susan became aware of first.

Damp stone and rust, mildew, wet moss. Surely it had been drier and warmer when she went to sleep?

Then she remembered.

Wingbeats and strange voices. The balcony window bursting in. Barbara's cry. Strong hairy arms seizing her, and a liquid soaked rag giving off a cloying vapour being pressed over her nose and mouth. A sensation of falling. Then darkness.

As the fog in her mind slowly lifted, she realized she was resting on something even more lumpy than her previous bed. A coarse blanket had been thrown over her. There was a sour taste in her mouth. She felt sick and thick-headed. With an effort, though they seemed gummed together, she managed to force her eyes open.

The outline of a stone block swam into focus a foot or so away. After a moment the shape made sense; she was facing a wall. Pale daylight from some high, narrow source illuminated it. Her eyes followed the stonework up to the ceiling, some eight or nine feet above her. Cautiously, she raised her head from the straw-filled sack that substituted for a pillow. Not far beyond the foot of her crude mattress was the inner wall of the room, with a low, heavy door in its centre. There was no lock or handle on the inside. Carefully turning to see more of the room, she found she was not alone.

Another rough pallet like her own lay beside the opposite wall. Sprawled on it was a woman's figure, half covered by a blanket. Like Susan, she was wearing a nightdress, though of finer material. Her head was turned away, but a long loose mane of golden hair, slightly waved, flowed down her back, over the pallet and on to the floor. Rolling on to her hands and knees, not trusting herself to stand yet, Susan crawled over to the figure so that she could see her face. It was Princess Mellisa. Obviously she had been chloroformed, or whatever the local equivalent was, as well.

For a couple of minutes, Susan concentrated on breathing deeply and gathering her wits. Then she stood up, bracing herself against the wall. The flagstones were cold and slightly greasy under her bare feet. She had hoped she could see out of the window, but the sill was above her head. Also, the inside of the sill sloped downwards from the window opening itself, so she could get no hold on the edge to pull herself up. Stepping back, she saw that the recess was a good three feet deep, with the narrow slotted window closed by one vertical iron bar. Beyond was nothing but a strip of sky. The outer wall curved slightly, she noted, suggesting the cell was in a round tower. She could guess whose. With an effort she forced herself to remain calm.

The Princess stirred slightly and moaned, as though she was having a bad dream. As Susan knelt beside her, she flung out her arms, struggling blindly, and gave a choking cry. Then her eyes flickered open.

'It's all right,' said Susan, taking her hand and trying to sound reassuring, 'they're gone now. You'll feel better in a minute. Just lie still.'

The Princess blinked at her, her wide green eyes looking confused and frightened. She licked her lips, and asked faintly, 'Who . . . who are you?'

'My name is Susan Foreman, I was at the banquet last night but we hadn't been introduced. I'm with a party of travellers from a long way away. Sir Stephan may have mentioned us.'

'Travellers?' The Princess frowned. 'Yes – four people in a box – I remember . . .' She started to take in her surroundings. 'Where is this place?' She suddenly gave a little gasp as memory flooded back. 'The apes! No! Keep away!' she shrieked, shrinking into the corner. Susan stroked her shoulder in what she hoped was a comforting manner.

'It's all right, they're gone. We're in a cell in some kind of tower. I think it must be Dhal's.' Gradually the Princess relaxed, making a visible effort to regain her self-control, though she was clearly frightened.

'Please, excuse me. I remember now. A tower. Yes. Dhal has one on Scud Moor.' She was regaining her poise rapidly, shaking her head to clear it. She tried to sit up, despite her dizziness. Susan helped her, and she rested her back against the wall, her face still very pale. 'Thank you – I will be all right.' She licked her dry lips. 'Is there anything to drink?'

'Not at the moment, but I'm sure we can get something. I mean, there's no point in bringing us here just to let us die of thirst, is there?'

Mellisa shook her head. 'Unfortunately, that may be Dhal's intent. He may try to force me to plead with my father to grant him what he wishes.' Then her chin took on a determined set. 'But I will not. Whatever he does to me!'

'But your father will try to rescue you, won't he? I know my grandfather and my friends will try to find me . . .' she trailed off, a frightening possibility having just occurred to her. 'As long as they're still all right.'

For a moment their eyes locked in mutual fear for family and friends. Then the Princess said deliberately: 'We must believe they are still all safe. Fluxford castle is very strong. I do not think even those flying creatures could have taken it alone. If they had, then we would not be here. No, it is like you said Susan, they have brought us here as hostages.' Then she frowned. 'Your pardon, but are you somebody . . . important? I understand why I am here, but what would Dhal wish with you?'

Susan hadn't thought about this. 'I really don't know. I'm not important in the way you mean. Perhaps they took me by mistake, or they were just after anybody else they could get?'

The Princess looked troubled. 'It is said that Dhal does nothing without good reason.'

Susan shuddered as she wondered what Dhal might want her for. She thought of the image of the man who had appeared at the banquet. Even though she had seen him only briefly, she recalled the aura of arrogant power that had surrounded him. There was nothing such a man would not do to achieve his goal. Trying not to think about the unpleasant possibilities, she said, 'Well, we'll have to get out of here before he gets a chance to do anything, won't we?'

'Nobody escapes from Dhal.'

'Well at least let's try. For a start, we can find out what's outside. Do you feel well enough to stand up?'

'Yes, I think so.' With an arm up from Susan, she got to her feet. 'Brrr,' she shivered. 'The floor's so cold.' She walked up and down the few paces their cell allowed to steady herself, looking about her at the door, then the window. 'But how can we see out?'

Susan made a stirrup with her hands. 'If I give you a leg up, you can reach the bar, then I'll push your feet and you pull yourself as far forward as you can get.'

Within half a minute, after some scrabbling and shoving, the Princess was wedged as far into the window aperture as she could, her face pressed up beside the bar.

'From the look of the light, I believe it is still morning,' she reported. 'We must be very high, because I can see a long way, I'm sure it's Scud Moor, there's lots of gorse and green boggy patches, and just a low rocky hill in the distance.'

'How high up are we?'

'About two hundred feet.'

'What's right below?'

Mellisa twisted about. 'I can't see straight down, but there are two small towers a little way off. They seem to

87

have a hole in their tops, like large chimneys. There are men, I think, standing sentry on them.'

'Isn't there any outer wall?'

'No. There is a low ditch and bank joining the towers. Maybe they're turrets whose linking walls haven't been built yet.'

'What else can you see?'

'Some paths tramped through the gorse. Closer to, there are rocks. The Black Tower is built on a rock outcrop, I recall. And that's all.'

Susan helped her down and for a moment the two of them looked glumly at each other.

'We cannot possibly get down that way,' the Princess stated, 'even if the window was unbarred. There is no escape.' She lifted her chin bravely. 'We must accept our situation with courage and patience. My father and Palbury will come in time and lay siege to this place because they cannot accede to Dhal's demands, nor can they now dare leave him be.' Quietly she added, 'Even though doubtless my life, and maybe yours, is forfeit by such actions. But at least we can face death with dignity.'

'Well I'd rather face life with hope!' Susan responded earnestly. 'At least promise you'll be ready to take advantage of any chance that comes our way.'

The Princess looked at her curiously. 'There is a strange quality about you, Susan Foreman, that I have only seen in people of rank and breeding. Are you sure you are not of high birth?'

Susan half smiled. 'Well, we do have a sort of title, but I'm not sure how much it means here –'

There was the sound of footsteps outside their door, and the rattle of a heavy bolt being slid back. They shrank back against the far wall as the door swung open.

A pair of apemen stood outside.

These were larger than their winged brethren, standing about five foot six, and had flatter faces. Their stooping postures took away some of this height, but they still looked very broad and strong. They also seemed to be better dressed than Susan's hazy memories of the ones who had abducted her, wearing simple red tabards, belted at the waist, which bore the symbol of a black tower. On their feet they wore broad and rather oddly shaped soft leather boots. They each carried a sword and a short whip hanging from their belts.

The leading apeman tilted its head to one side and narrowed its eyes. 'Urr, you awake now,' it growled heavily. 'Master says take you to him when you awake. You come now!' It beckoned them. Susan and Mellisa hesitated. The apeman frowned, and unhooked his whip from his belt. 'You not come, you feel this. Then you come anyway!'

Susan bit her lip. 'We'd better go. There's no choice. Remember what I said.'

Cautiously they edged past the apeman and out of the door. They were on a gloomy circular landing ringed by similar heavy doors, at the centre of which was a wide stone spiral staircase, with cantilevered treads turning about a massive central core. Daylight filtered down from the very top of the stairwell, while from its depths came only the flickering shadows of torchlight and the faint echo of an animal cry. Susan wondered if the shaft ran through the whole tower. The ape guards gestured for them to ascend.

They passed an open landing before they came to a floor where the stairwell was enclosed, with only one door leading off it. The apes urged them through.

The chamber beyond was lofty, occupying two levels of the tower, with the stair shaft running through its centre. Susan estimated it was over sixty feet in diameter, and lit very dimly by six narrow slotted windows set evenly around its outside wall. It was full of racks and shelves and tables, clustered in little islands about great iron candle trees that were caked with ancient rivulets of wax. A complex chemical odour hung in the air. Several shelves were neatly stacked with rows of books and scrolls, many marked with slips and tags, while others carried flasks containing preserved specimens of animals, either dried or suspended in liquid. She saw row after row of bottles filled with many coloured powders, or the dried leaves and seeds of plants. On one worktable, a jumble of flasks, bottles and dishes were scattered about a mortar and pestle and a set of scales, as though a compound was in the process of being mixed. On a clear section of floor, an elaborate pentagram had been marked out. Against one wall was a rack of small, very finely barred cages, containing what seemed to be tiny creatures, which Susan could not identify from where she stood.

As they tried to take in the strange scene, a voice said: 'Ah, I see my guests have arisen. Bring them over here.' The apemen urged them over to a study table bearing a large white sphere, before which was set a high backed chair facing one of the windows. Dhal was reclining in it, looking exactly as his image had appeared the night before, his handsome, arrogant features even more distinctive seen close to. Susan felt his amused, dark, hard eyes upon her, and shivered. Dhal turned his gaze to Mellisa. 'I'm sorry to have spoiled your wedding day, Princess, but your father was so unreasonable, I really had to try to make him see sense. I do hope you understand?' His voice was smooth, sardonic and teasing.

Mellisa replied with dignified contempt. 'This is the end for you, Dhal, you realize that. My father will not be influenced by threats against me. Do what you like, but I will not plead for my release, and in the end you will surely be destroyed!'

Dhal chuckled lightly. 'Such spirited defiance! You really are too good for young Palbury. But you have quite the wrong idea. I have no intention of trying to extract such a plea from you by crude means, entertaining as the process no doubt would be. No, you will both serve me perfectly well merely by being here. You will be my guests for the next few days and amuse me in my leisure moments. Frankly, my creations,' he nodded towards the apemen, 'though fine loyal creatures, are not the most stimulating company.'

'This girl is of no use to you,' Mellisa said firmly. 'There is no need to keep her here.'

Dhal appeared moved. 'Oh, how noble and self-sacrificing!' he exclaimed, turning to Susan. 'She is trying to save you from your fate, even though that would leave her all alone.'

'It's a kinder gesture than you will ever be capable of,' Susan retorted.

Dhal shrugged off her insult with a smile. 'More spirited defiance. But I'm afraid I intend to keep you anyway. Until yesterday, I would have been satisfied with any of several possible companions for the Princess. But then you oldworlders arrived in that remarkable box. And escaped from my dragon, which was very annoying. I heard of your strange story, and so arranged for you to be brought here. I want to know more about you, in case your presence may have a bearing on my plans.'

And he began to stare with unnatural intensity. Susan felt his cold eyes bore into her as though he were peeling her open layer by layer. She turned her head aside, but her ape guard twisted it back to face Dhal again.

'Good,' he said at length. 'You are young, healthy and intelligent. You will suit my needs admirably.' He smiled. 'If I have time, I may make a more detailed physical examination to determine if oldworlders differ from us in any ways.' Susan shivered.

'You beast!' exclaimed Mellisa. 'What sort of man treats helpless women this way? When my father comes for you he will –'

'He will do nothing!' Dhal said sharply. 'He is powerless against me. Would you like to see the forces at my command? Come!'

He sprang to his feet and strode from the chamber. The ape guards pushed Susan and Mellisa after him.

They descended the spiral stairway through so many turns that Susan began to feel dizzy. Daylit alcove

91

windows vanished to be replaced by wall-mounted torches, and she realized they had passed the ground level. Coursed stonework became hewn rock. Then the stairs ended in a tunnel floored with sand and gravel that pricked her bare feet. Water trickled down the walls. Grunts, moans and jabbering echoed about them, and there was the stink of animal pens in the air that reminded Susan fleetingly of a trip to London Zoo. A few paces along and the tunnel opened out into a much larger cavern. White daylight shone mistily through a hole in the centre of the arching roof. Of course, she thought. The chimney-like opening in one of the sentinel turrets.

'Behold, my army,' said Dhal proudly.

The cavern was ringed with stepped ledges, on which were laid out sleeping pallets. Resting on these, rather look a rookery, were hundreds of ape-bats, filling the air with their whooping chatter and sudden snarls of anger.

'This is but one company of my lightest aerial infantry. Would you like to see some of my heavier troops? Follow me.'

They were prodded after him as he strode towards one of several tunnels opening into the cavern. Susan realized the rock of the tor must be honeycombed with such caves. Dhal led them briskly along a broad, torch-lit gallery connecting a row of lesser chambers. The mouths of some were dark and heavily barred, but in one Susan glimpsed a row of large glass vats tended by a team of ape workers. Tiny mannequin forms floated in coloured liquids. She realized they were miniature versions of the ape-bats.

'My growing rooms,' said Dhal casually. 'Once I have combined the characteristics I wish for a creature in my workroom through spellcraft, they are sent down here to mature.'

Susan felt sick and stumbled on. There were other shapes floating in the vats she could not begin to recognize.

The gallery opened out into a second cavern, similarly

illuminated by the turret shaft in its roof. Here the ledges around its perimeter were carved far broader and deeper, and for good reason. Twenty full-grown dragons lay sprawled upon them. Susan and Mellisa edged uneasily backwards, even though they saw massive collars and chains secured each creature in its place.

Dhal smiled at their reaction. 'Have no fear. They are presently all drugged to keep them from fighting amongst themselves. But you can be sure they will be fully alert when the time comes. Well, Princess, what do you say now?'

Mellisa looked defiant. 'Even if every cavern under your tower is similarly stocked, it will not be enough, Dhal. You may take Fluxford or even Glazebry, but you will never conquer all Elbyon. And the prize you seek can never be won by force!'

Dhal chuckled. 'We shall see, Princess. We shall see.'

'Hail, Bron of Westhold,' said one of the two men striding across the castle yard to where the wagon was loading. 'As our lords promised in the council, we have been chosen to accompany your quest, so that all free peoples of Elbyon may be represented.'

'Greetings, Alammar,' said Sir Bron, clasping his hand. 'And to you, Thurguld. It cheers me to know I have such stout company on this mission.'

While Bron made introductions, Ian sized up their new companions. Alammar of Silverwood was a tall, golden-haired, golden-eyed elf. He wore a bow and quiver across his back and a long, rapier-like sword on his belt. Thurguld Thongarson was a stocky, bearded, compact dwarf, dressed in mail and a steel helmet. He carried a heavy, double-edged battle axe. It looked well used. Yes, he agreed with Bron. They seemed stout company.

'Climb aboard, my friends,' said Bron. 'Our boat awaits us, and we have a fair way to travel before day is done.'

* * *

The black cat circled the remains of the burned-out hamlet twice before it ventured closer. There were fresh graves in a small clearing outside the stockade. Inside were many footmarks on the ground, which it sniffed at curiously. The wandering poultry had now been rounded up and removed, leaving the ruins utterly deserted. The cat padded out of the gateway again, giving the dragon's footprint in the soft earth a wide berth, and headed purposefully off down the track again.

Back in the tower workroom, Susan and Mellisa watched while Dhal sat before the white globe. He produced a vial containing a glittering powder, which he sprinkled over it. 'With the right knowledge, one can make use of the eyes of others to see things far away. A person's eyes are harder to use, but an animal's are quite easy. Let me see if I can show you something I was watching earlier. Ah, here it is.'

The globe became transparent before Susan's amazed eyes, and it was as if she was looking down from the air on countryside rolling underneath her. Dhal reached out to touch the globe. 'Literally a bird's eye view,' he commented. 'Let me see if I can make it go lower.' His eyes narrowed in concentration.

The ground swelled and treetops flashed past. A road ran between the fields. There was a company of mounted troops moving along it at a steady gallop. The spy bird swooped down and passed across in front of the leading riders. Mellisa gave a little gasp. At the head of the column was Edmund Palbury.

'Yes, it's your intended, as hot-headed and impetuous as ever. He's on a road about ten miles outside of Flux-ford, determinedly heading this way to keep watch on my tower. Perhaps he hopes for the chance of some dramatic rescue. Or at least to pine away under your window to prove his love. But really, he'll wear out his horses if he keeps that pace up much longer. Besides, I did leave a clear warning that I wouldn't stand for any intrusion into my domain. I think I must take steps to dissuade him —'

'No!' gasped Mellisa. Dhal looked at her expectantly, but she lowered her head, lips pinched tight. Susan reached across and held her hand gently. The image on the globe shrank as the spy bird rose higher, and its view shifted to show what might have been a flock of birds flying low over the tree tops. Except these were far too big to be ordinary birds.

'I decided that some of my creatures should stay in the vicinity of Fluxford after last night. Just in case.'

In the globe they saw the flying apes swoop down on the horsemen, who scattered for cover under the trees. The apes followed. As the spy bird circled the scene, they saw snatches of a confused battle, with loose horses and sprawled bodies of both apes and men. Mellisa leaned forward, desperate and fearful for a glimpse of Edmund. Dhal smiled at her expression, and touched the globe again. The picture blurred and swirled, and suddenly it showed a view of jetties and ships bobbing at their moorings, with men hurrying up and down gangplanks and adjusting rigging.

'No. Bring it back!' cried Mellisa.

'All in good time,' said Dhal. 'Meanwhile I have noticed much activity in Fluxford dock I do not approve of. They seem to be preparing for war. I think a little reminder that I am aware of their activities would not go amiss here either. Do watch closely. This will be rather amusing.' His eyes narrowed.

In horrified fascination, they saw the water swell and boil around one of the ships. A monstrous head broke the surface and arched into the air on a smooth, sinuous neck. Susan saw a dragon face, but different from the one in the forest. This was flatter and broader, with a wide, gaping mouth and more tendrils trailing from its brow and chin. Slotted snake-eyes gleamed greenly, and on its head were three horns. The two on its crown were small, but rising from its brow between its eyes,

95

was an up-curving spike like that of a rhinoceros.

'A freshwater guivre,' explained Dhal. 'I've been raising one or two of them as pets.' Men were fleeing in panic. The guivre arched forward and plucked one off the rigging. For a moment his legs kicked wildly, then he disappeared into that terrible grinning mouth. The beast sank back out of sight for a moment, then the ship rocked violently, as though it had been struck underwater. Slowly it started to list. The water swirled between the berths, then another ship trembled and rocked, bumping against the jetty wall. It also began to settle in the water. Soldiers appeared along the dockside, watching for the slightest ripple. Harpoons and arrows began to cut the waters of the dock.

'I think we can leave them to their fun,' said Dhal, 'they will think twice about using the river now.' He looked enquiringly at the Princess. 'Would you like to return to see how young Palbury is doing?'

'Please!' Mellisa begged unashamedly.

The globe swirled and they were looking down on the woods once more. There was no sign of the flying apes, only soldiers regrouping, calming horses, tending their wounded. For a moment Mellisa stared in despair at the scene, then she pointed at a figure. 'I see him! He's not hurt!' She sagged against Susan, weak with relief.

'How touching,' said Dhal. He passed his hand over the globe and it clouded to opacity. He faced the two young women, a satisfied smile playing about his lips. 'You have seen but a small sample of my power. While your people, Princess, have dithered in futile inaction, I have prepared and planned. Let your precious Edmund come to my gates. He will learn, too late, that he has been wasting his time. Now, you'd better return to your room. I'll have some food and water sent along in due course. We shall talk again later.'

The apemen led Susan and Mellisa away, silent and dejected.

* * *

96

Ian watched the green waters swirl past the prow of the small barge. They were already a couple of miles down-river from Fluxford, thanks to the favourable wind which filled the craft's neat sprit-sail. The barge's six auxiliary oarsmen had needed to add little extra effort to maintain a very fair rate of progress. At this speed they would be in Fluxmouth port by sundown, where, assuming the carrier pigeon message had been received, they should find a ship waiting for them. As Avalon had no significant tides, there should be no delay in setting sail for the Shadow Isles. Then the quest really would begin. Despite his concern for Susan, Ian suddenly smiled at the direction his thoughts were taking him.

'Something amusing you, Chesterton?' enquired the Doctor, joining him at the prow.

'I couldn't help it,' Ian admitted. 'I just remembered a fantasy tale about a group of people setting out on a sort of quest, and they included a wizard, a human warrior, and a dwarf and an elf. They also travelled down a river for part of the way.'

'Indeed. And was their adventure successful?'

'Only after much sacrifice on their part, and several battles.'

'I see. Well we must hope to avoid their mistakes then. I trust you remember the story well, it might prove useful.'

'It was only a work of fiction.'

The Doctor lowered his voice. 'So is much of Avalon's history, I suspect, though I wouldn't want our friends to know it. Anything connected with ancient myths and legends may have relevance here, so you would be well advised to – my goodness, how remarkable!'

Ian turned to see what the Doctor was looking at. The river was presently running through a twisting, steep-sided gorge that clove through a line of hills, exposing sheer faces of reddish rock on either side of them. Into the eastern wall, like a giant frieze, had been carved seven towering figures.

Even at a glance he could tell they were ancient. Moss and grasses and even small trees had colonized the upper slopes, and weathering stains and generations of birdlime ran in long streaks down their outer surfaces. Some of the figures overlapped and the finer details of their features or costumes had long since faded into mere suspicions of contours and lines, leaving it hard to tell what they were meant to be doing. From their poises they might have been playing some game or sport, or even engaged in battle for all he could tell. Whatever it was, it seemed to be active. Something about their proportions put Ian in mind of American Football players, though he couldn't say exactly what.

'Sir Bron,' the Doctor asked, 'what are these figures called?'

The knight stepped over to them. 'They are the Seven Companions, Doctor. Though whose companions I'm sure I have never heard. They are very old, that is certain. Some say they date from before landfall, and are the work of ice giants who lived here before men, and who Merlin drove back to the north, during the Cold Years, before towns and castles, when the land was wild.'

'That is most interesting,' said the Doctor, his eyes narrowed in thought. 'I would like to learn more of any similar artifacts, and also of these "Cold Years".'

Bron smiled politely, as though puzzled by the Doctor's interest. 'I'm sure we will have time to talk of such things if you wish, though what use talk of the past is in our present situation, I cannot imagine.'

'Perhaps a great deal,' replied the Doctor. He looked up at the huge carvings again. 'Yes, perhaps a very great deal indeed.'

12

Lights in the Sky

Electric blue sparks danced and crackled across the surface of the TARDIS in response to the blow. Barbara lowered the stick to the ground and leaned on it again, resting her leg. She took out Susan's key and carefully inserted it in the lock in the manner the Doctor had described, and twisted it in the unlocking sequence. The door remained firmly shut. She sighed and replaced the key around her neck, then turned to find she was no longer alone. Queen Leonora and Gramling had just entered the little yard. A stick and a bad leg did not allow for a graceful curtsy, so she made do with a slight bow instead.

'Good morning, your Majesty, master Gramling.'

The Queen was not a tall woman, but she carried herself with an inner assurance that seemed to add inches to her height. Her present demeanour seemed perfectly controlled, but Barbara noted the carefully concealed puffiness about her eyes and knew she had been crying.

'This is Barbara Wright, your Majesty,' said Gramling, performing the introductions.

The Queen regarded her intently. 'You are a friend of the girl Susan, who was taken with my Mellisa?'

'I am, your Majesty. Please accept my wishes for the Princess's safe return.'

'Thank you.' The Queen looked at the TARDIS. 'And this is the magical box you arrived in. There hardly seems room enough for four persons within.'

'It is hard to explain, but it's much larger inside than out, your Majesty,' said Barbara. She had the feeling that the Queen was making conversation for some reason.

'That is most remarkable,' she said. 'I wish I could see such a wonder for myself.'

'Unfortunately, the door refuses to open,' admitted Barbara. 'Even master Gramling couldn't shift it.' The old wizard stiffened slightly.

'In that case he must try again,' said the Queen firmly. 'I have an idea, mistress Wright. We shall leave him to concentrate on the task, while we walk in the gardens.'

'Your pardon, your Majesty,' said Gramling, 'but both Sir Stephan and the King desired you not to venture out unaccompanied. After the attack on the docks this morning, and the continuing danger of the flying ape creatures –'

'Wizard,' said the Queen, with a distinct edge to her words, 'we shall only be a few yards away in the orchard. There must be fifty archers watching the skies, and I doubt a guivre could make its way up here from the river unnoticed. In any case, I do not believe it is any safer inside the castle' – her voice caught for a second – 'as I learned to my cost last night.' She rallied again: 'In any case, I desire some fresh air. You shall attend to this device, and I shall walk in the orchard. That is all.' And taking Barbara's arm, she strode determinedly away, leaving Gramling standing by the TARDIS.

They passed through a gateway into a large walled orchard, planted with rows of apple and pear trees. Raspberry canes were trained up the inside of the walls, and in a corner Barbara noticed traditional hump-backed beehives. It seemed very peaceful, with the overhanging boughs hiding the towering mass of the keep and the battlements of the inner bailey wall. The Queen said nothing until they reached a bench set between the trees, but then looked at Barbara intently.

'I have reasons for wishing to talk to you alone and away from my ladies or other ears, mistress Barbara. Things I wish to ask as a mother, not as Queen.'

Barbara nodded: 'I understand.'

The Queen smiled slightly. 'Do you? Have you any children of your own?'

'Not yet. But I teach many children. I think I know what you are feeling.'

'You cannot,' said the Queen simply, but not unkindly. 'However, it is enough that you are understanding and of sympathetic heart. First, your friend Susan. Like as not she is my daughter's only companion in an evil place. I know my child will be strong and behave as fits her rank, but what of Susan? Will she be a support to her?'

'Well – Susan is kind, and intelligent and is naturally cheerful. She can also be very brave, when she has to be. And she's resourceful. In fact, if I know her, she'll already be working on some means of escape even as we speak.'

The Queen's taut features relaxed a little. 'Your words cheer me. I have little hope that two girls may escape Dhal's Tower, but it is good to think my daughter has such a companion in her present adversity.'

Barbara smiled encouragingly. 'Don't be too hasty about dismissing their chances. Susan has a lot of her grandfather's determination in her, you know.'

'Yes, her grandfather. The Doctor he is called, I believe.' The Queen became more intent again. 'He, and your friend Ian, showed great interest in the Helm, once its purpose had been explained. They insisted on joining the quest to recover it, I understand, despite the many dangers they may face.'

Barbara swallowed, trying to keep a steady face. The Doctor and Ian had made light of the risks of the journey. Now she wondered if they had been trying to save her further worry.

'But does their presence increase the chances of success?' the Queen continued. 'My husband and Sir Stephan seem to think well of them, even after a few hours acquaintance. Is their faith justified? Might I hold out some hope yet for my child?'

Barbara had to steel herself, and she hoped her words came out evenly, without revealing her new apprehension. 'Yes, there is always hope. Ian and the Doctor are both very single-minded and determined in their own ways. They will do everything possible to help get Susan, and your Mellisa, back safely. You can rely on that.'

Queen Leonora sighed and allowed herself a fuller smile. 'You do give me hope, mistress Barbara. Thank you.'

A fresh thought seemed to strike her. 'It occurs to me that you must be lonely without your friends. You must take your meals with us, and we shall continue to hope together. Perhaps you can divert us with tales of the oldworlds –' She paused. 'You realize that not for one moment will my daughter truly be out of my thoughts. Today should have been her wedding day – but I must seek some respite from worry, or else go mad. The nights, I think, will be the worst. My husband's fear is just as deep, you may be sure, but he can show it even less than I, and I must be there for him when he needs me . . .' She hesitated, peering intently at Barbara. 'That is a most private admission for me to have made, but as a woman, I think you understand what I mean.'

'I do. The best of men are just as vulnerable as we are in such matters.'

'Yes, but at least men can lose themselves in planning for battle, or going off to adventure, whereas we can only wait.'

'But for this leg,' Barbara assured her, 'I would have gone with the Doctor and Ian.'

'Would you really?' the Queen asked curiously. 'Yes, I believe you would. But, the danger –?'

'I'd be terrified,' admitted Barbara, 'but I'd still have gone.'

'Is this the way now, on the oldworlds beyond the veil?'

'Yes, I think generally it is.'

'Much has changed then.'

'Oh, yes,' agreed Barbara, 'you, er, you wouldn't know the place.'

102

'I can see we must talk more about this betimes. But I think now we must be getting back to Gramling. I was firm with him earlier for my own purposes, but we must not forget the task he may face in but a few days. He deserves our consideration for that and his long service to the Steward, so I must make amends.' As she spoke, there came a crackle of electricity from the other yard, and a muffled curse. 'Besides, I do not believe he is having much success with opening your travelling machine.' Barbara smiled.

They started back through the orchard.

'Is there aught else I can do to make your stay more comfortable here? With the confusion of guests leaving and troops being mustered, you might find the hospitality of Fluxford castle passes you by unintentionally, and I know Stephan would never forgive that.'

'Thank you. But I'm quite all right as I am – except, I would like to be able to use the castle library, if there is one.'

'Why yes, there is a fine large library. Is it solace in words that you seek?'

'I do love books. But actually the Doctor suggested I might do some research to find out anything that might help against Dhal.'

'For such a purpose, Barbara Wright, you may have all the books that you require.'

That afternoon, Barbara stood in the library of Fluxford castle, looking about her with a mixture of fascination tinged with disappointment. She had forgotten that 'fine' and 'large' were relative terms. For a quasi-medieval society, no doubt it was exactly that. However, the library held, she estimated, less than two thousand volumes. They were substantial volumes, of course, mostly leather bound. Some of the larger ones probably weighed fifteen pounds or more. They took up a lot of shelf space.

Harding hovered nervously at her side. 'Is there any assistance you require, Lady Barbara?'

Barbara did not know how she had been promoted suddenly to the status of an honorary 'Lady', and suspected that the news had spread rapidly about her being in the Queen's favour, and dining with the royal party. Well, a little influence wouldn't do any harm.

'Just a table I can work at, and a pen and paper, thank you. And is there a catalogue or index? I want to look up some specific subjects.'

'Certainly, Lady. This way, if you please.'

Very soon she was set up in a comfortable alcove with everything she required, including a page boy in attendance who would fetch and carry the larger tomes for her. Harding then made his excuses and returned to the administration of the mobilization. Barbara rolled up her sleeves, both figuratively and literally, and opened the catalogue. Very shortly, the page was searching for the first book.

The afternoon wore on. The library grew warm and drowsy, while Barbara struggled to read handwritten texts of differing degrees of legibility and variable spelling. Gradually she realized something unusual about them.

All the books were either copies of older texts, or written about events after Avalon had been settled. There were no actual books from Earth, or wherever the settlers had originally come from, to be found anywhere. This was odd as she would have expected at least a few to be preserved as treasured mementos of the past. Surely all the originals could not have been lost.

Then there was the strange bias of the earlier works. They were almost all versions of Terrestrial heroic tales or mythological fantasies, mainly of European subjects, but treated as valid histories. She had come across a distorted prose version of Spenser's *The Faerie Queene*, which some later reader had seriously tried to date by the 'Old Calendar of Earth', as though it was historical fact. Where genuine history did intrude, it was usually incredibly distorted; as she realized when she found herself reading an account of how King Arthur defeated the Nazi

104

Armada off the coast of Cornwall with the aid of Merlin's remarkable, but unexplained, 'Atome Fire'. This event seemed to be related to the 'last battle', which had caused the migration to Avalon, though the details were oddly obscure.

In fact, Arthur and Merlin appeared so often in the accounts, she realized they had become eponymous heroes, credited with almost every military triumph or new invention the writers could think of. Unfortunately, she had yet to find more than a passing mention of the Helm. Still, the work did stop her worrying about Ian, Susan and the Doctor.

By early evening, when she put down her quill, she felt at least she had made a sound start. She had also made a minor discovery which indicated how some historical detail could be distorted. 'Elbyon' was a corrupted form of Albion: the old name for Britain. So perhaps 'Glazebry' derived from Glastonbury?

The evening meal was eaten taken in a smaller chamber than the banquet hall of the previous night. Most diners were too preoccupied to enjoy their food, but the King had decided they should set an example by maintaining a regular domestic routine despite the emergency. The King and Queen sat with Palbury, Giles, and their senior knights and captains, and those guests who had remained in the castle to play their part in the confrontation to come. They all made dutiful, desultory conversation. Barbara noticed there were fewer women about now. Through the day, many of the wives and children had been hastily packed away back home. Everybody knew Fluxford was going to be the focus of Dhal's attentions shortly, in one form or another. Gradually the talk drifted on to questions of offence and defence, and Barbara began to feel guilty about spending so long in the library while around her people had been dealing with far more urgent matters.

Then she heard Sir Peridor, who was seated next to her

again, talking to another knight about the problem of defending the castle against further attacks by the flying apes, and how there were too many windows to bar or shutter, and what could be done about the exposed battlements? Suddenly, the mood and problem seemed almost familiar.

'Wires,' she said aloud, almost without thinking.

'Your pardon, Lady?' said Peridor, with a polite frown.

'To stop the flying apes. You do make wire, don't you? You wouldn't need anything like as much material as bars use. Stretch a few fine wires across a window and the apes will get tangled up in them. At night they wouldn't see them at all. And you could string some along the battlements from posts, I should think –' she realized half the table seemed to be listening to her and faltered '– they wouldn't be able to swoop down low like they did before, if you see what I mean, with their big wingspans.'

There was a moment's thoughtful silence, and she was afraid she had said something foolish. Then Peridor nodded.

'Yes, that might well work. What a surprise for our winged friends. Thank you, Lady. Where did you get such an idea from, may I ask?'

'Oh, I was thinking of the blitz spirit and barrage balloons. Never mind, it's rather complicated.'

And she kept silent and listened to her idea being discussed and amplified, while she pondered over something she had just realized. These people were generally unused to change and responding to new situations. This was a society frozen in a mimicry of an unreal past, which had not significantly altered for eight hundred years. But what was holding them back? Magic, whatever that was, or some subtler force she had not yet recognized?

She heard Sir Stephan saying enthusiastically he would find out how quickly new wire could be produced. From the head of the table, Queen Leonora nodded in approval. Barbara smiled back.

* * *

The last glow of sunset was at their backs as the ship slipped out of Fluxmouth harbour and into the Circle Sea.

Ian had seen little of Fluxmouth, as the light was already fading when their river barge had arrived. He had the impression of a smaller town than Fluxford, rising up the cliffs about a natural harbour formed by the arms of two curving promontories. As they tied up at a wharf, its blocky houses and steep, twisting streets, now being delineated by freshly lit torches, reminded him of a Cornish fishing village. A lone tower broke the skyline above the cliff top, with bright lantern light shining from its topmost floor.

The message from Fluxford had evidently got through, for they were met by the harbourmaster himself, who personally escorted them to a ship berthed a little way along the dock. Ian's knowledge of sailing craft was insufficient to classify it accurately. She had three masts, and resembled a very compact galleon, with superstructure fore and aft and open deck space between. At least it appeared reassuringly substantial and seaworthy.

A distinctive figure met them as they stepped aboard. By the light of the deck lanterns, they saw he was a stocky man with a full black beard, touched with grey, and a weather-beaten complexion. Ian was curious to see that, though otherwise dressed in conventional tunic and hose, he wore a large hat folded and pinned very much in the tricorn style. Clearly an incongruous period detail had become absorbed into local fashion.

'I am Captain Tristram, and I welcome you aboard,' he said, in gravelly tones. 'The order from his Majesty commanded that the best ship in Fluxmouth be put at your disposal, ready provisioned for sailing. The *Merrow* is that ship,' he added, with a touch of pride.

Sir Bron presented Tristram with a wax sealed scroll.

'Your commission and sailing orders, Captain.' Tristram took the scroll under a lamp, broke the seal, and read the contents carefully. As he did his face fell. He turned back to

107

them somewhat less composed and self-assured.

'The Shadow Isles is it then?' he said, in a way that suggested he hoped he had read wrongly.

'You will be well compensated,' Bron reminded him.

'Oh, no. Reward enough to serve his Majesty,' Tristram insisted hastily. 'Only, well, it's the crew, you see, sir Knight.'

'Do you have a discipline problem, Captain?' said Bron levelly. 'Men should go where their master commands. And you are going where your King commands. Whose loyalty should I doubt, that of the captain or his crew?'

'No, no! Follow me anywhere, these lads. Best sailors on the Circle Sea. But the Shadow Isles. There are these stories about them.'

'Then we will have the opportunity to find out whether they are true or not,' said Bron.

'Didn't I just hear say,' added Kilvenny Odoyle, 'something about this being the best ship in Fluxmouth?' Beside him, Thurguld was fingering his axe handle thoughtfully, while Alammar fixed the *Merrow*'s captain with a golden-eyed stare.

Tristram looked unhappily at the determined group before him. 'Prepare to set sail!' he bellowed to his crew.

Mooring lines were cast off and drawn aboard. Orders were shouted. Eight long, broad-bladed oars were unslung and slid out through sockets in the bulwarks into the water. With two men working each oar, they slowly pulled the ship away from the dockside and out across the harbour towards the sea. As they reached the harbour mouth, a breeze started to fill the sails and the *Merrow* began to make headway without assistance. The oars were shipped, and they glided on into the night, trailing a slight phosphorescent wake through the indigo waters.

Ian watched the lights of Fluxmouth shrink and fade into the great sweep of the coastline that curved away to the horizon on either side of him. This was it. They were on their way towards – what?

The Doctor and Odoyle joined him at the rail. The leprechaun hopped up, with effortless nimbleness, and seated himself with his feet dangling over the side. He lit another pipe. Ian realized he never actually saw him re-fill his tobacco pouch, yet it always seemed to be full.

'A fine night to set out on such a journey,' Odoyle observed, after a few minutes contented puffing.

'Most gratifying,' pronounced the Doctor. 'We must hope the weather holds for us all the way to the Shadow Isles.'

'And all the way back,' Ian added.

'Naturally, Chesterton,' replied the Doctor testily. 'I had not forgotten the necessity of a return trip.'

Ian smiled, and watched the stars come out as the last of the dayglow faded. The great blossom of Guinevere's Veil swelled in the skies. A spread of moons displayed their different phases. Shooting stars again put on a fine show, and he began to count two or three a minute. The Doctor had apparently noticed them as well.

'Is this level of meteor activity typical?' he asked Odoyle.

'I would say tonight was much as usual.'

'You mean you have a regular shower at this time of year?' said Ian.

'No,' the leprechaun chuckled. 'At certain times of the year, the sky is far more busy than you see it now.'

'Really,' said the Doctor, half to himself. 'Most interesting.'

Ian had turned back to the sky again. 'It certainly makes our night sky seem boring by comparison,' he admitted. 'A nebula, six moons, shooting stars like fire-works. You couldn't fit much more into it, could you?'

The Doctor suddenly remarked dryly, 'I believe you have spoken too soon again, Chesterton. Look!'

A glowing curtain of light seemed to be falling out of the night from the north, reaching almost halfway to the zenith. It billowed, as though disturbed by some stratospheric wind. As Ian watched, he realized the rippling,

109

shimmering ribbon was turning across the sky like a spoke in a ghostly wheel, with its hub set on Avalon's pole. A second curtain twinkled and sparkled into being, turning after the first. Then a third appeared. Ian gazed silently at the breathtaking display for several minutes, before looking at Kilvenny Odoyle again.

'You must be getting very tired of this question, but is this also a typical spectacle for an average Avalon night?'

'Surely it is,' said the Leprechaun simply. ' "Guinevere's Tresses", they are sometimes called, in keeping with her veil, do you see. But you must journey to the northlands sometime, to Thule and Borea. There the sky is ablaze, often in full daylight.'

'Why didn't we see this last night if it's so common?'

'Because our rooms faced south, Chesterton,' explained the Doctor patiently.

'But we're only in the mid-latitudes. Aurora are not usually visible from here, are they?'

'Apparently they are on Avalon,' said the Doctor, staring intently at the phenomenon. Between the light in the sky and the ship's lanterns, Ian once again caught the suspicion of a knowing gleam in his eye.

'Right,' said Ian decisively, 'are there any other surprises in the night sky I should know about, or is it safe to go to bed without missing something?'

The leprechaun tilted his head thoughtfully on one side. 'No,' he said, 'I think we're about done now –'

A voice called out from the poop deck: 'Captain. Look – near the moon!'

'There now, you've made me tempt fate,' chided Odoyle. He slipped down from the rail and skipped lightly up the steps with the others close behind.

Captain Tristram was peering up at the sky through a long brass telescope by the time they reached him, looking as though his worst fears had already been confirmed. Ian saw it almost at once. A bright moving blob of light between two of the moons. He stared. It was moving faster than the moons, catching them up. He narrowed

110

his eyes further. It wasn't one object, it was several, travelling close together. The Doctor had the telescope now, and was studying the new arrival with interest.

'I take it this is something new?' Ian asked Odoyle.

The leprechaun nodded.

The Doctor handed Ian the telescope. The lens was poor, and uncorrected for chromatic aberration. But it was sufficient to confirm his suspicion. As he watched, the group of light specks passed in front of the black limb of a moon. There were five of them, quite distinctly arranged.

'It's a fleet of spacecraft, isn't it?'

'Yes,' said the Doctor, 'that is precisely what it is.'

The bolts of their cell were shot back, and Susan and Mellisa were suddenly awake and blinking in the light of a lantern.

'You, dark hair, come,' said the ape guard. 'Master want talk with you now!' Hardly giving her time to stand up, the guard grabbed her arm in one large hairy paw, and pulled her from the cell. He seemed to be in a great hurry and Susan stumbled trying to keep up with him. They practically ran up the spiral stairs and through the door into Dhal's workroom. Dhal himself was sitting at his table, staring at an image in the seeing globe. As she was dragged to his side, he spun round to face her.

'Tell me what you see!' he commanded.

Obediently, Susan peered into the depths of the globe. What creature's eyes Dhal was borrowing to make the image, she could not imagine, but she could see blackness and starlike points drifting across the field of view. Centred in the middle was a regular pattern of five objects, shining brightly as though they were reflecting the sun. Looking closer she saw they were each formed of a series of spheres and spars, with smaller modules supported on outrigger pylons.

'Well, what do you make of them?' Dhal demanded.

'They're spaceships. Quite large ones, I think.'

111

'You mean skyboats?'

'Yes, skyboats.'

'What do you know of them?'

'Nothing – what do you mean?'

'You are from beyond the Veil. Have they followed you here?'

'No! I don't know why they're here. They're nothing to do with us!' She felt his eyes burn into her and wanted to turn away, but it was impossible. His gaze was hypnotic. 'I don't know anything!' she kept repeating tremulously. Then he suddenly turned back to the globe and she sagged in relief.

'No,' said Dhal, 'I do not believe you do.' Then half to himself: 'But why have they chosen to come now? Oh, take her back to her cell,' he ordered dismissively.

As the ape led her out, Susan realized that Dhal's supreme self-confidence had been dented. This was something quite outside his plans. For the first time he had actually seemed worried.

13

Task Force

'Standard low orbit about objective planet has been achieved, Admiral. Squadron maintaining formation.'

'Thank you, Captain. Are the energy flow readings between the planet and its moons still constant?'

'Yes, sir.'

'Any idea what's causing it yet?'

'No, sir, but it's too steady to be natural, I'd say. I've got a tech team working on it right now.'

'Good. And be sure to relay all data to Captain Shannon's team, of course.'

'Understood.'

'Could the flow prove any danger to our systems?'

'It's within shielding tolerances, sir. Most of the flow appears to follow magnetic field lines down to the poles. No problem while we remain in this orbit.'

'And still no signals from planet surface?'

'None detected so far, wide band all channels search has been initiated.'

'Hmm, odd there isn't any traffic at all. Never mind, keep looking. Meanwhile maintain Amber Alert status. Begin photographic survey of planetary surface. Locate any signs of cities or major population centres. Prepare drone probes for reconnaissance of moons and planet. But planetary probes must only be launched on my order.'

'Aye, sir.'

Nyborg allowed himself to relax back in his chair for a moment, surveying the bridge of the carrier ISS *Prince Randolph* with satisfaction, while Captain Chandry efficiently proceeded to initiate his orders. A good man,

113

Chandry. A 'backbone of the Empire type', as people used to say. How he wished the mission was just the responsibility of himself and men like that. They would have seen it through all right, without all this cloak and dagger nonsense of Shannon's. Still, orders were orders, and Shannon's came practically from the Empress herself. And Nyborg had never disobeyed a legitimate order in his life.

The panoramic sweep of the main monitor screen showed the blue-white globe turning serenely below them. What is your secret, he wondered? On secondary screens were images of the rest of his squadron; the cruisers *Indus* and *Dorado*, and the destroyers *Valkyrie* and *Tigershark*. To some, their functional assembly of crew-spheres, drive units and weapons modules would have seemed crude. But to Nyborg they achieved a kind of beauty. They were the finest craft of their kind. The honest embodiment of Imperial power. Their specifications had hardly changed for a hundred years, dating from the old combined service days of the Imperial Landsknechte Corps. True, he knew some of the newly independent systems had begun producing their own designs, but give him a ship built in an Empire yard every time, even if spares and servicing had become somewhat erratic of late. Still, Imperial ships were built to last.

The squadron fell on along its endless orbit about Avalon. Electronic senses probed the world below. Inside the ships, they recorded, analysed and prepared.

Barbara was surprised to receive Gramling's invitation that morning. She wasn't sure the old wizard felt comfortable in her company, considering his continuing failure to open the TARDIS. However, she recalled the Queen's words about him, and decided the least she could do was try to be cheerful. Besides, she had never been in a wizard's tower before.

In the event, the steep climb up the spiral stairs to the top meant she arrived resting heavily on her stick.

Gramling met her in the doorway, his face, such as could be seen behind his flowing beard, full of concern.

'Oh, dear. Take my arm, Mistress Barbara, let me help you to a seat. There, there, I'd quite forgotten about your leg. How is it, by the way?' He seemed far more amiable and rather vaguer than before.

'Getting a little easier, thank you,' said Barbara. 'Stairs don't usually bother me like that.'

'No, they never bothered me when I was younger. Of course, my staff is my support now, but oddly I don't seem troubled by the walk up here. I suppose I must have got used to it over the years, and just go up at my own pace. I'm usually so preoccupied with some matter anyway, that I just seem suddenly to find myself at the top without remembering the climb. Probably a blessing really . . .'

As Gramling prattled on, Barbara looked about at his untidy, and rather dusty, chamber. Apart from the lounger with the stuffing coming through the splits which she sat on, and the creaking high-backed chair of Gramling's, there was a single bed in an alcove, imperfectly concealed behind a half-drawn, faded curtain, and a table cluttered with a few books and a large dead white globe. Against the walls were sagging shelves stacked with bottles and jars, containing various fluids and powders and what she was very much afraid were bits of preserved animals. One shelf held a small, tattered and well-thumbed collection of books. Mystic charts hung in the free spaces. On the floor was a very scuffed and faded pentagram, while in one corner sat an Avalonian orrery; a collection of tiny spheres rotating on geared arms, showing the motion of the planets and moons of the system about its sun. She wondered how having six moons complicated local astrological forecasting. Not that it looked like Gramling had practised much active magic in here for years.

She suddenly realized that Gramling had asked her something. 'Pardon?'

'I asked if you would like some wine, Mistress Barbara.'

'Oh, yes please.'

Actually, the wine was rather good, and Barbara found herself relaxing a little. Gramling, however, appeared to be noticing the state of his chambers for the first time.

'Um, I suppose I should have tidied the place a bit. Haven't had many visitors for — well, a long time. Not really much point now . . .'

Barbara's discomfort returned abruptly. How do you talk to someone who was probably going to sacrifice his life in a few days time? 'Is there no alternative?'

'Oh no. All the indications are that the power of the Helm is too much for the body to stand. I hope to last long enough to do what must be done, that is all.'

'I'm . . . so sorry.'

'No, no, you mustn't be. It's my responsibility. Dhal was my apprentice, and I should have recognized the signs earlier. But I suppose I was too busy with providing the knights' next quest, or defending the realm from invasion, or the deprivations of dragons.' He looked sad and wistful, staring into nothing. 'I have seen so many battles. So much blood. I sometimes wonder what it's all been for . . .' He appeared to gather himself. 'Anyway, now this old body is about done, so you see, I've nothing much to lose.' He saw her expression. 'Come, come, let us not dwell on the past. I invited you here for a reason, not denying the pleasure of your company, of course. May I ask if you looked at the sky last night?'

'You mean that little group of moving lights? Yes, I saw them.'

'Others have noticed them too. Do you know what they are?'

'I think they must be what you call skyboats.'

'Precisely. But they do not behave like any we have known before. I have seen the remains of three such craft over the years, and heard of others. Always they have fallen to earth killing their occupants. No one knows why, though the common folk have plenty of

116

superstitions about them and usually leave the remains alone.'

'We found the wreckage of a spacecraft in the forest.'

'Yes, that would be one of them. But now there are five of the craft together, and they do not fall. They are waiting. Look.' He touched the globe on the table which lost its milky whiteness and became a deep bluish purple. In the centre were the cluster of five spacecraft. The image was slightly hazy, but it was large enough to see details of their structure. 'I have been watching them each time they pass over us. The seeing is not so good as it was, though, now the sun is up.'

'But how do you get that picture?'

Gramling looked genuinely surprised. 'You do not know of seeing globes?'

'Not . . . exactly.'

'It is a simple enough magical art. We are presently looking through an animal's eyes. In this case those of a roc, nesting high in the mountains where the air is thin. I have influenced it slightly to hold the lights in its gaze.'

'A roc – like the giant bird?'

'Naturally.'

'Of course,' Barbara agreed quickly.

'But what,' continued Gramling, 'are the intentions of the skyboat's masters? Why have they come here now?'

'Perhaps they're looking for the lost spacecraft, but I can only guess at that. They're nothing to do with us, that's all I can say.'

'Can you communicate with them by any means?'

'There might be a radio, a machine for speaking over long distances, in the TARDIS. But that's no use, unless we can get back inside.'

'Ah, a pity.'

'Yes – oh, look. Something's happening!'

In the globe, they saw a small dot of light detach itself from the largest of the spacecraft and drop away. Gramling touched the globe and closed his eyes for a moment, and the picture turned to follow the dot as it fell, growing steadily larger and larger.

'Probe now at 75 miles. Powered atmospheric descent phase initiated, trajectory holding true.'

Nyborg and Chandry watched the screen displaying the view from the probe's camera. The planet swelled, the curvature of the horizon spread and flattened, becoming the boundary of a landscape, rather than a sphere. The skin of atmosphere showed as a purple and blue haze over its limb. Great swirls of cloud began to seem tangible, with upwelling thunderheads casting shadows like mountain peaks.

'Probe now entering stratosphere,' continued the controller's commentary, 'repulsors to half power – atmospheric sampling commencing.'

The first wisps of high cloud flashed across the screen. The black of space shaded into purple and then blue.

'Readings coming through: nitrogen, oxygen, ozone plus trace gases, all within normal limits. Pressure now reading eight millibars and rising steadily, temperature fluctuations normal for upper atmosphere. Probe now at twenty miles, repulsors on three-quarters.'

'Looks like it's all going smoothly, sir,' said Chandry.

'Let's hope so, Chandry, let's hope so.'

'Probe at ten miles. Entering troposphere. Pressure now – sensor telemetry link has failed!'

The image on the monitor screen suddenly flickered and went black.

'Camera link has been broken!' said a probe technician. Lights on control boards started to blink off, and others began flashing red. 'Attitude control has gone – repulsor drive command link has failed!'

'Switch to backup channel!'

'Switching – backup does not respond!'

'Visual tracking,' demanded Chandry, 'is probe still intact?'

118

The man at the ship's telescopic display screen checked: 'Probe still intact, but falling free.'

'Activate probe self-destruct,' ordered Chandry.

The probe controller flipped the cover off a red button and pressed. 'Self-destruct activated.'

'Visual?'

'Probe still intact and falling,' reported the telescope monitor. 'Still falling – impact!'

There was a moment's silence on the bridge.

'Probe lost, sir,' Chandry reported formally.

'Damn!' said Nyborg softly.

Barbara looked in dismay at the image in the seeing globe, which showed a thread of smoke rising from a distant forest. The roc had followed the probe's fall all the way to the ground.

'They seemed to lose control part of the way down. I hope there was nobody on board. It looked quite small, maybe it was an automatic landing craft.'

'Your pardon?'

'An unmanned machine to test the way is safe first.'

'Ah, that would be a wise precaution.'

'But why did it crash? Why did all the others crash?'

Gramling shrugged. 'Alas, I do not know.'

The *Merrow* sailed on under an almost cloudless sky. The coast had fallen away completely now, and the entire horizon was empty sea. The wind held steady from a little north of east, snatching the top off an occasional wave crest, but leaving the waters otherwise resembling rippled sapphire. Ian, leaning on the foredeck rail, the salt air breeze of their passage ruffling his hair, contemplated the scene with some satisfaction. Just let this weather hold, and they would reach the Shadow Isles in another two days. Off their port side, a school of porpoises broke the surface in a series of arching plunges and leaps, and he saw their sleek grey bodies surging through the clear water for a mile or more, playing about the *Merrow*'s bow, before

slipping away again on business of their own. He coul[d]
almost begin to enjoy the trip, if it wasn't for the constan[t]
worry about Susan.

Voices from the mid-deck disturbed his thoughts. Th[e]
Doctor had laid out some charts borrowed from Tristra[n]
on a hatch cover. Bron, Odoyle, Alammar and Thurgul[e]
were gathered about it curiously. 'Now, Sir Bron,' sai[d]
the Doctor, 'you promised yesterday that you would tel[l]
me about other artifacts like the 'Seven Companions''
And if you gentlemen also know of such things, I woul[d]
be very interested to hear of them.'

The long mosaic of photographs filled most of one wall o[f]
the *Prince Randolph*'s conference room. A continuous stri[p]
of Avalon's surface stretching over fifty degrees north an[d]
south of the equator had been recorded in some detail
with features of special interest displayed as enlargement[s]
to one side. Nyborg and Chandry sat at the head of the
table, with other department chiefs down the sides. A two[-]
way audio-visual channel linked the meeting to the ship'[s]
science stations and the rest of the squadron.

An hour before, they had lost a second probe, 9.4 miles
above the planet's surface, in circumstances identical to
the first one. There could be no possibility of chance
failure. But what had disabled them? Nyborg forced
his attention back to the briefing as the keen young
lieutenant heading the planetary survey section pointed
to the photo-mosaic.

'We have identified several centres of population so
far, linked by a sparse network of roads ... well, tracks
for the most part. Close-up views of some of the larger
settlements have shown structures which appear to correspond closely with terrestrial architectural forms typical
of the tenth to fifteenth centuries. The greatest concentration of these centres we've found so far is to the
north-west of this distinctive circular sea. Presumably, if
this is a lost Earth colony, that was the area of first landfall
and earliest settlement.'

'Any indication of an advanced technology?' asked Chandry.

'No radio sources, or power plant emissions, Captain. Everything is consistent with a medieval, pre-electrical culture of the horse and cart level. Except for these of course.' He tapped the enlargements. 'These don't fit in at all!'

'A pyramid three miles high, you say?' said the Doctor, marking the spot on the chart.

'Ay, the top rose straight through the clouds. But that is not the half of it,' insisted Sir Bron. 'Besides the sheer bulk of such a thing, there was also the precision with which it had been formed. The edges were as perfect and true as any rule, and the whole thing seemed to be made of one solid block of black stone, so hard it defied every attempt to mark it.'

'Remarkable,' said the Doctor, still scribbling.

'If you wish to hear of ancient marvels,' said Alammar, in his smooth and clear tones, 'then what of the Crystal Forest of Glissandor.' He pointed to a spot on the south-west of Elbyon. 'Imagine a sheltered valley filled with a lush forest of strangely shaped plants, but every plant, from greatest tree to smallest flower, sculpted from clearest glass. Yet with every grain of bark and vein of leaf perfectly formed, and the light endlessly reflected and twisted on every side as you walk through its crystal glades. A wonderful, yet deadly place.'

'Deadly?' asked Ian, who had come to stand on the edge of the group.

'Verily so, for it is not formed out of the tough stuff like that of the bridge of Fluxford, but glass as fragile as a window. The very grass underfoot may break and pierce your sole, and I know of many who have been cut to shreds by a falling branch. Yet it still draws many to wonder at it.'

'If you want a wonder,' cut in Thurguld, in his gruff tones, 'then speak of the Great Fountain of Largos,

121

which, exactly ten times every day, mark you, throws up a spout of water fully five hundred yards into the air, so chilling it, that it falls to earth as a rain of ice and snow in cooler weather!'

'Now that reminds me,' said Odoyle, 'of the river Dellberry in me own little corner of the land. A charming bubbling brook it starts as, twisting and turning by switchbacks down the side of a hill. And as you follow it down it gradually swells to a mighty torrent, which flows around the base of the hill as a wide river. Then, neat as you please, runs back up again until it is a brook, and starts all over.'

'Runs back up?' asked Ian uncertainly.

'Certainly. 'Tis a well known local sight. And very convenient for any who fall in, for their friends only have to sit down on the bank and wait awhile, and they'll be back around again to be hauled out!'

While Ian was pondering this apparent absurdity, the Doctor thanked the others for their help. They drifted away while he continued to make notations on his charts. Eventually he said: 'Well, Chesterton, what do you make of that?'

Ian sighed. 'I'd say it was the sheerest nonsense, if it wasn't for what we've already seen. Since they all claim to have seen these things personally I must believe them. But is it significant?'

'Of course! You don't suppose I was asking out of idle curiosity. Look at the charts. I've been able to plot a dozen different such incongruous structures or phenomena, drawing only on the direct experiences of four individuals. By extrapolation, we can assume that such things are scattered all over this planet.'

'So?'

The Doctor clicked his tongue in exasperation. 'It's a part of the puzzle, Chesterton. Hold it in your mind and see where it fits in. By the way, do you notice anything else of interest on these charts?'

'Well, the Circle Sea isn't quite circular, though it's

122

pretty close. The Shadow Isles are in the middle. It has a few circular bays cut out of it in places. Come to that, there are quite a few other rings and arcs of mountains on the lands around it, aren't there?'

'Exactly. But what do they remind you of?'

'Umm . . . oh yes. The craters of the moon!'

'Precisely. The remains of ancient meteor craters, most of which are now distorted by crustal movement, or worn down with age. Now, put that together with the other phenomena we have noted and you have two pieces of the puzzle.'

'And?'

'When we recover the Helm, we may find a third that links them!'

'Clearly, the planet was once subject to a high level of meteor activity,' said the lieutenant, 'so it would seem that the artifacts we have noted in our survey must –'

Chandry's table comm link buzzed: 'Captain, you wanted to be informed when the probe reached the moon.'

'Right, put it on the conference room screens.'

It looks like a sooty billiard ball, thought Nyborg, as the probe closed in. There was no sign of craters or mountains, just a curving expanse of dull matt blackness. The probe controller began his commentary.

Albedo, temperature and mass were all unusually low. The last of these anomalies might have been explained by the density readings, which were erratic: suggesting there were large voids within it. In contrast, electromagnetic readings began to rise the closer the probe got, as did the levels of raw radiation. The moon was surrounded by a cloud of radioactive particles.

'Is that radioactivity natural?' Nyborg asked.

'Hard to tell, Admiral,' said the *Prince Randolph*'s chief technical officer. 'Could simply have been gathered from the solar wind by secondary field effects. Certainly makes it an unhealthy place.'

123

'Deliberate? A way of discouraging visitors?'

'Perhaps, Admiral. Either way, a manned landing woul be risky.'

'A pity. I think we could learn a lot down there.'

Then the screen revealed a change in the perfec symmetry of the surface. A low dome, just as black as th rest of the landscape, made a shallow hump barely visibl against the stars.

'Probe control: head for that dome,' Chandry ordered

On the screen, the image of the black dome swelled. / fuzzy electronic snow started to cloud the picture.

'Transmission interference. Particle density and energ readings increasing,' the probe controller warned. 'Radia tion approaching maximum engineering tolerances .. There was a monstrous flash of light which briefly li up even the coal black landscape. The monitor pictur blazed white and went dead. 'Probe lost!'

'What was that!' exclaimed Nyborg. 'A weapon?'

'Just lightning, I think, Admiral,' hazarded the chief 'The potential difference between the probe and th moon caused a discharge through the particle cloud Need to make special adaptations if you want to sen another probe.'

The thoughtful silence that followed was broken by Nyborg's comm link.

'This is the special survey team, Admiral,' came Shan non's voice. 'We request that another attempt be made to reach the planet's surface, but with a class three probe. Everybody round the table, Nyborg noticed, was tryin; very deliberately not to appear to be taking too mucl notice of the conversation. The entire ship knew Shan non's team was something special and was keeping ar officially sanctioned low profile. Naturally this had only intensified the unofficial shipboard speculation as to thei purpose.

'Class three, Captain?' A class three probe was a simple ballistic unpowered shell, braking by atmospheric resist ance and a parachute triggered by increasing air pressure.

It delivered a very basic short life instrument package to a planet's surface that transmitted limited environmental data. 'Why do you believe it will be any more successful than the others?'

'It's just a possibility we want to test out, Admiral,' Shannon said. Nothing more. Uncomfortable glances were exchanged about the table.

Don't be a fool, Shannon, Nyborg thought. Give me a reason or let me tell them about your mission and who you represent. You can be anonymous or have rank here, not both. I can't be seen to grant requests blindly. That's not how it's done. Aloud, speaking as though the idea had just occurred to him, he said: 'It might be as well to make another attempt on the planet while we work on the problem of the moons. Please arrange that, Chandry.'

'Yes, Admiral,' said Chandry smartly.

Nyborg turned off the comm link without another word to Shannon.

Back in the library that afternoon, Barbara was diverted by the unexpected discovery of an Avalonian Bestiary.

It seemed to contain every wild animal the author knew of, listed alphabetically, together with some rather fanciful illustrations and notes about their habits. She wondered how all these animals had been brought here, along with all the Earthly plants. The *Prydwen*, if it had actually existed, must have been like Noah's Ark. Perhaps they had carried the animals as frozen embryos, or something?

What made the book unusual was that it listed ordinary creatures beside fantastic ones without distinction, giving no clue as to where they came from. She noted that dwarves, elves and leprechauns were not listed, and were clearly seen as people, at least by the author. But goblins were in their place: after giraffes and before gryphons.

Curious, she flipped through: Aardvark, antelope, ape, armadillo, bat (including, alarmingly, vampire), bear, boar (including a giant variety), bogie (a kind of shape-changing goblin), camel, cephlie, cheetah, crocodile, crab (including a singing kind!), deer, dolphins, dragons – ahh. There were several types of these listed. The fire herald, which they had encountered, was at the top, and reckoned to be the most dangerous. She shuddered when she discovered its tail could deliver a deadly sting! (How close she had come!) Guivres (sometimes also called knuckers), like the one that had attacked the docks, were described as wingless and legless water dwelling types, like giant snakes. Lindworms, which Bron had mentioned, had one pair of legs and were fast runners. Wyverns had eagle's legs and leathery wings and spread poison or disease . . .

Barbara shut the book firmly. Apart from interfering with her research, she would never sleep tonight if she read any more. She returned to her notes, and then paused. In the back of her mind was the suspicion that she had seen something significant. But she couldn't think what.

The probe fell like a meteor, with a burning tail searing across half the sky. This was quite intentional. As its heat shield burnt away, it lost energy and speed, slowing it down from thousands to mere hundreds of miles per hour. At a predetermined height, a pressure switch jettisoned the charred shield, and a parachute unfurled and snapped open. The small ball of instruments floated to earth to land with a slight bump in the middle of a patch of heathland. It transmitted data for almost a minute and a half before failing from, presumably, the same cause that had struck down its predecessors.

An hour afterwards, Shannon was facing Nyborg over the desk in his quarters once again. Nyborg stopped him before he could speak.

'We shall get one thing perfectly clear, *Captain* Shannon, or whatever your actual rank is. If we are to maintain this fiction, you will give explanations when I ask for them. Is that understood?'

For an instant Shannon looked puzzled, as though he couldn't see the point Nyborg was making. 'You must have known I would not make such a request lightly, Admiral.'

'But don't you see, I had to ask, man!' Nyborg found himself losing his temper, a thing he normally prided himself on never doing. More evenly, he continued: 'I'm sure you have your reasons for wearing that uniform, even though I may disagree with them. But while you are in it, you, like the regular marine contingent on board, are under my ultimate authority. I do not blindly grant requests from junior officers. You're a military man of some sort, so you must know that's how service discipline works. Next time you make such a request in public, be sure to have at least a plausible excuse for doing so. Do I make myself clear?'

'Yes, Admiral.' Shannon's face was expressionless.

If Nyborg had expected an apology, he was disappointed. Though not entirely surprised, he realized. For the first time he began to wonder what the Empire was coming to when people like Shannon held such positions. Did the fragmentation of the services after the fall of the Landsknechte contribute to such indiscipline? For a moment the image came to him of the Empire fragmenting the same way. He marshalled his thoughts. 'Very well. The probe was a qualified success. What have you learned from it?'

'That a properly sealed vessel can reach the planet's surface before whatever it is disables the control systems. Also there is a pattern to the way whatever it is affects the systems, approximately in order of exposure to the atmosphere. Purely mechanical moving parts do not seem to be affected at all.' He handed over a list. 'If these modifications are made to a standard Delta landing craft, I believe my team could be ready to make planetfall in eighteen hours. Once the method is proved, you can provide me with support and supplies as required.'

'But you can't intend simply to land at random and hope to find what you're after.'

Shannon pulled out a folded graphic printout from his pocket and smoothed it out on the desk before Nyborg. 'Your scanning teams produced this about half an hour ago. They were fine-tuning their equipment to detect details of the moon-to-planet energy flow, and discovered a secondary network of energy transference fields across the surface of the planet itself.' The printout showed an outline map of the continents, overlaid with an amorphous tonal pattern indicating energy concentrations. 'They were just going to tell you about it,' continued Shannon pre-emptively, 'when I said I'd inform you myself.'

Nyborg made no further comment about protocol. Besides, the discovery was fascinating. There were energy frequencies and notes on observed fluctuations printed beside the map. He'd never seen anything like them before. 'All right. But how does this help you choose a landing site?'

A rare flush of excitement coloured Shannon's cheeks. 'The resolution is not very high yet, but they're working on it. But you can already see that some of the areas of highest concentration correspond to the anomalous structures we found on the photographic survey, while others match with centres of habitation. At the moment, the most active region is around here.' He tapped a spot on the map. 'I think that would be a good place to start. If we find out how this energy is being used, we can learn how it is controlled. The answer is down there, and I'm going after it!'

The realization struck Barbara just as she was considering finishing for the day.

She was feeling slightly annoyed, having been frustrated by several gaps in Avalon's history after the first landing. There was mention of the 'time of giants', and sometimes the 'cold years', and then the structure of

128

Avalonian society as she now knew it seemed to suddenly come into being. It was rather odd, if nothing else. She had at least found more references to Merlin's Helm, which bore out the general view that it was an item of tremendous potential power, but deadly to its user. However, there was no clue yet as to how it got to the Shadow Isles, and she wondered if Gramling had those sources in his own library, together with other works on magic. Should she ask him, or persevere a little longer on her own? She suspected, as the Doctor obviously had when he suggested the research, that the old wizard might be secretive about such things.

Then it happened.

The nagging matter of what she had subconsciously seen in the Bestiary inverted itself in her mind. What was there that should not have been, became what should be here but isn't.

They would have realized sooner, if it hadn't been for Susan's kidnapping and subsequent events. They might even have suspected something when they first saw Fluxford from the hillside, if their minds hadn't been filled with thoughts of dwarves and dragons. She remembered the panorama, with the walled city, the river and the castle rising on the hill high above it. But what other tall building should have been there, dominating the skyline of the city, as it would in a true medieval scene, where it formed an integral part of the society? Who had not been at the banquet? What had she found no mention of in any book in the library?

Fluxford had no cathedral, monastery or church.

There had been no clergyman of any kind at the feast.

She had seen no religious texts, or mention of religious thought or teaching in any book in the library.

14

The Stolen Hour

The bolts of the cell slid back, the door swung open, and Dhal and two apemen, carrying lanterns, walked in.

Susan and Mellisa did not stir.

They had piled their straw pallets one on top of the other to make a more comfortable bed, and had doubled up their thin blankets, under which they huddled close together to keep warm. They were very still. Susan's hand had slipped out from under the blanket on to the cold stone floor. Dhal nudged it with the toe of his boot. She stirred slightly, but did not wake. Dhal looked at a tray resting on the floor bearing empty plates and a pitcher of water, and he smiled.

'The drug has taken effect most satisfactorily. The same dose tomorrow at the same time, understand?'

'Yes, Master,' grunted the apemen.

'Now, carry them up to my chamber. But note how they are resting first. They must be returned here and replaced in exactly the same positions, understand?'

'Yes, Master – uh, why must they be same, Master?'

Dhal sighed. 'Because they must not suspect anything has happened to them. The process will not work if they fight it, so they must not know there is anything to fight! Now do you understand?'

'Uh – yes, Master.'

Dhal stripped the covers from the sleeping figures. 'See how they are lying? That is how you will put them back when I have finished with them. You will do exactly the same thing for five nights. Now, take them to my chamber.'

With surprising gentleness, the apes carefully picked up Susan and Mellisa and carried them out of the cell.

Slightly less than an hour later, the apes returned with their burdens and laid them back on their bed, positioning them as they had been before. The two young women were still asleep, and did not stir until morning.

15

Descent

For the third morning, the TARDIS's defence shield crackled and its door refused to open. Barbara was not really expecting otherwise, but it would have been nice to have at least one problem resolve itself. Queen Leonora, this time escorted by Sir Peridor, came by as she was finishing her examination of the ship, and they walked again in the orchard. It was obvious the Queen needed somebody to talk to and, as was sometimes the case, it was easier to let her feelings show before a near stranger. Peridor maintained a discreet distance while they conversed. Barbara thought he understood.

Afterwards, after a token protest from Peridor, they climbed the long stairs leading up to the battlements of the inner walls. Barbara saw small masts being fitted into place along sections of the wall walks, and learned with a modest glow of pride, that they were for 'Lady Barbara's wires'. Peridor confirmed that fresh wire was being drawn in all the available forges, and would begin to be strung within a few days.

The outer bailey looked more like an army camp now. There were a few of the colourful knights' pavilions still visible, but they were outnumbered by the more utilitarian shelters and tents being erected to provide for the growing army now camped within the castle walls. It must be like this in castles all over the South Share, she thought; troops being mustered to prepare for whatever came after Dhal's deadline passed. She saw a squad of horsemen gallop out of the gateway, and, shortly afterward, a company of foot soldiers march in. All the roads and boundaries were being regularly patrolled. Two days

132

had passed without a sign of further intrusions by Dhal's creatures, but this may only have been part of his strategy. No one believed he had given up his ambitions.

And suddenly Barbara felt strangely isolated from the activity below, looking down from the high castle grounds. How she wished for a radio-phone, so that she might talk to Ian and the Doctor and know they were making progress. Something must have shown on her face, for the Queen turned to her.

'You look very pensive.'

'I am thinking about my friends, your Majesty, and wishing I could talk to them. It's a shame Gramling can't find a way. And then also I . . .'

'Yes?'

'Well, I'm beginning to feel cooped up in here. Not that I'm complaining about the hospitality, but I'd like to get out. My leg is feeling better, and I think I could ride, if that were possible.'

'Excuse me, Lady,' interjected Peridor, 'but it is not wise to venture forth beyond the walls. We know not what foul creatures of Dhal's may next assail us, or when.'

'And that doesn't help either,' replied Barbara sharply, 'to know I'm well protected behind several thick, well defended walls, while there are people out there with far less protection. It makes me feel a bit guilty.'

'If I may point out, Lady,' said Peridor, 'the castle itself is more likely to be the focus of any attack than the town.'

'Well if it's just as dangerous here, why do you keep wanting us to stay inside?' Barbara put in quickly, leaving Peridor momentarily lost for a counter argument.

The Queen smiled gently. 'I believe I understand your feelings, my dear, but what can we do?'

'Well at least we could show ourselves outside the walls, to let the people know we're sharing the danger with them. Inspect the troops. Maybe ride around the town.'

'My husband and Stephan ride out regularly to do that

133

very thing, of course. But tomorrow they will go to the field where they are preparing for the midsummer fair. Those creatures of Dhal's that stole away Mellisa also fired several houses, and what with the guivre in the docks, there is much fear. Some small entertainments may prove a diversion. It will not be as grand as it should have been, but Stephan thought it would give some cheer to the townsfolk.'

'Exactly. Good for morale. We should go too!'

'You know, Barbara, I think we shall.'

Peridor looked dismayed, but wisely said nothing.

They began to walk back to the keep. Barbara thought for a minute, then asked: 'Your Majesty, may I ask you a question which you may find a little – strange?'

'Certainly.'

'What do you believe lies beyond life?'

The Queen frowned. 'Beyond life? I do not quite understand your meaning.'

'An afterlife. The existence of the spirit after the body dies. Going to heaven.'

Peridor, who had also heard her question, was looking as bemused as the Queen.

'I'm sure what happens when we die is a mystery, Barbara. Perhaps it is only an eternal sleep. We can only be certain of the life we have, so we should value it and live it to the full, and face its end with courage and the knowledge that we have done our best. If there is anything of us that survives death, surely that is a matter beyond our comprehension. Is that not what people hold to where you come from?'

'Some do. But others try to prepare specially for death, to ensure the survival of their spirit, by following special rules governing their behaviour during their life.'

'But how might that help?'

'Well, they think when they die they are judged on how well they held to those beliefs.'

'Judged? But who could possibly judge them once they are dead?' exclaimed the Queen.

In the circumstances, Barbara could think of no suitable reply.

On the road a few miles from Fluxford, a pedlar, pushing his handcart of wares bound for the midsummer fair, flinched at a sudden insistent mewing. A black cat was seated primly beside a milestone. At the sight of him it sprang down, advanced purposefully, and circled about his cart. When it had the man's curious attention, it walked a few steps into the forest, and looked back at him meaningfully. The pedlar swallowed nervously. He had heard too many stories over the last few days about troubles around Fluxford, to follow any strange cat into the forest. Besides, he didn't like the look in the beast's eyes. He clasped the handles of his cart and set off again at a rather brisker pace than before, determined to be safe inside the city walls before evening.

The hangar deck of the *Prince Randolph* seemed positively cavernous after the days Jen had spent in the warren of the ship's crew decks. It was also an incredibly busy place. A host of mechanics were at work on the ranks of landers, shuttles and sleek fighters. Engine panels hung open to the probing of inspection torches. Fuel and power cables snaked across the floor. In workshop bays, welding torches sparked with eye-searing intensity, to the accompaniment of rivet guns and echoing voices exchanging instructions and commands in their own obscure technical sub-language. But Jen's attention focused on one particular craft that was just being wheeled into position before the big airlock. She felt her palms begin to sweat. She glanced at Ivanov standing by her side, and could see a pulse throbbing in his temple. They shouldered their personal packs and began the long walk across the hangar floor, slightly encumbered by the bulky outer coveralls of their survival suits. As they approached the lander, Jen felt the surroundings of the hangar seemed to fade away into the background as a sense of unreality overwhelmed her, trying to deny the fact that she was committed to stepping on board it.

The Delta lander was not a large craft, being less than fifty feet long. It had the same solid, curving, stubby lines that all such craft had borne for a thousand years; dictated by the unchanging laws of aerodynamics that determined the optimum form for a vessel capable of surviving the re-entry fireball of an unpowered descent from orbit through an atmosphere. Jen noticed there had been some modifications to its tail thruster unit, based on the analysis they had made of the previous probe flights. Theoretically they should allow them to make a safe landing. Theoretically.

Once the craft was in place before the airlock, a gang of mechanics descended on it again to make last-minute checks. Its side hatch swung open to reveal Shannon, also dressed in a survival suit.

'Fifteen minutes to launch. Get stowed away and strapped in,' he commanded curtly.

Beside her, Ivanov cleared his throat and passed a tongue over dry lips. He tried to force a smile. 'After you, Doctor Komati.'

'Ah, come in, come in,' said Dhal effusively, as the apes ushered Susan and Mellisa into his workroom and lined them up before him. 'I'm afraid I neglected you yesterday because I had a few pressing things to attend to. But I trust you slept well and are quite comfortable?'

They had slept, but hardly comfortably. They were beginning to feel grubby with only their nightdresses to wear, and their cold, slightly damp cell was becoming oppressive. Mellisa voiced their feelings with undimmed spirit. 'Why do you continue this cruel game, Dhal? We are not your guests, we are your captives. If you truly cared for our comfort, you would give us a better room, and clothes and a chance to wash ourselves.'

Dhal smiled. 'You find the accommodation rather basic do you? But as you point out, Princess, you are my

136

captives, and, believe me, conditions could be made far more uncomfortable for you if I wished.' He paused to let the implication sink in, then continued: 'Besides, if you let prisoners have too many home comforts, they tend to take liberties with your hospitality, and ungratefully try to escape. Quite futile, of course, but it is annoying. So you see, the secure, unfurnished simplicity of your present quarters gives me peace of mind.'

'Can we at least have enough water to wash in,' asked Susan, 'and a comb –' she bit her lip, 'please?' Her own hair was tousled, but Mellisa's long tresses were tangled and straggly.

Dhal considered. 'I suppose I might allow that, since you ask so politely. What about you, Princess? Is there anything you would like to ask for? Another vision of your precious Edmund, perhaps?'

Mellisa started slightly, but controlled herself. 'I will not beg, Dhal, if that is what you expect,' she said stoutly.

'Never mind, I was going to tell you anyway. I relented after my first warning, and let him have an easy journey. His little band has made good time, and will probably be camped within watching distance shortly, like the intrepid scouts they are. As long as they keep their distance, I will leave them be. Actually this is quite a day for visitors,' he continued, turning to Susan, 'the people in the skyboats I showed you have been trying to land their machines on Avalon. I've been keeping a close watch on them . . .' he paused, as though listening to something that was beyond their senses, 'in fact, I believe something is happening even now. How convenient. Would you like to see how I deal with unwanted visitors?'

He faced the seeing globe and conjured up an image within it. On the table beside it were several small jars and bottles, presumably containing magical ingredients, and a cylindrical glass tank two-thirds filled with water. In the globe they saw a stubby deltaform shape dropping out of the purple void. As it fell, a hazy aura started to envelop it, growing more intense and streaming out into a funnel of thin rippling air behind. Red shaded to orange and then yellow and the landing craft disappeared in a ball of fire.

Jen saw the flames licking about the lander's tiny viewports, shivering and crackling as though fanned by the fiercest wind she could imagine. She could hear their roar as well, but it was curiously distant and muffled. The craft started to tremble and shake as a continuous drumming vibration began to pound away under the supports of their semi-reclining seats. The deceleration pressure grew, pressing her down into the contoured padding. She and Ivanov had the two rear seats in the cabin, while Shannon and Monadno sat in front of them before the control panels; Monadno in the left hand seat as lander pilot, his hands steady on the chair arm joysticks. Mounted between them was a newly installed auxiliary control box, fitted with heavy manual levers, switches and plungers, connected to a bank of hydraulic pressure bottles mounted between the two rows of seats. Running out of them were armoured conduits that snaked away and vanished through the hull and into the engine compartment.

Two minutes after beginning atmospheric braking, the vibration was getting worse. They were coming in steeply to reduce their descent time to the minimum. The fire outside blazed as brightly as before, pushing the tolerance of the heat shield to the maximum. Jen tried not to think of what would happen if it failed. Out of the corner of her eye she saw that Ivanov had his eyes closed and appeared to be mumbling to himself. She was glad she was wearing her suit gloves. It hid her own hands that were gripping the chair arms with white-knuckle intensity.

Three minutes into braking. The vibration gradually began to die away. The fiery glow about the windows faded and was gone. Jen heard faint pings and creaks of

138

cooling metal through the hull as the heatshield contracted. They had made it! Outside the viewports, purple blue sky had replaced the black of space. A wisp of thin cloud flashed by. Monadno banked the lander on to a course for the target zone. Its thrusters droned and Jen felt herself being pressed back into her seat once more. They were in a hurry to get down.

Thirty seconds of powered flight.

Forty-five seconds.

One minute.

The drone of the thrusters stuttered and died away unevenly.

'Main drive control lost,' announced Monadno calmly. Red lights started to appear on his control panel. The lander began to wallow. 'Attitude thruster control gone.'

'Initiating bypass,' said Shannon, throwing a lever on the alternate control box. There was a hiss of hydraulics. The lander's wings unfolded and bit into the air as more lights on the control board flashed red. 'System failure spreading,' noted Shannon. How did he remain so infuriatingly cool? wondered Jen.

'Going to manual,' Monadno confirmed, pulling the emergency manual control yoke out of its recess and locking it into place, abandoning the electronic joystick controls. The wallowing died away as the wings locked into place at maximum extension, cutting their airspeed but giving them stability again. The cabin lights flickered and went out. The last control board light died. 'Total power failure,' said Shannon. Monadno was now flying the craft like a high speed glider, without any power assistance, purely through manual linkages. The only instruments left functioning were those without electronics; the magnetic compass, altimeter, artificial horizon and air speed indicator. A thousand years of flight technology wiped out in moments, thought Jen. They flew on in a strange calm, with only the soft rush of air caressing the hull.

'Airspeed dropping,' said Monadno, 'we'll be short of

target zone. We need a boost. Ten second burn. Brace yourselves!' He pressed down on one of the control box plungers. There was a pop and roar from the rear as a chemical trigger ignited a solid fuel rocket tube, slamming them back in their seats. The lander surged forward nose up, climbing, velocity increasing. 'Frisky,' remarked Monadno, fighting the controls to hold them steady. The solid fuel rocket burned out and the peaceful whisper of air returned. He scanned his few functioning instruments. 'Speed good, height good, bearing . . .' he banked the craft slightly, then straightened up ' . . . good. Target zone dead ahead.'

'How persistent they are,' Dhal commented, watching the lander glide onward in his globe. 'They have tamed demons of fire and wind to drive them on. Unfortunately I cannot allow outsiders to influence my plans at this stage.'

He unstoppered a vial and poured the contents into the water tank. It billowed and spread like black ink. Speaking a complex rhythmic verse under his breath, he took up a rod and stirred. Then he emptied a tiny pot into the water. It seemed to be full of silver glitter. He stirred again, still chanting.

The storm came out of nowhere.

Through the cockpit window Jen saw puffy white clouds boiling up into great seething thunderheads, filling out and darkening, coalescing. In moments, a solid wall of black cloud was rolling towards them, blotting out land and sky as surely as a drawn curtain. Lightning forked about its leading edge.

'What the hell!' exclaimed Monadno, for an instant his professional calm deserting him. Then he slammed down a plunger. A fresh rocket exploded into life, pressing them back into their seats. Monadno pulled back on the controls, lifting the lander's nose, trying to get above the storm.

140

It was too late.

With a banshee wail the wind struck. The impact threw them against their seat harnesses, almost as though they had hit something solid. Daylight was snatched away to be replaced by a grey half-light. The lander shuddered as the wind screamed past them, bucking and tossing as Monadno fought to keep control. There was a brilliant flash of light all about them followed by an almost simultaneous deafening thunderclap and smack of exploding air. Something broke loose and rattled about in a storage locker. The rocket tube burned out. Over the constant howl of wind came a creaking groan from the wing sockets.

'Retract the wings or we'll lose them!' shouted Monadno.

'How will you land us?' Shannon bellowed back.

A lightning bolt exploded against the hull, searing purple after-images of the viewports into their retinas, the concussion rattling their teeth. The lander pitched wildly, and Monadno struggled to bring it level again.

'I can't, captain. We have to abort this target!'

For one ghastly moment, Jen thought Shannon was going to order him to land anyway. Then he nodded, lips drawn tight in a grimace of anger. He pulled a lever and with a hiss of hydraulics the wings retracted. Monadno's hand hovered over the rocket tube plungers. 'Trying for a sub-orbital hop to another target zone. It's going to be rough!'

He pushed down a spread of plungers.

Lightning exploded against the hull.

The ship tumbled.

Something cracked inside the cabin, filling the air with the smell of ozone.

Jen had the fleeting impression of Monadno's hand jerking wildly, trailing sparks. Then there was a boom from the rear of the ship and a concerted roar of sound as every remaining rocket tube burst into life. The shock wave slammed Jen back into her seat, her head thudding

141

into the rest. The flesh of her cheeks was tugged backwards. A terrible weight seemed to settle on her chest, driving the breath from her lungs. Her eyeballs distorted under the pressure, squeezing her field of vision into a narrowing grey tunnel.

Which mercifully faded into blackness.

The image within Dhal's crystal disappeared in a swirl of wind-torn cloud and stabbing spears of lightning. For a moment, a ruddy glow suffused the leaden depths of the maelstrom, then it was gone. 'I believe I have discouraged them successfully, don't you?' said Dhal with satisfaction.

Admiral Nyborg stared in dismay at the telescopic display being projected on to the main bridge screen. A moment before the landing zone had only one tenth cloud cover with light winds, according to the met sensors. Now he was looking down upon a black spiral of clouds thirty miles across, in which a force twelve storm was raging.

There was a spark of light.

A meteor seemed to burst improbably up out of the boiling cauldron and rise like an arrow towards the south-east and into the stratosphere.

'Lander detected. Wings retracted. Under maximum thrust!' reported one of the scanner team. The tail flare faded and died fitfully as the differently graded rockets burned out one by one, and the craft's trajectory began to curve over in a shallow arc. On the infra red display, the lander still glowed. 'Readings indicate internal damage and possible cabin fire.'

'Keep tracking!' Chandry snapped. 'Plot an intercept course and prepare for emergency manoeuvring. Ready the gravitic tractor beam –'

'Cancel that order!' Nyborg was shaking his head, staring at a graphic display of the lander's trajectory and the flickering figures beside it. 'Sorry, captain. They won't quite make it out of the atmosphere, and we daren't risk the ship going down after them until we know how this disabling effect works.'

'I – yes, admiral.'

Nyborg watched the plot of the lander as it reached its maximum altitude and started the long plunge back towards the planet. Their only hope was an unpowered landing now. It would need fine piloting. If there was anybody still capable of piloting it. He saw where the display projected the lander's touchdown point would be and stiffened. 'Wings still retracted?'

'Yes sir.'

Come on, thought Nyborg, open those wings and get some control. I don't like you, Shannon, but nobody should die like this.

Barbara looked out of the library window. A change in the quality of the light had disturbed her. Over the battlements to the west she could see a mountain range of black cloud rising over the horizon. She thought she heard the drawn out rumble of distant thunder. Looks like we're going to have a summer storm, she thought, pulling the window to and returned to her studies.

Not only had she still found no mention of any religion or god, by any name, but she realized that traditional symbols of evil had also been adjusted to suit Avalonian conditions. In the ancient past during the time of the first landing, it was the Ice Giants, long since driven back to the far north. If there was disease or pestilence, wyverns got the blame, and so on. Could atheism have swept away all traces of religion before these people left Earth? Surely not. There should be some mention of religious thought somewhere in these people's history. But there wasn't. After talking to the Queen and Peridor, it seemed the very concept was strange to them.

She sighed, realizing she would have to put the matter aside for the moment, and turned her mind to the problem of magic and Merlin's Helm. She wished she could find out more, especially about the origin of the

Helm. Then she brightened slightly. It occurred to her that she didn't need to go to Gramling to find out what books he had used for his research after all.

Tristram and Odoyle leant over the rail talking to the figures in the water, while the others kept a few feet back so as not to alarm them. This was annoying to Ian who would rather like to be able to claim, even though no one would ever believe him, that he had once talked to a mermaid.

In fact only two of the sea people were mermaids. The other three were mermen, or merrows, as he learned they were called. They had none of their companion's beauty, having faces that combined the jaws of a moray eel with the features of a bulldog. However, they seemed to be talking intelligently enough to Odoyle and Tristram; the latter making great play of the fact that he had named his ship after their kind.

The strange meeting had been instigated after Tristram announced they would reach the Shadow Isles in another day. He had conferred with Odoyle and Sir Bron, and they had decided it would be wise to contact the sea people to check the accuracy of their charts of the isles, and also see if they could enlist their aid as guides through the dangerous waters of the outer isles. The problem was, Ian discovered, that relations between mer-folk and seamen were often acrimonious, due to accidents with fishing nets, claims of deliberate wrecking and enchanting humans into the sea. However, the attempt was made. The *Merrow* reefed her sails and Tristram took a belaying pin and began rapping it in a complex rhythm against the ship's side for several minutes at a stretch. Interspersed with this, Odoyle stood at the prow and sang softly something that might have been an Irish lullaby, his voice drifting out across the blue sea. Either the song or Tristram's drumming had the desired effect, for twenty minutes later, a woman's blonde head rose cautiously out of the water a few yards off their bow. A moment later, the ugly snout of a merrow surfaced beside her. Soon they were joined by three others, and the negotiations began.

Shortly afterwards the *Merrow* gathered speed again as the steady breeze filled its sails. Two of the sea people, as agreed, now swam before them, effortlessly keeping pace with the ship. Porpoises had again appeared and seemed to frolic with the mermen like dogs out for a walk with their masters. Ian stood by the bowsprit, watching glittering scaled tails and sleek grey flanks flashing under the water. Avalon had again surpassed itself for novelty. And yet, as the Doctor said, it was all part of the pattern. If he stayed here any length of time, would he begin to take such wonders for granted?

He turned away from the bow, and as he did so, a dark spot in the sky off their port quarter caught his attention. For a moment he thought it was a large bird, for he was sure he could make out wings. Then he realized it was trailing a thin streamer of smoke behind it.

He raced to the gangway leading to the mid-deck and clattered down it, shouting to attract the others. The spot was growing steadily larger every second. It was definitely an aircraft of some kind, with a flattened, oblate body, seen nose on. Nose on? It was coming straight at them! On the poop deck, Tristram took one look over his shoulder and spun the wheel madly. The *Merrow*'s decks heeled over as the ship began to turn. With a rising scream of air the strange craft flashed past their beam hardly a hundred feet over the waves. Ian had a momentary impression of a compact rounded fuselage sprouting long, narrow wings like a glider, with a cluster of tubes projecting from its stern leaking black smoke. Then it was streaking away before them, dropping lower every second, wings dipping one side then the other as though the pilot was fighting desperately to keep her level.

They rushed to the rail to watch helplessly as the inevitable crash came. The craft kissed the water once in a shower of white spray and skipped like a skimming stone.

It touched a second time and ploughed a longer furrow through the waves. The third time it stayed down, sending up twin walls of spray, and trailing steam from its tail. One wing cut deeper into the water and the craft slewed about, juddered side on to the sea and came to rest, bobbing in the swell, half a mile off the *Merrow*'s bow. Even as they turned towards it, the craft started to settle a little lower.

The ape guard carefully put the large bowl and pitcher of water down on the cell floor before the two subdued young women, while his companion placed a folded towel and comb beside it. 'Master say you can have these,' the first growled. 'You make selves clean and hair straight again.'

'Yes – thank you,' replied Mellisa woodenly.

'Make hair long and shiny again?' queried the second ape.

'Yes – that's right, I will.'

'Golden hair nice,' observed the first ape.

'Thank you,'

The two apes nodded to each other slowly, as though a weighty aesthetic point had been agreed, and withdrew.

'I think you've got an admirer there,' Susan whispered with mock confidentiality, trying to lighten their gloom. For a moment Mellisa looked at her in bafflement, then they broke into mutual giggles.

Jen felt herself stumbling through events as though in a dream, still dazedly recovering from the high 'g' force blackout. There was blood in her mouth. She'd bitten her tongue as they had hit. Dimly, she was aware of the craft settling in the water, and the cabin floor tilting backwards as the engine compartment began to flood. She saw Shannon and Monadno release their safety harnesses, Monadno fumbling over it because his right arm was still numb from the shock he had received. Beside her, Ivanov groaned and clutched his head.

'Unstrap,' Shannon ordered crisply, his commanding voice cutting through their daze, setting fingers reaching for harness buckles as though of their own accord. He was sliding out of his control chair and reaching up to the emergency hatch in the cabin roof, as he spoke. 'Grab your number one packs and be ready.' He released a handle on a long length of cord, stood back and yanked hard. There was a sharp bang of explosive bolts and the hatch panel blew out and disappeared. Sunlight poured in through the aperture. Shannon opened a locker, pulled out the tightly folded bundle of an inflatable raft and a lightweight ladder, which he hooked over the edge of the hatch, and rapidly scrambled up, boosting the bundle ahead of him, then drew himself effortlessly out on to the fuselage. 'Ivanov. Pack first, now yourself. Move!'

The professor clattered up the ladder and was hauled out of sight. Lightheadedly, Jen threw her pack after him and followed, stumbling up the steps. Shannon's strong hand caught her by the collar of her suit and almost lifted her bodily clear. She stood teetering on the slippery curve of the fuselage, trying to keep her balance on the angled surface. Steaming bubbles were rising from the tail of the lander, which was already awash. The bright sunlight glinting off the incredible sapphire blue sea dazzled her, and the freshness of the salty breeze was almost shocking after weeks of canned and reprocessed ship air. There was a hissing sound, and she realized the raft, tethered to a safety-line eyelet beside the hatch, was already in the water and automatically inflating.

'Into the raft,' Shannon ordered. 'Get ready to catch whatever we can salvage!'

As the bulging shape unfolded and flipped upright, Jen and Ivanov slithered down the fuselage and jumped into the water, grabbing for the hand loops around the raft's outer ring. Their survival suits kept them dry and buoyant as they awkwardly hauled themselves aboard.

147

They had hardly managed to sit upright before Shannon was throwing the other number one packs over to them. Then an equipment case, spare med-pack and ration boxes were tossed over in quick succession as Monadno scavenged from their stores. With a fizz and turgid rush of bubbles the lander began to slip lower, its nose lifting skyward for the last time.

'Get out!' Jen screamed. 'It's going under!'

Shannon reached down as a wave broke over the rim of the hatch and hauled. Monadno scrambled out into the open air. Shannon released the raft tether and they slithered across and leaped clear of the fuselage even as the waters closed in over it. There was an explosive rush as gouts of air erupted from the hatch, breaking into a brief plume of spray. As the marines reached the side of the raft the waves met across the lander's nose with a rush and slap. With a last plume of bubbles and upwelling of displaced water, which briefly set the raft rocking, the lander was gone.

The two hauled themselves into the raft and sat with their heads bowed for a moment, taking a few deep breaths to recover from the adrenaline surge the crash had generated. Jen wondered if their armour of professional cool had been cracked, and they might actually admit how close they had all come to dying just then. But if they felt like opening up, it became clear they did not intend to do so before two quasi-soldiers like Ivanov and herself. Shannon merely gestured to Monadno's arm. 'How is it?'

Monadno flexed his fingers. 'Feeling's coming back. Just a secondary zap from the charge that blew the rockets . . . ' he looked over Shannon's shoulder. 'Captain. We've got company.'

They all twisted round. The antique sailing craft they had glimpsed seconds before impact was now perhaps four hundred yards away and bearing down upon them. 'Maybe they're just coming to rescue us?' Jen said hopefully.

Shannon unsnapped the cover of his holster. 'Maybe, but we won't take any chances.'

'My God!' gasped Ivanov, pointing to one side. 'What's that?'

Ten feet away, a hideous head balanced on human shoulders had risen from the sea to stare curiously at them with goggling fish eyes. Another rose beside it. Their jaws were full of needle sharp teeth. Shannon and Monadno had instinctively drawn their guns when Monadno swore, tapping the power gauge on the base of the barrel. 'Charge reads zero!'

'Mine too. How are the stunners?' Shannon snapped at Jen and Ivanov. They fumbled their lesser weapons from their holsters and found they were also dead. Shannon started to rummage in a pack for something, appeared to think better of it, and grabbed one of the folding paddles instead, raising it as a makeshift club. Monadno did the same. Jen thought she saw a glint of scales under the water and a third head broke the surface. This one was strikingly female, with long, blonde hair, into which appeared to have been plaited strings of pearls. For the first time Shannon actually showed surprise, giving Jen a small glow of satisfaction as it provided company for her own shocked disbelief. As they stared in amazement at the latest arrival, a faint voice floated across the waters from the approaching ship.

'Leave them be! They only want to help you!'

The words were understandable but slightly stilted, with an intonation that made Jen think of historical telefictions. The speaker was leaning over the ship's rail shouting through what seemed to be a metal trumpet. Shannon and Monadno exchanged questioning glances, then slowly lowered their paddles.

'Were there any more in your craft?' asked the voice from the ship. She could make the speaker out now. He was wearing a strangely shaped black hat.

Shannon cupped his hands together. 'No,' he shouted back.

149

'Then, if you are able, we shall heave too, and you can make your way over to us.' They could hear orders being shouted, and saw activity in the rigging as sails were taken in. The ship began to lose way, slowly drifting to a gently wallowing stop some thirty yards away. A heavy rope net was thrown over the side.

Shannon started paddling, and Monadno followed suit. 'They may be friendly, but stay alert and keep together,' he directed.

Jen saw the fish people and the woman following them a few yards off. There was something odd about the way they swam. She could see no sign of kicking legs, just glinting scales and an occasional flicker of fins. She began to feel queasy. Perhaps it was seasickness. But the feeling of unsettling unreality grew stronger as they tied up alongside the ship. Its hull was actually made of separate sections of real wood, she noticed. Cautiously they clambered up the net to the deck.

The strangest group of people were waiting for them.

'No, Lady Barbara,' said Harding, 'I do not recall Master Gramling using the castle library much in, oh, let me see . . . five years.'

'But I understood he had done some research quite recently. I was wondering if there was any record of his references I might borrow.'

'As I say, I know of none, Lady.'

'Is there a library in Fluxford he may have gone to, or some other place?'

'Gramling has only infrequently stirred from the castle in years, Lady.' He lowered his voice discreetly. 'His age is telling, I believe. Many a time I have come across him in the grounds dozing, on some seat, or else staring ahead of him at nothing . . . ' he trailed off awkwardly. 'You understand, I mean no disrespect to his past achievements. But I believe when the treachery of Dhal was fully revealed, he was never quite himself afterwards.'

'I see. Thank you.'

She was obviously going to have to ask the old wizard directly, after all. Well, he couldn't object as it was all for the common cause. She pictured the handful of books she had seen in his room. It shouldn't take her long to look through those.

16

Objectives

Tristram's cabin was crowded, but it seemed more appropriate to talk in here than out on the open deck. At least it was light and airy enough, with the afternoon sun streaming in through the open sterncastle windows. Besides, they might have to discuss things that Bron would rather the crew did not hear. He studied the four newcomers carefully, noting the differences between them and the Doctor's party. There was clearly much variety in the peoples of the oldworlds. That two of them were soldiers was obvious from their bearing before they gave their ranks during the introductions. The woman and the thin, scholarly man were puzzles, falling in their manner somewhere between the soldiers and the Doctor and Ian. He wished he understood more fully what being a scientist truly meant. It was a word they had used several times already. There was an aura of power about it, rather like 'wizard', and it suggested things beyond the capabilities of ordinary people. He saw the Doctor was as keenly interested in the newcomers as he was, and Bron let him carry the conversation for the while, as he felt he understood them better. At the moment, the Doctor's fingers met in a thoughtful pyramid under his chin as he stared across the table at Shannon, who seemed to do most of the talking.

'So,' the Doctor concluded at length, 'you are now marooned on Avalon like we are. Still, it was fortunate we happened to be around when you crashed, or else you might have had a long wait before you made landfall.'

'After all our rockets blew we couldn't make it back to

the coast again,' explained Monadno, 'so we were trying to reach some islands we'd seen from orbit.' He looked thoughtful. 'I guess that's where you're going too, from the way you were heading.'

'We are, as it happens,' admitted the Doctor. 'But you mention rockets. Rather primitive for your type of craft, I would have thought. Reactionless impellers or thrusters would be more suitable. Unless you were expecting trouble, of course.'

Shannon smiled tightly. 'We had already lost some test probes, so we knew something was wrong.'

'Such cautious use of probes suggests you already had your suspicions about Avalon even before you arrived. And you have come in squadron strength as well. Did you envisage the likelihood of a military confrontation?'

Monadno cut in, trying to sound helpful. 'It is very simple, Doctor. Over the years several ships have been lost in this sector. At last the likely source of the problem was narrowed down to this system. Since it was possible that an enemy of the Empire was at work the military got involved. Now it looks like some natural phenomenon is responsible, we can let the scientists study it.'

Bron noticed the reactions of Monadno's companions while he spoke. Shannon and Ivanov quickly nodded as though to reinforce his explanation, but Komati sat still, staring fixedly at a knot in the surface of the table.

'But you were not expecting Avalon to be inhabited, were you?'

'Clearly a lost colony world, Doctor,' Shannon said firmly. 'The Empire will be glad to take it back under her protection.'

Bron scowled at the implication, but the Doctor spoke first.

'Forgive me, but I do not believe your empire was in existence when these people's forebears left Earth. After eight hundred years of isolation, they must surely be accorded the status of a fully independent world, must they not?'

153

'Of course,' Shannon said quickly. 'I'm sure the Interstellar Court of Justice will rule that is the case. But in the meantime –'

'In the meantime, we must remember we are guests here, however unwittingly, and behave accordingly. We have been treated with every courtesy by these people, and I'm sure such consideration will be extended to yourselves. Which means any further investigations into the nature of this world can only be undertaken with their permission. That is only civilized, do you not agree?'

Shannon nodded fractionally. Monadno was noncommittal. Komati continued to stare at the table top. Ivanov spoke up.

'Naturally, Doctor, we shall respect local feelings. But it is surely in everyone's best interests to understand what is going on here. We must learn how this disabling effect functions, and whether it has any other properties we should know about. As a scientist you must understand that.'

'And have you discovered anything yet?'

'Be fair, Doctor. We've only just arrived.'

'But you have had the opportunity to observe Avalon from orbit and send down probes. What results have you obtained from that?'

'Nothing conclusive. So far.'

'And what of the moons? Have you probed them yet? I'm sure you'll find a closer inspection most rewarding.' The Doctor was leaning forward intently, his eyes glittering with little diamond points, ready to pounce on any new scrap of knowledge.

'They are being examined, of course,' admitted Ivanov, noncommittally, his eyes turning aside from the Doctor's.

There was a silence which Shannon broke quickly by asking: 'If your spacecraft is back in this place called Fluxford on the mainland, why are you on this ship, Doctor? Is this a pleasure cruise – or have you some special reason for being out here?'

Bron frowned. The man was no fool. Well, it would be impossible to conceal their objective anyway, once they reached the island. They would have to stay on the ship as there was nowhere they could safely be put ashore. At least it was certain these people were no agents of Dhal.

'I must explain,' he began, 'that a state of war exists in the South Share of our land . . .'

It was the last free cabin on the *Merrow*, and cramped with the four of them inside, but at least it afforded a measure of privacy. They stacked their packs in a corner and sat on the narrow bunks. Even Shannon and Monadno seemed to feel the need to think quietly for a moment, while Ivanov was scowling fiercely at the timber bulkhead. For herself, Jen Komati felt her head would burst with the effort of trying to take in the improbable story they had just been told. War with a magician! A quest for a mythical relic! Yet the image of that leprechaun sitting at the table calmly smoking his pipe kept floating before her eyes. Then there was the dwarf and the elf and the sea people (she could hardly make herself use the word mermaid). If they had been the most grotesque aliens they would have been easier to accept. But these were humans. Or rather, they were *not* humans. Eight hundred years of isolation could not have caused such changes to the original colonists, but where else could they have come from?

'Are those freaks out there for real?' Monadno said at length, giving vent to his mounting exasperation.

'They certainly appear to be corporeal enough,' observed Ivanov.

'But elves and mermaids from fairy tales! It's got to be a con. I mean, hasn't it?' Jen was surprised to see the fear and resentment in his eyes. His icy professionalism and nerve, so evident while piloting the lander, seemed to have deserted him. It was a form of xenophobia, she suspected. 'I remember,' he continued, 'that there used to

155

be a fashion for people changing themselves like that fifty years ago. Maybe that's what's going on here.'

'Body-bepple,' Ivanov confirmed. 'But it was largely abandoned after the city riots. It had unexpected side effects. It also needs a level six culture to support it at a minimum, lieutenant, and this is at best level three.'

'What about,' said Jen, forcing herself to think reasonably, 'the planetary energy field? It's operating on some unusual frequencies. Prolonged exposure could lead to genetic instability.'

'There might be a slight increased incidence of mutation,' agreed Ivanov, 'but it could hardly explain both the diverse and particular nature of the humanoid species we have seen. All we can say is that it cannot be chance they resemble such mythological types as they do.'

Jen sighed. She hadn't really believed the possibility either, but she was trying to cling to at least a semblance of rationality. The alternatives were too wildly improbable to consider.

'It doesn't matter,' said Shannon firmly. They all turned to him. He was looking resolute and certain once again. 'We're not here to study the indigenous population. If what we're after has anything to do with these changes, we'll investigate that later.'

From an inside pocket of his survival suit, he withdrew a waterproof wallet, took out a map of the planetary energy field patterns and laid it on the floor between them. 'Look,' he pointed, 'we're about here, heading for what they call the Shadow Isles, where they think some sort of ancient artefact is hidden. But, on one of the islands we had already plotted a steady point source node within a discontinuity in the energy flow. I even considered it as a secondary target briefly, but dismissed it because it was not showing any activity. But if the locals also think there's something there, something powerful, then it's worth looking at.'

'But they say they need it for use against this wizard,' Jen protested. 'He has hostages –'

'They are not our concern, Komati. Your sworn loyalty is to the Empire, remember that. Our mission takes priority over everything else, understand?' His eyes blazed with absolute conviction and determination. They were not easy to defy.

Jen nodded dumbly.

'That reminds me,' said Monadno, cooler again now they had put the matter of the mutations to one side, 'what about this Doctor and his friend? Curious thing, other offworlders turning up here just before we did. And they also seem pretty keen to go after this Helm thing.'

'But the Doctor's granddaughter is one of the hostages,' Jen said. 'Of course he wants to find the Helm if he thinks it will help her.'

Shannon regarded her with barely concealed contempt. 'Use your brains, Komati. That's just what he told us she is. It could be a trick to get in with the locals.' Jen marvelled, appalled at the paranoiac twists of his thought processes. 'We'll watch them with the rest,' he continued. 'They must not be allowed to interfere with our objective. If this Helm, or anything found with it, is associated with the energy field, then we must be able to study it first. That is a priority.'

With an effort, Jen replied moderately: 'I don't see the locals letting us take it quite as easily as that. Our weapons don't work here, remember?'

Shannon allowed himself a thin smile. 'I had allowed for that possibility. We will be able to back up our demands with whatever force is necessary if we need to. By then we should also be able to call down any additional support from up top.' He glanced at his watch almost by reflex, then cursed sharply. The shockproof, waterproof, immensely accurate, immensely rugged sliver of micro electronics on his wrist was dead. So was everybody else's.

Jen could forgive his oversight. Watches were so reliable and ubiquitous you never thought about them failing. But whatever it was about Avalon had affected them too. She wondered how long it had taken. Did they

157

fail when the lander systems went down, or did they last longer? It would have been useful to know.

'Hey, Captain,' exclaimed Monadno, 'the Doctor and his friend were wearing some kind of antique watches, weren't they?'

'So?' Shannon snapped, still angry with himself for not anticipating the problem.

'So their old mechanical watches were still working. I saw the Doctor pull out that fat pendulum on a chain to check it.'

'An interesting observation,' agreed Ivanov.

'More than that. It looks like they came prepared, doesn't it? But they said they landed here by accident.'

Shannon's eyes narrowed. 'Maybe we're all after the same thing. But we must get it first!'

Barbara was able to speak with Gramling after the evening meal, as they walked back to their rooms. She asked politely, with due deference and apologies for any inconvenience, if she might look at the books he used into his own researches into the Helm. And was there anything about the origins of magic in his collection, while they were on the subject.

'Of course, Lady Barbara,' he replied, with absent-minded amiability, 'I shan't be needing them again. They are all there, indexed and cross referenced . . .' Then he paused, blinking, with the oddest expression on his face. 'No. I am sorry, I should not have said that. It will not be – appropriate for you to see them.'

'But why not?' Barbara exclaimed in bewilderment. 'How can it hurt? I may find something useful. I know I'm not an expert, but a fresh mind, a different point of view; it might help.'

'I'm sorry,' said the old wizard stiffly, 'but it is simply not permissible.'

'But how can it do any harm? You know my reasons. Look, forget what I said about magic. I'll just look at anything to do with the Helm.'

'I should have made myself clear,' said Gramling, with iron in his words. 'It is not possible for you to look at any of those books.'

Barbara set her clenched fists on her hips angrily. 'Well why on earth not?'

'Because I have burnt them all, that's why!' And he stomped off, his staff clicking on the flagstones.

The most inconspicuous spot on the *Merrow* at night was in the shadows by the rail of the mid-deck. Here Shannon waited silently until the cluster of lights that marked the orbiting starships rose into view over the horizon. Then he took a heavy, torch-like object from his pocket, held it out over the rail well clear of his body, and pulled back a sliding switch. The dome covering the end snapped open. Keeping the torch pointing at the cluster of lights he began tapping his thumb rapidly on a second button switch. After several minutes he closed the end of the device. From another pocket he withdrew a thick pair of goggles which he put on, continuing to stare fixedly at the spacefleet. After a minute, he used the torch again briefly. Then, replacing torch and goggles, he slipped silently back through the door that led to his cabin.

In their own cabin, the Doctor and Ian were still talking even though the light was out.

'I don't trust that man Shannon,' said Ian flatly. 'He and his party are up to something much more important than tracking down lost spacecraft.'

'Regrettably, I must agree with you, Chesterton. The trouble is, we don't know exactly what. They were certainly concealing something earlier. You noted that Shannon grew increasingly interested as Bron told them about the Helm. He's a dangerous man. As loyal and committed to his own cause as Sir Bron is to his.'

'Well it's obvious that thirtieth century weapons don't work here, and Shannon's party are outnumbered, so I

159

don't think they'll try to start a rough house.'

The Doctor pursed his lips. 'Nevertheless, we'll have to take care. Something about this world has caught the attention of powerful forces. But why? What are they really after?'

Nyborg and Chandry read over the transcript of Shannon's signal several times. Then they called the *Prince Randolph*'s chief engineering and weapons officers to the briefing room, together with their counterparts from the marine corps contingent. The conference lasted nearly two hours. Then the work began in earnest.

17

Into the Shadows

Shortly after dawn, the black cat trotted through the gates of Fluxford new town and made its way steadily down the long high street, skipping lightly from side to side to save its tail from cartwheels and careless feet. It trotted over the glass bridge and started up towards the castle. A dog, loping out of an alley, growled threateningly. The cat spared it one baleful flash of its eyes. The dog whined and backed away. As the cat reached the castle's outer drawbridge it slowed down, as though it was beginning to feel uneasy. Reluctantly, it crossed over with a squad of soldiers and made its way up past the confusion of the outer bailey and under the arch of the next gateway. The towers of the keep rose before it. The cat halted. For an unhappy minute it paced up and down, flicking its tail irritably. Then it hissed, backed away, and bounded out through the gate again.

In the middle of the morning, the King, Palbury and a company of knights rode slowly down through the winding streets of the old town, across the glass bridge, and along the broad high street. The people applauded and cheered warmly when they saw that the Queen accompanied the party. Barbara even received a few cheers herself, which she tried to respond to by copying the Queen's gracious wave. But most of the time she concentrated on staying upright on her horse. She had never mastered the art of riding side-saddle, and it was more difficult than it looked.

They took nearly two hours over the exercise, making a point of riding along all the main thoroughfares, and stopping several times in squares and by towers in the city walls to reassure the people and review the guards. Eventually they passed out through the city gate and across the wide green meadow where the midsummer fair was to be held. Tents and stalls were already being erected, and pitches marked out as the first of the traders and entertainers began to arrive from across the share. Some had brightly painted wagons, others led laden donkeys, and a few were simply tinkers, with all their wares in a single pack on their backs.

'It is good to see news of Dhal's activities has not turned all folk back along the roads to whence they came,' observed Sir Stephan, with a slight smile. 'Matters of business and the simple desire to enjoy oneself still prevails over his black arts.'

But for how long, thought Barbara.

They made a dutiful circuit of the field, watching the posts and rails go up to mark the jousting rings and stock pens. A large pavilion tent had been erected, inside which a long table had been laid. Here the party sat down to their luncheon. It could hardly be called a carefree picnic, but Barbara felt better for having got out of the castle. She was beginning to feel stuffy working in the library. Besides, she wanted time to think after Gramling's surprising revelation the previous night. The King also seemed to feel the exercise had been a good idea, as far as strengthening the populace's morale was concerned, and thanked her for her participation. Watching the royal couple, Barbara thought they were displaying as much ease and good-natured resolve as could be expected in the circumstances. She wondered how much effort such a front took to maintain. There were moments, as she caught the Queen's unguarded expression, when she thought she knew.

After the meal, the party walked about the field once more on foot, gathering quite a crowd, as some people had decided to follow the royal example and leave the shelter of the city walls. Barbara saw several well dressed couples carefully placing themselves in the path of the royal party, then bowing low with the deepest of reverence. Barbara smiled at the ingratiating tactics of transparent social climbers, which were, even in the thirtieth century, apparently still going strong.

And then, on the edge of the crowd, she saw Susan.

The bank of fog stretched for miles across the *Merrow*'s course. Its cold grey wreaths contrasted strangely with the blue sky. Oddly, the steady wind, which had been their constant attendant all through the voyage, seemed to have no effect on it. They sailed on. The sky grew duller, and the sun faded to a murky orange ball. Ian, standing on the foredeck, shivered, pulled his quilted jerkin more tightly about him, and made his way aft. As he crossed the mid-deck, he passed Bron, Alammar and Thurguld, who were standing alertly by the rail, weapons resting beside them at the ready. Ian touched the handle of his own sheathed sword, which Bron had given him, and wondered if he would have to use it. Komati and Ivanov, he noticed, were leaning on the opposite rail, staring out into the grey murk. Komati gave him a slight, uncertain smile.

From the helm, Tristram ordered the sails to be reefed and the oars to be unshipped. To the accompaniment of the regular wash of water over blades, they edged into the greyness. Visibility shrank to a few yards beyond the prow. The tops of the masts were invisible. The grey fang of an upthrust rock glided past and was lost in the fog again. If it had not been for the guidance of the mermen they would hardly have dared move in such conditions. Even with their help, Tristram had a crewman taking regular depth soundings with a lead-weighted line.

A table had been set up beside the wheel displaying charts of the islands, such as they were, together with Gramling's own maps and other items he had provided to help them reach their goal. The Doctor was bending over

163

it, while Odoyle held up a flat piece of metal shaped like a fish, suspended from a piece of thread. As he swung it to and fro it twisted to point almost directly ahead, rather like a compass needle. The leprechaun took note of the direction that the fish's head was pointing in and consulted with the others, who checked the charts and nodded. The Shadow Isles were surrounded by a ring of small islets and treacherous reefs, through which there were few known clear channels. Hopefully they were heading for one of them.

Standing to one side of the navigators, watching the proceedings with keen, if suspicious, interest, were Shannon and Monadno. Ian was wondering whether it was worth trying to make conversation, when there came a call from the man on the prow, and a relayed message from the mermen. Tristram adjusted their course slightly and slowed the stroke rate. Ian became aware of a deeper, darker greyness to either side of them, and the sound of sluggish waves breaking languidly against rocks. More instructions came from the mermen and the course was changed again. As *Merrow* glided on it grew darker. He realized they were in the channel now, moving between the sheer cliffs of two close-set islets.

All seemed peaceful, if rather gloomy, at first. But gradually the weight of the unseen rock faces seemed to press in on him. He felt the hairs of the back of his neck begin to lift. A dreadful sense of anticipation began to steal over him. He could see it in the eyes of the others as well. Odoyle whispered something to the Doctor, who picked up an item from the table and held it ready. Ian realized Odoyle was clasping his silver hammer. There were shouts from the water bidding them a hasty farewell, and their mermen guides were gone.

There was a distant rumbling, groaning sound. Water suddenly swirled and slapped against the hull. The rumble came again, but louder this time. Rock grated against rock. Pebbles rattled and clattered down the cliff and splashed into the water. Then with a booming roar of shattering stone, the cliff sides began to collapse on top of them.

The sight of Susan stunned Barbara, and for fully ten seconds she stood with her mouth gaping wide in astonishment, heedless of the crowd that surged around her. Recovering herself, she was about to call out, when she saw Susan put her finger to her lips in a secretive gesture, beckon to her urgently, then slip away between the stalls. Bemusedly, Barbara looked around, realized she had fallen behind the main party and nobody was paying her much attention for the moment, and followed.

She emerged on the other side of the stalls to find Susan was already running lightly towards the trees on the edge of the field. Barbara realized she was still wearing her white nightdress, making her a distinctive figure. Susan ran past one of the guards patrolling between the fair and the woods, but he seemed to take no notice of her. Barbara hesitated uncertainly. Susan turned and beckoned her on again. Barbara picked up her skirts and ran after her, still confused but convinced, for some reason, that she must not lose sight of her. Thankfully her leg seemed to have stopped aching. She also passed close by the patrolling guard. He glanced over curiously, then his attention seemed to slide past. Susan disappeared between the trees and a moment later so did Barbara.

'Row lads, row!' yelled Tristram as the rocks began to rain down. The men heaved on their long oars. Crashing boulders threw up plumes of spray, the impacts sending the *Merrow* tossing and pitching in the waves. Odoyle gestured upwards with his hammer. There was a blaze of light, and a huge mass of toppling rock that threatened to crush them was dashed to one side. The Doctor leaned over the stern rail and threw the object Odoyle had given him into the seething waters.

There was a rush of bubbles and the water rose beneath the *Merrow*'s stern, bulging upward as though a monstrous wave was being born in the narrow channel. The deck tilted crazily and everybody staggered to remain on their feet. Even as the *Merrow* started to slide down the liquid slope, the huge swell rolled forward through the collapsing canyon, bursting against the rock sides and throwing breakers back at them, carrying the ship along with it oars akimbo, sheets flapping in the sudden blast of displaced air and shreds of fog as the ship was practically thrown out from under the falling cliffs. Ian, clinging to a rigging line, had one brief crazy image of the ship skimming the wave tops like a misshapen surfboard. Then they burst out of the canyon into open waters once more. The tumult of crashing rocks behind the *Merrow* subsided. The wave they rode collapsed into a thousand lesser wavelets and a tracery of spreading foam, leaving the ship bobbing gently to rest.

Kilvenny Odoyle dusted off his knees and straightened his hat. 'Just like a merry ride on the Dellberry,' he commented mildly.

'What *was* that?' Ian asked.

'A token containing an imprisoned water elemental, apparently,' explained the Doctor, also regaining his feet. 'Gramling thought it might come in handy, and it seemed he was proved right, wouldn't you say?'

Ian caught sight of the expressions on the faces of Shannon and Monadno. They were looking at the Doctor and especially Odoyle. Cynical curiosity had been replaced, if only briefly, by a measure of awed respect. There's nothing like a brush with death to make a believer out of one, Ian thought.

The trees, interspersed with tracks and clearings, gradually thickened into denser woods. Susan continued to dance on lightly ahead of her, ignoring Barbara's occasional cries to stop and talk. Every so often she would pause to put her finger to her lips again, and beckon her on. Try as she might, Barbara could not get closer than ten yards. At least her leg was holding up, she thought

166

again. And she herself was running strongly. Actually, now that she came to think about it, she felt curiously detached from any strain, moving with a slightly dream-like quality. There was a lingering notion in the back of her mind that she shouldn't have left the field without telling someone, but that was rapidly buried under the overwhelming desire to catch Susan. She had to catch Susan.

They ran on.

The wall of fog fell away behind them. The sky brightened a little, and a light wind picked up, filling the *Merrow*'s sails and giving the rowers their rest. On the horizon were the smudges that marked the positions of the central isles of the group. The metal fish in Odoyle's hands, which Gramling had sensitized to the nullifying field surrounding the isle, pointed towards them. Ian could feel the unease of the crew, but Tristram kept them busy with their tasks and stood by the wheel with fatalistic determination, waiting to see what would come next. Ian had by now heard enough of the stories about the isles to know that falling rocks were only one of its hazards. On the mid-deck he saw Shannon's crew conversing in a huddle. He wondered what the spacemen and scientists were making of life on the seas of Avalon.

He became aware of a steadily growing roaring sound.

There was a yell from the forward lookout: 'Rough waters ahead!' Followed a moment later by: 'Whirlpool Captain! Whirlpool dead ahead!'

Barbara had no sense of time left. The sun was lost in the trees and she did not notice its movement. All she could do was keep on running after the ever elusive Susan, deeper and deeper into the forest. She was vaguely aware that her dress was being torn by the brambles, and that what she was doing did not actually, at some fundamental level, make sense. But by now it seemed impossible to stop. She thought Susan was beginning to show signs of tiredness, and several times she appeared to be talking to someone Barbara couldn't see. Then she ran on again. But however much her footsteps dragged, Barbara could not catch her.

The keep of Fluxford castle would have disappeared in the whirlpool. Before they could change their course the current had them, dragging the *Merrow* into the long spiral that could only end in the plunge down the curving wall of water to the booming blue and purple depths. The growing thunder made speech all but impossible. The crew frantically tore at the water with their oars, but they could only slow the inevitable. They saw a huge rotted tree trunk protrude from the wall as it spiralled down and was gone. A school of fish leaped high in the air in their desperate bid to swim clear. A ghastly paralysis seemed to take hold of them as they edged inexorably over the funnel edge of the maelstrom and looked down into a pit of darkness. Incongruously, Ian noticed there was a rainbow sparkling in the spray, arched perfectly over the vortex of death.

At last she saw Susan slow down and stop, panting; bending over to clasp her hands to her knees. They were in a hollow between the trunks of some massive trees, far taller than any Barbara had yet seen. It began to impinge upon her how gloomy it all seemed. Then her leg began to hurt. She realized she was panting herself, gasping for air in fact. A stitch stabbed her side. Suddenly her legs felt as if they were on fire. How far had she run? Where was she? Her torn dress was stained with sweat. A red mist tinted her vision and she sank to her knees. 'Susan . . .' she croaked, through a parched and raw throat. She saw a puzzled Susan appear to look right through her.

Then she faded away into nothing.

For a second Barbara gazed in horror at the place Susan had stood. Then unnaturally suppressed exhaustion claimed her and she collapsed unconscious to the forest floor.

Odoyle sang.

> 'Rainbow of light, beauteous and clear,
> Carry us on your ray,
> Vision's delight, spare us from fear,
> Fashion a smoother way,
> Wondrous sight,
> Shimmering bright,
> Carry this bark away.'

Over the roar of the whirlpool his words should really not have been audible, but somehow they were. Ian thought the tune sounded a little like the *Skye Boat Song*.

And the rainbow over the funnel of cascading water changed.

It turned about and laid down on its side and unbowed. One end seemed to swoop towards them as they swung around the pit. Suddenly they were no longer riding on water, but on a sparkling bridge of light that arched over the depths and carried them, awestruck and silent, half a mile clear of the turbulent waters before setting the *Merrow* gently down again. And all the while, Odoyle kept singing.

Then, when they were safely clear, he collapsed to the deck, his tiny body making a peculiarly pathetic bundle, so different from the vitality he radiated normally. The Doctor was by his side in two quick strides, kneeling down to examine the little wizard.

'He's passed out,' he concluded rapidly. 'The effort of sustaining the spell must have been tremendous. Let's take him down to the cabin. I'm sure all he needs is some rest.'

'Thank goodness he managed as long as he did,' said Ian, carefully scooping up the leprechaun in his arms. 'Let's just hope we don't come across any other obstacles.'

'I'm very much afraid that we will encounter at least one more,' said the Doctor darkly.

'How do you know?'

'The significance of the number three,' he said mysteriously.

When Susan had recovered her breath she said angrily: 'Why are you doing this?'

She was standing in the pentagram in Dhal's chamber, with one of the ape guards just outside it with his whip trailing on the floor to ensure she co-operated. For hours, it seemed, she had been obeying a string of pointless orders; running on the spot, standing with her finger to her lips or beckoning absurdly to Dhal. The longer the strange exercises went on, the more confused she became. Half the time he seemed to be ignoring her, or had his eyes closed, or else he had been staring fixedly into his seeing globe.

Now a smile touched his lips. 'For my own purposes, naturally. And, you might say, for your friend Barbara.'

The colour drained from Susan's face, and she took a step towards Dhal only to be caught in the firm grip of the guard. 'What have you done!'

'I have been projecting your image into her mind. Nobody else could see you. With a little additional help from me, she's taken quite a long trip into the forest, from which, I fear, it is unlikely she will emerge for some days, if ever. It can be quite dangerous, you know, especially if you are lost and exhausted as she is. They will send out search parties to look for her, of course, which will be something else to keep them occupied. And serve as a useful reminder of my powers.'

He broke off, his eyes unfocusing, as though he was seeing or hearing something which she could not.

'Take her away,' he snapped abruptly, and turned once again to his desk.

It was half an hour after leaving the whirlpool that they sighted the monster.

At first, when he heard the cry of the lookout, Ian

thought it was a string of small islets off the bow. Then a monstrous head lifted clear of the water. It was the king of sea serpents. Its features were somewhat dragon-like, but there any resemblance ceased. It could have swallowed the dragon that had pursued them in the forest whole. Glassy eyes as wide as his outstretched arms swivelled to focus on them. The head was thrown back and the beast gave vent to a bellowing, moaning foghorn cry, which actually sent shivers across the waves. Then the neck arched and plunged down, and ripple after ripple of sinuous body looped after it, heading straight towards them.

'A kraken! Break out the harpoons!' yelled Tristram to the terrified crew. It was a futile gesture, as though harpoons would mean anything more than pinpricks to a beast of that size. But they obeyed. Bron also seized one, as did Thurguld and Alammar.

'Aim for the eyes!' Ian heard him shout.

Beside him, the Doctor rummaged amongst the magical artifacts Gramling had supplied. Odoyle was still recovering in his cabin.

'Will one of them help?' gasped Ian.

'I don't know!' the Doctor snapped back. 'Their functions have not been explained in full.'

'Well make a guess, Doctor. We've got nothing to lose!'

The Doctor snatched one of the items up at random. 'That is precisely what I was going to do!' He ran to the ship's rail.

The kraken's head erupted from the sea not thirty yards away, water cascading from its body as it rose up. And up. Ian felt his neck crick as the thing towered over them. One blow from the beast would shatter the *Merrow* to matchwood! A harpoon bounced futilely from its scales. The Doctor swung back his arm to throw the magical token –

A pale pink tentacle as thick as a tree trunk whipped up out of the water and coiled about the kraken. A second

171

followed it, coiling the other way. The kraken roared and plunged its great head down into the water after its new enemy. For a moment it disappeared from their sight under the boiling swell. Then its sinuous scaled body burst forth again. But now it twisted and arched in mortal combat, held within the horrible embrace of a nest of writhing tentacles.

'Some form of giant squid, or octopus!' the Doctor shouted above the breaking waters.

The sea exploded as the two behemoths fought. A shower of spray drenched the *Merrow*. Surging waves threw the ship on to its beam ends. Tristram yelled orders and spun the wheel, trying to steer them clear. Men slipped and staggered across the pitching decks to deploy the oars once more, pulling with all their strength. The tip of a huge tentacle lashed across the ship's side, snapping an oar and tearing away ten feet of rail. Two crewmen were knocked halfway across the deck by the blow, while a third, crushed against the shattered timbers, crumpled and fell over the side and vanished under the surging waters. Through the sheets of water and billows of spray thrown up by the titanic struggle, Ian glimpsed a pale, sack-like body as big as the *Merrow* fastened to the underbelly of the kraken by its many-suckered arms. He saw the flash of a huge, startlingly human eye, and a great beak, like a parrot's, snapping and tearing into the serpent's flesh. The foam began to run pink and red, even as the kraken caught a loop of tentacle between its jaws and severed it with one bite.

An oar from the other side was brought across to replace the one that had been lost. Thurguld's axe cut away the debris, allowing it to be crudely lashed into place. Bron and Alammar threw down their harpoons and helped pull on it. Ian saw Komati at the side of one of the injured crewmen, applying an emergency bandage from her suit's medical pack to a deep wound on the man's arm. After a moment's hesitation, Ivanov helped her. Shannon and Monadno stood alert but uncertain by their salvaged dinghy which had been lashed to the middle of the deck. Another tentacle flailed close to the ship. Monadno reached into an inside pocket, but Shannon stayed his hand.

Gradually, painfully slowly, the *Merrow* began to draw away from the incredible conflict.

Then, with a clash of waves, the two beasts submerged again, leaving only spreading rings of foam to show where they had been, and the occasional uneasy upwelling of water to tell that the mortal combat continued into the depths, which could only result in the death of one or both of the monsters.

With the sun dipping in the east, the *Merrow* limped onward.

It was almost totally dark under the trees when Barbara awoke from her exhausted sleep. The glow of sunset was so filtered by the lofty forest canopy, that night already seemed to be creeping out of the shadows all around her. With an effort she sat up, and began massaging life back into her aching limbs, looking anxiously about as she did so. For the moment, however, bitter anger was keeping fear at bay. It had to be Dhal who lured her out here, she realized, there was no other explanation for what she had seen. Or rather, thought she had seen. How he had induced her to run so far without tiredness she did not know, but she had to admit it was a cunning way of making somebody lose themselves. Because she was certainly very lost. In fact, her recollections of entering the woods were so confused, that she was not even certain which way Fluxford lay.

A pale shape flitted silently through the trees, making her start in fright. Then she heard an owl hoot, and relaxed again. But she knew the forests of Avalon contained far more dangerous things than owls. She had to find some more secure shelter for the night, and quickly while there was still some light left. Climbing a tree would have been better than nothing, but the monstrous trunks surrounding her offered little chance of that. Her legs still felt like rubber, so she rolled on to her hands and knees and shuffled over to the skeletal form of a dead branch a few yards away. A minute's pushing and pulling broke off a reasonably stout stick about four feet long. Resting on it, she hauled herself to her feet. It would be her support, and means of testing the way when it got darker. And a weapon, if it came to it.

In the gloom an unidentified animal yelped in pain or fright, making her jump. There was the distant sound of pattering feet.

Stiffly, she hobbled away into the gathering darkness.

As the last molten red sliver of the sun slipped below the horizon, the *Merrow* sailed into the harbour of Helm Island. Seen close to, there could be no doubt it was the place they sought. Everybody on the ship had crowded the rails as they approached, taking in as much as possible while the light lasted.

Once it had probably been just an island like the others in the group; a rock about three miles long by one wide, rising to a summit a few thousand feet above sea level, lightly encrusted with vegetation.

Now it looked machine-made.

The contours of the old island had been preserved, but cut into five massive terraces, rising in decreasing size, in a series of perfectly vertical walls and flat plateaus, without any sign of vegetation. The base terrace rose sheerly from the sea for two hundred feet before turning a precise forty-five degree chamfered edge to form the first plateau. The second terrace rose even higher, as did the third. The only visible link between each level was a staggered series of single, soaring, impossibly slender free-spanning arches. They sparkled like glass, and Ian was reminded of the bridge at Fluxford. On the lowest arch they could just make out the fine divisions of steps. It would be a long climb to the top.

Each stairway had an odd detail. Halfway up it pierced

the centre of a vertical disc of glass that entirely surrounded the arch structure. The image struck Ian as being disturbingly familiar, and it took him a moment to recall where he had seen it before. Copper discs were slotted over the mooring ropes of ships in dock to prevent rats climbing up them to get on board. Yet, there would be no point in the incredible stairways if there was not some way through or round the obstructions. Perhaps they would discover it when they climbed them, for that was obviously the way to their goal.

The top of the highest precipice forming the apex of the island was not flat, but curved smoothly into a regular dome-like cap, perhaps two hundred yards across. As the last rays of sunlight touched the dome, they could see it sparkle through great slotted windows in its sides. Clearly it served as the repository for something of great importance.

Without some means of aerial transport, even making a landing on the lowest level would have been next to impossible, had it not been for the discovery of a narrow inlet, just a hundred yards deep, which cut into one end of the island forming a sheltered, if rather claustrophobic anchorage. At its head was a wide glass staircase rising up to the first terrace. Here they dropped anchor.

'We will begin our ascent at sunrise,' declared Bron. 'We need a few hours rest to prepare ourselves for the climb. In any case, such a task would best be undertaken in daylight.'

Tristram looked uneasy. 'That, er . . . that would not be all of us, Sir Knight? I mean, someone's got to stay with the ship. To keep it safe, that is.'

'I do not believe there will be any further physical threats to your ship, Captain,' the Doctor assured him. 'I suspect the only tests we now have to pass are purely immaterial ones.'

Bron smiled. 'In any case, you will not be required for the journey, Captain. That is the task of the chosen seekers.'

175

'What about us?' said Shannon.

The Imperial party had been keeping so much to themselves over the last few hours that Ian had almost forgotten about them. Now he realized Shannon had been taking a keen interest in everything that had been going on.

'What do you mean?' Bron asked.

'We came here to find out what caused our ships to crash over the years. Maybe this Helm of yours has something to do with it. We have a duty to find out.'

'The Helm can have nothing to do with such events.'

'It won't matter if we have a look at it, then.'

Bron scrutinized him closely for a moment. 'You may look,' he said at length, 'but you understand it is destined to serve a vital purpose elsewhere. There can be no delay in returning with it.'

'I understand,' said Shannon crisply, and walked stiffly away.

Bron turned to Ian and the Doctor. Alammar and Thurguld, who had been listening, also drew closer.

'He is not telling all that he knows,' the knight said softly. The others nodded. 'I agreed that his party should accompany us because I would rather have him where he can be watched. Take care. As he reminds us, he too has his duty to perform, and I think he is a man who takes such obligation seriously.'

18

Stairway

There was a dreadful brooding presence in the forest. Barbara could feel it as she stumbled blindly on, her dress torn, her legs scratched and bruised by several falls. It felt like an amalgam of all her worst fears and nightmares, coalescing and taking tangible form, ready to creep up behind her. She kept twisting round to see it, but there was nothing there, just the ever present imminence of the thing. It was that fear, more than anything else, that drove her on. After the first hour she had given up hope of finding any shelter, and now she only staggered on because of what would happen if she stopped and *it* caught up with her.

In what remained of the light from Guinevere's Veil and the shimmer of the aurora, after it had filtered down through the branches, she saw the recumbent form of a fallen tree. It was a good eight feet thick. Might it be hollow? Cautiously, she probed about between its splayed roots. Yes, the heartwood had rotted away. Dizzy with relief, she started to edge inside. Then she became aware of a warm, animal scent. Four pairs of eyes flicked open in the darkness. There was a shrill chattering. Barbara scrambled out of the hollow in alarm, tripped over a straggling root and fell heavily. The stooping, bulbous-headed form of a cephlie emerged from the tree to jabber angrily at her for a minute, before seeming to lose interest and slouch back into its shelter again.

'Please – let me in,' Barbara begged. 'I won't hurt you.' She tried edging closer to the entrance again. There was more shrill chattering, and the cephlies began to throw

177

small sticks and twigs at her. Wretchedly, she stumbled away again into the darkness.

At some point not long after this, though whether it was five minutes or an hour she could no longer tell, she slipped down an unexpected bank and fell into a small, muddy stream. For a moment she sat there in the water without the strength to pull herself out, feeling more miserable, desperate and frightened than she could ever recall. Surely things couldn't get any worse.

Then she heard the light patter of paws, and a snuffling, panting noise. With a stifled gasp she dragged herself out of the stream, up the shallow bank, and pressed herself into the shadow of the nearest tree. Dimly she saw a pale form lope across a tiny clearing not thirty yards away. Closer to she thought she saw the glow of red eyes. Then there was another flicker of movement through the trees, and another. The snuffling, rustling sound grew louder. She turned and ran. An urgent howl rang out in the darkness and with the patter of many feet the wolf pack followed her.

Even as she ran for her life, Barbara knew she was only postponing the inevitable. Unless she could find some sort of cover there was no escape. Desperately, she lunged upward in an attempt to grab the lowest of the overhanging branches, but it was far beyond her reach. She staggered, nearing the end of her strength, and half fell into the best shelter she could find, which was the hollow between two massive splayed tree roots. Grasping her stick firmly, she turned to face the pack. Half a dozen pairs of feral eyes gleamed at her as the wolves fanned out before the tree. She waved the stick at them and shouted, but they edged closer. The boldest one, the leader, gathered itself to spring.

Then came an incredibly shrill and furious cry.

A small dark form streaked out of the night, leaped and fastened itself on to the lead wolf's head in a spitting, screeching ball of teeth and claws. The wolf howled in pain, rolling about and clawing at his small tormentor, while the rest of the pack drew back in surprise. Then the creature sprang clear and the wolf, whimpering in pain, staggered away. The pack growled at the intruder, pawing the ground uncertainly. The creature hissed back at them, whipping its tail to and fro, as though daring them to challenge it. Slowly, with a few unhappy whines, the pack drew back into the shadows and was gone.

The creature turned to Barbara, and she realized for the first time that it was a large black cat. She also saw why the wolves had been afraid of it. Its eyes were yellow, but not the reflected yellow of an ordinary cat's. Its eyes actually *glowed*, as though lit from within. They also seemed uncomfortably intelligent. She half raised her stick again as it approached her, but it merely rubbed itself about her legs in a polite manner, purring fiercely. Then it walked away a few steps and turned back to look at her questioningly.

'You want me to follow you, don't you?' asked Barbara, too dazed by shock and relief to care if she sounded foolish. If the cat had answered back she wouldn't have been surprised.

It contented itself merely with purring again, but with a new, distinctly satisfied rhythm. *At last*, it seemed to say.

Jen was roused by Monadno's hand on her shoulder. She blinked awake to find he and Shannon were already dressed, while Ivanov was putting his outer coverall over the lighter crewsuits they had been sleeping in.

'Suit up and bring your basic pack,' Monadno said softly.

Jen found herself obeying while still half asleep. 'What's happening? I thought we were waiting for dawn?'

'They are, we're not,' Shannon said simply.

'It makes sense,' Ivanov explained reasonably. 'These people can have no idea what they have here, with all their talk of mythological fantasies. We must examine this

179

Helm first to see what it really is. It might be the key to everything.' His thin face flushed with excitement.

'This island is no fairy tale,' added Shannon. 'And it wasn't chiselled away by hand, either. It was built with advanced technology to shelter something important in that dome on the summit, and make it damned hard to reach. If I'd looked closer at the recon photos I might have given it a higher priority.'

'Maybe that storm wasn't so unlucky after all,' Monadno speculated.

'Maybe. Now we're here, we're going to find out exactly where that energy point source is coming from. All ready?'

He blew out the lantern, and quietly opened the door.

There was no reply to her knocking at the door of the tiny, ramshackle cottage that huddled in the heart of the forest. The cat wove impatiently about Barbara's ankles. She tried the latch, which opened stiffly, and the door swung open with a slight squeak. The cat brushed past her and trotted inside.

'Hallo,' she called out uncertainly. 'Is there anyone there?'

There was no reply. She could hear the cat purring impatiently in the darkness, so she stepped gingerly inside. All she could see was the faint glow of light coming through two small lead latticed windows. After a moment her eyes adjusted, and she made out a table set before one of them, on which stood a half burned candle. Beside it was something she had become familiar with in the last few days: a metal tinderbox. She felt her way over to the table across a flagstoned floor, opened the box, and fumbled with the flint and striker. After a few showers of sparks, she managed to get the cup of dry moss glowing redly, touched the candle wick to it and blew until it caught. Yellow light flooded the small room.

And Barbara found herself staring straight into the face

of an old woman in an apron and black dress, sitting stiffly beside the table.

'Prepare yourselves!' said Bron, putting his head round the door of the Doctor and Ian's cabin after a peremptory knock.

'What's the matter?' said Ian blearily, throwing back his covers.

'The watchmen have been struck down and Shannon's company are missing. They must have gone after the Helm.'

'The fools,' exclaimed the Doctor, already hurriedly dressing, 'they cannot imagine the power that might lie in that dome. We must stop them before it is too late!'

She was not dead, as Barbara had first thought. Her skin was cool, but not cold, and her breathing incredibly shallow; no more than three a minute, she estimated. If it was sleep, then it was so deep that nothing Barbara could do would wake her. How long had she been like this? There was an outline in the dust on the table where Barbara moved one of the woman's hands aside. Her arm felt stiff, though not with the rigidity of rigor mortis. Was it a stroke, or was it some kind of seizure? An epileptic fit, perhaps? Barbara realized the cat was playing with something underneath the table. It suddenly rolled out into the light. Barbara picked it up. It was an apple with one bite taken out of it. She looked about her and saw a basket of similar apples on a tiny kitchen dresser. It suddenly made her realize how hungry and thirsty she was.

'I'm going to try to make you comfortable,' she said, just in case the old woman was aware but unable to respond. 'But I'm terribly hungry, so if I could just have a drink and a bite of something first.' She took a step towards the dresser. The cat gave a low, moaning yowl. She took another step and it bounded across the floor, sprang up on to the dresser and stood guard over the apples, hissing.

'Look, I'm going to do what I can for her, but I need to eat too –' she frowned, then went back to the bitten apple she had left on the table. Unless somebody had just dropped it, it must have been lying on the floor for days. If so, why wasn't it rotten? On an impulse, she gently prised the woman's jaws apart. There was a sliver of apple resting on her tongue. She pulled it out. The old woman seemed to relax slightly, settling less stiffly in her chair. A slight sigh whispered from her lips.

Barbara decided not to eat an apple after all.

Ian had never seen such a perfectly flat surface as the island's lower terrace. The grey pre-dawn light only emphasized its strangeness. With the sheer walls of the next level rising above them, and the dome-topped tower of the last level above that, it reminded him of a vast plaza skirting the base of a skyscraper, except the surface they were crossing was not paved. Something had cut through the living rock like the proverbial knife through butter, leaving it so smooth as to be almost slippery. He began to appreciate the vast forces that had shaped this place.

'Come on, Chesterton,' said the Doctor impatiently. 'We've got to catch them up!'

He followed on after the Doctor, Bron, Alammar and Thurguld. Kilvenny Odoyle had remained on the *Merrow*, still recovering from his exertions over the whirlpool. 'In any case, my skills are no good here,' he admitted, a blanket still wrapped about him, puffing away at a restorative pipe. 'Can you not feel the power of the place?' Now, striding along towards the base of the first staircase, Ian realized he could. It was not an entirely pleasant sensation.

Seen up close by the light of their lantern, the staircase seemed to be made of exactly the same material as the glass bridge. It was ten feet wide, with no hand rail, only a low coping running along either side of the steps. He looked up at the transparent arch, soaring up unsupported for over five hundred feet, rising at about fifty degrees at first, then arching over to touch the lip of the second terrace. A spot of light glimmered far up the arch above them. Shannon's party had already passed the first of the mid-point discs.

Without a word, they started up, the Doctor showing his usual vigour by setting a brisk pace. Ian did not think they could maintain such a rate, however. How many steps had they to go? Assuming they had to climb twenty-five hundred feet, and each step was about eight inches high, that would be three thousand seven hundred and fifty steps. At an ideal steady two steps a second, that would mean over thirty minutes continuous climbing. He guessed it would be more like forty-five minutes to an hour in practice.

They pressed on. Already he thought he could feel the tendons along the back of his legs begin to ache.

With an effort, and taking several rests, Barbara managed to half drag, half carry the old woman upstairs to the cottage's single bedroom, and made her as comfortable as possible in the narrow wooden frame bed she found there. The cat watched the procedure intently, with apparent approval.

By the time dawn was colouring the sky, she had a fire going in the kitchen hearth, water drawn from the hand pump outside the back door, and had a soup heating in a pot made from the vegetables she had to hand. Even if the old woman couldn't take any yet, Barbara felt she needed something substantial herself. The only other food she had found was hard bread and cheese in a cupboard, which had done little to satisfy her. While the soup warmed she sat in the old woman's kitchen rocking chair and wondered what to do next.

She had to let the others know she was all right as soon as possible. They would probably be making some kind of search for her, of course, but that would take up valuable time and manpower that could be better spent strengthening the castle's defences. Maybe that was why she had been lured away. It added to the confusion and uncertainty even more than an outright killing, which, presumably, Dhal could have quite easily arranged. He was playing games with them, and Barbara didn't like being used as a pawn.

She had noticed a faint path leading away from the cottage when she had gone out for water. Presumably it led somewhere. Even if she was ten miles from Fluxford, she should reach it if she set out early enough. She didn't like the thought of another walk in the forest, but at least it would be light. In any case, she felt she had to tell someone about the old woman. And the apples. Did they have any part in the overall scheme of things, or were they just coincidental? She wondered vaguely if anything that happened on Avalon was truly coincidental . . .

It was at this point that she fell asleep.

She was woken by the sound of soup boiling over and the smell of burning as it put out the fire.

The first of the glass discs was even more impressive seen close to. It was over twenty-five feet across, and would have been almost impossible to climb round. There was a hole in its centre large enough for one person to pass through at a time. But as they stood on the steps below the portal, massaging their calves, they hesitated. They could all feel the aura of power surrounding it, pressing at the edge of their consciousness.

Are you determined? Are you worthy? Is your cause true?

They knew it would be impossible to pass through unless they could answer those unspoken challenges honestly.

Bron look resolute. 'I am here on a noble and just mission for my King and country,' he said boldly. 'I do not fear to carry on.' And he stepped through the portal. One by one the others followed.

Ahead of them, Shannon's party had reached the second terrace.

* * *

'I've made her as comfortable as I can, and now I'm going to get help, do you understand?' The cat continued to stare at Barbara with feline inscrutability and did nothing to indicate whether it approved or not.

'I've left this window hooked open, you see, so you can get in and out if you need to.' The cat tilted its head as it took in her explanation. She was beginning to suspect the animal of condescension. 'And the fire's banked up and I've put the guard around it,' she finished, determinedly. 'And now I'm going. I should be back before dark, or at least somebody will, I hope.'

The cat padded up to her, brushed around her legs for a moment, then trotted away and bounded up the cottage's tiny twisted stairs. And that is goodbye, she thought. She let herself quietly out of the door, closed it firmly behind her, took a deep breath and set off along the path that snaked away between the great trees.

It was as they began the ascent of the last stairway, the tallest and steepest, that they saw Shannon's group pause at the portal disc. They had gained slightly on them during the ascent, but they were still tiny figures, several hundred feet above. Now they saw them milling about in some confusion. Then three of the party passed through the portal and continued up towards the summit, while one sat down on the stairs; even at this distance, the posture communicating every sign of weary dejection.

The last portal had defeated Jen Komati. Whatever mental field the structures generated had become stronger each time, testing her resolve and belief beyond endurance. There was a limit, she discovered, to her sense of duty, loyalty to the Empire, and fear of Shannon's wrath. It was a joke, really. Even he couldn't force her through. It was hardly the place to start a struggle, and he had no time to stage a court-martial, or whatever, which she knew he would have preferred. He had to be content with giving her one last look of uncomprehending contempt, before passing through the portal. Neither he nor Monadno had any difficulty with that, they were armoured by their sense of duty and purpose. She suspected that if they had sheltered any secret desire to use whatever they found for themselves, the portals would not have let them pass. But that was one thing you could not have accused them of; they were true patriots of the Empire. Ivanov gave her a slightly more sympathetic glance before passing through in turn. He was protected by a different sense of duty and altruism. The quest for knowledge for its own sake, without concern for the consequences. As the mission progressed, she had seen his courage grow as he began to appreciate the scientific value of what they might find; but he seemed blind as to how it might be used in reality. Of them all, he was the one who disappointed her most. No scientist should be that certain and single minded, there should always be doubt; and now she had that in plenty.

So she sat, her head in her hands, with the rising sun making the stairway glow like fire, while their pursuers toiled up the steps towards her.

'I'm sorry,' she said miserably, as they arrived panting and moving stiffly. 'It was wrong. Whatever's in there doesn't belong to us, and it might be incredibly dangerous. I must explain –'

'Later, my dear,' said the Doctor, not unkindly. 'We must stop them if we can. You wait here.'

One by one, the party passed through the portal and continued on up towards the great dome.

'Be careful,' she called after them. 'I think Shannon and Monadno have some kind of weapons.'

Ian tried not to look down as they climbed. The view *through* the very stairs he was walking on was disconcerting. Even though he knew, intellectually, that they must be made of some incredibly strong substance, there was the nagging fear that one heavy footfall would shatter them like plain glass, and he would plunge hundreds of feet to the hard terrace below. He kept his eyes fixed ahead, where Shannon, Monadno and Ivanov kept slipping almost out of sight behind the bow of the stairs. It was ridiculous. This close they should be running after them, but the ascent up the great stairways had reduced both parties to the same rubber-legged plodding pace.

Then he saw their quarry disappear through the entrance of the dome itself. How far ahead were they? Three minutes . . . four? How long would it take them to find Merlin's Helm in the dome? Was it mounted in splendid isolation on a plinth in its very centre for all to see and pick up at will, or would it be concealed or protected in some way? He realized that all their efforts had been focused on simply getting here, and that he really had no idea of what they might find. Well, they would know soon.

The dome swelled over them, glowing warmly in the low morning sun. The stairway entered through an archway in its side, just where the sheer side of the tower that supported it began to curve over. They were twenty yards away when Monadno appeared in the archway with an old-fashioned automatic pistol in his hand.

'That's far enough,' he said.

The path seemed to peter out about half a mile from the cottage in the middle of a dell, ringed by trees hung with streamers of ivy and trailing beards of moss. There were several possible ways out, but they were hardly more than animal tracks, with no indication of which led to the nearest settlement. Barbara had not exactly been expecting a signpost, but she had hoped to strike a more substantial path by now. She shrugged, made a note of the way she had come should she need to return this way to the cottage, and set off along one of the paths. She didn't notice what appeared to be a tussock of long grass beside the path lift itself up on to spindly legs and watch her go by with bright mischievous eyes.

* * *

'You cannot hope to leave here again,' Bron called out to Monadno. 'You will be marooned. How will that aid your cause?'

'We've got rations for a few days,' came the calm reply. 'Our people in orbit are working on modified landers that will get us back up there again. There's plenty of flat ground here for them to touch down. Now, I don't want to hurt you people, so just stay clear, understand?' They hesitated for a moment, and he fired a single shot at the steps in front of them. It ricocheted off the glass leaving a splash of lead and whined away into the sky.

Bron motioned to the others, and they retreated a little way down the steps.

'I thought their weapons did not work here?' he said to the Doctor.

'They must have brought others in case of such an eventuality. These are of a far more primitive type but still deadly. They use the expanding gas from a fast burning powder to fire small metal pellets. They will penetrate ordinary armour.'

'And now they will surely take the Helm. None could resist such a prize,' he said grimly.

'But it will be of no use to them without the proper ceremony,' Alammar pointed out.

'They would not believe that if we told them so, and how long will it take them to learn the truth for themselves, after they have carried it back to their skyboats? We cannot afford any delay in returning to Fluxford.'

'Then we must act now,' growled Thurguld, unslinging his shield and clasping his axe. 'Ready your bow, Alammar, while I draw him out. The rest of you must be prepared to rush him. If I fall, tell my lord I died well.'

Ian swallowed. The dwarf's action was almost suicidal. 'Hold your shield at an angle. The bullets may glance off.'

Thurguld smiled grimly. 'Thank you, friend Ian. I will do that.' And he advanced, crouching behind his shield. It made a hard kind of sense, Ian realized. Of them all, he made the smallest target. Alammar unslung his slender elf bow and notched an arrow to the string. Bron drew his sword. Ian loosened his own sword in its scabbard, wondering if he could use it to strike down a man who was only doing his duty as he saw it. Then he thought of Susan and the Princess, and tightened his grip.

To do Monadno credit, he called out a warning before he fired his first shot. It struck Thurguld's shield, but did not seem to harm the dwarf. Thurguld shuffled quickly to one side, trying to spoil the man's aim, and draw him out of the shelter of the archway. Monadno fired again. A hole appeared in Thurguld's shield and he jerked as though he had been hit. Alammar loosed an arrow which rebounded from the side of the arch, causing Monadno to flinch back. Thurguld advanced another few steps, rapping his axe against his shield. 'I am coming for you, sky warrior. Prepare yourself!'

Then it happened. Monadno and Alammar fired almost simultaneously. Thurguld gasped and slumped down on the steps, while Alammar's arrow caught Monadno in the shoulder and he staggered backwards. Bron and Ian charged forward. Weakly, Monadno raised his gun. Alammar strung and loosed a second arrow with incredible speed. It struck Monadno in the chest and he fell. Alammar ran after Bron and Ian as they entered the dome.

The Doctor paused for a moment as he reached Thurguld. The dwarf was still and there was a spreading red stain on his chest. The Doctor shook his head sadly, and followed after the others.

In the entrance he found Ian in the act of picking up Monadno's gun. Monadno, quite evidently dead, lay on the floor. Bron and Alammar were running down the corridor leading to the heart of the dome. As they reached its far end they halted in amazement. A moment later Ian and the Doctor joined them.

They were standing on a broad walkway that circled

the inside of the dome, which was golden lit by the rising sun shining through the great slotted windows. But now they realized the dome was the cap of a great funnel cut into the heart of the rock. Almost filling it was the squat column of a huge, steel-grey space craft. Its prow rose into the cup of the dome high above, while its tail was lost in the gloomy depths hundreds of feet below. On its side was the boldly emblazoned name: *Prydwen*.

'The ship of our ancestors!' breathed Sir Bron.

'No time for sightseeing!' said the Doctor sharply.

Another glass bridge extended out from the walkway to touch the hull of the ship just below an open hatch. They crossed over and cautiously stepped through the hatch, which proved to be the outer door of an airlock. Beyond the inner door they found themselves in a wide corridor branching three ways.

'We'll try the control room first,' said the Doctor.

They headed down the centre corridor. Metal deck-plates rattled under their feet. Ian realized the lighting panels set in the ceiling were all dead, yet, mysteriously, there was a soft glow coming from the walls themselves. It suggested the way had been prepared a long time before. He shivered. They came to a central well containing stairways rising through the core of the ship. The sound of voices came from somewhere above. They silently climbed two levels until they came to a wide doorway. There was movement beyond it. Weapons ready, they slipped inside.

It was clearly the *Prydwen*'s control room. Banks of instruments and monitors were racked against every wall of the room, with heavily padded chairs set before them. But the controls were still and filmed with dust, while the monitors gaped blankly like empty eye sockets. One chair alone, set at the centre of the room, still had an occupant: the desiccated corpse of a man in a stained and faded coverall. A pile of books was stacked on the floor by his feet. The Empire men stood beside this strange tableau. Shannon must have heard a sound, because he drew his automatic and spun round even as Ivanov reached for the thing resting on the corpse's head; the thing that was no part of the standard equipment of any colony ship.

It was a large silver skullcap that seemed to glitter even in the soft light that shone from the walls.

Merlin's Helm.

Ian and Shannon held each other covered in a classic stand-off. But Alammar had an arrow strung again and the tip was also pointing at Shannon. 'Don't be stupid!' Ian warned Shannon. 'One of us will get you. He's a very good shot.' Shannon's gun never wavered.

'Both your comrade and ours are dead,' said the Doctor bitterly. 'Let us have no more needless bloodshed!'

'My sworn duty is to serve and protect the Empire,' said Shannon, unmoved by his plea. 'And I've never failed to do my duty yet. This device may be the key to preserving that Empire and nothing is going to stop us taking it.'

Bron said: 'And *I* am sworn to serve my King and country, and in that duty neither have I ever failed. We must have the Helm to save our Princess and defeat an enemy of the realm. You are outnumbered. It is hopeless. Surrender now and you have my word you will not be harmed.'

Shannon smiled grimly, his stance unchanged. 'Even if you take me, the fleet knows where we are and what we're after.'

'No communications equipment can work here,' countered the Doctor.

'I have a radiation torch. No circuitry. Crude and slow but detectable by the right sensors from orbit. They replied by infra-red laser, which can be seen with sensitized goggles. Believe me. They'll track your ship, and when they've modified the landers as I instructed, they'll be down after this thing, you can count on it.'

Ian felt his nerves fraying as he stared down the barrel of Shannon's gun. 'Look, after we've used it, perhaps you can work out some sort of compromise and borrow it for study –'

'No, Chesterton,' said the Doctor sharply, 'that would be exceedingly unwise.'

Then it happened.

Disturbed by vibrations and air currents it had not been subjected to for over eight hundred years, the corpse in the chair simply crumbled to dust before their eyes. As it tumbled, Ivanov who was nearest, instinctively caught the Helm.

The rest of them froze, uncertain yet expectant.

Ivanov turned the Helm over, examining it. Ian could see padding inside. 'It has to be part of some control system, doesn't it, Doctor,' Ivanov said, almost absently. 'But there are no connection sockets or terminals inside or out. Direct telepathic control, perhaps . . .'

The Doctor caught the gleam in his eye. 'No! It's not meant for you!'

But Ivanov had slipped the Helm over his own head.

His eyes rolled up until only the whites showed, then closed.

He swayed almost drunkenly.

His arms jerked as though animated by electric shocks.

Then, slowly, he broke into the most satisfied smile Ian had ever seen.

'Of course . . . how *simple*. It's obvious now. The possibilities! You could move mountains just by thinking . . .' he flung out his arms.

His eyes opened.

They were glowing.

Then the look of supreme contentment was wiped from his face to be replaced by stark horror. He screamed and clawed at the Helm.

A wind sprang up from nowhere, tearing at their clothes and shredding the remains of the ancient corpse.

The walls of the control room rippled as though drawn by some invisible hand, then tore out; metal screaming against metal, as control units, panels and stanchions were blasted into intervening compartments to punch out through the hull itself. Distantly there came the crack and rumble of shattered stone.

And the mountain moved.

Slowly, inexorably, the dome began to collapse about them.

19

The Dancers and the Ring

The faint pathway Barbara had been following disappeared unexpectedly into a clump of rhododendron
bushes, leaving her staring about in puzzlement. She
seemed to have moved into a part of the forest with more
undergrowth between the trees, which was making it
harder to keep a sense of direction. Shrugging, she turned
back the way she had come, thinking she would return to
the dell where several paths divided and try another way.

After fifty yards of retracing her footsteps, she found
the path had disappeared behind her as well.

The *Prydwen* shook as fragments of the dome began to
strike its hull.

Bron and the Doctor both sprang towards the body of
Ivanov.

Shannon turned towards them, gun blazing, even as
Alammar's bow twanged. Ian pulled the trigger almost by
reflex and his own gun thundered in the confined space.

A section of wall stove inwards and the ceiling began
to buckle. A beam snapped and swung loose on the end
of a length of cabling, catching Ian across the chest and
knocking him flat. The ship trembled as thousands of tons
of rock shattered its upper decks and began to beat them
flat. Bron's strong hand caught Ian under the arm and
hauled him to his feet. In his other hand was the Helm.
The deck pitched and the whole ship tilted as they all
staggered out into the corridor. Behind them the control
room caved in and the doorway filled with wreckage.
The Doctor was clutching a book he had snatched from
the pile beside the corpse. Alammar's arm was bleeding.

They half fell down the stairs as the upper levels collapsed under the weight of the debris. A cloud of dust billowed after them. They reached the entrance level. At the end of the corridor they saw the glass bridge bouncing as rocks shattered and rebounded from it, but amazingly it remained unbroken.

Gradually the shriek and clamour of stone and metal subsided. Slowly the reverberations died away and the *Prydwen* became still once more.

They looked into each other's faces and saw the relief of being alive. Ian straightened up carefully. The ceiling was battered in above them. He walked back to the central access core, which was impassibly choked with debris.

'Shannon!' he shouted.

There was no answer.

He imagined the state of the levels above, shook his head resignedly, and returned to the others. Bron was tying a strip of cloth around Alammar's wounded arm. 'Well, that's that then.'

'Not quite, Chesterton,' said the Doctor, dusting off his coat. He glanced around keenly for a moment then started investigating the rooms on their level. Rents in the hull now illuminated those not lit by the still glowing walls. After a few moments they heard him utter a small cry of satisfaction, and he shortly emerged carrying a laboratory microscope.

'There was sure to be one around somewhere,' he confided. 'This was a self-contained colony ship, and they would have been prepared to make tests on soil samples and that sort of thing.'

'But why do you need it?' asked Ian.

'To confirm a theory, my boy,' he said, as they made their way towards the hatchway. 'It is time we had some answers.'

'But we've got the Helm.'

'Yes. And we know without doubt how powerful it is. But it doesn't tell us how it operates. Ivanov knew, before

195

the end, poor man. I think he knew almost everything for a moment. But the shock was too much. I hope to solve part of the puzzle by less drastic methods.' He tapped the instrument in his arms. 'For the rest, I hope that young woman waiting on the stairs will tell us.'

Barbara was trying not to allow panic to overcome her, but it was getting harder by the minute. She had taken special care to note the way she had come precisely to avoid getting lost again, yet here she was in just that situation. She was in a slight clearing that she was sure she had come through not five minutes before. Except then it had been quite open, and now it was half full of bushes. It couldn't be the same one, or could it? Determinedly, she searched around until she found a sharp-edged stone and scratched an arrow in the bark of the nearest tree on its sunward side, pointing in the direction she was heading. Then she strode off purposefully.

Behind her, the bushes rustled.

An hour later the *Merrow* was slowly rowed out of the inlet of Helm Island. As the ramparts of its geometric cliffs fell away, a breeze sprang up and filled the sail.

'The wind has turned and is in our favour once again,' declared Tristram. 'Is this your doing, Master Odoyle?'

'Not mine,' replied the leprechaun. 'I've had a wind spell ready, but we've not needed it yet.'

'Well keep it handy,' said Ian, morbidly. 'We're bound to need a push getting back through that avalanche canyon. If a whirlpool or sea monster doesn't get us first.'

'Somehow, I think we shall have an easy return journey,' the Doctor suggested. 'I doubt landing-craft from the Empire ships will be ready to intercept us at sea, whatever Shannon said. The technical problems they must surmount are considerable. Any further challenges will come after we reach Fluxford. Just in time for the finale. The final confrontation, you might say.'

Ian looked at him suspiciously 'You're sounding very

lyrical all of a sudden, Doctor. What makes you think that?'

'Because it would be more . . . appropriate, that way.'

He said no more for the moment. Bron, standing with them at the stern rail, also seemed wrapped up in his own thoughts. Silently, they watched the summit of the island, capped now by the jagged rim which was all that remained of the dome. Up there, they had also left cairns of dome rubble covering the bodies of Thurguld Thongarson and Lieutenant Vincent Monadno.

The *Merrow* sailed on and was soon lost in the grey of the fog bank that surrounded the Shadow Isles.

On the summit of Helm Island the wind whistled eerily through the jagged ruins of the dome that now filled half the funnel that held the *Prydwen*. The torn and smashed upper decks were laid open to the skies.

Then there was a movement amid the remains. A piece of metal plate scraped and fell aside, revealing a hole leading up through the tangled wreckage, out of which a scratched and bloody hand appeared. Shannon's head emerged. Painfully, he dragged himself clear and lay sprawled across a section of hull panel, panting and exhausted. But his gaze turned upward to the open sky, and he smiled through his cracked lips as he fingered the radiation torch in his pocket.

Barbara groaned in dismay as she found the arrow scratched in the tree. She was sure she had been going in a straight line. How could she have circled back on herself?

Looking round in desperation, searching for some clue as to the right path, she noticed the tree opposite also had an arrow scratched on it, but pointing in the opposite direction. She walked over to examine it. Yes, it seemed like one she had made. Then she saw an arrow on the next tree, pointing at an angle to the other two. How could she have made this one as well? In the next five minutes she found twenty trees marked with arrows, no two of which quite pointed the same way.

'Come in, my dear ladies,' Dhal said heartily. 'I trust you slept well?'

It was Dhal's usual, half-rhetorical enquiry. But they were too preoccupied to respond. Susan was worried about Barbara, while Mellisa had been spending long periods squeezed into the window embrasure looking out over the moor and thinking of Edmund.

Dhal was sitting before his seeing globe, and waved them closer. The image within was of Fluxford as seen from the air.

'I thought you might be interested to see this. Note the activity on the roads. Patrols constantly leaving. Fields and woods around the town being searched. All this for your friend Barbara.' Susan looked up hopefully. 'But I'm afraid she has not yet been found.' Susan's head dropped again. 'And now I'm going to make their search a little more . . . mmm, challenging, just in case they might have thought I had forgotten them.'

'You mean more of your beasts shall be let loose to terrorize and destroy,' said Mellisa contemptuously.

Dhal smiled. 'I see you have grasped my methods. Yes, there will be more of that, including some novel distractions for tonight that I will enjoy telling you about later. But never, of course, enough to interfere with the gathering for the convocation that will be taking place shortly.'

'My father will never give you what you want!'

Dhal smiled. 'But he has sent word to the appropriate dignitaries, and they are on their way. Fact, I assure you. Also, a heavily guarded caravan has set out from Glazebry. What do you think that contains, eh?' Mellisa fell silent and uncertain. 'Meanwhile to business,' Dhal continued briskly, laying his hands on the globe.

They had to endure a full quarter hour witnessing Dhal's creatures bursting out of their hiding places about the countryside around Fluxford, and falling upon soldiers or farmers working their fields. Susan tried not to show the depths of her dismay when she realized how long and thoroughly he had been planning his actions. How had all that preparation been concealed from Palbury or Gramling?

Suddenly Dhal looked distracted for a moment, passed his hands over the globe and the image changed. It showed the orbiting space fleet. As they watched they saw three small points of light were falling away from the formation and growing larger. The globe tracked them as they fell.

'These oldworlders are persistent, I see. But cautious after what befell their previous manned vessel. These are but mechanical devices again, I believe. They can do me no harm.' Tolerantly he watched the craft descend in balls of fire, switching to the eyes of another of his spy-birds to see them deploy parachutes just two thousand feet above the ground. Widespread shock-absorbing legs sprang out and the three craft landed safely within a mile of each other.

But then, unexpectedly, the upper section of one of the craft immediately spouted flames and blasted away into the sky again. Dhal glowered angrily and peered closer at the globe. A minute after the first one, an upper stage lifted from the second probe. A minute after that, the third did. The rockets of the third ascent craft failed when it was only a mile up. The probe curved over and began the long plunge to earth again. Dhal smiled. The first ascent stage fared little better, failing at ten miles up. But the second blasted on, soaring rapidly upwards. Only when it was over fifty miles up did the rockets splutter and die, as it at last succumbed to the mysterious disabling force. But it had made a low orbit, Susan realized, even if it was not a stable one.

She saw the scowl on Dhal's face and inspiration struck.

Boldly, she leaned forward, resting her hands on Dhal's

199

desk, as though to emphasize her words. 'I know what they're doing. They're finding a way to make a safe return to orbit. That means very soon they'll be landing larger forces, and you won't be able to stop them all. They might bring advanced weapons you cannot even imagine. If they find out you sabotaged their first landing craft –'

'Get her out of here!' Dhal roared, losing his temper for the first time. Susan sprang back from his desk with her arms wrapped around her, as though fearing a physical blow. The guards caught hold of them and dragged them away. Dhal returned to contemplating the globe, a dark scowl on his face.

'I didn't choose to come here. I'm not really a soldier. I want to explain.'

Jen Komati sat in Tristram's cabin. Before her were the Doctor, Ian, Bron, Alammar and Odoyle. How much the native Avalonians would understand of her story she was not sure. Mainly she spoke to the Doctor. She had a feeling he would understand everything.

'This region of space was pretty well unexplored until recently. We didn't even know a colony ship had landed here. I suppose it must have been one of the twenty-second century diaspora. A lot of them were never heard of again. All we did know was that a few private prospecting ships had got lost around here over the years, and there had been a garbled emergency transmission saying a ship was going down over a planet because its controls had failed. But the full co-ordinates were never received, so it could never be followed up.

'What was most interesting was the nearby nebula. When a science expedition finally got around to examining it, the Empire began to take serious interest. That's where Shannon and the military come into the picture. You see, they discovered the original star should never have gone nova in the first place, at least, by all the rules of stellar evolution we know of. Even the shape and longevity of the remnant are unusual. So they analysed the local inter-stellar dust clouds, corrected for shift over time, and discovered an ancient ionization trail leading back to this system. It seems, two thousand years ago or so, an energy beam of incredible power projected from here made that star explode. You can see why the military took an interest. The first survey showed this planet was strange, with macro-engineered moons and unexplained energy fields. Obviously the most likely source of the beam.'

The Doctor was nodding sadly. Sir Bron was struggling to understand.

'The stars are but suns seen a great distance off, that I know,' he said slowly. 'And worlds are warmed by them and turn about them, as Avalon does. Your warriors wanted control of a weapon that would destroy a sun?' Komati nodded. 'And all its worlds with it?' She nodded again. Bron looked appalled. 'Where is the honour in that? That is not how men should fight!'

'I didn't say it was honourable.' Komati sank her head in her hands again. 'Please don't think I agree with it. I didn't know any of this at first. They didn't tell Doctor Ivanov or myself until we were almost here. I'm sorry I didn't have the courage to refuse to co-operate earlier. But it was my duty . . .' she sighed. 'We were brought along because the whole thing was arranged so quickly and secretly. They needed specialists for the initial lander team. They thought it might be tough getting down, so the team would have to be small, physically fit, and encompass as many useful disciplines as possible, in view of what they thought they would find here. The remains of an extinct alien civilization probably. Well, we were both healthy enough. Ivanov has – *had*, degrees in fusion engineering, cybernetic control systems and astrophysics. I'm qualified in microtronics, physics and xenotechnology. Together we fulfilled the requirements for the ground-breaking team. Later, when they'd solved the landing problems, larger teams would have come.'

'General weapons technicians, I presume,' said the

201

Doctor coldly. 'To operate the equipment you had identified as the control mechanism for the nova trigger device.'

'Or to dismantle it if it could be installed elsewhere,' she conceded wearily. 'When Shannon heard about the Helm, he guessed it might be something to do with the control system, as it linked in with the energy fields we'd already detected.'

'But why should your Empire need such a weapon?' exclaimed Ian. 'Are you at war?'

Komati looked at him sadly. 'Only with time and change. The Empire is simply dying for want of anything better to do. It has been for fifty years. Longer, probably, only people didn't see it. We expanded as far as we could and became too cumbersome to rule efficiently. Technical progress slowed and became moribund. We turned inwards and became soft. Classic signs. It's coming to pieces now. Old colonies are breaking away and declaring independence. New alliances are forming and other powers are just waiting for the big fall, or the senile whimper, whatever. But there were still fervent patriots, like Shannon, who realized with a weapon like this . . . you can guess the rest. You can't blame him, I suppose. He was only doing his duty.'

There was a long silence after she had finished. Then the Doctor spoke up in his carefully considered tones.

'Humanity is not mature enough to use such powers responsibly. In a million years, perhaps . . . perhaps. But that is only half the story Avalon has to tell.' He picked up the book he had rescued from the control room of the *Prydwen*, and started to turn the pages. 'Stellar manipulators may be the least of your worries.'

As the door of their cell closed behind their guards, Mellisa looked curiously at Susan. She had walked back from Dhal's chamber with her head down and arms still wrapped about herself. But as soon as the bolts rattled to, she raised her head to reveal an unexpected smile. She withdrew her hands from her armpits and opened them triumphantly. A small glass vial rested in each palm. One held a clear fluid, the other oily yellow.

'How did you get those!' Mellisa exclaimed.

Susan grinned. 'They were in the clutter on the table. I just picked them up when I leaned over to speak to Dhal. It was easy.'

'But what good are they?'

'I'm hoping they might be acids. He must have some amongst all those chemicals. We can try them on the window bar or the door hinges, maybe.'

'What are acids?'

'Liquids that eat metal, amongst other things. We might be able to break out of here.'

The Princess was looking at her intently. 'How do you know such things? Are you skilled in the wizardly arts like your grandfather?'

'No, we're scientists.'

'What are they?'

Susan sighed. It was not an easy question to answer on Avalon. 'Well, I suppose they are a bit like wizards, but they do things by different rules.'

Mellisa, suddenly worried, asked, 'What if Dhal notices they're gone?'

'We'll have to hide them.'

Mellisa looked around their bare cell. 'But where?'

'We may never know the name of the writer,' said the Doctor, flicking through the book. Ian noticed the pages did not rustle like paper. They seemed more like very thin plastic. 'It is clearly a diary of some kind, but the earlier pages are badly faded.' He fished his monocle from his pocket and used it like a magnifying glass. 'I can only make out occasional words and phrases. It seems to be a journal of the first landing on this planet and its early settlement. Perhaps written by the leader of the colony. I can make out a date 28 September 2145.'

'That is the year of landfall by the old calendar,'

exclaimed Bron. 'But, were those Merlin's remains we saw?'

'No, my friend,' said the Doctor gently. 'Please bear with me for the moment. You will understand in time, though I fear the truth may seem disturbing at first.' Bron frowned. The Doctor continued: 'The entries become erratic, and the writing less distinct. I can make out *power failure* and *creatures . . . in the woods . . .* the rest is very confused. Ahh. Something different.'

Leaning over, Ian could see the faded handwriting ceased, and on a new page, bolder, clear letters appeared. They almost looked as if they had been burned on to the plasticized sheets.

'This is most extraordinary,' said the Doctor solemnly. 'I will read it in full:

' "I know I'm dying. Hard to think straight. This metal cap focuses so much power and knowledge. Dangerous. Too much for one man's mind. But I can't remove it now. I've done what I can to safeguard it. Nobody can use it unless it's life or death. Now I must explain, if I have time. The words are appearing on the page as fast as I can think them. With the cap you can work miracles. I moved the ship and shaped this island in minutes. But the effect also works with group subconscious. Gradual at first. Didn't realize. It had been dormant a long time when we arrived. Then our machines started breaking down for no reason. People started seeing things. It was a terrible winter. Electronic readers failed. My books were only real ones left. Read old stories to children. Just my hobby, to give names to these new lands. But they believed. And what they believed started to come true. People in the outlying settlements are changing, getting smaller or taller, and others are starting to work magic. I know what it really is now, but better magic than the other. Forgive me if I have sinned! I had to take the knowledge away and make the changes. So many minds I touched. I feel unclean. But safer this way. They must never think like that again. I'd put it all right again but there's no time. I've done my best, really. It was when they prayed, you see. They imagined gods and they got them! Manmade in his own image! But they fought. They would have destroyed us for our imperfections. Had to stop that. I'd found the helmet in a cave that had once been a great hall. Could feel it was old and powerful. Knew everything as soon as I put it on. Wish I could destroy the whole system, but only they can do that. But it's been so long, perhaps they've forgotten how. Too late now . . ."'

The Doctor looked up gravely. 'It ends there,' he said simply.

To get lost once in a forest may be regarded as a misfortune, Barbara paraphrased with grim humour; to do so twice looks like carelessness.

But she hadn't been careless, that was what made it so unfair. She almost sobbed aloud, and tried to get a grip on herself again. But the forest showed no sympathy for her plight, and continued to press in closer. Somebody was playing games with her. Was it Dhal again? She had begun to think she was being watched, and kept twisting round suddenly to try to catch it . . . them, whatever. But there was nothing there, only flickers of movement in the corner of her eye. She stumbled on uncaring now. Only wishing she could arrive wherever it was and get it over with.

Susan and Mellisa looked up as the door of their cell was suddenly thrown open. Marton Dhal strode briskly in followed by four of his ape servants.

'Take them outside and search them,' he gestured impatiently. Two of the guards caught the young women by their arms and dragged them unceremoniously out of the cell to the landing, where they proceeded to pat and prod for anything concealed under their nightdresses. In response to this treatment, Susan and Mellisa struggled and complained with appropriate indignation. From inside the cell they heard rustling and scrapings as their few belongings were examined. 'Are you sure they're not in the bedding? Look for any cracks that are large enough . . . you, check the window ledge . . .' A minute later Dhal emerged, frowning uncertainly, to stand before them. 'Anything?' he asked the ape guards.

'No, Master,' they chorused.

'What is the purpose of this, Dhal?' Mellisa demanded, with suitable hauteur.

'I find I am missing two vials of potion, and it occurred to me that you might have taken them, for some foolish reason.'

'As you can see, we have not.'

'Apparently so,' Dhal admitted grudgingly.

'Perhaps you've simply forgotten where you put them,' suggested Susan simply, but with a condescending edge to her words. 'You've been working so hard at your nasty plots and schemes that you've probably overdone it a bit. I mean, I don't suppose even you claim to be infallible.'

Dhal swelled with annoyance, but contented himself with stalking away back up the stairs to his chamber without another word.

The apes locked them back in their cell, where they silently straightened up the disorder left by the search. When they were quite sure the landing was deserted, Mellisa stood with her back to the window, made a stirrup with her interlocked fingers, and boosted Susan up into the window recess. Susan edged as far forward as she could, reached out of the window and to one side, grasped something held in the cleft between two stone blocks, and carefully brought it back inside the cell. The two vials were linked by a length of golden thread, formed out of several long strands of Mellisa's hair plaited together, tied about their necks. In the middle of the thread was an overtied knot large enough to catch in the crack between the wall blocks.

Mellisa smiled broadly. 'It was worth being handled by those creatures to see the expression on Dhal's face.'

Susan grinned back. 'I really think he believes he must have lost them himself now. Anything we can do to make him uncertain, even in a small way, is worth the risk.'

'But can you use these as you said to remove the window bar or the door hinges?'

Susan examined the contents of the vials carefully, holding them up to the light from the window, then unstopping them and cautiously sniffing. 'They could be acids, but there are so many different kinds and strengths. I'll experiment on the bar first, and we'll just have to hope for the best. Help me up again.'

Wedged into the window recess, Susan carefully deposited a few drops from both vials on to the joint where the bar was mortared into the window masonry. She looked closely at the result. Yes, there was a definite bubbling where the fluid touched the metal. That was encouraging. She replaced their stoppers, returned the vials to their hiding place, and slid back down into the cell.

'We'll give it a while,' she said quietly, 'but I think it's working.'

Mellisa's face lit up. 'That would be wonderful. I am sure this chemistry you have spoken of is but a branch of sorcery not known to the magicians of Avalon. You might have something to teach them. It is a shame you could not become one.'

'It's only very simple chemistry,' replied Susan lightly, then frowned. 'And what do you mean, I couldn't become one?'

'Well, you could become a witch, I suppose, though it is hardly a fitting calling for a lady.'

'I'm sure if I knew how he did it, I could do anything Dhal does. Or Gramling, for that matter. Grandfather is certain there is a rational explanation for everything magical that we've seen. It's just a question of looking hard enough.'

'But you are a woman.'

'So?'

Mellisa looked at her thoughtfully. 'I do believe you would do this if you could.' She smiled. 'I wish you luck, Susan Foreman, but I fear you will be hard pressed to find your explanations. Magical practitioners are loath to reveal secrets of their art to any but their chosen successors. It has always been that way.'

Susan considered what she had seen of the practice of magic so far. It passed the time and at least it was better than pointlessly fretting over their predicament. 'What is it that wizards and such actually do?' she said, half to herself. 'When they cast a spell they concentrate, chant a bit, wave their hands about and . . . hey presto! as they say on Earth, something amazing happens.'

'They have staffs, and use potions and powers as well,' Mellisa pointed out.

'But not all the time. Dhal hasn't used a staff yet, that I've seen. And Kilvenny Odoyle has that little silver hammer. Besides, if it was just a question of staffs or potions, wouldn't people simply steal them for their own use?'

'Nobody would dare steal a magician's staff,' Mellisa said firmly. 'And no potion will work if it is not fairly obtained.'

'But do staffs make magicians, or magicians make staffs? Where did the first magician come from?'

'Well, Merlin was the first on Avalon, of course.'

Susan wondered if this was an appropriate time to tell Mellisa the truth about the past. It might be a shock to her. She edged round the point. 'I mean, where do new magicians come from? Can anybody be taught, or is it simply a talent that some people have? Perhaps it's a bit of both.'

Mellisa was giving her that uncertain but wondering

208

look again, which meant she was behaving in an un-Avalonian manner.

'I do not believe I have heard anybody speak of the thing in such a way. To us, magic is simply part of life. Magicians are what they are. It has always been so. You seem to want to pull the matter into little pieces and find out how it works. Is this what your chemistry is all about?'

'A lot of it, like most science. In fact, it was through the efforts of people long ago trying to make what you would call "magic" work, that scientific methods were discovered. That sort of thing happens all the time all over the universe.' And as she spoke, she felt she was on the brink of an important insight. If she only knew what it was.

The objects on the microscope slide were smaller than dust motes. They varied in detail between themselves, but were all regularly formed and bi-laterally symmetrical. A few appeared to be moving; beating tiny hair-like rods about their sides, like the *cilia* of some protozoa. Except those objects were not animal or vegetable.

They were not living organisms of any kind.

Ian relinquished his place for Komati to have a look. The native Avalonians followed on curiously.

'All right, Doctor,' Ian conceded. 'You've shown us half a dozen slides of clothing, food and seawater, and I agree these things are in all of them. But what are they?'

The Doctor's eyes twinkled. 'I believe Doctor Komati knows. They are related to one of her own specialities.'

'But I never dreamed I would see them in such profusion,' she admitted. 'Microscopic self-replicating machines. Microtons or nanobots, they're sometimes called. Are they really everywhere?'

'I believe the planet is saturated with them, from high in the atmosphere to deep underground. They feed off and control the energy fields you detected. Sensors, actuator mechanisms, force generators, power and matter transmitters all combined in one pan-global network, whose countless trillions of component parts are too small to see with the naked eye. The ultimate multi-purpose machine!'

Komati said slowly: 'So it's these things that interfered with our probes and lander controls. Even our watches!'

'Exactly. They are programmed not to tolerate other electronic mechanisms, even to the extent of actively penetrating and neutralizing them; no doubt to avoid any danger of interference or contamination of the system.'

'That's why the TARDIS wouldn't let us in!' Ian exclaimed.

The Doctor looked pleased he had worked it out for himself. 'Precisely, Chesterton. We would have brought the nanobots in with us. The TARDIS has a force field to filter the air, but they would have already been embedded in our clothes, even within our lungs by then, so it had to lock us out and seal itself completely.'

Komati suddenly looked appalled. 'But, how can we ever get off this planet again if we carry these things with us?'

'Ah, perhaps you begin to appreciate the danger now. Until we learn how to neutralize them, we dare not.'

'*Valkyrie* to flagship. Have recovered ascent stage of test probe gamma as ordered. Returning to squadron, ETA twelve minutes.'

'Roger, *Valkyrie*. Good fishing. Status of probe?'

'Systems read dead, *Randolph*. Holding it in grav beam lock until we can transfer to your science module as per specified handling instructions.'

'Confirmed, *Valkyrie*. We'll take it from there. *Randolph* out.'

The music was faint at first, but slowly Barbara made out the wistful note of pan pipes and the plucking of harps. They seemed to settle her mind, and her fear gradually fell way. She stumbled unthinkingly towards it. The music was so pure and clear she wanted to hear it up close, to drink it in, to bathe in it. She passed swathes of ivy trailing like curtains and tapestries. The great trees began to line up like the columns of some lofty arboreal hall. Flowers spotted about the path, glowing in colours and variety she had never seen before. Their scent filled the air with a heady aroma more delicate than the offerings of the finest perfumer. Through the darkening green veils ahead she saw a light dancing like a will-o'-the-wisp. She followed it, arms outstretched.

'*Valkyrie* to *Randolph*, come in.'

'*Randolph* receiving, *Valkyrie*.'

'Minor problem, *Randolph*. Main grav beam projector has failed. The probe slipped away from us for a while until we could snag it again with the secondaries. Back on track now. ETA now eight minutes.'

'Understood, *Valkyrie*. Just as long as you get it here. The techs want to check its data recorders soonest possible. *Randolph* out.'

The company of fair folk ringed the glade. Or was it a hall? For a moment Barbara thought they were seated on grassy banks, but then she realized they were actually long couches draped in forest green cloth, decorated with flowers of golden thread. Some were robed in silk while others were clad in dresses of petals and woven leaves and a few wore only a nimbus of glowing light. There were handsome, slender, regal men and women as tall as she, then smaller, grotesque beings with large noses and long ears. Some had donkey tails and goat-like, shaggy haunches with cloven hooves. Tiny creatures flew on insect wings. And they talked and sang with sweet voices. Then she found a golden goblet in her hand, and all were watching her, urging her to drink. She sipped. It was the sweetest nectar. She drank some more.

* * *

'*Valkyrie* to *Randolph*. Emergency! Emergency! Come in *Randolph*!'

'*Randolph* receiving. What is your emergency, *Valkyrie*?'

'Massive systems failure spreading through ship! Can't stop it. Main computer down, life support failing . . . there go the main lights . . . putting on emergency suit . . . may have to abandon ship, understand, *Randolph*?'

'Understood. Notifying command of your situation. We can be in your position in three minutes.'

'Hearing you . . . suited up now . . . main transmitter starting – switched to the portable reserve unit. Do you read, *Randolph*?'

'Still reading, *Valkyrie*. Hang on.'

'Central air has just died. Sealing helmet . . . Lifeboat stations sounding . . . The Captain says . . . hell . . . main comm has cut. It's spreading . . . Oh God. If it reaches the power core and the containment fields! Listen, *Randolph*, we think it started in the grav beam generator room . . . uhh . . . emergency lights have gone now. My torch . . . no . . . that's fading. The grav beam, understand? Maybe when we –'

The atomic fireball that consumed the *Valkyrie* brought a brief, false dawn to half the night-time hemisphere of Avalon.

There was a ring of toadstools in the grass. Or was it a carpet? The fairy dancers were prancing and leaping about within, circling round and round. The music was louder, and they waved and beckoned her to join them. Barbara clasped small hands, and stepped inside. Her feet seemed to leave the ground and she was whirled away with the rest. The tempo increased and she spun faster. She became dizzy. The nectar was warm within her. The fairy faces began to blur and change. Then there was only the light and timeless music left.

20

Nightmare in Orbit

The Doctor had been sitting staring into nothing for some time. Now he faced the other occupants of the cabin again.

'From what the diary has told us, together with my own observations, I believe I can now extrapolate the history of Avalon before the *Prydwen* landed.' He looked at Bron, Odoyle and Alammar. 'I'm afraid this may come as a shock for you, but I am sure the principal facts are correct.'

'We do not shy from the truth, Doctor,' said Bron, 'even if it is hard to comprehend.' He glanced at his fellow Avalonians. 'We realize something is amiss here. The *Prydwen* is a great craft, but it is just a machine. If it bore the remains of Arthur and Merlin we would feel it. But we do not.' He looked grave. 'I have touched the Helm, but it also feels . . . wrong, somehow. Not of human origin. I cannot believe Merlin ever made or wore such a thing. Neither were those remains Merlin's, and that account was never written by him. It tells a strange story, which I but half understand. But is it the truth?'

'You can speak frankly, Doctor,' confirmed Odoyle. 'We're not children, you know.'

'Then I will tell you the truth. Arthur and Merlin are characters from historical myth. They never came to Avalon. They probably never even existed.'

Komati was nodding. 'They're just legends. I read about them when I was at school. Sorry.'

Ian admired Bron's self-control. The foundation of his world was being demolished, but all he said was: 'Continue, Doctor.'

'Very well. Thousands of years ago, a technologically advanced race lived on Avalon. They made two crucial inventions. The first was a system of gathering and focusing solar energy on a planetary scale to deflect or destroy the unusually large and dangerous numbers of meteors and asteroids in this system. The Circle Sea was the result of one such ancient impact, and the shooting stars you see every night are but remnants of this process. They built the moons to become part of the system, which also supplied their whole planet with power. This was then used to energize the second of their inventions: the nanobots you have just seen. Eventually their numbers and sophistication meant that, at the right mental command, energy, force or matter could be directed and manipulated at will. Creation directed by pure thought! They no longer needed to work, and every wish, within reason, could be granted. And *that* is what you call magic.'

'You're saying,' exclaimed Odoyle, 'that I make all those little motes do the work for me? But if so, why am I tired after casting a powerful spell?'

'Because the system was designed for alien minds to use. It takes other beings continuous effort to maintain control and ability must vary from person to person. Some, I suspect, would never be able to interface with the system at all.'

Odoyle clicked his tongue. 'Well, I'd never have guessed.'

'But it was their downfall. It was the last invention they ever needed to make. It destroyed true creativity and ingenuity. They began to decline. The nearby nebula suggests their ordered lives came to some violent end: war, or some ill conceived experiment, perhaps. But something changed, or else how did the colonist get hold of the Helm, which, I suspect, is a master control and amplifying device for handling more complex tasks.' He looked at Bron. 'Your ancestors, when they arrived here, inadvertently fed the system with their new ideas from

214

history and legend. Especially the children. They had heard tales of knights and castles and fantastic creatures. After the destruction of their machines by the nanobots, the system began to give their dreams and fantasies form, which stimulated their imaginations in turn. And so the Avalon of today was born.'

There was a long, thoughtful silence.

Cautiously, Ian asked: 'What did the diary mean about the gods? Was that literally true?'

'I fear so. It said the system responded to group consciousness. Or unconsciousness. But it had no sense of discrimination. Think of intense religious belief given tangible form. The writer meant people had begun to create gods in their own images! Imagine rival gods fighting? Imagine being forced to live by a set of values enforced upon you by a mockery of a living God? A God given virtually unlimited powers by the nanobots. It must have been a nightmare. So in desperation he wiped such knowledge from their minds and records, leaving only a dim memory of war with the ice giants. That was what he felt so guilty about. It was, many would say, a crime, though we may not judge too harshly, for he was clearly dying when he made the choice he thought best. The choice of the lesser of two evils. He could not deactivate the system itself. Only its makers could do that. So the ideas he had unwittingly let loose had to continue. They shaped Avalonian society, with magic as a sort of safety valve. At least its use by individuals would never result in total domination. Except, of course, for the Helm. Its potential power, even with safeguards, poses a grave threat.'

'Gramling must use it as planned,' Bron reminded him. He was feeling dazed by the Doctor's revelations. Just what were 'gods' anyway? But he clung firmly to his original purpose. Whatever the truth of the past, he had his duty to the present.

'But afterwards it must be dealt with somehow,' the Doctor insisted.

215

Komati said firmly: 'It must never leave here. If any of this spreads to other worlds – the chaos and damage it could cause does not bear thinking of!'

'One thing, Doctor,' Ian asked. 'These people who created the Helm and the nanobots in the first place. What happened to them?'

The Doctor smiled enigmatically. 'You shall see, Chesterton, in due course.'

The faces around the *Prince Randolph*'s conference table had never been grimmer. A wretched, numbing business, thought Nyborg; the post-mortem on the loss of a ship and two hundred and fifty crewmen. He had known Captain Selmon for five years . . . He pulled himself together. Time for personal grief later.

'It was not sabotage in the ordinary sense,' the *Randolph*'s chief engineer stated. 'Not any sort of conventional failure that I've ever seen. We received enough of their emergency telemetry before the end to know that. We can plot the breakdown spread through the ship. It does look like it started in the main grav beam unit as they said. Then it grew from secondary sources in an almost exponential curve. It reached the power core before they could shut it down, and when the containment fields cut . . .' He spread his hands expressively.

'It wasn't just a computer failure?' somebody asked.

'Not until it reached the main bank itself. Actual physical breakdown of multiple units and conduits in linkage sequence. Like the way the first probes went down.'

'We are forced to suppose, then,' said Chandry, 'that somehow the *Valkyrie* became "infected", for want of a better word, by the same agency responsible for those and the other crashes. But the *Valkyrie* never entered the atmosphere, even when it recovered the probe ascent stage. The only contact it had with the probe was purely immaterial through its grav beam – oh.'

Nyborg voiced their suspicions.

'Could something have entered the ship through the grav beam projector mount? Something brought up from the surface with the probe? It destroyed its systems, then was drawn along the beam to the *Valkyrie*, where it somehow got inside and did the same there.'

'We're talking about a physical entity then, Admiral,' the engineer speculated. 'But too small to see, or else the *Valkyrie* would have spotted it on the probe. It almost behaves like a virus . . . hell! Of course. Sorry, sir, but that's what it is: a microscopic agent, either a biological mutation or a synthetic nanobotic replica. It must be programmed to seek out and attack any foreign mechanisms. Probably feeds off them, replicating itself as it goes. Power conduits would be ideal sources of new material, energy and a means to spread further.'

Chandry looked appalled. 'How can we stop it, chief?'

'Right at this moment, I don't know, sir. That was what the probes would have told us. We packed in multiple shielding on general principles, trying out different systems to see what worked best. The gamma probe almost made it back, which tells us something. But if these nanobots are programmed to actively penetrate any mechanism or component unlike themselves, then any type of shielding will break down eventually, or else be so massive it impairs the function of the equipment it's protecting.'

'Well, work on it, chief. We must have some way of shielding it out or neutralizing it. At least some foolproof decontamination procedure. Otherwise we can never recover our landing party.'

'Best if I had some sample nanobots to work with, sir.'

Chandry smiled grimly. 'Tinker up some of your own, Chief. We can't risk collecting any more samples.'

'Meanwhile,' said Nyborg, 'no craft will go within one hundred miles of the planet's surface except on my specific orders. If we weren't acting under conditions of strictest secrecy, I would put this planet under galactic quarantine.

217

The thought of what might happen if a contaminated craft ever reached another world is horrendous.'

'But what about the landing party, sir?'

'We can keep them supplied with one way, unmanned cargo landers for as long as necessary.'

'And if they call for marine back up?'

'That would have to be on a volunteer only basis. They would have to know we may never be able to lift them off again. Next time we are in contact with Shannon we must explain the new situation. We must halt the work on the lander modifications for the moment to give priority to this new problem –'

His table comm unit beeped: 'Signal received from Captain Shannon, Admiral. Priority prefix and coded.'

'Relay to my screen.' Nyborg entered his decode and studied the message. Around the table, the others saw a look of amazement cross his face. Eventually he turned back to them. 'It seems I am forced to countermand my previous orders. Captain Shannon has discovered something of immense potential value to the future security of the Empire. The securing of this item must take absolute top priority. The solution of the nanobot problem must wait. Meanwhile, the modification of additional landers and weapons systems must be stepped up. Mobilize all technicians. Call in extra personnel from the other ships if required. Shannon is no longer on the sailing craft, but it must still be constantly monitored. It should be returning to its home port on the north-west coast of the circular sea. Our aim is to intercept it before it reaches that destination!'

Susan woke sluggishly as a thin sliver of morning light struck the back of their cell and started to work its way across the wall. The window was on the north side of the tower, so only in the morning and evening did they see any direct sunlight. She shook her head dully, realizing she had slept heavily again, despite the uncomfortable conditions. Her arm itched, however, and she saw insect bite marks had appeared overnight. They had unwelcome guests! Perhaps Dhal would allow them some fresh straw for the mattresses.

Mellisa stirred into wakefulness, and turned to face her, shivering slightly under their thin blankets, but smiling gamely. 'Good morning. Brrr . . . I suppose we must be thankful that Dhal chose summer to put his plans into action. Oh, how is the window bar? We must see how your potion is doing before the guards start their morning rounds.'

After a minute's stretching and bending to work the kinks out of their muscles, Mellisa helped Susan up into the window aperture to examine her handiwork. To her delight, she found the bar half eaten through where it was bedded into the mortar. She retrieved the vials from their hiding place and added a few more drops to complete the job, then lowered herself back into the cell again to report the good news.

'I think what you have done is wonderful,' admitted Mellisa, 'but what good will it do when we are still so high up? Even if we made ropes out of the blankets, they would not stretch a tenth of the way. Would it not be better to try to open the door, so we might have a chance to escape down the stairs?'

'The acid will eat through the hinges, but it'll be no good if the guards come in when it's half done. It might come loose in their hands!'

'Then you must apply it last thing at night, so that we may escape in the early hours.'

'Where to? There's certainly no way out through the pits, and the main doors will be guarded night and day for sure. But outside, all the sentries will be looking away from the tower and there's some cover amongst the rocks and gorse, so if we could get down unnoticed, we'd have a chance to stay hidden.'

'But there is no way we can descend the outside of the tower. At least we have a chance by the stairs. Why do you cast doubt upon the obvious choice?'

219

Susan frowned, chewing her lip. 'I don't know myself really. I just have this feeling that it's the . . . *appropriate* way to do it.'

'A strange choice of words.'

'Sorry.' Susan looked about her at the few items in the room, Mellisa and the vials in her hand. 'But I really think it's the best way I can put it. We have everything we need here to get down safely, if we use it correctly. I know we have. Trust me.'

'I still do not understand. But I do trust you. What shall we do?'

'Keep watch out the window as often as we can and note anything that might be useful to us later. When we can remove the bar, we can see further either side.' She looked at the two vials of acid and frowned again. 'I wonder if there's anything else I can use these for?'

'More of your chemical magic, you mean?'

Susan smiled. 'Possibly, yes.'

Mellisa scratched her leg, which had also suffered from the attentions of the mattress bugs. 'Is your magic capable of ridding us of these pests?' she asked hopefully.

Dhal was seated in his high-backed chair, his eyes closed, his breathing slowed, reaching out with his mind. He had felt the change the night before. There had been a shock, an upheaval in the world-shape of the latent magical field that surrounded and permeated everything. All magic users could sense this to a greater or lesser degree, but he prided himself on being specially sensitive to its fluctuations beyond his shielded tower. Every time one of those craft had descended from the sky he had felt the alien intrusion, the strangeness of the thing, before the essence of Avalon permeated it. He had been frustrated that their parent vessels had circled the world beyond his reach. But now, something had caused the aura to extend itself, tenuously, beyond its normal bounds. Now they were no longer so inaccessible.

* * *

The glade in the forest was cold and empty by the morning. There was no sign of the fairy company who had invested it with light and music the night before. Barbara lay in the hollow of an earthy bank as though asleep. A light dew had settled on her, and a spider web glistened across the folds of her dress, but she did not stir. A tendril of ivy curled itself about her ankle.

The *Merrow* sailed on peacefully. The wind was at their backs once more and Tristram strutted about the decks cheerfully. They had passed through the fog bank surrounding the Shadow Isles without encountering kraken, octopus or whirlpool. The passage through the narrow channel between the sentinel islets had proved entirely uneventful. Ian wondered if these hazards were only triggered when a ship tried to enter the Shadow Isles. Or perhaps the Helm, locked away in a chest in Bron's cabin, granted them some sort of immunity. He would have questioned the Doctor about it, but curiously, the old man seemed to be staying in his cabin for long stretches, or else holding private discussions with Odoyle in quiet corners. What was he up to now?

By mid-morning, the base of the window bar was completely eaten through, leaving a dark stained socket hole in the stonework. Susan thought she might have to apply acid to the top of the bar as well, which would have been far more awkward than the base. But once the bottom was free, she found the top could be worked loose by rocking the bar to and fro, and turning the base around in a circular motion, gradually cracking away the damp mortar. She and Mellisa took ten-minute turns, one working on the bar, while the other listened at the door for the guards. So far today, they had received their meals, but not their usual summons to Dhal's chamber. One of the ape guards had asked how they slept, presumably on his behalf. Perhaps he was too busy with something else. Still, while they were undisturbed they could work on. They got blisters, but slowly the bar began to loosen.

In the glade, a second strand of ivy had twined itself around Barbara's leg, and a third had begun to circle about her outstretched arm. From the top of the bank, a questing bramble stalk was bowing lower and lower over her.

Artificer first class Harley Zelk was collecting electronics spares from the racks of *Prince Randolph*'s stores when he felt he was being watched. The hairs on his neck prickled, and he turned round expecting the quartermaster to be standing over him. There was nobody there. Puzzled, he walked to the end of the stack and peered down the passage between the ranks of shelves. There was the sergeant in his office at the end. Frowning, he went back to filling his list, rolling the cart with his selections over to the next stack. He felt it again. Somebody watching him from the shadows.

'Buzz – is that you?' Buzz Garton was capable of playing the fool even with the present workload and after what happened to the *Valkyrie*. There was no response. But he saw a dim figure through the shelves moving silently down the next aisle.

'Quit messing, I see you.' The figure vanished into the shadows. Zelk ran to the end of the stack and looked down the aisle. Nobody there. Then he saw a movement through two intervening racks. 'Sarge,' he called out uncertainly. 'Is there somebody else down here?' The air seemed to chill. He edged along the rack ends and peered cautiously around the corner. There was a dim figure standing with his back to him. He was wearing some kind of robe. What was the fancy dress for? Who was this joker who'd been trying to give him the shivers anyway? Indignantly he strode up behind him and reached out for his shoulder.

'All right, you've had your fun –'

The figure turned round.

It's face was horrible.

Zelk sprang backwards with a yell even the dozing quartermaster heard; tripped, fell over, cracked the back of his head on the corner of a shelf and lost interest in events for the next two hours.

Two levels above on the hangar deck, a technician installing new hydraulic lines in a landing craft failed to notice a loop of cable rise up behind him, as though held by invisible hands, until it dropped over his head and tightened remorselessly about his neck. When he was found later, his fingers were still locked about the cable as though trying to tear it free.

Shortly afterwards, on the *Dorado*, the thermostatic controls in a bank of shower stalls failed, and suddenly discharged scalding water. Four crew received first degree burns.

The head cook on the *Indus*, preparing a tossed salad for high table in the officers' mess, continued, inexplicably, to vigorously slice Aldebaran red celery for at least half a minute after severing three of his own fingers, before noticing his error.

On the *Tigershark*, the second lieutenant was seen to run screaming down a corridor, enter an airlock, and frantically attempt to open the outer hatch without wearing a spacesuit. Fortunately, somebody hit the override in time. When they finally got him back inside again, his only explanation was that he thought he was on fire, and that the airlock led to a swimming pool.

On the hand-weapons range in the *Prince Randolph*, a marine firearms instructor of fifteen years experience calmly turned one of the antique-pattern automatic rifles he was testing upon the others using the range, and shot five marines precisely through the chest, just as though they had been cutout targets at the end of the range. Which to him, for ten seconds, they had been.

'Nyborg to all ships! Emergency manoeuvring command. Increase orbital parameters by fifty miles immediately!'

The ship trembled as the main reactor drive cut in. On the screens, Nyborg saw tail flares lance out from the other ships as they followed his order. Something half-seen, half-felt moved through the control room of the *Prince Randolph*. It brushed past the operators at the consoles and stirred papers on the chart table. A monitor screen flared with sparks. For a moment a manlike shape seemed to be standing before it.

Then the image faded, slipped away and was gone as the squadron lifted to a higher orbit.

With a final heave, the bar came away in Susan's hands. She twisted around in the window recess and waved it triumphantly to Mellisa.

'Well done! Can you see more outside now?'

Cautiously, Susan leant out of the aperture. The evening sun was lowering and shining into the window once more, but she doubted if any of the guards would see her up here. Twisting around she saw the tower rose fifty or sixty feet to end in the overhanging lip of the battlements. No escape that way. Below was a dizzy drop to the rocks that formed the tor, but there were no walls or other surrounds. If only they could get down! She could now see four of the squat turret chimneys ranged about the base of the rock. The ditch ran continuously between them, but it was no impassable barrier. There were several patches of scrub within the perimeter, and the ground was uneven, with worn paths and hillocks. The cover was there, if only they could use it.

'Right,' she said, slithering back down into the cell. 'First we must make up a plug of straw to pack out the lower socket hole, to hold the bar in place when we're not looking out.'

'What are we looking for?'

'The routine of the guards. Any regular patrols. The best possible route with the most cover. We must learn the ground like the back of our hands so we can cross it in the dark. We know your Edmund is out there somewhere and the only chance of reaching him is at night. And we've got three nights left before midsummer.'

In the gathering gloom of the glade, Barbara was now half-enveloped in a shaggy cocoon of ivy. Several bramble stalks had already coiled loosely about her, but they were slowly, inexorably, tightening their grip. An early fox on the prowl trotted into the glade, paused curiously and pricked up its ears, then slowly padded over towards her still form. He got within ten feet of her when he sniffed suddenly and saw the toadstool ring on the grass. He turned and ran and in a moment had disappeared through the trees. The forest waited on.

'Whatever it was,' the *Prince Randolph*'s chief engineer admitted forlornly, 'it could work through our shields, at least at low power. But they didn't register any penetration.'

'Things may be different with shields on full, chief,' Chandry suggested.

'I hope so, sir.'

'Meanwhile we seem to have got beyond the range of the . . . er, effect, whatever it was.'

'Six dead, several minor injuries and a serious loss of morale and operational efficiency,' Nyborg stated flatly. 'All achieved within ten minutes, possibly by some half-seen ghost, which may or may not be responsible for illusions and psycho-kinetic manifestations. Or it may have been merely another illusion in itself.' He glowered down the length of the table. 'There was no prior attempt at peaceful communication. These are deliberate acts of sabotage. From this moment on, we must consider ourselves at war with persons or forces, as yet unknown, on the planet below. I am open to suggestions as to how we may deal with this situation. For a start, is it connected with the nanobot presence on the planet?'

'Theoretically,' said the chief, 'nanobots in large enough numbers could project electromagnetic, or gravimetric pulses that could simulate what we experienced, without the need for actual physical contact. But it would eat up a lot of power, and only function over a relatively short range.'

'That's something to be thankful for, at least.'

'If we can ascertain the exact time and duration of these events,' the head of planetary scanning suggested, 'we may be able to match them with specific energy fluctuations on the planet's surface. Assuming there is a fixed point of origin to these attacks, we can then identify it.'

Nyborg brightened. 'That sounds promising, lieutenant. We're operating blind here. The enemy can see us, but we can't see him. But if we have a definite target,' his voice dropped, 'then they shall learn the cost of assaulting ships of the Empire!'

21

Amateur Magic

For the first time, Dhal did not enquire how they had slept. This was probably for the best, as they had taken turns watching out of the window through most of the night, and so were quite tired. As it happened, Dhal didn't look as though he'd had much sleep himself. He was unshaven, there were dark circles under his eyes and his clothes were crumpled. The workbenches of his chamber were littered with a jumble of magical paraphernalia, and the smell of strange potions hung in the air.

'The other day you taunted me with the threat posed by the oldworlders,' he said to Susan. 'That was very impolite.' He let an ominous silence develop until she swallowed uneasily, fearing he was going to take some sort of revenge for her impudence. He smiled at her anxiety. 'I just thought you might be interested in the steps I have taken against them,' he finished mildly.

The images of the orbiting ships hung within his seeing globe. 'You notice they are smaller than they were,' he pointed out, almost as though he were giving a lecture. 'My actions have caused them to move further away from Avalon's surface. They have learned, I believe, to respect my powers. Unlike some,' he added meaningfully.

'But there are only four ships,' Susan exclaimed. 'You haven't . . .'

'I cannot take the credit for that,' Dhal admitted candidly. 'The other skyboat may have simply left, but I suspect they may have been careless and come too close to our world and suffered the same fate as all such vessels do. Still, by whatever means, there is one less for me to worry about. If they all leave, they are of no further concern. If they approach again to land more of their small boats,' he smiled, 'then I am well prepared. I have learnt what vessel to keep special watch on. Would you like to see what I have prepared for it?'

On the workbench next to his desk was a box-like shape, about a foot square, covered by a thick black cloth. Dhal stepped over to it, motioning them after him, and drew the cover off with a flourish. They instinctively flinched away when they saw the thing inside the tiny cage. Yet there was a terrible fascination when they realized it was, improbably, in a real sense, alive. They couldn't help but lean closer to stare disbelievingly.

'Engaging little creature, isn't it?' said Dhal proudly. 'They're quite hard to capture and keep securely, as you can imagine. Feeding, of course, is no problem. You just have to be sure it doesn't eat too much or it has a tendency to grow out of control. But then, that is the nature of the beast.' He picked up the box with a pair of long tongs and carried it over to the centre of the pentagram marked on the floor, and carefully set it down. 'I am prepared to send this to them, if necessary. It will be an effort, but the thing is so nearly immaterial already that I'm sure I will manage the task. But its cage, I fear, will be beyond me. They will have to catch and tame it afresh. I trust they will find it diverting.'

Susan and Mellisa looked at him in horror as they realized his intent.

'Would you like to watch?' he enquired considerately. 'I promise to have you brought up here if there's time. No? Oh well, please yourselves.'

There was a sharp bang from below decks, making everybody on the *Merrow* flinch. Thin streamers of white smoke drifted out of the ship's ports and swirled away behind them. There was a shout of *fire!* and a rush for buckets. Ian and Jen clattered down the steps from the upper deck only to meet Kilvenny Odoyle emerging from the companionway, coughing slightly.

'No need for alarm,' he assured them. 'Just a minor mishap. No damage. No fire,' he assured Tristram and the bucket laden crewmen who dashed up to the doorway.

'What is going on?' Ian demanded. 'The Doctor's up to something, isn't he?'

'Ah, well, my friend, you'd better ask him that for yourself. And if he's a mind, he'll tell you. But I'd wait a while longer, if I were you.' And the leprechaun smiled and winked, and returned down below once more.

A snail had crawled across Barbara's face in the night, leaving a glistening trail over her cheek. She had not stirred. There had been a brief shower of rain, soaking the grass and her dress. She slept on, the rhythm of her breathing so shallow as to be almost imperceptible. The ivy had totally enveloped her lower body, binding her legs and arms to the ground, and working its way across her chest with a tightening web. Soon it would reach her throat, but there was a length of green and supple bramble already circling her neck, slowly tightening. Already it had drawn the first pinprick drops of blood on its thorns. As it did so, its stem was infused with a scarlet tint.

Back in their cell, Susan's face still burned with anger as she thought of what Dhal planned.

'I am so sorry,' Mellisa said sympathetically, 'but even your fellow oldworlders are doomed if they oppose him. We can never match his power.'

'No,' Susan replied determinedly. 'I'm sure there's nothing impossible about what he does, as long as you know the trick.' Yes, she thought, but what *is* the trick? Well at least I can try. What is there to lose?

'Is your chemical magic powerful enough?'

'Maybe! For a start I'll . . .' What? Something simple. Something not too unlikely that she could believe was almost conventionally possible. '. . . I'll get rid of the bed bugs!'

Well, it was mundane, but it was a start. Even as she

spoke she was aware that she had no real idea of how to do what she so confidently claimed was possible.

But, perhaps, absolute knowledge was not actually necessary. Did Dhal or Gramling really know how their spells worked in every detail? Or were they like the drivers of those wonderful antique twentieth-century cars she had ridden in during her time on Earth? Few of them knew what went on under their bonnets, but they could still drive them perfectly well. A few simple actions made a far more complex, but hidden, mechanism work. They believed that turning a key and treading on a pedal would make the car go, and, usually, it did. But was belief in itself important here? Some instinct told her it was. It was bad science to think belief could affect the outcome of such an experiment. But perhaps it was good magic.

'Right. We've got time before they bring the meal round,' she said briskly. 'We'll get the bottles back inside. Stand the mattresses up against the wall.'

In two minutes they were ready. The base rim of the upturned washing bowl gave her a simple mixing crucible. She had plucked a few protruding straws from the offending mattresses for symbolic effect, and had crumbled them into it with a little water. Now she had the vials ready to pour. There were many gases that such a reaction might genuinely produce which would serve her purpose, of course, but hardly in the quantities required. Never mind. This was not conventional chemistry. She knew what she wanted to happen. All she need do was give it a nudge in the right direction. She swallowed nervously knowing this would only work if she had total confidence. She knelt before the bowl, concentrated, gestured, poured a few drops from the vials. A rhyme! What should she say? And then some simple words fell into place:

'Compounds combine upon this plate,
to make a smoke that will fumigate.
Cleanse the filling of this poor bed,

230

so in comfort I may rest my head.
Rid us of bugs and mites that bite,
so we sleep easy for once all night.'

A fountain of glowing green smoke rose from her improvised crucible, spiralled in the air for a moment, then streamed into the mattresses and vanished. There was a faint hissing, like hundreds of tiny insect bodies simultaneously popping, then the sound died away.

There was a long silence in the cell while Mellisa looked at her in awe.

'You really did it. You *are* a magician!' she said at last, her face alive with wonder and hope for the first time in days.

Susan, still slightly dazed by her success, felt herself smile foolishly for a moment before common sense reasserted itself. She had to face facts, even if it meant disappointing Mellisa. 'I made one very simple spell work, that's all. If you think I can simply fly us out of here right now, forget it, because I daren't risk anything that complicated. I've got a day and a bit, at most, to use what little we have to get us out of here. I just hope Dhal's too busy to notice what we're doing right under his nose!'

On the screens and graphic displays of the *Prince Randolph*'s bridge, they watched first the *Tigershark*, then the *Dorado* make a low orbital sweep over half the hemisphere of Avalon. Their retuned and amplified scanners strained to record any fluctuation of the energy flow across the planet. Nothing interfered with the passage of the vessels that anybody could detect. Crewmen waiting by open comm lines, ready to call out at the first sign of abnormal behaviour or any inexplicable incident, saw nothing.

'They're not buying it, Admiral,' said Chandry.

Nyborg was very much afraid that he was right.

The *Indus* made her pass with the same anticlimactic results.

'All right, Bob. Let's make the bait more tempting. Prepare to make the pass ourselves. Remind the crew of the drill.'

It was the first time Chandry could remember the Admiral calling him by his Christian name on the bridge.

Dhal saw the largest of the ships leave formation and start its run in. He smiled and closed his eyes in concentration. He spoke the words of power and mixed the waiting powders. He pushed with his mind and felt the living aura of the planet bend to his will. It was a strain when he tried to accomplish such a feat. But soon that would all change. There. It was done!

The little cage in the middle of the pentagram was empty.

Fire in hangar deck! Emergency! Fire in the hangar deck!

The alarms wailed. Isolation doors slammed shut. Crewmen rushed forward with extinguishers spraying clouds of foam and gas. But the spinning, dancing fireball, which had popped out of nowhere, seemed always to elude them.

Then it stetched and uncurled.

A figure of fire a foot high pranced before them. A perfect little man of red and yellow flame, who skipped and cavorted through the cavernous hangar deck. And everywhere his feet touched, if it was remotely flammable, they left tiny burning imprints that flared up and spread. Across work benches and through the hatches of the landers under modification it flitted, and the trail of fire followed. Metal scorched and blistered. Supposedly flameproof plastics melted, smoked and flared briefly.

But still it was frustrated. Nothing burned really well here. The fire sprite danced on, hungrily searching. Some strange sense attracted it towards a long metal container resting on the floor beside a lander.

CAUTION: EXPLOSIVES: MARK 3 SOLID FUEL BOOSTER UNITS.

The sprite could not read, but it knew what food smelt like.

It sprang for the lid, searching for the slightest crack. Extinguisher foam sprayed over it. The little figure seemed to shrivel and then it was gone. The fire crew smothered the case in foam and stood back. Nothing happened. They turned to each other, foolish grins of relief showing behind their masks.

The case lid blew upwards.

A solid fuel rocket erupted from within, flared into life and cartwheeled across the hangar. The sprite rode it like a bucking bronco, but facing backwards; washing its hands in the blazing exhaust as it lashed across men and machines. And it was growing even as it tumbled about on its blazing wild broomstick. Two feet tall, three feet, four feet.

A second rocket ignited in the case, blowing out the sides and scattering the rest of the tubes about the hangar, some already igniting as they went. The hangar filled with smoke and unquenchable oxidant-fed fire.

Rows of explosive bolts blew in the hangar's huge inner airlock door, releasing a panel only slightly smaller than the door itself, which hinged down and dropped flat. Beyond was the outer door. A second string of bolts blew out its central panel in turn, and tons of air pressure tumbled it away towards the stars.

The hurricane wind of decompression blasted through the hangar, picking up everything loose in its path. Smoke, blazing rocket tubes, small tools, scraps and work sheets, trailing cables and the sprite, now eight feet tall, were all carried away; tumbling and whirling end over end out into the void.

And with them, eight men.

A ninth was trapped within an open lander cabin and was rescued by the emergency crew. He lived, but anoxia and explosive decompression would leave him permanently brain-damaged.

* * *

The sharp pricks of pain and a terrible sensation of being squeezed tighter and tighter at last penetrated the depths of Barbara's unnatural slumber. Feebly, she began to struggle, as though she was caught in the throes of a nightmare and desperate to wake up; but she could not break free or even open her eyes. She started to choke, and the world began to slip away. The last thing she was aware of was a small, rasping tongue licking her face, and, distantly, a voice saying: 'Here's a fine pickle for a young lass to be in . . .'

Sir Bron was worried about the Doctor. Over the week that he had known him, he had grown quite fond of the old man. For all his irascibility and impatient mannerisms, he respected his obvious wisdom and stalwart determination. Yet, just when he could have done with wise council to help him reconcile the strange truth that had been revealed about Avalon, he had shut himself away in his cabin, seeing almost no one but Kilvenny Odoyle. And now he had come to him with a most peculiar request. Would he compensate Tristram for the price of some small bolts of material the captain had in the hold, unsold from his last trip? And who could he borrow scissors, needle and thread from? Oh, yes, and some wire if possible. Puzzled, Bron had agreed to cover the cost, and the Doctor had retreated to his cabin again. Oddly, he could not see that the Doctor's own strangely fashioned clothes needed repairing. In any case, what would he want with several yards of red silk?

The inspiration came to Susan as she watched Mellisa comb out her long hair with the carved bone comb Dhal had provided.

They had taken to washing and trying to keep as neat and clean as possible once they were locked in for the night, and would not be disturbed again until morning. Combing out her striking mane of hair was something the Princess clearly took great care over. In the mornings

234

Susan plaited it for her, taking time over the task. Any diversion to fill the long hours of their incarceration was welcome. But now another association clicked into place in Susan's mind, and she grinned broadly. 'Appropriate' had indeed been the right word.

'I know how we can get down from here,' she announced brightly. Mellisa paused in mid-stroke.

'You have a spell? That is wonderful! What is it?'

'Just a minute. We must decide when to go first. It has to work first time, you see. We won't be able to wait and try again later.'

'Why not tonight?'

'I want to get out of here as much as you, but I think it might be sensible to wait until tomorrow night.'

'But that is almost the last minute. The next day is midsummer when Dhal's ultimatum expires.'

'Exactly. And the nearer we escape to that deadline, the more chance we have of spoiling his plans. Look, you know there's a chance they'll capture us again before we get very far, and, even if we do reach Edmund, we might not make it home anyway?' Mellisa nodded glumly. 'But the closer to the deadline the more likely it is that Dhal will have other things on his mind. Midsummer may have some magical significance for the handing over of these treasures. Whatever reason he wants us there for, that will be the time when we can hurt him most.'

Mellisa was silent for a long time, then she nodded. 'Yes, Susan, I see your reason in this. I will resign myself to being apart from my Edmund for one more night. At least we are safe here until then. But now you must tell me, how can we get down?'

'Well, you will have to make a small sacrifice, I'm afraid . . .'

Nyborg turned a grey face towards the lieutenant in charge of the scanner team.

'Have you found it? This bloody mess had better be worth it.'

'Yes, Admiral. We've correlated against previous read-ings and matched the event with the flow patterns.' He pointed to a spot on the printout map of Avalon. 'Just there. An isolated tower-like structure, in the middle of this open moorland.'

Nyborg stared at it for a long time in silence. Finally he said: 'We shall synchronize our response. As soon as we've repaired the damage, and have a sufficient force of modified landers ready, they will go in after our prime objective. But before they leave the ship, we shall obliterate that tower from the face of the planet!'

22

Witch Craft

Consciousness did not return easily to Barbara. For the first time in days, it seemed, she was warm and comfortable. She simply didn't want to wake up. But there was a sound troubling her; a regular clicking that seemed irritatingly persistent. Its rhythm stirred a vague recollection of being lost in the forest and dancing. And then . . . She jerked up with a start, pushing at the ivy that wrapped about her.

Except it was not ivy but blankets. She was staring up at the low, sagging, black-beamed ceiling of the tiny bedroom of the cat's cottage.

'There, there, me dear. Don't you fret now. I've tended your hurts. It's all over.'

Sitting in a rocking chair beside the bed, was the old woman she had found in the kitchen. She put down her knitting and offered Barbara a sip of water from a china mug sitting on the tiny bedside table. Her eyes were now as black and bright as blackberries, Barbara realized; so different from the glaze she had last seen over them.

'Thank you,' Barbara said faintly. 'I remember . . . you found me in the woods.'

'Nearly gone, you was,' the old woman admitted. 'But cat found you. Soon as I came to myself, he was bothering me over you. He knew you'd met trouble, and he was right.'

'I got lost. I made marks on the trees, but somebody must have been playing tricks, because more kept appearing. I was only trying to get help for you, and get word to Fluxford that I was all right.'

'Some puck or bogie having his prank, no doubt. But you should never have wandered into the fairy ring, specially near midsummer.'

'I didn't know. They offered me something to drink, and I was so thirsty by then.'

The old woman sucked in her breath through her teeth censoriously. 'Never take food nor drink offered to you in a fairy revel. They has funny ways with intruders. You were lucky they only left you for the forest to claim, or else . . .' she trailed off darkly. 'Still, who am I to talk, seeing how I was caught by a weasly trick myself. And it was kind what you did, and really 'tis I who should be thanking you for taking care of me before, mistress. Ah, now, I haven't had your name yet.'

'It's Barbara Wright.'

'That has the ring of a sound and sensible name. I'm Anni. Old Anni, they sometimes call me round here. Anni Glassfeather in full.' She smiled, ''Cos I sees clearly, goes lightly, and is harder than I looks.'

Barbara liked her smile. It was reassuring. Despite her wrinkled features, Anni seemed to glow with vitality. Perhaps she had seen so much of life that she had stored it up within her. 'Do you live out here all alone?' she asked.

'Of course. 'Tis only right and proper considering my calling.'

'Oh, what do you do?'

'Why, I'm a witch, of course.'

I shouldn't be surprised, Barbara thought. Really it was only a matter of time in a country like this. Still, it sounded odd to hear the word spoken so matter-of-factly. Aloud she said: 'Sorry, I didn't realize. I'm from . . . abroad, you see.'

'I could tell you wasn't from around these parts. But do you know what's afoot in the land? You mentioned Fluxford. There is a nasty taste to the air from that way, and I'd say it was wizard magic. Is it that Dhal? I reckon he was the one who tainted those apples. Should have known they was too fresh to have kept over winter natural, like, when I bought them.'

'They were poisoned, then?'

'They were coated in faerie sleep. Not unlike what made you swoon.'

'But why not actually . . . well, poison you?'

'Not so easy to tell as poison, see. And anyway, he knows killing me would cause ructions. Others in the sisterhood would sense it and come to see what had caused it. No. Better have Old Anni out the way snoozing till it were all over. Might it have been him, then?'

'Probably. He's given the King an ultimatum to make him the royal sorcerer, and he's kidnapped Princess Mellisa and a friend of mine, and —'

'Whoa, there, Mistress Barbara. You've a long tale to tell, that's for sure. Tell it to me slow and steady like, and then we'll see about making Marton Dhal rue the day he were born! Faerie apples indeed!'

There was no reason why Queen Leonora should not have attended the war council meeting in the Stewards Room. It was simply that the Queen of Elbyon was expected to attend to other matters at such times.

Today she decided she no longer cared whether it was expected or not.

The comfortable order she had known for so long was sliding away. They had received visitors from beyond the veil in a magic box. Now the circling skyboats of others could be seen every night. Gramling was unsure of their intentions. How would they influence Dhal's plans? Whatever the outcome, something different would take its place. Now was not the time to blindly obey protocol. Besides, decisions made at the meeting might mean the difference between life or death for her daughter. So she simply told Magnus that she would attend that day, and he made no fuss, the poor man was so tired. So they sat together at the table while the reports were read, and opinions given; and she commended where she agreed, and countered where she thought otherwise. Halfway through the meeting, she felt her husband's hand slip into hers under the table, and give a little squeeze. Then she knew she had done right by coming. She had Barbara to thank for the inspiration. Poor Barbara.

'The search for Lady Barbara has had to be abandoned, I regret, Sire,' Peridor reported. 'Keeping the roads open, maintaining order, and the protection of the surrounding farms is making too great a call on our time. However, there has been a great exodus of folk of many types from the forest, driven out by Dhal's creatures, and we are questioning all we can for any news of her. At least we have heard nothing untoward as yet.'

'I understand. What of our military strength?'

'The build-up continues, though some forces have been harried on their way here and delayed. The muster as of this morning was three hundred knights, eight hundred skilled archers and some two thousand trained foot soldiers. In addition, there are perhaps as many again half-armed yeomanry. The main body of troops from Glazebry has yet to arrive. They have suffered most from assaults and delays, no doubt the work of Dhal. They cannot be expected before the morrow.'

'I see. Thank you, Peridor. Captain Morgane?'

'The additional defences are almost complete, Sire. Lady Barbara's wires . . . your pardon, but that is what they are being called, have been strung over all main battlements and windows. Extra javelins and crossbow bolts have been made ready. Dhal's flying apes shall not enter the castle so easily a second time!'

'Of that I am sure. Now, Palbury, should this become a siege, how long would we and the town last?'

'Master Harding has been keeping check of the exact totals. In general, however, I believe we could last a month, no more. In this time before harvest, the stores in the castle and town are low. If additional supplies of fresh game and forage were cut by siege, and with extra

240

mouths to feed sheltering within our walls and those of the town, it cannot be otherwise. Concerning which, Sire, many goblins, cephlies and others have also been driven out of the forest and are seeking shelter. There has been some trouble over the common folk objecting to sharing with them. If food becomes a problem –'

'We shall shelter *all*,' the Queen interjected firmly, 'whatever their natures. Dhal's creatures make no distinction, neither shall we. Please allow them to stay within the outer walls, Stephan, if the town will not have them.' Palbury inclined his head in assent.

'It may not come to a siege, of course,' the King pondered. 'I do not see that Dhal has the patience. Though to be sure, he has been a long time in planning this confrontation. Wizard, have your arts been able to penetrate his stronghold and gain any insight into his plans . . .' he faltered '. . . or any news of the Princess?'

'Sadly, no, Majesty. He has shielded his fastness against such spying as I am holding this castle against his. But as you say, he has prepared long for this day. How one wizard, even one as powerful as he, can have created such forces I do not know. When this is over we may learn who has aided him, for he must have had aid. But time enough for that later. Our best hope, still, I feel, must lie with those sent after Merlin's Helm. That will be a weapon which Dhal cannot resist.'

'Sire,' said Palbury, 'the river has been made dangerous again by further attacks of Dhal's creatures on watercraft. Should we not send a message to Fluxmouth to warn Bron's party on their return, so they may be prepared?'

'A wise precaution. When might they return at the earliest?'

'If they have met with no unexpected delays and the weather has been kind,' Gramling answered him, 'then it is possible for them to return today. But more likely it will be tonight or even tomorrow. I could make divination for them, but I hesitate to do so lest it leave the

241

castle unguarded, or even draw Dhal's attention in their direction.'

'That must be avoided at all costs,' the King agreed. 'Their only chance is to remain inconspicuous and unimportant should he come across them. But I fear it will be a close run thing.'

'It was always going to be so, Majesty,' Gramling agreed solemnly.

A few hours rest had left Barbara feeling fully recovered again. She had no idea what sort of ointment Anni applied to the many minor injuries picked up during her time in the forest, and thought it best not to speculate about what it contained, but scratches and bruises alike had practically disappeared. Even the dragon scar on her leg had faded, and it no longer ached.

In the early afternoon, she climbed down the narrow creaking stairs of the cottage to find Anni busy in the kitchen. Many of the bunches of herbs and odd looking plants, previously strung from the beams, were now scattered about the table. Several pots hung on the hooks over the fire, bubbling merrily. The cat was stretched out on the mat in front of it, one cocked ear swivelled round to follow Barbara's footsteps, but otherwise it did not stir. Anni, wearing her apron once more, was frowning over a large, yellowed book propped up on the table, while she chopped and ground different coloured seeds, leaves and powders. An assortment of small bottles and tiny draw-stringed bags waited to be filled with the end results of her labours.

'Ah, you be looking better, me dear,' said Anni cheerfully, without actually looking up from her work.

'I am, thank you. Are you cooking something special?'

'In a manner of means. I'm cooking, dear, but more truthfully I'm potioning.'

'Sorry?'

'A wizard has a workroom to prepare his potions in, but a witch's workroom is her kitchen. Besides, it's convenient if I get peckish while I'm busy.'

'So all these ingredients are for, uh, magic potions?' She couldn't help hesitating. It still sounded foolish out loud.

'Will be, if they're mixed proper,' Anni replied practically.

'But what are they for?'

'They're for just in case, me dear.'

Shortly, all the liquids and powders had been decanted, the pots were off the fire, the table was cleared, and Anni was putting the last of the bottles and bags into her apron pockets. A simple cloth bag with an over-the-shoulder strap bulged with the rest.

'Now, we've got to look the part,' she continued, surveying Barbara critically. 'Good thing your dress has seen a bit of dirt, recently, 'cos I don't know that I'd have anything to fit. Hmm, just a scarf and you'll do, I'd say.' She opened a cramped cupboard under the stairs, took out a headscarf of indeterminate colour and handed it to her.

'Do? Do for what?'

Anni had retrieved a traditional tall black witch's hat from the cupboard. She frowned at the point for a moment, then pressed it firmly and it concertinaed down until it resembled a crumpled boater. This she tied on with a length of black ribbon under her chin. 'Why, paying a visit to Marton Dhal's tower, of course. You want to get your friend back, don't you? Not to mention Princess Mellisa, poor dear.'

'Yes, of course. But at Fluxford, they thought it would take an army to capture Dhal's tower.'

'Well, what of it? That's typical of men to think of sieges and great battles. Who wants Dhal's tower anyhow? We just want to get the girls out.'

'But how?'

'Wizards and kings can only think of going in the front door. But witches are used to going in the back.'

'Just the two of us?'

Anni pulled a tin bucket and mop out from the cupboard, stood them ready, then reached inside again. 'Couldn't carry no more, could we?'

'Oh.'

The last two items Anni retrieved should really not have surprised her, in the circumstances. After all, how else had she thought they were going to travel?

23

Flight

It was early evening when the *Merrow* finally glided into Fluxmouth harbour and made her berth.

There were waves and cheers from the quayside. Where the *Merrow* had gone was a mystery, but the people were relieved to see her back. The gangplank was slid out, but even before they could step ashore, the harbourmaster had run on board and thrust a carrier pigeon message slip at Sir Bron, with as much deference as haste permitted. 'Said it must be given to you as soon as you docked, sir,' he puffed.

Bron read the message and grew grave. 'The river way to Fluxford may now be unsafe. It may be better if we return overland.'

'That'll take too long,' Ian protested.

'It may be the only way. We must hope to make it in time.'

'I believe I may be able to manage something,' said Kilvenny Odoyle, thoughtfully. 'I think I can fly us back.'

Ian thought of the leprechaun passing out after flying the *Merrow*. Obviously five people would be easier, but they would presumably still need to ride *in* something, and the journey would be far longer. 'Are you sure?'

'It won't be easy, I admit. Flying spells need a lot of concentration. But I have the makings with me. Now if we can have a few of those gull feathers over there, and borrow a row boat, the lighter the better, then we're away.'

'If you want a really light boat,' said Komati, who had been listening on the edge of the group, 'then you're welcome to our raft.'

Odoyle beamed. 'A fine idea, lass. A boat of air to ride the air. 'Twill make the job half the strain.'

'On one condition,' she added.

Bron looked at her suspiciously. 'What is that?'

'That I go with you.' She looked up at the sky for a moment. 'They won't give up, you know. Shannon told them enough to find this Fluxford of yours, and gave an idea of what the Helm might be. They'll come after it. Maybe I can help. At least I can try to talk to them.'

'Very well,' Bron agreed.

Ian had also looked upwards. The sky was clouding over. In fact, it was beginning to look ominous.

Barbara would have pinched herself to check if she was dreaming, if she had not been gripping the shaft of the broomstick quite so firmly with both hands. I'm flying on a witch's broomstick. No. On her spare broomstick, she corrected herself, feeling a grimace of panic tug up the corners of her mouth. It was ridiculous. Unfortunately, that didn't stop it being real. Anni Glassfeather, who was calmly sitting on a second broom ten feet away, glanced over.

'That's better, dear; you enjoy yourself.'

The next solid object beyond Anni was the ground, perhaps two thousand feet below. Barbara had never had any fear of heights or flying until now. But then, being enclosed in a solid fuselage was not the same as perching on an inch and a half thickness of broom handle. And yet, it wasn't quite as simple as that either.

She had to admit it was more comfortable than she'd expected. Some pressure seemed to be supporting her and spreading the load, so that she was flying with the broom, rather than wholly resting upon it. The rush of air past her was also reduced to a light breeze. How? And for that matter, why hadn't Gramling or anyone else in the castle mentioned Anni before? Was it unconscious male chauvinism? And could only witches and women ride broomsticks? More mysteries.

They flew on. The sky was filling with clouds, it looked like they were going to have a storm.

Bron and Ian took the oars and hesitantly pulled on them. Odoyle muttered something under his breath and shook some powder on to the inflatable's bulging prow. The feathers tied to the oar blades fluttered. There was a slight scraping and the raft rose silently off the deck of the *Merrow* and into the air. The sailors waved and shouted. 'Farewell!' Tristram called after them. Fluxmouth shrank below as they turned sedately inland towards the mountains.

Ian saw the Doctor's face. He was sitting beside Jen Komati, who looked slightly green. The Doctor, however, seemed perfectly calm. No longer annoyed or irritated; almost as though he was thinking how easy it all was when you knew how. On his knees was a tightly wrapped bundle of red silk.

Barbara and Anni touched down on the moor a few miles from Raven's Tor. Staring at the expanse of rolling, boggy ground they now had to cross on foot, Barbara suddenly found herself missing flying. She had actually begun to tolerate travelling on the broomstick, and, though Anni was obviously helping guide her stick, she was quite pleased with the way she had pulled up its nose just as they touched down and slipped off to finish her flight smoothly with a few running steps. With a bit of practice, she might even come to enjoy it.

'Edmund's company of scouts should be around here somewhere,' Barbara said.

'Well we'll just have to avoid them, won't we, lass? Dhal's bound to be watching them.'

'So we sneak past them and up to the door of the tower –'

'No, me dear. We watches where we puts our feet, walks boldly up to the door and knocks.'

'And they just let us in?'

'Dhal don't rely on other people, see, just these creatures he's made, and they're quite stupid outside doing what they're told. With a little persuading they'll take us for what we look like. Remember what I said about back doors? Why do you think we brought the mop and bucket?'

Barbara hadn't liked to ask. Now she began to understand. It was absurd. But perhaps no more so than the broomsticks.

Shannon stood in the ruined dome of Helm Island staring up at the sky. At his back the sun was going down but the stars were not yet out. Through his sensitized goggles he read the pulsing spot of light that marked the position of the squadron.

PREPARE FOR RECOVERY WITHIN NEXT THREE HOURS.

At last they were ready!

He sent an acknowledgement with the radiation torch, then awkwardly slung his pack. One arm was in a sling, and he limped as he walked. His survival suit was torn and dirty, but his bearing was still erect and upright. Before he left the dome through the passage to the head of the stairs, he paused by Monadno's cairn and saluted it. At least they had treated his comrade correctly. When this was over, he would see his remains were returned to Earth for a proper funeral. He saluted Thurguld's cairn as well, as one warrior to another. Besides, he had no argument with the dead.

Then he limped off towards the stairs.

Shardrog, commander of the third turret, did not know what to make of the insistent banging on the heavy outer door, which a puzzled guard had called him about. Hardly anybody used the paths now all the linking tunnels were complete. What stupid ape was outside at this time? He looked down from the battlements and saw, in the gathering gloom, two human women carrying brooms, bucket and mop.

'Come on! We ain't got all day,' the older and smaller of the two called out. 'He said to be here before sundown and we're nearly late already and you know he doesn't like to be kept waiting.'

Even through his bafflement, Shardrog knew who 'he' was. But what were these two doing outside? He looked about anxiously at the landscape being swallowed rapidly by purple shadows. There was no sign of any besieging force, and in any case, he was fairly sure armies were not usually preceded by women with buckets who knocked at the door first. Actually he would have preferred an army. This was more complicated. 'What you doing here?' he asked doubtfully.

The older woman raised her broom and shook it in the air. 'We've come to clean up his quarters, of course. Special job. Wants them clean for tomorrow. Special day tomorrow.'

That was true. They were all preparing for it down below. And the two couldn't have got past the traps on the moor without knowing the safe path, or setting off alarms. But he wished he'd been told. 'Over there is tower,' he growled down at them. 'Why you come here?'

''Cos we want an escort across all those paths and rough ground up to the tower door and see we get let in. That's only right and proper when going to an important place like this, isn't it?'

And Shardrog suddenly realized that *was* the proper way, and wondered why he hadn't remembered. A feeling of panic swept over him. He mustn't keep *him* waiting. He must send down an escort.

'You women wait there. Guard come down quick.'

'Thank you, dearie.'

Dhal had been watching the skyboats in his seeing globe for some time. They had adjusted their orbit slightly, and he suspected they might be trying another approach. Because they could move so fast, he only dared take his

249

eyes off them for a minute or two. Briefly he changed to a view of Fluxford to check on progress there. At least that was going well. His attentions had reduced it to a city under siege. Then he changed to a quite different scene before he returned to the ships.

And now he couldn't find what he was looking for!

He started searching, with a growing sense of panic, ignoring the ships. There were only so many routes, surely. Ah, that explained it. But they had gone further than he expected. How long until . . . ?

His plans for tomorrow dissolved in a glorious and frightening realization.

It would be tonight!

Susan and Mellisa heard the beginning of the commotion not long after final lock-up. For a moment they were paralysed with dismay. It was as though the tower was coming alive. There were distant muffled orders being shouted, the drumming of many feet, the clink of armour and deep moans and roars from the pits. A sense of panic seemed to drive the activity. Were they under attack? Or was Dhal making his move earlier than they had thought? Whatever it was, it was too soon for their plans.

Susan could not read Mellisa's face in the last of the grey light that filtered in through the window, but she could sense her anguish. The guards might come for them at any moment. It was probably hopeless. But what was there to lose? Taking a deep breath she said firmly: 'We go now!'

'But it's —'

'Now!' Susan put all her determination into the word. Mellisa obeyed.

They assembled the necessary items almost totally by touch. They had practised it earlier, planning to make the attempt in the middle of the night. Susan had made a very limited test of her spell, the satisfactory result of which had been stuffed into the mattress so the guards would not see it. Now they would know if it would work for real. They were ready. She took a deep breath, poured the last drops from the vials, and began to speak her rhyme.

The ape guard had led them halfway from the perimeter ditch to the base of the rock when the activity began. For a moment he was horribly undecided which way to run, knowing it was a call to arms, but having been ordered to take the two servant women to the tower. The older one helped him make up his mind.

'Don't you worry about us,' she said cheerfully. 'I'm sure you've got lots more important things to do. You run along now. You *forget* about us . . .'

And in a moment he had. He ran off, taking the lantern with him.

Anni drew Barbara into the cover of a straggling gorse bush. 'Fair buzzing like a wasps' nest stirred with a stick,' she observed.

'*Randolph* to *Dorado*. Arm warhead and begin your approach run. Good luck and good shooting.'

'Fetch my cloak,' Dhal commanded his servants, marshalling the confusion into order. 'You! Put the globe in its carrier . . . don't drop it, fool. Take it to my personal mount. You two, fetch the women and take them below. Hurry!'

'This is Admiral Nyborg to all Marine commanders: confirm your men are boarded and ready. Departure on my signal.'

The bolts slid back and the cell door was thrown open.

'You come with us now,' growled one of the apes.

There was no response. Its companion unhooked a lantern from the wall beside the door and held it aloft.

The prisoners were gone.

They stepped inside and looked about them in

251

astonishment. There was a slight scraping noise. They saw the window bar was now wedged horizontally across the aperture. About its middle was knotted what looked like the end of a golden rope, extending tautly out into the night. Even as they watched, the rope trembled slightly.

With a grunt of alarm the first ape leaped for the window, grabbed hold of the bar, and began tugging at it. His companion took his shoulders and added his weight. Slowly the rope was drawn back into the cell. Then the tension vanished and the apes fell backwards, pulling a length of slack rope after them. In the light it was obviously a continuous plait of blonde hair, but pierced through at regular intervals by foot-long spikes of bone to serve as rungs. The apes looked at each other in horror for a moment, then scrambled to their feet and left the cell in a shambling run. Lying unnoticed in a corner of the cell was a comb. Most of its teeth were missing.

Susan and Mellisa rolled down the bank of thin turf that skirted the tower base until they reached a level stretch and came to a halt. They lay gasping for a moment, shocked and winded by their forced drop from the hair rope. They had grey blankets tied about their necks as camouflage. Weakly, Mellisa pulled hers over her head, concealing a mop of golden hair now as short as Susan's.

Determinedly, Susan got to her feet and pulled Mellisa with her. 'Come on,' she hissed. 'We must keep moving!'

They scrambled down the rocks, skidding and slipping and taking desperate risks in the darkness, which was now almost total. Only a faint glow penetrated the heavily overcast sky, and, so far, only a few torches glowed on the tower and its outflung perimeter turrets. That at least was to their advantage. But Susan wanted to be well clear before those few torches turned into many. If only they hadn't been discovered so quickly. In another minute they had reached level ground. How long would it take

252

for word to spread and the search to start in earnest? Should they make a run for it, or conceal themselves within the perimeter, where they could sneak out later behind any search parties?

Even as they hesitated, an unseen door opened in the rock of the tor itself, catching them on the edge of a widening fan of light. They dashed off into the darkness, but a grunting cry told them they had been spotted. Booted feet pounded after them. They heard more shouts. Torches began flickering across the crest of the tor. They stumbled on across the rutted ground, heading for the open moor. If they could just cross the ditch they might have a chance. Then they saw lights around the bases of the turrets, and knew the net was closing about them. The running feet following them were getting closer.

There was an odd popping, crackling sound, followed by a sharp hissing. The jerking torches behind them became blurred and hazy as a cloud of thick smoke billowed up from nowhere. The cries of the guards became confused shouts of rage and alarm, interspersed with coughing. Susan and Mellisa halted uncertainly as there were more firecracker explosions. Within moments, the tower and turrets had vanished in a pall of smoke.

Then a figure appeared out of the gloom.

'This way, quickly!' It was Barbara's voice.

For five days, Edmund and his small company had camped uncomfortably in the shelter of the jagged rock outcrop some three miles or so from the tower. It had been a frustrating, anxious time, spent circling the tor from afar, probing its defences. He had sent regular messages back to Fluxford detailing its situation and the pits, bogs and other traps they had discovered that protected it, and noting the comings and goings of Dhal's flying beasts. But that was all he could do. It was anguish, knowing Mellisa was so near, yet quite beyond his reach.

He was dreaming of her when the sentry roused him.

Sounds of confusion were drifting over the marshy plain.

Through his spyglass he surveyed the flickering torchlights, strangely hazed, as though by fog or smoke. The details were maddeningly indistinct. If only there was more light!

It was as though his wish had been granted.

A sparkling green point sped upwards from the top of the black tower like a shooting star, reached the underside of the cloud sheet and burst. It was as though the whole plain were illuminated by a continuous lightning flash diffused and reflected by the clouds, casting a sickly green half-light back to Earth. Now he saw clearly through his glass the hurrying specks of four figures beyond the turret ring. As he watched they grouped into pairs.

Then rose into the air.

Even as he followed the flying forms through his glass, wild hope growing within him, he saw an incredible sight. For a moment he thought the sentinel turrets were burning, as some dark rushing mass appeared to be boiling out of them like smoke from chimney pots. Then he realized the mass was composed of living creatures. The pits of Raven's Tor were discharging their spawn.

There must have been hundreds, perhaps thousands, of the small flying apes, together with dozens of larger animals with massive wingspans. Dragons and even stranger beasts he had no doubt. The host rose in streamers up into the sky, still lit by the unnatural green fireball. Over the tower they merged into one mass of beating wings, like a wheeling flock of monstrous birds; circling, waiting. Waiting for their master?

Edmund found his voice, and called to the man who kept the carrier pigeons: 'Send word to Fluxford – Dhal is coming with a great force of flying beasts – be quick!' But could the bird reach Fluxford before Dhal?

There was movement in the air over his head. The

figures he had seen escaping were now circling the outcrop, riding two apiece on . . . broomsticks?

'We're safe, Edmund. Take care of yourself now!'

It was Mellisa!

'I'd keep your head down, lad!' came an older voice from above. Then the riders shot off low across the moor towards the east and were lost in the night.

As he turned back to the tower, dizzy both with relief and amazement, he realized Mellisa and the other riders were being pursued. The main body of the host still circled over the tower, but flying low and furiously after them were two winged beasts somewhere between dragons and huge bats. Mounted on them were riders carrying slender lances.

'To your bows! They must not pass!' he yelled.

It was doubtful if the riders realized the rocks sheltered their enemies, or else they would have flown higher. But they were only intent on their prey. Until it was too late.

A hail of arrows rose to meet them. One beast squealed and tumbled from the sky, mortally wounded, spilling its rider as it crashed to earth. The second received only minor damage as quarrels passed cleanly through its membranous wings. But its rider was struck in the leg and side and reeled in the saddle, losing the reins. Uncontrolled and confused, the beast flapped down heavily to land in the shallow valley beyond the rock outcrop.

On a wild impulse, Edmund sprinted towards it, calling back over his shoulder to his men: 'Take cover! Your job is done!'

He reached the flapping, jittery beast in half a minute. He ignored the teeth in its gaping, bloated frog mouth, which snapped at him, and the wild glare in its red eyes. The beast's ape-like rider swung feebly at him with a long, spike-ended riding crop. He ducked under the blow, caught the ape's leg and heaved it up and out of the stirrup. It crashed to earth with a thud on the other side, dropping the crop. Edmund snatched it up, gathered the

255

trailing reins, and vaulted into the saddle. He had never ridden such a beast in his life, but he would not let his new mount know that. He spurred it like a horse and flicked the crop across its flanks. It hopped forward, wings beating heavily, then launched itself into the air after the broomstick riders.

Dhal's mount resided in its own pit within the caverns, beneath the widest of the turret chimneys. It was a golden dragon with wings spanning eighty feet. No saddle would fit such a girth, so he rode a high backed chair mounted over its dorsal spines, and enclosed within a canopy. Secured by a hoop mesh to one arm of the chair was his seeing globe. Upon his command the dragon spread its wings and rose up through the turret chimney and out into the open air. As the fireball above them started to splutter and fade, the dragon took its place at the head of the airborne army. The circle broke as he turned towards the east, and the lesser beasts and ape-bats trailed after it. Within his aerial palanquin, Dhal focused his thoughts on the seeing globe, looking for the keen eyes of the beasts pursuing the broomstick riders. The two girls had to be recovered safely. If that interfering witch was involved in their escape, then he would deal with her once and for all! But he could only find a single beast in pursuit, and, far from catching up with the broomstick riders, it was being left behind. Curse the old besom! No, wait. Dhal pondered. Perhaps interception was unnecessary. They were all headed for the same place. They would be to hand when he needed them.

Then he felt the intrusion into the planetary aura.

The skyboats! He had ignored them for too long. Even as he cast about for some counter measure, he sensed a smaller object separate from the main vessel and plunge earthward at a speed far greater than anything he had previously known.

Far behind them now, the lonely spike of the Black Tower rose from the rolling moor. A blue-white spear of light burst out of the clouds like a thunderbolt and struck precisely at its base.

There was a flash that lit up the sky for fifty miles around, and punched a hole through the clouds into the clear sky above. The tower vanished in a red and yellow tongue of fire that licked upward, erupting into the void, scattering splashes of molten rock like ejecta from a volcano. Unseen, the shockwave expanded through the caverns beneath the tor, venting red hot from the turrets in secondary blasts that shattered them into piles of smoking rubble. Then the earth heaved, the cavern roofs gave way, and the remains of Ravens Tor collapsed into a glowing crater half a mile across.

24

Invasion

Air was hissing from two arrow holes before Bron managed to convince the castle defenders of their identity. Gently, the unlikely craft spiralled down into the central courtyard of the keep and grated to rest on the gravel. Odoyle looked relieved, and mopped his brow with a spotted handkerchief.

'Well rowed, lads,' he commended. 'My, but that was getting a bit of a strain towards the end, there.'

Ian smiled, massaging his aching arms. 'Next time, we use an outboard motor.'

Captain Morgane and a handful of guards ran up to them, gaping incredulously. 'Is it really you? I could hardly believe it.'

'I can scarce credit it myself,' Bron admitted. 'But what has been happening here? We saw fires in the town and folk sheltering within the walls. Has it got so bad?'

'Yes. Creatures appear and work their mischief then disappear into the forest again before we can respond. When our forces pursue them, many do not come back. The river is hazardous and many roads are closed to all but parties of great strength . . . But none of this matters now if you have met with success. Have you?'

Bron lifted a small locked chest from the raft.

'Merlin's Helm . . .' he hesitated, glancing at the Doctor for a moment. 'What we were commanded to find is in here.'

Gramling emerged from an archway and hurried over to them, his staff scraping over the gravel.

'You arrived much sooner than I thought. Is it in there?'

'That it is, my friend,' confirmed Odoyle. 'We brought home the bacon and no mistake!' His tone grew serious. 'Now 'tis up to you . . . if you're still determined?'

Gramling stiffened, looking resolute. 'I am. Please inform his Majesty the convocation may start in one hour. I will now go to prepare myself.' And he turned and walked away.

Ian was looking around the courtyard amongst the small crowd that had gathered. 'Where's Barbara? Doesn't she know we've returned yet?'

Morgane looked grave. 'Forgive me for not speaking sooner, but I have sad news for you . . .' In a few words he told of Barbara's disappearance and the subsequent fruitless search. Bron, Alammar and Komati listened sympathetically.

Ian's lips became pinched and white and his fists clenched. 'We've got to go out and look again –'

'No, Chesterton,' said the Doctor. His words carried the weight of timeless authority that commanded attention. 'You know that would be a futile, quixotic gesture in the present circumstances,' he continued gravely. 'You saw the state of the surrounding countryside when we flew in. If you went out now, we would only lose you too.'

'But we must do something!'

'Of course. But to help Barbara, we must resolve the matter of the Helm first. Believe me, everything rests on that. Once it is successfully concluded, a full scale search can be resumed. Think hard, Chesterton. Don't let your heart rule your head in this. You know it's the only way.'

Ian took a deep breath, and slowly nodded. 'All right, Doctor. What do you suggest we do?'

'First, I have a small task for you, but a vital one, nevertheless.' He drew Ian a little aside and spoke quietly but rapidly to him. Ian looked surprised, but nodded. The Doctor turned to Morgane. 'Captain, can you spare one man to go with my friend and allow him to pass through to the outer bailey? I assure you it is most

259

important. With any luck it will help bring an end to this whole sorry business.'

Morgane looked doubtful for a moment, glanced at Bron, then nodded. 'Certainly, Doctor, if that is so.' He detailed a guard to accompany Ian, and the two set off.

'Now I must present the Helm to the King,' said Bron.

'And I must accompany you to give my account of Thurguld's death to his lord,' said Alammar, 'if he be in the castle.'

'He is indeed, Master elf,' Morgane assured him as the three and their escort walked away. 'Together with dignitaries from far around. All are gathered again for the convocation. Dhal may believe it is to grant him power. But after your success it will have a finer purpose!'

'Well, I'm off for a drink myself,' said Odoyle. 'And then to put me head down for half an hour. I'll be seeing you at the ceremony then.' And he walked wearily away.

Suddenly left alone, Komati glanced uncertainly at the Doctor. He smiled back, not entirely reassuringly. 'You had best come with me, Doctor Komati. I assure you we will not miss anything. Like a classic drama, you see, all the players will be gathered together for the final resolution. For good or ill.'

There was a rumble of thunder from the heavy clouds overhead. Jen shivered, though the air was becoming close and oppressive. 'Well, there's a gathering storm at least.'

The Doctor looked up. 'Yes. The symbolism of the storm. And when it breaks? Signs and portents. How appropriate.'

'Scanner team, anything yet?' Nyborg demanded.

'Still waiting for the effects of our missile strike to clear, Admiral . . . ah, beginning to get something now. Patterns are coming through . . . Yes, they've changed. Whatever was in that structure on the moor is no longer part of the energy web. Flow lines are now bypassing the site.'

'Good.' Nyborg opened another channel. 'Admiral Nyborg to all lander crews: your attention please. I can now confirm the source of the hostile interference on the planet's surface has been destroyed. You can proceed with your mission without any further worries from that quarter.' He paused, then continued in slightly softer tones. 'You are all volunteers, and have been fully briefed on the situation down there. You know why you have to use special arms and equipment, and why it may not be possible to withdraw you from the surface for some time. But let me assure you that we will be up here giving you all the support and backup you require for as long as it takes. Never doubt that what you do today may be the finest service you can render to the Empire which we all serve. In the name of the Empress, good luck to you all!

'Lander one: proceed with recovery mission. Immediate launch. Main force: Ready for launch in two minutes for prime target.'

Dhal flew on at the head of his army. Shock began to fade. His tower was gone, and that was it. He had only one possible objective left. But success was still in his grasp. If all went well, nothing that had gone before mattered anyway. Then he would show them all who was master. And the interfering oldworlders would be the first to taste his revenge.

The keep guards, already jittery after the sudden appearance of the flying raft, loosed several more arrows at the four broomstick riders, until they realized they were firing at a royal princess and her friends. The party glided down out of the night to land in the courtyard beside the deflating and abandoned raft, which Susan and Barbara regarded with special curiosity. The news of their safe return spread rapidly through the castle, already roused by the arrival of the Helm. Before Mellisa could leave the courtyard, people started opening windows and coming on to balconies to call down to her. Others poured out of doors. Soon she was in the middle of a welcoming throng. Then the crowd parted and the King and Queen hurried up and embraced her. Many freely wept with tears of joy, and not just the royal family. And then the Doctor was at Susan's side, hugging her to him. Barbara saw the relief clearly written across his face. For a moment she thought she heard them exchanging quick words in some strange language, but it was soon drowned by the general cheering and jubilation.

When she could finally interrupt them, she asked anxiously: 'Where's Ian? Is he –'

'Chesterton is quite all right. He's within the castle walls running an errand for me. You'll see him shortly. Meanwhile, I must thank you for helping bring Susan back safely to me. If anything had happened to her . . .' The old man trailed off, for once at a loss for words.

Embarrassed, Barbara said lightly. 'Well, you really should thank Anni Glassfeather, not me. She was the brains behind it all.'

The Doctor was introduced to Anni, who had been standing on the edge of the throng, beaming upon the reunited families and friends in a satisfied way. The Doctor exhibited the gallant charm he was quite capable of when he chose, and Barbara thought he came within a fraction of kissing Anni's hand. The witch, flattered by his attentions, blushed almost coquettishly.

'I understand, madam,' he continued politely, 'that you are a practitioner of the magical arts; a field in which I have recently become most interested myself.'

Susan piped up: 'But Grandfather, I was trying to tell you. I've found out how to work magic myself. Ask Mellisa.' But the Princess was still within the embrace of her parents, while reassuring Sir Stephan that Edmund had been safe the last time they had seen him. Then she spoke more urgently to her father, and suddenly the King was calling for silence above the chatter.

'People of Fluxford castle. This should be a time of joy unconfined, as those who were lost have been returned to

262

us. But my daughter has just given me news that requires us to put personal feelings aside and return to our duty. The renegade Marton Dhal is approaching Fluxford even now with a great army of winged beasts, no doubt intent on taking by force what he could not win by threats and kidnap. But this castle must be defended while the ceremony of convocation is enacted. Then the mightiest tool of our ancestors may be turned to good purpose, and we shall be rid of his villainy for ever. Now to your posts and do your duty!'

There was a loud cry of resolute approval and the throng started to disperse. Then came a cry from the highest tower. Everybody looked up. A yellow fire trail arced across the sky, then another and another. They did not move like Avalon's typical shooting stars.

'Landing craft,' Komati said despairingly. 'They know you've got the Helm, and now they want it for the Empire!'

Ian was in the outer bailey, having just found what the Doctor requested, when he heard the roar of retro-rockets. For a moment he thought it was another roll of thunder, then he saw the flare trails. There was a flash of lightning, and he saw a dozen deltaform bodies, wings extended, frozen by the lightning strobe in the act of swinging around for their landing run. These were much bigger than the lander Shannon's party had arrived in.

The castle guard who had accompanied him gasped: 'They are Dhal's creatures come for us!'

'No,' Ian retorted grimly, 'but they still mean trouble. Come on, we've got what we came for!'

They started quickly back up towards the inner gateway amid the fresh cries from the refugees sheltering within the walls. Fortunately, after some initial protest, Ian's new charge allowed itself to be led along docilely; looking around but otherwise seeming unmoved by the growing commotion. Behind them, five of the landers extended their wheels and bumped down on to the turf of the outer bailey. Their breaking rockets blazed, pulling them up quickly within the confined space, sending the refugees and soldiers alike running for cover. The rest came down outside the walls, as far as Ian could tell. Was this chance, or deliberate? Had they put sufficient forces inside to open the gates for the rest if needed?

They passed through the inner gate complex. The gates and portcullis closed behind them. By the stairs leading up to the gateway turrets they met the Doctor, Komati, Bron and Alammar. The Doctor was still carrying his mysterious bundle, Ian noticed.

'I'm going to try to talk sense to them,' Komati said quickly.

'But if they do not listen, we shall be ready to fight!' exclaimed Bron, and he and Alammar ran up the stairs.

'I've got what you wanted,' said Ian to the Doctor.

'Yes, I can see that. Good. Go to the Great Hall, the ceremony is starting shortly. But keep it out of sight for the moment. If there's any chance, you know what to do.'

'And it'll end it?'

'Oh yes. I think it will be pleased to. By the way,' he beamed, 'you'll find Barbara waiting for you.'

'What!'

'Yes. She and Susan and the Princess arrived back safely a few minutes ago. No time to explain now. Well go on, my boy; don't delay!'

With a deeper boom of thunder than any before, the rain started to fall.

Only one end of the Great Hall was well lit, focusing all eyes and all thoughts upon it. That was intentional, Barbara realized.

She was standing with Anni and Susan near the front of the sparse crowd of attendants witnessing the ceremony. She realized that they must look rather bedraggled in their stained and torn clothes. At least cloaks had been found for Susan and Mellisa to replace their blankets, and slip-on pumps for their bare feet. Anni looked the most dignified of the three of them in her black dress. She still carried her broomstick, and that, together with her tall hat, made it unmistakably clear who, and what, she was. She had received some puzzled glances, but a respectfully wide berth.

At the head of the hall, an empty chair had been placed on a small dais. Resting on a cushion on the chair was the Helm. Seated in concentric circles around the dais were two dozen dignitaries and nobles, representing the various peoples and castes of society in the South Share of Elbyon. The royal family and Palbury were there of course, together with Kilvenny Odoyle, lords of the elves and dwarves, barons and elders of the city of Fluxford. In turn, each would stand, walk up to the Helm, state clearly their name and position, and then repeat the same phrase:

'I hereby freely commend the use of this Helm of power to Gramling, Wizard of Fluxford, to use as he may without let or hindrance.'

The wording of the ceremony had been discovered by Gramling during his researches, Barbara remembered. Researches. She smiled to herself, remembering her own labours in the library. Had that only been a few days ago? She would never be sure now if she had found anything useful, except more questions. And she never had got around to searching for the Doctor's suspected spy. Perhaps if she'd not been lured away like that . . . Out of the corner of her eye she saw a hand waving over the heads from the back of the hall. Leaving Susan with Anni, she pushed her way through the intent crowd until she reached Ian. She was so pleased and relieved to see him, that they had hugged for at least ten seconds before she realized he had a most unexpected companion.

And suddenly she knew what she had seen in the bestiary that shouldn't have been there.

From the gateway turret Bron watched the stationary landers through the steady downpour. A few arrows had bounced off their hulls before the order was given to cease firing. Catapults and heavy bolt guns were being turned to bear upon them. In a moment Morgane would order them to fire. He was waiting for the last of the refugees to get into shelter around the far side of the castle. But why didn't they attack? Bron wondered. They had forces inside close to the gates. If they took those, they could open the way for the rest. He turned to the Doctor and Komati.

'What manner of weapons will these soldiers have? Are they so powerful they can afford to wait while we prepare to smash their vessels with our catapults?'

'I don't know why they're waiting,' replied Komati. 'They can't use energy weapons down here, but the marines probably have old style guns, like you saw on the island, but which fire more shots and with greater power. And grenades – uh, larger charges of the explosive that propels the bullets, which can blow holes in wood or even stone.'

'Do these marines wear armour?'

'Body armour, yes.'

'And is this amour proof against sword or arrow?'

'Probably . . . it's a light synthetic. Very tough.'

'Does it have joints?'

'Yes.'

'Hah!' exclaimed Bron, clenching his fist. 'Where there is a joint there is a weakness. Tell your men, Morgane. These oldworlders bleed just like us. I have seen it. Get in close and they die just as easily.'

'But they won't let you get close!' said Komati. 'They'll shoot you first.'

'Do they carry an endless supply of these bullets?'

'No.'

'They must stop to replenish their quivers then?'

'Their magazines. Yes, of course.'

'Then we shall get in close,' Bron said fiercely.

'It is possible they underestimate your strength or determination,' suggested the Doctor. 'They may plan a demonstration of power to awe you into submission without the need for all-out war. But if they wish to parley, keep them talking. With a little more time, all may be resolved without further bloodshed.'

'Of course. Gramling can use the power of the Helm to smite these people as easily as he will Dhal!'

The Doctor made no comment.

'Look!' said Komati.

The flare of braking rockets marked the arrival of another lander. It glided in low over the castle walls, touched down, and ran along the turf up beside the other craft.

'Perhaps this is what they were waiting for,' said the Doctor.

The lander's side hatch swung open and a ramp extended slowly, as though it were being wound down by hand, and touched the ground. A voice called out: 'I wish to speak with someone of authority.'

Komati went pale. 'That sounds like . . . Shannon!'

Bron frowned. 'We shall see.' He shouted down: 'You may come out to speak. We will not shoot. You have my word.'

Shannon stepped out of the hatch and down the ramp. He was clad in black segmented body armour now. He held one arm stiffly, and there was a suspicion of a limp, but he still carried himself erect. He walked across until he stood opposite the turret on the edge of the moat.

'We thought you dead,' Bron said. 'Or we would not have left as we did.'

'I believe you,' Shannon replied, as though the matter was of no importance any more. His eyes flickered across the line of faces looking down upon him. 'Lieutenant Komati, are you being held here against your will?'

'What? No, I –'

'Then you will be charged under military law with cowardice, desertion, and conspiring with the enemy,' he said, crisply and coldly.

'The woman may stay here as long as she wishes,' said

Bron. 'She has made her peace with us, and we do not hold her responsible for your actions. Now, what have you to say?'

'You know what we want. We have weapons far more powerful than you can imagine. Do you wish to see them in action? Give us the Helm and we will leave you in peace.'

'Captain Shannon,' the Doctor said, 'you dare not take the Helm off this planet. There is a type of microscopic contamination here –'

'I know about the nanobots. We will find a way to neutralize them. The Helm may even be the key to their control.'

'But don't you see, you cannot simply walk off with the Helm. The nanobots and the nova trigger are indivisible. It's an integrated system. The planet itself is part of it. At full power the beam is probably focused using Avalon's energy field. You cannot have one without the other, and you cannot risk spreading nanobotic contamination.'

'Maybe you're right. That's for the scientists to decide. But the Helm's still a vital part. And if it takes a month or a year, we'll learn how to control it. We can call down all the support we need for as long as necessary. So hand it over peacefully, or we'll take it from you.'

Bron laughed dryly. 'Do you think us such fools? Even if we gave you this thing, could we be sure you would never turn it against us, supposing you could make it work?'

'Your society is of no importance to us. Why should we trouble you again?'

'Because it is in your nature. I have heard a little of your history over recent days. You wish to rebuild your Empire, and empires only grow by conquest. With such a tool as the Helm, what else would you use it for?'

'How it would be used is not my concern. My only objective is to recover it safely.'

'How can you be so cold-blooded!' cried Komati.

268

'I'm just following orders, lieutenant. Something you should have done.'

'Eventually you've got to think for yourself!' she retorted spiritedly. 'I don't trust anybody with the power of this thing. But at least these people only want it for self-defence.'

'Will their intentions always remain so modest?'

'I don't know. But I do know what the Empire will use it for. It's more dangerous than you can imagine! Let me explain –'

'If they will not give it up, there is nothing more to say, lieutenant. You will die here with the rest, or face trial in due course.'

'If we die,' Bron called out, 'at least we do so defending our home! We are not as helpless as you think. In the last resort we will turn the power of the Helm on you. Remember what it did on the island!'

'If you had it ready now, you would not have let us land, therefore it is not yet operational,' Shannon concluded. And he turned away and strode back to his lander.

'Wait!' the Doctor called after him. 'You still don't know the real danger of the Helm!' But Shannon ignored him.

Bron spun round to the Doctor and Komati. 'Curse my foolish words! He will move all the more swiftly now! Go to the hall at once,' he commanded. 'The parley ends the moment he is inside his vessel.'

There was no arguing with him. Komati and the Doctor ran down the steps.

They heard the crackle of an automatic weapon. In response came the swish and thud of a catapult.

'But why have you brought it in here?' Barbara whispered.

'It was the Doctor's idea. He said . . . well, maybe you'd better ask him yourself. I've only had the potted version so far. He probably thinks we should work the

269

rest out for ourselves like a class exercise.'

Barbara smiled ruefully. 'Isn't he infuriating like that. Where has he gone anyway?'

'Trying to talk peace with the Empire landing force —'

There came the sound of gunfire and explosions from outside.

'It sounds as though he's failed,' Barbara said flatly.

'They'd better get a move on in here, then. How long does this take?'

'It's about half over, I think. When they've finished this part, Gramling will be called in and the Helm will be offered. They want to be sure it's safe. At least, as safe as it can be.'

'I can't blame them, I suppose. I saw what it did to somebody unprepared.'

'Does it really kill its user?'

'Yes, but that's only the half of it. Talk to Jen Komati and you'll hear a definition of a real terror weapon. That's what the Empire wants, apparently.'

'I meant to ask about her,' said Barbara with a touch of coolness. 'Just how did you meet —'

The Doctor and Komati entered the hall at that moment. While the doors were open the sound of fighting was noticeably louder.

'Useless, useless . . . !' the Doctor was muttering.

'He wouldn't listen,' said Jen.

'Who?' asked Ian.

'Shannon. He's still alive. He seems to be commanding the marines out there.'

'But we thought —'

'He doesn't care about that! That's what's so frightening. All he wants is the Helm. And he'll stop at nothing to get it!'

An explosion blew open the outer gates and the rest of the marine force poured in. Grenades tossed on to the wall walks cleared them of defenders. Arrows rained down, but most rebounded from the invaders' armour.

270

One or two marines fell when an arrow found a weak link, or were beaten down by a hail of stones flung from a catapult. A lander was crushed by a heavy catapult stone and pierced by dragon gun bolts. Fire arrows set it alight and exploding munitions blew it apart fitfully. But the invaders still advanced.

Bron could admire their discipline even as he strove for their deaths. They held a quarter section of the outer bailey and were moving towards the inner gateway. Surely the moat would slow them down? But as their comrades kept up a hail of covering fire, others reached the moat's edge. Rifle grenades started to rain down on to the walls and into the turret rooms. Some were loaded with explosive charges, others with smoke or choking, stinging gas. That, at least, was one weapon that did not work as they planned, Bron realized. The rain damped down the gas and smoke alike, but still they came on.

Rocket-propelled grappling irons flew over the moat and locked into place between the merlons of the battlements. The attackers swung across the moat and began to climb, even as the defenders tried to dislodge their purchase. Many fell back, but others climbed on and some reached the top. Then it was a hand to hand battle on the wall walks. At last Bron could reach them with *Invictus* and lay open those chinks in their armour as he promised, and he felt the fierce lust for battle burn within him as he became one with his sword and shield. Others felt it too, he knew. Morgane was everywhere, dashing along the ways, rallying his guards, hacking at the heads which topped the parapet. And when the marines slowed, pausing to refill their weapons, Alammar and the other archers, at closer range now, would pour deadly accurate arrows down upon them. More began to fall.

At last they were holding them back!

Then came a huge explosion.

The entire gateway disintegrated in a sheet of red and yellow fire.

Masonry blocks were hurled about like pebbles.

Alammar and Morgane vanished from his sight as the blast knocked Bron off his feet and threw him ten feet back along the walkway. Through the ringing in his ears he heard cries of: 'They're through! The gate is lost!'

Even as he struggled to regain his senses, his hand scrabbling automatically for *Invictus*, he realized that a black-armoured marine was standing over him, rifle levelled at his chest.

They heard the explosion in the Great Hall, even as the escort was sent to the ante-room to fetch Gramling. The sounds of combat grew louder and closer. Several men present unobtrusively edged towards the doors and slipped out, drawing their swords as they went. Ian fingered the grip of the sword he had worn during the quest.

'They'd better hurry up,' he said quietly.

With a shrill cry a winged creature soared over the walkway. The marine instinctively raised his gun to cover it. Bron kicked out at the man's knee and he fell against the parapet, swinging his gun back again even as Bron's hands closed on *Invictus*. A figure seemed to fall out of the air, tumble as he hit the walkway, and come up thrusting a sword into the marine's throat. The man kicked and gurgled, then was still.

'Come, Bron, we must move! Dhal's host is at my heels!'

It was Edmund Palbury.

Barbara, who had rejoined Susan at the front of the gathering, found a lump came to her throat as Gramling walked in with dignity, dressed in his finest robes, his pointed hat no longer looking as absurd to her as it had the first time they met; his staff clicking on the flagstones. 'I'm going to miss him,' she admitted in a whisper to Susan. 'He was quite sweet, really. Even if he did make a fuss about his books.'

'What books?' Susan asked absently, as Gramling took his seat.

'Oh, just references about magic and the Helm.'

'Dhal had loads of books. All neatly set out with lots of bookmarks in them.'

'Gramling only had a few really, all very untidy . . .' She trailed off. A slow chill seemed to rise up her spine. In a faint voice, she asked: 'Did Dhal have a seeing globe?'

'Yes, he was always using it.'

But Barbara was pushing her way through the congregation. 'Doctor . . . Doctor!'

But a new sound rose above the alien chatter of automatic weapons and the crump of grenades. It was the whirr of many wings and the roar of dragons.

Dhal's beasts set down where the Empire landers could not: within the inner yards of the castle and upon the keep itself. Hordes of the winged apes tried to land as they had before, but the wires that stretched across walkways, windows and balconies, almost invisible in the dark and rain, trapped many. Dhal raged. In his haste he had forgotten to warn them of the new hazard. But it didn't matter now. The wires snapped under the bulk of his larger beasts as they smashed their way in, opening a pathway for him into the heart of the castle.

Bron and Edmund ran towards the keep through an incredible confusion. Winged apes flew thick overhead, casting down their throwing stars or flasks of oil that splashed liquid fire as they struck. Larger beasts smashed through the walls of the yards. Some dragons breathed fire, while others blew jets of green smoke that bleached white all it touched, and seared the lungs. Some, bizarrely, exhaled clouds of freezing vapour that chilled the life from whatever it touched, turning men to statues of ice. Petrified in mid-stride or swing of sword, they toppled and shattered on the ground like glass.

But men fought back. They saw castle guard and

Empire marine suddenly standing side by side against a common, indiscriminate foe. Winged apes dropped from the sky, feathered with arrows or punctured with bullet wounds. Arrows and swords stabbed the great beasts, while grenades tore gaping wounds in scaled reptilian flesh or severed limbs and long, sinuous necks. Blood laced the rain puddles.

Inexorably, the conflict spilled over into the rooms and corridors of the keep itself.

'Doctor!' Barbara almost shouted above the clash of arms that rang out from the corridor. 'It's Gramling! I think he –'

King Magnus placed the Helm upon Gramling's head.

'Gramling, wizard. We freely grant you the power to save our land from the evil of two enemies now at our very doors. Act swiftly!'

Gramling's eyes glazed.

A grey veil seemed to envelop the castle and its grounds. The very air seemed to thicken. Raindrops slowed their fall, flames flickered and died, sounds became muffled. Swords dragged in mid swing and stopped, bullets in flight became visible, slowed and trickled to the ground as though they were falling through treacle. And every combatant, man or beast, found themselves locked rigidly within an invisible cocoon, as though the air had solidified around them. Bron and Edmund, frozen in mid stride, fought in vain against its tightening vice. Consciousness began to slip away as the sluggish air flowed ever slower into their lungs.

Inside the hall, they heard the sounds of conflict fade away to an unnatural silence.

'He's done it!' somebody called out, in wondering, uncertain relief.

Then they heard a single pair of footsteps approach along the corridor outside. The double doors swung open. Marton Dhal, robed in black and silver, stood smiling triumphantly at them from the entranceway. A clear tunnel was visible in the thickened grey air behind him.

There was a long moment of stunned surprise, then the King turned to Gramling: 'Wizard, your treacherous apprentice is here before you. Destroy him!'

And Dhal threw back his head and laughed.

25

Turnabout

A translucent floor-to-ceiling curtain materialized within the Great Hall, shimmering like Avalon's own aurora.

It enclosed the doorway where Dhal stood, the dais and Gramling's seated figure. Peridor, sword drawn, lunged at it. There was an electric crackle and he was thrown back in a shower of sparks. Odoyle had pulled his silver hammer from his belt while Anni Glassfeather reached into her pocket for a potion bottle. Dhal laughed again. 'This shield draws on the power of the Helm, against which you are quite powerless, as you well know.' He strode confidently towards the dais. The shimmering curtain contracted to follow him until it formed a circle about its base, while he stood beside Gramling's chair.

'You are wondering, perhaps,' Dhal continued, addressing the room at large, 'why my late master does not smite me down? That is because, some years ago, he incautiously probed too deeply into my affairs through his seeing globe. And I was able to take over his mind. He has been my tool ever since!'

There was a stifled groan of horror and dismay from the assembly. Barbara felt her stomach knot. Beside her the Doctor and Ian were both tight-lipped and impassive. 'A fifth column by proxy!' Komati muttered. The Doctor motioned her to be quiet.

With an effort, the King said firmly: 'Your victory is only temporary, Dhal. Only while Gramling lives. In that time you still cannot force us to grant you the position of court sorcerer, nor will you ever gain access to the treasures pertaining to that position.'

Dhal's mocking smile merely deepened.

'Have you still not realized?' he said contemptuously. 'It was the Helm I wanted all along!'

There was dead silence, broken only by the Doctor's faintest murmured: 'Of course!'

'The other baubles are nothing in comparison,' Dhal continued. 'Ever since my researches uncovered its location, I wondered how I might make the Helm my own. But it was well protected and could not simply be taken. So I created the circumstances where it would be recovered for me, then be freely given for the use of my agent here.' He smiled down at Kilvenny Odoyle. 'I trust your party had a pleasant voyage. I kept watch over you as often as I could and ensured favourable winds, and of course I knew Gramling had provided every aid to success. Naturally, should you have been delayed, I would have permitted unobtrusively, every possible extension of my deadline. Sorry about the close call with the kraken, but I was able to induce that octopus to intervene in time. Your unexpected oldworld guests were, I admit, inadvertently my fault. I was quite surprised to see where they turned up. But you managed to cope with them in the end.'

'Thurguld died through their actions!' Odoyle retorted.

'Did he? Well, everything has a price, they say.'

'Gramling is paying the price for you, Dhal,' Odoyle said with a sneer, 'but he cannot last more than a few minutes longer. Anything you plan must be done by then, because when this shield falls –'

'Really! Do you think I have not anticipated that?' He raised a beckoning finger. 'Come forward, my dears.'

Two cylinders of the misty shield formed within the assembly, causing those nearest to recoil in alarm.

They enclosed Susan and Mellisa.

Their faces had suddenly slackened into mask-like blankness.

With a fearful cry, Queen Leonora clutched desperately at her daughter, but was repelled by a crackling discharge of sparks. The two young women moved like automata, the shields following them. Ian and Barbara instinctively started forward, but the Doctor held them back.

'Not yet!' he hissed. 'Wait!' Out of the corner of her eye, Barbara saw him unroll the parcel he had been carrying, then slip back into the shadows.

A bolt from Odoyle's hammer burst against Mellisa's shield, while glittering powder cast by Anni Glassfeather sparkled futilely against Susan's. The two walked on, their shields merging with the one surrounding the dais, until they stood beside Dhal.

'More of my servants, you see,' he said. 'I took great care over their conditioning to ensure they are completely under my control. This is how I circumvent the binding on the Helm. Before Gramling dies, he will, at my command, nominate one of the women as his successor, conferring his right to use the Helm, and she in turn will pass it on to the other. But always they will be my creatures. I think, by the time they are all spent, I will have secured my position on this world beyond any possible interference.'

Queen Leonora, half cradled in her husband's arms, screamed out: 'No! Take me, not Mellisa!'

Dhal smiled pitilessly. 'I fear, your Majesty, you would not be suitable. But now, as my colleague Master Odoyle pointed out, time is running short. First, I think I will take a little revenge.' Those nearest flinched away. He laughed. 'Present company excepted, for the moment.' He rubbed his hands together in a ghastly, gleeful gesture. 'First, I am feeling particularly annoyed with the vessel of the oldworlder's that destroyed my tower.' He gestured. A ten-foot wide black sphere appeared hanging in the air over the assembly's heads. Within it, like a seeing globe, hung the images of the starfleet ships. 'Now, which one was it? Ah, yes . . .'

It was pure chance that Nyborg noticed the secondary monitor image. He saw the web of light briefly glow into being across the face of a black moon and flow into a dome in the centre of its disc. And he knew the power to destroy a star was about to be unleashed on those who had come to take it for themselves.

'All ships! Maximum power to shields!'

A brilliant blue lance of raw energy lashed out across space towards the squadron. It punched through a force shield as though it had not been there, and turned the cruiser *Dorado* into a swelling fireball of white heat. The shockwave transmitted by the expanding vapour cloud was so intense it sent the rest of the formation tumbling wildly through space.

Clinging to his chair, Nyborg shouted: 'Evasive action!'

The surviving ships' drives glowed and in moments they were scattering across the sky.

'That will keep them occupied for a while,' Dhal concluded with satisfaction. 'And now –' Gramling stirred and groaned, and slumped a little deeper in his chair. 'Ah, the strain is telling. Gramling is not what he was.' He leaned over the old man. 'Speak now. Nominate the girl Susan as your successor!'

Barbara clenched her fists in helpless horror.

Then it happened.

A mistiness seemed to envelop the heads of apprentice and master. Dhal jerked away, clutching at his temples, crying out in pain. The haze followed him, thickening. For a moment it seemed as though pale wreaths streamed between the two wizards' heads. Then Gramling moaned and jerked wildly in his chair, while Dhal straightened up calmly.

But, somehow, it was not Dhal.

He extended his hands before him, turning them over as though seeing them for the first time. Then he looked at Gramling, who was struggling ever more feebly, trying to remove the Helm. He moved to stand over him.

'You have no idea how long I have planned for this moment,' he said softly.

279

The voice was Dhal's, but the intonation had changed.

'Don't do this!' The old wizard's face was ghastly.

'Do you remember what I said when I chose you for my apprentice?'

'Please master . . . please . . .' Gramling gasped.

'I said we would have a great future together.'

'No, don't . . .'

'Well your part has ended now. You had your proxies but I had you. Did you really think you could take over my mind so easily? And you never realized that the Helm was capable of this, did you? But I did. At least, I hoped so. But then, I had nothing to lose. And now you're too weak to reverse the process. Too weak to prevent my controlling *you* now.' Gramling's old face blanked and the clawing hands froze. 'I prepared for this a long time ago, you see, but I had to wait for the right moment.'

Palbury had stepped forward to the edge of the shield curtain. 'Gramling? Is it . . . really you?'

Dhal's eyes now animated by Gramling's mind stared coldly back at him. 'It is, my lord.'

'It is incredible,' he said in a wondering voice. 'Then . . . you have triumphed! It is over! Let down this shield and release the captives!'

For one long, agonizing moment, Gramling hesitated.

'I'm sorry, my lord,' he said, softly.

The body that had once been Marton Dhal's reached over to grasp the Helm, ready to lift it clear. His glance flashed at Susan, and she obediently knelt down beside the chair to receive it.

'What are you doing? I command you to stop!' cried Palbury.

The wizard ignored him.

'Gramling . . . why?' It was Odoyle who spoke; his voice dulled by shock and incomprehension.

'Greed, plain and simple,' Anni pronounced. 'It's taken many a better man before him this way, I'm sorry to say.'

'Is it greed that I simply want to live to fulfil a purpose? Is that so hard to understand?' Gramling retorted. 'Because

280

I still have work to do, but no longer the strength? I was old in your father's time, Palbury. How long ago that was . . . I have stretched my life as far as I can. Now, at last, the chance for real power, the chance for —'

'But at the cost of these innocent lives!' said the King. 'You have triumphed over Dhal. Stop now for pity's sake!'

'And lose the Helm? No. Never! It will be worth the cost, I promise. There will be unity; a better order. There will be no more war or conflict. I can make Avalon a paradise, you'll see. There will be nothing beyond us —'

The shield curtain around the dais flickered. Barbara saw Odoyle and Anni tense.

Then a remarkable figure pushed past her and strode masterfully towards the dais. She heard gasps of surprise from the assembly.

It was the Doctor.

But his frock coat was now covered by a flowing red robe with voluminous sleeves, decorated with stars. On his head, its wire stiffening a little crooked after being wrapped in a bundle for so long, was a wizard's hat. His eyes locked with Gramling's.

'If you attempt to put the Helm on my Susan, I swear you will die!' the Doctor said simply. His tone left no doubt that he was speaking the absolute truth. Barbara had never heard such icy determination. 'I too am a magician, you see, and I will use all the power I command to strike you down!'

'It's true,' Odoyle spoke up loudly in confirmation. 'I coached him on the journey back here, and he's a mighty fast learner. The Doctor has the skill for sure.'

'You can't use the full power of the Helm just before changeover, can you?' the Doctor continued. 'Even if your natural power is combined with that of Dhal's, I don't believe you have the strength to hold us all at bay! Listen to me, Gramling, before it's too late! I understand the temptation, and your aim may be a noble one, but this is not the way to build a better world. Nothing built upon the calculated sacrifice of innocent lives can be! And what would you gain? The power of the Helm is a trap, a dead end! It destroyed its builders by granting too much! Show us you have more sense and courage than your apprentice. Don't let it destroy *you*!'

A momentary flicker of doubt passed across Gramling's face, causing Barbara to catch her breath. Then he shook his head, almost regretfully. 'No, it is too late, Doctor. If you had shared even the briefest moment of what I have already experienced through the Helm, you would understand. The only justification for what I have already done is to go forward. There is only one path for me now.'

Then Gramling's old body died.

The shield curtain flickered away.

Gramling snatched at the Helm.

Outside, the veil lifted from Fluxford castle. Men and beasts fell gasping to the ground as the air flowed freely once more. At the head of the advancing marines, Shannon struggled grimly to his feet.

'Get inside the main building. Find it!'

Gramling thrust the Helm towards Susan. Odoyle, Anni Glassfeather and the Doctor struck at him. Eldritch fire streamed from silver hammer, broomstick and the Doctor's sapphire ring.

Free again, Bron and Edmund stumbled, gulped down fresh air, picked themselves up and ran on. Amid the tumbled yard walls and churned earth of the castle orchard they found an advance party of three marines, lying crushed and torn beside the carcass of the dragon that had died slaying them. Bron snatched up a pair of their automatic rifles and tossed one to Edmund.

'I have seen how these work,' he cried. 'Let us turn them to our own use!'

* * *

Fire flared off Gramling's personal shield. He staggered back, shocked but unharmed, dropping the Helm. Susan and Mellisa shook their heads dizzily as the control over them slipped.

'Get down!' Ian yelled, and they leaped off the side of the dais and fell flat. Chairs tumbled over as the assembled dignitaries scrambled clear of the magical conflict.

Gramling snatched up his own staff which had been laid beside his chair, even as Anni tossed a potion bottle at his feet. Thick green tendrils of ivy erupted from the boards of the dais and twined about Gramling's legs, pinioning him to the spot. He pointed his staff at the floor under Anni's feet. The flagstones lifted and tossed her aside as red-brown chitinous forms expanded beneath them. Three five-foot long earwigs were suddenly standing amid the shattered stones, shifting about uncertainly, their huge rear pincers snapping menacingly. The Doctor pointed upwards. His ring sparkled. A spider dropped down from a beam on a thread of silk that became a rope as it swelled to enormous size. It fell on to the earwigs and started to entwine them in its web.

Odoyle turned his silver hammer on a hanging candle wheel. It began to spin, snapping its chains, and dived towards Gramling hissing like a flail. Gramling caught the wheel on the end of his staff and it became a child's spinning top, which he whipped back at Odoyle so fast he had to duck and tumble out of the way as the missile screamed over his head and shattered against the far wall.

Anni had scrambled clear of the earwigs. Now she cast a bag of sparkling powder over a jumble of fallen chairs by her side, and muttered a few words. The chairs seemed to unfold and twist in a complicated fashion, becoming stick figures that stalked stiffly towards Gramling as he struggled clear of the ivy around his legs, and began to club at his staff, trying to knock it from his grasp. He gestured with his free hand. A crossed pair of ornamental axes detached themselves from the wall and flew through the air to start hacking at the animated chairs. The Doctor pointed his ring and a row of hanging shields bearing assorted coats of arms swooped in front of the axes. The hall rang with the clang of metal on metal.

Odoyle's body elongated and his head swelled. He became a huge, emerald green snake. Forty feet of sinuous body suddenly uncoiled, writhing around the side of the hall, sending the cowering guests leaping for fresh cover. It reared up behind Gramling as he was guiding the axes against the Doctor's flying shields and Anni's chair warriors, and struck. Gramling disappeared as coil after coil enveloped him.

They tightened slowly, immobilizing Gramling.

'Now I have you!' Odoyle hissed. 'Sorry it should come to this, my old friend.'

Then there was a blaze of flame and heat that lit up the hall, radiating out from between the coils.

Odoyle's eyes widened and his snake body writhed. 'No . . . !'

Then it burst apart; disintegrating into a mushroom of green vapour which rolled up into the roof.

And Odoyle was gone.

In his place, towering over them, was a replica of the dragon that had pursued them in the forest. Flame streamed from its gaping jaws, setting fire to a hanging tapestry.

Anni threw a potion vial down at her own feet. There was a pop and billow of bright orange smoke. She grew in size with the rising cloud of smoke, her pointed hat spearing upwards until it brushed the ceiling and she was as tall as the dragon. Swinging her broom vigorously, she began to drive it back into a corner, knocking its huge head left and right, bringing forth roars of pain and fury. Desperately it flamed again, setting her broom alight. As Anni beat at the flames it lashed out with its tail, catching her in the ribs and sending her crashing against the wall, cracking the stonework. She slid down to the floor limply, slowly shrinking back to her normal size. The dragon roared in triumph.

The Doctor pointed at the stained glass window by its head. A section of ultramarine glass representing the sea suddenly spewed a torrent of water with such force that it knocked the dragon sideways, quenching its flame. The Doctor gestured at another window containing a section of sky. A blast of wind whistled forth, setting everybody in the hall shivering. A glistening, frosted cocoon formed about the dragon, freezing it rigid even as it struggled upright.

For a moment everything was very still in the hall, but from outside they heard the sound of fighting once more. It was getting closer.

Sheltering at the back with Barbara, Komati and their temporary charge, Ian strained his eyes in the faint light of the remaining candles. He saw Susan and the Princess crouching in the far corner beyond the dais behind some upturned chairs, apparently unhurt. But where was the Helm?

Then the ice shattered about the dragon and its quasi-solid form boiled away into noxious steaming slime. The vapour dispersed and there was Gramling, looking tired and dazed. As soon as he saw the Doctor he raised his staff, even as the Doctor extended his ring-hand in a spell-casting gesture.

'So. It is down to you and me, Doctor,' Gramling said.

The Doctor also seemed drained by his efforts, but his voice was still firm. 'You can never use the Helm now. Susan and Mellisa know about the conditioning and will resist, and that would make them unsuitable cat's paws, wouldn't it? Why continue this madness?'

Gramling laughed without humour.

'Perhaps it is fated, or perhaps I have gone too far to turn back. Or, just possibly, it is personal. You humiliated me at our first meeting, Doctor, remember? The old Gramling had no time to bear grudges, but now I find my sense of pride renewed afresh. Retribution appeals to me once more. And now you have interfered again and cost me dearly. I really can't leave that unpunished.'

'That is Dhal speaking, not Gramling!' the Doctor riposted. 'Gramling spoke of nobler aims than petty revenge, however misguided were his methods. Perhaps there is still a little of Dhal left in you?'

For a moment Gramling looked uncertain and clutched his brow. 'Don't try to confuse me! I know who I am! I am the master, Doctor, and you are but an upstart apprentice!'

Fire seared from his staff.

The Doctor's ring blazed in blue-white brilliance.

A hot wind sprang up and howled through the hall, blowing out the remaining candles, shattering windows and filling the darkness with the eerie glow of the fierce magical emission. Chairs began to scrape and slither across the floor, driven back by the discharge. All illusions and animations were abandoned, as though they had only been preliminaries; preparation for the ultimate confrontation between wizards. Now it was simply a battle of raw energy as they drew more and more from the global power web.

Challenging each other to see who would burn out first.

Outside the rain grew heavier. A vortex of cloud swirled over the keep. Lightning forks began to stab down at the clustered towers and the struggling forms of beasts and men.

Peal after peal of thunder reverberated through the Great Hall. The Doctor and Gramling had almost vanished behind glowing shields. The air between them crackled and flared with criss-cross bolts and spears of energy, lighting up the whole chamber with arc-lamp brilliance, and sending crazy shadows dancing about the vaulted roof. Creeping tendrils of electricity writhed and earthed. The flagstones about them cracked and melted and the boards of the dais began to char and smoulder.

And then Ian saw the Helm, caught in the angle between the dais and the floor.

This was it. Now or never!

Dragging their frightened burden between them, with Komati helping push it forward, Ian and Barbara forced their way towards the dais, stumbling over the tumbling chairs and toppling candle trees. The scorching wind beat them down, drawing sparks from their hair. Crawling, they clung to cracks in the flagstones, pulling the struggling creature along with them until they could move no closer to the dais.

The hall doors burst open. Gunfire could be heard.

Ian lifted his head. 'Susan!' he yelled, 'can you reach the Helm?'

Sheltering in the far corner behind upturned chairs, Susan shielded her eyes against the fearful blast of heat and light. The Helm was perhaps twelve feet from her, but the pressure of the discharge was already fearsome at this distance. How could she get closer? Could she move the Helm by magic? No, she couldn't concentrate amid the noise and confusion. Desperately she looked around. There was a halberd lying on the floor, fallen from its display hooks. Its shaft had to be eight feet long, surely. She scrabbled towards it.

Backing into the howling gale came Bron and Edmund, firing their captured weapons.

Susan grasped the shaft of the halberd and pulled it to her.

Bron ran out of ammunition and drew *Invictus*. They fell back to one side of the doorway, sheltering in the jumble of scattered furniture. Shannon and a marine appeared at the doors, dazzled for a moment by the light of the magical discharge.

Susan stretched forward, extending the halberd towards the Helm, biting her lip as the heat scorched the exposed flesh of her arm.

Edmund fired and the marine beside Shannon fell.

The tip of the halberd touched the Helm. It rolled free, was caught by the wind and tumbled and bounced away.

Edmund's rifle clicked empty.

Ian snatched at the Helm as it sailed past, but missed.

Shannon swung his rifle to cover Edmund and Bron, saw his magazine gauge, and hesitated.

Komati, a few feet behind Ian, caught the bouncing Helm by pure reflex. Ian reached out his hand. Komati began to crawl towards him.

Shannon, still covering Bron and Edmund, snatched a glance at her.

'Bring it here, Komati!' he commanded, his words cutting through the thunder and crackle of energy.

'Give it to me,' shouted Ian. 'I can finish this thing!'

Komati looked helplessly from one to the other.

'It's your duty, lieutenant!'

'Stop telling me my duty!' she yelled. She threw the Helm to Ian as Shannon twisted and fired. The impact sent her sprawling jerkily across the floor like a rag doll as Ian caught the Helm.

Shannon's gun turned to him.

And clicked dryly.

As Shannon grabbed for a fresh magazine, Bron lunged forward, swinging *Invictus*.

Ian tore the padding from inside the Helm, and, as Barbara held their squirming captive, he thrust it into place.

The Helm fitted the contours of the cephlie's head perfectly.

Sounds of combat outside ceased abruptly. The blaze of energy around the magicians dimmed and was gone. The heat was snatched out of the half-melted flagstones at their feet as though it had never been there. The searing wind became a whisper and died away. Outside the last rumbles of thunder faded. Silence and darkness seemed to ring in Barbara's ears.

All the candles in the hall sprang alight.

By the dais, Barbara saw the Doctor still standing, but looking utterly exhausted. Gramling was slumped to the ground and lay very still, his robes blackened. His face . . .

288

she turned away.

Slowly, as though half dazed, people began to move. She saw Ian examine Komati's still form and shake his head sadly. Then Edmund stumbled over to Mellisa, with the King, Queen and Palbury beside him, and kissed her; while Susan ran over to the Doctor and hugged him. The Doctor lifted his head and murmured reassurance. Barbara saw Anni stirring, and she and Ian helped her to her feet, as Peridor was giving a supporting arm to Bron, who stood, swaying slightly, over Shannon's body.

Then they all turned to the cephlie who stood impassively in the middle of the Great Hall.

No longer a furtive or hangdog creature.

Purpose and intelligence seemed to radiate from it.

With an effort, the Doctor straightened himself up, brushed off his robe, and approached it.

'Do you understand what has occurred?' he asked gravely.

The cephlie spoke in clear and precise tones. 'I know of every action made upon our world since the system was created.'

'Then you know why it must be shut down, or else its influence will spread to other worlds.'

'I understand. Its end shall be ours as well.'

'But is there no other way?'

'Not for us. We are too closely bound up with it. Do not concern yourself. It is all we crave now. My fellows are coming. I have called them . . .'

And to her amazement, Barbara saw cephlies emerging from the shadows out of the corners of the hall. Bron flinched as they pushed past him. Surely they had not come in through the door? A dozen, twenty. How could they have got there? Where did they come from so quickly? She would never know. Silently, gravely, they clustered round the cephlie wearing the Helm.

'The starship's weapons have been neutralized, as have those of their ground forces. There will be no more fighting.'

It turned its gaze to the Doctor again. 'You have learned most of our story, Doctor. We place the rest into your mind now. Tell it in full when we are gone.'

'I will,' the Doctor promised solemnly. 'Thank you for putting matters right.'

'Ultimately it was our responsibility,' it said simply. 'You will need a representative from the Empire forces to be present to talk of peace,' it added. 'We will arrange that.' The cephlie turned to the King and Queen, who returned its penetrating gaze uncertainly. 'Take care of this world. It truly belongs to you now. But do not make the same mistake we did. Do not force perfection. And learn when to move on.'

And it lowered its head.

Barbara felt the change wave surge through her.

The sky blazed.

In the *Prince Randolph* they looked up from wrestling with unaccountably locked weapon circuits to see the moons grow searingly brilliant. Torrents of stored energy radiated away into space. Briefly Avalon was encircled by a necklace of miniature suns. Then the light slowly faded. The moons cooled, sinking through orange and red and down into the dull blackness of dead and empty husks.

Then a technician called to Nyborg: 'Sir, look at the planet . . . Admiral? *Admiral!*'

A shockwave of light expanded out from Fluxford and swept across the globe.

Night became day once more as the whole world glowed.

Barbara felt herself lost in a mist of light and cold brilliance. It burned within her. Tiny firefly pinpricks spilling out with her breath; flaring and dying. Her hands glittered with them. The air about her sparkled with millions of them. The people around her were figures of fire.

Then the light faded and was gone.

And so were the cephlies and the Helm.

In their place, still seated in his bridge chair, was Admiral Nyborg.

The Doctor, formidable in his magician's robes, was standing over him, scrutinizing the dumbfounded Empire officer closely. Then he said commandingly: 'Sir Bron?'

'Yes, Doctor?'

'Please escort this man into the castle grounds. Let him tell his men there will be no more fighting. Show him the dead, so he may understand what has been done in the name of his Empire. Then bring him back here.' The Doctor turned to the King and Palbury.

'And then you will all talk of peace together.'

26

The Legacy of Avalon

It was the dawn of midsummer's day.

'I think it is time for us to go,' said the Doctor gently. 'They do not need our help anymore.'

'We'll miss a wedding . . . and some funerals,' Ian said. 'Alammar, Komati . . . and Odoyle. He was . . . well, so full of life.'

'I will miss him too, Chesterton. I will miss all of them. The price has been high, and must never be forgotten. But the Avalonians must learn to forge their own destiny now, without magic or outsiders to aid them.' He breathed in the fresh morning air. There was distant birdsong. 'I believe it is going to be a fine day. I trust this is a good omen. Now, have you all got everything?'

Susan, Ian and Barbara nodded. They began to pick their way through the battlescarred grounds to the TARDIS.

'I said goodbye to Mellisa and Edmund,' Susan confirmed. 'But they were too busy gazing into each other's eyes to take much notice.'

'Sir Bron was just going into the talks in the Steward's Room when I left him,' said Ian. 'The King and Palbury are there, with the Admiral and his advisors. They're negotiating reparations. His Empire may be falling, but I reckon Nyborg will behave decently. I think what the cephlies did rattled him a bit.'

'I trust they will reach some amicable compromise,' said the Doctor. 'They may need each other shortly. Avalon's isolation is ended, and it needs the Empire's protection for a while. But they do have something to bargain with, as I pointed out to the King.'

'What's that?'

'Land. This is a sparsely populated world. With the Empire fragmenting, there will inevitably be people looking for simpler lifestyles on new worlds. It is best to organize such things from the start in an orderly manner.'

Barbara smiled. 'Queen Leonora will make sure of that,' she confirmed. 'Oh, and I said goodbye to Anni on our behalf. She was setting off back to her cottage. She was worried about her cat. I suggested to Peridor that he arrange for some transport, as she can't use her broomstick again. Still, she seemed cheerful enough, in the circumstances.'

'She struck me as a most practical woman,' the Doctor commented, ignoring the others' sudden grins.

Then Barbara frowned. 'The magic really has gone completely, hasn't it?'

'Certainly. And, if I may say so, good riddance to it!'

'But you can't deny the system behind it was an incredible invention,' said Ian.

'A dead end, Chesterton,' the Doctor responded firmly. 'It reduced the cephlies to a brilliant futility, living in a sterile paradise. They had god-like powers with no outlet but building self-indulgent follies, culminating in the destruction of a star for purely aesthetic purposes. What value true creativity and ingenuity then?'

'Still, it's a pity something couldn't have been saved.'

The Doctor looked at him despairingly. 'The system, had it spread through nanobotic contamination, would have brought about the fall of all other technologies, and hence galactic civilization itself!'

'But if people knew how to use it, they wouldn't need anything else. They needn't have gone the way of the cephlies.'

The Doctor regarded him with mild exasperation. 'You still don't appreciate its true power, do you?'

'Surely there's nothing else!' exclaimed Barbara.

'Something so obvious, we didn't realize it. On Avalon, normal cause and effect and self-determination were subject to the prevailing expectations of the dominant

293

mythological structure. The incidents and supposedly chance encounters we experienced from our first day, the crash of the lander close to the *Merrow*, perhaps even our arrival itself at such a crucial time, were not simply coincidental. The system shaped everything to fit the pattern!'

Barbara looked shocked. 'I had a feeling people here were set in their ways, but I never realized we might be affected.'

'We were agents of change,' said the Doctor. 'Our new ideas upset the established order and possibly influenced others. But if the system had survived, and we had stayed long enough, who knows?'

Susan nodded understandingly. Ian shook his head in amazement, then suddenly said: '*That* was what you meant about the significance of "three" on the *Merrow*!'

'Yes. It seemed a suitable token number for a series of encounters in those circumstances. Now, would you really like everyone to live their whole lives subject to such arbitrary forces?'

'All right Doctor, you've convinced me,' said Ian fervently. 'Good riddance to magic! Still, it will be a pity to think there'll be no more dragons.'

'Speak for yourself!' said Barbara with feeling.

'Oh, I expect the dragons and such will live on,' said the Doctor, 'but merely as large reptiles. The fire breathing and the flying was all due to the nanobots enhancing their abilities to produce the appropriate image.'

'That was the word I thought of, Grandfather,' said Susan. 'When I was wondering how to escape from Dhal's tower when I remembered the story of Rapunzel.' She smiled. 'That had to be appropriate. But belief was also important. Mellisa believed in me, and I found it easier to work the spells. Those vials I stole from Dhal may not have been acids after all, but I hoped they were, and convinced Mellisa, and gradually they began to work.'

'Yes. All the spells and potions did was to concentrate

294

the user's mind on what he *wanted* to happen. Only the cephlies could integrate with the system fully, of course. But some people . . .' he paused modestly, 'with the right talent, and suitable application of method, could obtain satisfactory results.'

'That explains your magician's costume,' said Barbara. 'You had to look the part, so that people believed in you!'

'Exactly. I was convinced there would be some final confrontation, though I could hardly have guessed its form. It was obvious that presenting myself as a magician at the crucial moment would be advantageous, but I had to do so in the "appropriate" manner.'

They arrived at the TARDIS. The Doctor took out his key and turned it in the lock. The door opened smoothly. He beamed at them.

'But how did you know the cephlies were indigenous to Avalon?' Ian wondered.

'They were the odd ones out in the bestiary list!' said Barbara.

'Quite so,' the Doctor confirmed. 'They were not creations like Dhal's hybrids, nor legendary creatures from Earthly myths. They had to be natives, the *only* natives we encountered, so they had to be special. And their name. The similarity to "cephalic", pertaining to the cranium. Surely a fragment of a longer scientific description which could only have been given by the first colonists before the fall. We actually saw further proof when sailing down the river, Chesterton. "The Seven Companions" remember?'

'Of course! A cephlie sculpture! I thought the proportions were a bit odd.'

'Yes, and thousands of years old. They had to be the original dominant race here.'

'And now they've just . . . died,' said Barbara.

'They wanted an end,' the Doctor said simply. 'They were very old, as individuals, I mean. The system had been extending their lives artificially. All those we saw may have been older than the blackout disaster. Virtual immortality. Yet, for all its potential, their system did not have enough safeguards. It could be overruled by people who had long forgotten, through laziness, the consequences of their actions. Until they almost drained the system of energy for several months to fulfil a foolish whim. Those that survived never recovered from the shock, and feared further contact with the Helm, or similar devices, even though that was the only thing that could bring them release. From then on they existed, but nothing more. They had forgotten change is part of life, without which there is only stagnation. The Empire will also learn that fact soon, I believe . . . but that is another story.

'Now, shall we be going?'

Susan and Barbara slipped inside the TARDIS, but Ian paused.

'The way you've summed up, Doctor, almost makes me believe you had it all worked out from the start.'

'Not quite, Chesterton,' he replied modestly, 'but I did hold one key fact firmly in mind which proved useful.'

'Oh, what was that?'

'That there is no such thing as magic,' said the Doctor.

They entered the police box and the door closed.

A moment later the deep thrumming pulse of dematerialization sounded in the yard. And, almost magically, the TARDIS faded away.

Available in the *Doctor Who – New Adventures* series:

The next Missing Adventure is *Invasion of the Cat-People* by Gary Russell, featuring the second Doctor, Ben and Polly.